the Potluck Club
Takes the Cake

the Potluck Club

Takes the Cake

A NOVEL

Linda Evans Shepherd

and Eva Marie Everson

Revell

Grand Rapids, Michigan

Published by Fleming H. Revell
a division of Baker Publishing Group
P.O. Box 6287, Grand Rapids, MI 49516-6287
www.revellbooks.com

Second printing, August 2008

Printed in the United States of America

Library of Congress Cataloging-in-Publication Data
Shepherd, Linda Evans.
    Takes the cake : a novel / Linda Evans Shepherd and Eva Marie Everson.
       p.   cm. — (The Potluck Club)
   ISBN 10: 0-8007-3074-7 (pbk.)
   ISBN 978-0-8007-3074-1 (pbk.)
    1. Women—Societies and clubs—Fiction. 2. Female friendship—Fiction.
  3. Prayer groups—Fiction. 4. Women cooks—Fiction. 5. Colorado—Fiction.
  6. Cookery—Fiction. I. Everson, Eva Marie. II. Title.
PS3619.H456T35 2007
813'.6—dc22   2006100323

To Preston L. Purvis (1931–2006)—my daddy—who loved the stories of the Potluck Club and looked forward to the next installment. I love you and miss you more than I ever imagined possible.—"Ree-Baby"

Eva Marie Everson

To Eva and all my dear friends of the Advanced Writer's and Speaker's Association. What a team of encouragers you are. How glad I am that you are in my life.

Linda Evans Shepherd

Contents

Contents

1

Buttered Biscuits

A lot had happened to the ladies of the Potluck Club.

A lot.

Then again, a lot had happened to Clay Whitefield, ace reporter for the *Gold Rush News*, though neither the job nor the title kept him going. What really buttered his biscuits was keeping his eyes and ears open to whatever was happening to his favorite ladies of Summit View, Colorado. The ladies of the Potluck Club.

Evangeline Benson, chief potlucker, had started the club in the dining room of her home years ago when she and the late Ruth Ann McDonald gathered for coffee cake and prayer. By the time Ruth Ann had passed on to glory, the club had grown, adding Lizzie Prattle, high school librarian and wife of Samuel, president of the Gold Mine Bank; Vonnie Westbrook, retired nurse and wife of Fred; Goldie Dippel, one-time homemaker, now legal secretary and wife of Coach Jack Dippel; and Donna Vesey, a deputy sheriff. Finally, and most recently, Lisa Leann Lambert, Texas transplant, had added herself to the mix.

Back up. The other thing that kept Clay Whitefield on his reporter's toes was the aforementioned Donna Vesey, the youngest member of the Potluck Club.

Clay got up from the scarred desk in his tiny one-room apartment overlooking Main Street, which he shared with his two gerbils, Woodward and Bernstein. He needed a break from the notes he was tapping into his laptop computer, so he walked over to the single window overlooking the touristy town he called home and peered down to the snow-blown streets below.

He wondered what those ladies of the Potluck Club might be up to now. That's when it hit him. It was Saturday. And not just any Saturday. Potluck Club Saturday. Rumor had it the venue had been changed to Lisa Leann's home so as to blend a baby shower with the monthly potluck and prayer meeting.

Lisa Leann, his newest and most controversial columnist over at the *Gold Rush News*.

His stomach rumbled a bit as he spotted Fred Westbrook's pickup truck heading down Main Street and turning toward where Lisa Leann lived. Clay cocked a red brow. Fred wasn't alone. But who was that with him?

Could it be . . . nah . . . it couldn't be.

Or could it?

Lisa Leann

Crushed Pineapple Fruitcake

Ingredients:
3/4 cup butter
1 cup white sugar
2 eggs
2 cups all purpose flour
2 tsp. baking powder
1 tsp. salt
1 tsp. almond extract

2

Tea for Two

I had to admire how clever Clay was to stalk his story about Vonnie and her "secret" son all the way through my front door and into my daughter's baby shower. I could picture his headline now: "Hollywood's David Harris's Mother Is None Other Than Our Own Vonnie Westbrook! Ta-da!!"

I would have spilled the scoop to Clay myself if it hadn't been so risky. (As the newest and only uninvited member of the Potluck Club, that kind of spill would have gotten me the boot for sure.)

But Vonnie's story is so prime time it might even bring in the TV news trucks from Denver, not to mention the crew from *Hollywood Nightly*. And to think, it was Summit View's own Clay Whitefield who broke the story.

I made sure I was in earshot as Clay interviewed the players of this little drama as they sat in a corner near the fireplace.

First there was David, the son of Harmony Harris, the actress often considered the queen of the Hollywood musicals. Her frenzied fans had hounded both her and her secrets, trysts, and fortunes her entire career. Much as they did with Elvis, the press continued to unravel the seams of her private life even after her recent death to cancer. Their fascination with her was centered in part on the "who"

12

of David's father. In fact, the names of her most famous male costars were often linked to his paternity. So, this revelation that David was actually Harmony's adopted son would cause a sensation.

And to think David's birth mother was none other than our own ho-hum Potlucker Vonnie Westbrook, Sunday school teacher and retired nurse. Astounding.

As it turned out, Vonnie had been secretly married to a Latin hottie, a Joseph Ray Jewell, who'd been killed in 'Nam. And to think, poor old boring Fred, Vonnie's current husband of thirty-five years, had never suspected his dear wife had been married before, much less had a child.

But surprise! He'd made the discovery in recent weeks, and now it looked like he was starting to come to terms with it. I mean, he was the one who'd picked David up at the Denver International Airport this afternoon and brought him to Mandy's little baby shower. Bless his heart.

I pulled up a chair, with my back to Clay's interview, and took in every word.

Clay asked the questions I would have asked myself, like, "Say, Fred, how'd it feel when you found out your wife had been secretly married to another man?" "David, what was it like to grow up with a movie star for a mother?" "Vonnie, why'd you keep your first marriage a secret?" "Did you really believe your baby died at birth?" You know—all the interesting stuff.

I tried to be a fly on the wall, but my other guests kept demanding my attention. That was to be expected, as this was the first time the Potluckers had been over to my luxury condo for a meeting. Of course, I knew I'd read the interview in the paper soon enough. But I wanted to see how Clay would translate it into print. And since I was the local paper's newest advice columnist, I had a lot I could learn from such a scoop still in progress.

After Clay pulled his camera from his Jeep and took a few photographs of the reunited pair, I insisted he help himself to a plate of food.

That spark of appreciation in his eyes quickly faded as he watched David Harris make a beeline for Donna, who though dressed in black sweats, still looked adorable, especially now that her buzzed hair was growing out in blonde curls.

When I turned back to Clay, his crestfallen countenance told me it was just as I suspected: he was sweet on the girl deputy. Why, I'd seen those two not that long ago locked in what appeared to be an intimate embrace right on the sidewalk outside of the Higher Grounds Café. Thank goodness my wedding shop is just across the street so I can watch the locals for signs of romance.

It's not that I'm nosey, but as a wedding consultant, romance is my business, so knowing about any public displays of affection would only improve my bottom line, if you know what I mean.

While the girls were helping themselves to dessert, I managed to sit down next to Clay. The poor boy could hardly keep his eyes off David and Donna. I kept my voice low. "Clay, you look absolutely lovesick."

His eyes turned to me. "What? No I'm not."

"Yes, you are, and darlin', don't be embarrassed. I've known your secret for a long time now."

His freckles seemed to stand on end. "My secret?"

"Clay, I'm a trained professional, so some things are more obvious to me than to others."

He folded his arms over his denim shirt and cocked his head. He seemed both nervous and amused. "What sort of things?"

"Why, Clay Whitefield, you're absolutely smitten with Donna."

Clay blanched. "Uh, well. We grew up together, you know. Of course I care about her."

"Honey, you're head over heels."

A burst of laughter from Donna caused Clay's head to snap in her direction.

I tapped his shoulder and leaned in. "Dear, you've got it bad."

Clay looked a bit sheepish. "Let's say you're right. Let's say David Harris and I are after the same thing. From where I sit, I'd say Harris is winning."

I gave him my sweetest smile. "What you need is a romance coach."

Clay looked tempted to go for his notepad. "Say that again?"

"A romance coach."

Clay grinned and leaned forward. "And I suppose you know one?"

"Yes, darlin', I'm one of the best. My methods not only helped me snag my husband Henry, but they've helped to launch a thousand marriages."

Clay turned his full attention to me. "I've never heard that term, but it's an interesting concept. Maybe I could write an article explaining that you're offering this service at your shop."

"That sounds great, and while I'm at it, I'll give you some suggestions to try yourself. Deal?"

"Me?" Clay shrugged. "I'm open to hear what you have to say. As a reporter, of course."

Donna laughed again, and Clay's head spun back to the couple on my pink velvet loveseat.

I smiled. "I'll explain everything, and if you follow my advice, you'll be as good as engaged."

Clay looked skeptical, but I could tell he was more than interested. Else why would he agree to interview me?

While I was conferring with Clay, I'd failed to notice some of my guests were ready to dash off into the afternoon. When I glanced out the window, which was swagged with lace and pink ruffles, sure enough, the angle of the bright sun was just starting to cast a few shadows. Hard to believe it would be dark in only a few hours.

Vonnie and Fred waved from the front door. "Thanks for everything, Lisa Leann, we had a wonderful time," Vonnie said.

I jumped up, almost spilling my cooling cup of coffee. "You're leaving already?" I said, rushing to the door.

I set my cup on the hallway table and stopped to help Lizzie Prattle slip into her coat. She gestured to her daughter-in-law. "That goes for me and Samantha too. We simply must get home."

Before I could say good-bye, Donna then Goldie Dippel hurried down the stairs behind the Prattles. Goldie looked so good after that makeover I'd given her, it was hard to guess she was a woman in marital crisis. How her two-timing husband could have looked outside his own bedroom door for company was beyond me. I could hardly believe she was going to go away with him for the weekend. I shuddered. She'd probably catch some VD if she let him have his way with her.

"Thanks for coming," I called after them as they waved a good-bye.

When I turned around, I found Evie with her hand on her hip, giving me a glare so hard it made me jump. She said, "Well, so much for working on the Christmas tea this afternoon. But never mind. I was Jan's right hand on this event for years, so it would be best if I just took over the project myself."

"Evie, dear," I said in a voice I hoped would soothe her ruffled feathers. "My helping you on this task is no bother at all. It really *is* my cup of tea, if you'll pardon the pun. And since the pastor made us co-leaders, why don't you and I confer for a few minutes and work out the details."

"Honestly, Lisa Leann, I've decided to cancel the event. Traditionally, we've held our tea the week before Christmas, and here it is, already Saturday of the week before the week before. So, there's just no time."

"Nonsense," I said, knowing Evie had no intention of dropping the event. This "sudden cancellation" was a power grab if I ever saw one. I played along. "But I'm perfectly happy to accept your resignation. After all, you've had quite a week, what with being engaged to two different men. You need a break, for sure." I patted her arm. "So, the tea will probably go better if I run it myself anyway. I'm thinking I'll host the event the Wednesday between Christmas and New Years. That should work great since there will be no service that night. It'll give our ladies a lovely break during the holidays. And the best part is we'll be able to announce it both Sundays."

By now, David and the Westbrooks had headed out the door. Clay walked to my side. "Thanks for letting me stay. The meal was scrumptious, especially the pineapple fruitcake. I don't always care for fruitcakes, but when I heard you made it, I knew it would be delicious."

"Glad you liked it. It's my grandmother's recipe." I studiously avoided looking at Evangeline as I said, "In fact, I'm thinking of serving it at the annual Christmas tea the Wednesday just before New Years."

"So, this annual Grace Church event hasn't been canceled after all," Clay said with a grin. "Hey, I'll email you to get the details later tonight. If I get right on it, there'll be time enough to print the announcement in the paper. And the night of—I'll show up with my camera, if that's okay. This could be a great story about how a church is healing from the loss of their beloved pastor's wife. I bet I could get some excellent quotes from your ladies."

I ignored the fiery darts I was receiving from Evie and said, "Great idea. The tea starts at seven."

Before I turned back to Evie I could almost see the steam curling from her ears. As Clay slid into his parka and bounded down the front steps, Evie turned to me and said, "You had no right to go to the press before this was settled."

"Oh, I thought we'd just decided it. Besides, the press came to me."

I was just beginning to understand how the power of the press could become one of my greatest assets.

Evie stared back. "I have *not* tendered my resignation, and I'm still co-chair of this event. We may have to change the date and time as you suggested, but it will be held in the tradition it has always been held, though a tea held at seven instead of four might as well be called a dessert."

I could feel my eyebrows climb up my forehead, but I kept my voice honey sweet. "And what tradition is that, may I ask?"

Evie looked me up and down, making me feel as if my red fringed silk and velvet evening jacket, which I had slipped over a slinky black cocktail dress, was well beyond her admiration or comprehension.

She clenched her jaw. "Being a newcomer to our long-standing Grace Church Christmas tea, I guess you wouldn't know, would you?"

With that, Evie tossed her salt-and-pepper hair as she flounced to grab her worn-out wool coat, in beige, no less, a horrid color for her complexion. The hem of her new fuchsia print skirt peeked out from beneath the buttoned-down wool. As for the skirt, I'd say her clothing tastes were changing for the better, an accomplishment I took personal credit for, as I had made it my goal to spruce up the group.

I followed close on Evie's black flats. "Well, partner, since you're stuck with me, you'd better tell me your plans. It's the only way I'll reveal mine."

That stopped her in her tracks. She turned back to look at me. "Well, then, I'll call you tonight and we'll get started. Agreed?"

"*Agreed?* What could I say to such rudeness? Of course I agreed," I later told Mandy as she watched me pick up after the party.

"I wish you'd let me help you clean up," she said.

"Nothing doing, young lady. If the doctor won't let you fly home to Houston to be with your husband, I surely won't let you clean up my kitchen. I'll not have you flopping around on the floor again in need of another run to the ER. You do understand that, don't you?"

"Yes, of course I do," Mandy said as she sagged her strawberry curls onto the headrest of the rocking chair. She smoothed her lime green maternity sweater over her protruding belly. "It's just this wait is so boring, I can hardly stand it."

Poor baby. "It'll be over soon," I said. "Now might be a good time to catch a nap."

Mandy complied, and I turned up the stereo, which was playing Bing Crosby's rendition of "White Christmas," but not so loud as to disturb her. Then I busied myself in the kitchen, making a special plate of leftovers for my husband, Henry, who would be back from an afternoon of skiing over at Breckinridge soon, as the ski runs closed at three. Too bad he missed the potluck. If I'd known some of the guys were going to be there I'd have invited him as well. But I'm sure Henry had a lovely time skiing. Now that we were Coloradoans braving our first winter in the mountains, we would be doing a lot of dashing down those slopes in the coming weeks. I could hardly wait to pull out my white, fur-trimmed snowsuit. I'd be styling down the advanced trails (or "the blacks," as the locals called them) in no time at all.

Later that evening, Evie's phone call caught me as I was carrying an unopened box to the kitchen table, a box I'd garnered from the upper shelves of my garage. Nestled inside was part of my teapot collection. I'd given away so many of my treasures in our move from our rambling house in the Woodlands, an exclusive suburb near Houston, that I'd only managed to keep my very favorite tea sets. They would come in handy now, I dared say.

I pulled the tape from the top of the box and peeked inside, just before I picked up the phone call on its third ring.

"Merry Christmas," I said.

The crabby voice on the other end of the line no doubt belonged to Evie. "Lisa Leann, let's just get this over with."

"Merry Christmas to you too, and yes, I'm looking forward to working with you."

There was silence on the phone. "Okay," she said at last. "Let me tell you how it's going to be. Several pre-selected women of the church will be responsible for decorating their own tables."

"That will never do," I injected. "I've got the whole decoration theme mapped out. I've already made one run to Wal-Mart and picked up supplies."

"Return them. I've already made the calls, and the committee is already at work. So, there's really nothing for you to do."

"Hold on there a minute, Evie. What about food, a program, greeters? That sort of thing?"

"We always serve desserts and finger foods like cucumber sandwiches and the like. The same committee that has always taken care of the food has already volunteered."

"Evangeline Benson, why do I get the feeling that you are dismissing me from my co-leadership obligation to the pastor?"

"Well, sorry if it seems that way," Evie said, "but this event is tradition. There's really not much left for you to do, unless you want to decorate a table?"

"I certainly do, and what else?"

"I don't have a program together yet, so maybe you could ask the choir director to say a few words and conduct our annual sing-along. See that he does at least one Christmas solo."

"I'll handle that. Fine," I said.

"And about the auction?"

"The auction?"

"Yes, we always raise money for Toys for Tots, but again, you wouldn't know about that."

I ignored the dig. "Who's the auctioneer?"

I heard Evie sigh. "That's the main glitch. That job always belonged to Jan. It will take a special person to fill her shoes."

"I should say so. But, no worries. I served as auctioneer at several charities for my service sorority. So I'm your girl."

I could have sworn Evie said, "I was afraid of that."

"Pardon?"

She cleared her throat. "I said 'That will take care of that.'"

"Then it's set?"

"Yes. Let the tradition continue."

I hung up the phone, more than a bit miffed. What was wrong with that woman? Did she hate everyone or just me? You'd think after she finally convinced the sheriff to buy her an engagement ring her overall attitude would've improved. But then, some people are never satisfied. Not only did she want to run Sheriff Vesey's life, she wanted to run mine as well.

I shook my head as if to clear out the thorny vibes Evie had just presented me like a bouquet of thistles.

So, it will be "tradition," will it? Fine, I can play tradition, but some of the notes will be played from my tradition. If she thinks she can blow me off, well, she's got another think coming.

Besides, as usual, I already had a plan.

3

I'll Take the Works

Clay looked down at the pink sheet of paper in his hand, recently torn from one of Lisa Leann's notebooks and with her handwriting scrawled across it. It was his list of things to do—and do today—in order to begin the process of winning Donna's heart.

He frowned as he climbed into his Jeep and headed toward Silverthorne, where Lisa Leann insisted he go. Immediately.

He used his cell phone to call the first business on the list.

"Silverthorne Salon and Spa," the voice on the other end said.

"Ah. Yeah. Do you, uh . . . do you take men there?"

There was a pause. Man, he hated this.

"Take men?" the voice countered.

"You know . . . hair . . . uh, highlighting? Mani . . . manicures? Facials?" He nearly choked on the last word. "Waxing?"

There was a giggle from the other end. "Of course we take men," the voice said.

She sounded young to Clay. And pretty. Young and pretty.

He sighed.

"Any chance you have an opening? For, say, in an hour or so?"

There was another pause, followed by, "Yes, sir. I think we can fit you in. You want a haircut or just highlights?"

Clay looked down to the pink paper again, reading the bottom line. Underscored. Three times.

"The works," Clay read from it. "I'll take the works."

21

Vonnie

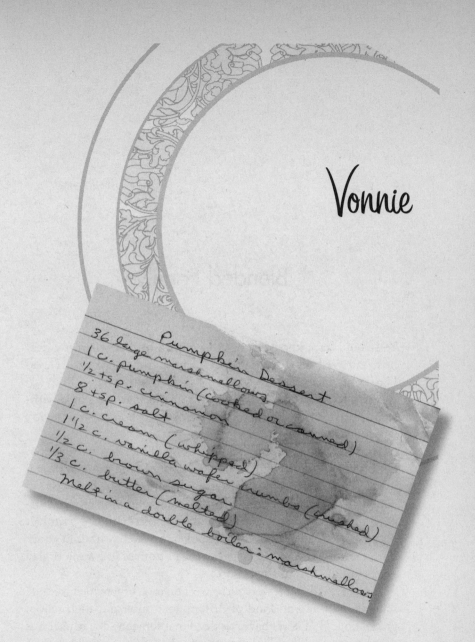

Pumpkin Dessert

36 large marshmallows
1 c. pumpkin (cooked or canned)
½ tsp. cinnamon
8 tsp. salt
1 c. cream (whipped)
1½ c. vanilla wafer crumbs (crushed)
½ c. brown sugar
⅓ c. butter (melted)

Melt in a double boiler; marshmallows

4

Blended Family

You could have knocked me over with a feather when my dear husband Fred showed up at Lisa Leann's front door with David Harris, my birth son.

Just a few days ago, I wasn't even sure our marriage could withstand Fred's discovery that I'd been married before—to David's father, Joe.

As far as I knew, Fred had no intention of meeting my son, ever. So, for Fred to surprise me with a visit from David was a miracle if I ever saw one. The only explanation was Fred must have been in conference with our pastor, Kevin Moore, who probably encouraged this encounter. As we'd just had dessert with the pastor, it made sense that Fred could have spoken privately with him about our situation. Regardless, I'd get to the bottom of it. I was just glad Fred's healing had finally begun.

You see, Fred and I, we'd been sweet on each other when we were schoolkids. But we'd kind of drifted apart after our high school graduation. He'd never have guessed I met someone else while I was away in nursing school. He says he was faithfully waiting for me. I say he should have called or written to let me know.

24

Not only did I meet Joseph Ray Jewell, I'd married him and had his baby. (Yes, in that order.)

My mother, who'd always had a firm grip of control over my life, was devastated, probably because she planned on me marrying Fred. So when she discovered I'd secretly married Joe and that he'd been drafted to Vietnam, she sent me packing, to live in LA with Joe's family. This move, though deemed as "punishment," had in fact been good for me. I cherished my time with Joe's family. Maria, Joe's mother, and I grew especially close. It was a terrible blow to both of us when the army chaplain showed up at our front door to tell us Joe had been killed in action.

I was almost nine months pregnant at the time and collapsed in shock. That's when the baby came. I was so heavily sedated, I didn't even realize little David had been born, much less been born alive.

That's how my mother got the upper hand. When she showed up at the LA hospital, she sent Maria packing. When she had me all to herself, she told me my baby was dead. She even had me sign some papers to release the baby's body for burial, or so I'd thought. I was too groggy to realize I was actually signing David's adoption papers.

I shivered and waved good-bye to Lisa Leann and my Potluck Club sisters then looped each of my arms through the crooks of David's and Fred's as we made our way down Lisa Leann's condo steps to where my Taurus was parked.

I stole a peek at each man who walked beside me as tears of relief and gratitude leaked from the corners of my eyes. How blessed could one woman be?

Yet, despite the warmth of the moment, my soul literally ached with bitterness. For the way I saw it, my needless heartache came from needless betrayal. Betrayal I wasn't sure I could ever forgive.

How could I? I hugged the arms of my men closer and tried to block out the pain of my past.

I wasn't successful.

Thoughts of my mother continued to torment me. Because of her actions, my entire life had been a lie, and why?

I knew the answer. My mother could not love anyone whose skin was darker than her own, even if that skin belonged to her own son-in-law and grandchild.

To think of the misery her conniving caused. Me without my baby, and my baby in the arms of that Hollywood woman, the actress known as Harmony Harris. It was all too much.

But even the thoughts of my mother could not completely rob me of enjoying the miracle of this moment with both my husband and son. My men saw me to my car, and David slipped beside me into the passenger's seat, while Fred headed for his pickup truck. David carried what was left of my pumpkin dessert and casserole dishes, reloaded with enough food for tonight's dinner.

Though David and I exchanged grins as we buckled up, I felt nervous. This was the first time David would see how simply I lived. My tiny house was filled with my collection of baby dolls and dust bunnies, a far cry from his and Harmony's Beverly Hills mansion I'd recently visited with Donna.

After living in such opulence, would David be ashamed of me?

Before I could think through this idea, I turned onto Main Street. *What's this?* I thought as I drove past the Higher Grounds Café. It looked like Donna walking down the sidewalk. I looked hard. Yep, that was Donna, looking almost giddy in a red outfit. But why hadn't she worn *that* to the baby shower, and what was it about her that looked different?

David said, "There's Donna. Honk. We're meeting for breakfast in the a.m."

The beep from my car caused Donna to turn and—upon seeing my son—exchange a wave with David. Her surprised but delighted expression was almost sweet. I scrunched my forehead into a map of wrinkles. "You two have a date? What about church?"

He smiled. "Church? I didn't know I was invited."

"Of course you are. Donna usually sits with Fred and me."

"Really? Well, I always wanted to see what church was like."

I looked at David out of the corner of my eye. His eyes told me his secret. He was smitten with Donna. So help me if I didn't sigh out loud. It's not that I was against the idea of David and Donna as a couple, but . . . with this lawsuit talk and all, she had too much going on to get involved with any man right now.

My reflection concerning Donna and her problems was short lived, because moments later, we'd turned into the driveway of our little Victorian, and Fred pulled up behind us in his pickup. I could already hear Chucky, our king kong bichon, as he yapped and danced on the other side of the front door.

The two of us scurried up the steps while Fred unlocked the door. Suddenly I saw how dim and shabby my home must appear. I'd always considered it so warm and comfortable until David stepped over the threshold. I looked down at Chucky, the white fuzz ball leaping at our feet.

Why hadn't I noticed he needed a bath before now?

David laughed and reached down to scratch my furry friend behind his ear. "Vonnie, you didn't tell me I had a sibling," he teased.

Despite my discomfort, I tried to smile. "That's Chucky. He was a stray who found us. Donna helped us rescue him."

David's eyebrows rose at the mention of her name, and he grinned. "Did she? Well, now."

Yes, there was no mistaking it, David was smitten. The look on his face was so obvious that even Fred noticed. "Uh, David," he said. "You're not interested in dating Donna, are you?"

David stopped petting the dog and stood up. He gave us one of his big grins and said, "Maybe. Donna and I, well, we're friends. Good friends, I hope."

Fred and I exchanged glances. "That's great," I said, not knowing if I meant it.

Fred handed David his suitcase.

"Thanks," David said, brushing off a few flakes of snow that had sprinkled the suitcase as if it were a powdered donut. "I forgot I'd tossed it in the back of your pickup at the airport."

I scurried to flip on the light switches and lamps, hoping the light would chase away the shadows as well as my home's shabby appearance. The results only stirred the dust covering my collection of baby dolls that lined the room. Feeling embarrassed at the sparkles of white that floated in the air, I turned to David. "Let me show you to your room," I said.

He followed obediently, Chucky close at his heels.

When I switched on the light to David's room, I felt a warm burn kiss my cheeks.

Oh, if only I'd known he was coming I'd have cleaned up this mess. Not only were boxes stacked on the bed, but dusty babies peered at us from every angle, the dresser, the rocking chair, the high shelf that ran around the top of the ceiling, not to mention the bed.

"Wow, it's like a doll museum in here," he said from beside me.

"Ah . . . yes. I would have prepared this room for you if I'd known you were coming. I've been using it to store some of my collection."

David turned to me and grinned. "So, you collect dolls. That's good to know. How'd you get started?"

I stared at him. "Overwhelming loss."

David stared back. "You mean, you collected these babies to replace the baby you'd lost?"

I nodded and wiped a tear from my eyes. "Silly, I know. But I could never get you out of my mind. So one doll led to another, and another, and . . ."

David gave a low whistle. "I see." He stopped and stared at me before wrapping me in his arms. "I'm here now. I'm not a baby anymore. But I'm here."

My shoulders began to quiver as he held me and I gave in to my tears. For the first time in a very long time, I couldn't feel my pain. All I could feel was love, love for my child and his love for me.

The moment was broken by the ring of the phone. I could hear Fred, who was in the living room, as he picked it up. "Yes, she's here," he said. "It's Evie," he called out to me. "She needs to talk to you about the Christmas tea."

I stepped back and wiped my eyes and reached for a tissue from the box on the dresser. "Tell her I'll call her back in a minute," I said.

I began to busy myself by picking up the room, feeling a bit self-conscious because I'd given in to such emotion. David seemed uneasy too. "How can I help you?" he asked.

"Stack those boxes in the closet, and I'll get some fresh sheets."

Within minutes we had the room ready. I could hear Fred already settled down in his recliner with his favorite show, *Truck Amuck*, a reality show about truck makeovers. I said to David, "Why don't you go sit with Fred for a while? I've got a phone call to make."

"Sure thing. Fred and I need a little bonding time. He was pretty quiet on the way here from the airport."

Hmmm. That didn't sound good. "Okay," I said. "I'll return Evie's phone call. We've got a couple of hours before supper. Hope you don't mind leftovers."

"Sounds good to me."

A few minutes later, I slipped the potluck leftovers into the refrigerator, thankful I had a microwave to heat up dinner later tonight. I paused a moment to smile at a burst of laughter coming from the other room. "My boys" laughing at the antics of the truck mechanics on TV.

I picked up the phone and dialed. "Evie, what's up?"

I could hear Evie turn down her Fox news program. How she could stand to run that all day long, I never knew. "Lisa Leann is what's up."

I sighed. "Now, Evie, dear, a lot of healing happened during her devotional at our meeting today. She offered to resign from the group, in an effort to make amends, and we wouldn't have it. Remember? You haven't changed your mind about accepting her apology?"

I could hear Evie sniff in that way she does when she's really steamed. "That woman. She just won't leave the Christmas tea alone. Well, I just won't have it!"

"Calm down, Evie," I said. "The pastor *did* make her co-leader on that project. You know that."

"But Lisa Leann is a newcomer. She doesn't know about our ways or our traditions. She thinks every situation, every potluck meeting, every Christmas tea, is all about her."

29

I smiled and changed the subject. "Speaking of which, Evie, you did notice my son David Harris today?"

A sudden silence filled the phone line. "I'm sorry, Vonnie. Here I am going on and on about Lisa Leann and totally ignoring one of the most important days of your life. What kind of friend am I?"

"A dear one," I said. "You're just a bit upset."

"You can say that again. So, where is David now?"

"He's with Fred watching one of his truck shows. They seem to be getting along."

"Seem to be?"

I giggled. "Well, when David indicated he was interested in dating Donna, Fred seemed concerned."

"David likes Donna?"

"It would seem so."

"How does she feel about him?"

"I have no idea, other than to say, I guess the two of them have been emailing one another."

"You don't say."

"Well, pretend I didn't. We don't want Lisa Leann to get hold of anything that could start a rumor."

"That woman," Evie said again.

"Now, Evie."

"I know. It's just that I could actually use her help, that is, if she would only do things the way they're supposed to be done." She sighed. "Here I am scrambling to get this Christmas tea together and I've got a wedding to plan. Say, did I tell you that Vernon and I set the date?"

"No!" I chided her. "And since I suppose I'll be your matron of honor, this is something I need to know."

"Of course you'll be my matron of honor. Who else would be? But you're not going to like it."

"Like what? The wedding?"

"No, the date. We've decided 'why wait?' Or, I should say, why wait any longer than we've already waited. We're getting married the end of next month."

"You mean January? This coming January?"

"That's right, and there's a million things to do, like selecting the bridesmaids dresses, renting the church, picking out the cake, sending the invitations. I mean, this is the wedding I never had, so I've got to do it up big. Plus there needs to be a bridal shower."

"That'll be my job," I said, giggling. "But honestly, Evie, you're not going to be able to pull off a big wedding in such a short time frame, not without professional help. Do you think?"

Uh-oh. The line sounded like it went dead again.

"You mean Lisa Leann's High Country Weddings, don't you?"

"Yes, dear. It's the only way. Besides, this could be the opportunity you two need to help you learn how to get along."

Silence again.

"Well, then, glad that's settled," I teased. "Talk tomorrow?"

"Yes, okay."

A couple of hours later, I pulled out my red Christmas placemats, the ones I'd gotten on clearance last year at Wal-Mart, and set the table with three Christmas plates loaded with hot microwaved leftovers. I lit my cinnamon candle centerpiece and put my cake and cake plates out on the nearby countertop before filling the glasses with ice and tea.

So despite the fact that my kitchen dining table was not located in a Beverly Hill's mansion, we actually had a lovely dinner, though a few awkward silences occurred between Fred and David during the meal. Once when David asked me about his father, Joseph Jewell, I caught David's eye and held my index finger to my lips as I tilted my head toward Fred.

I was glad Fred hadn't seen the gesture, but at the same time, David caught the meaning and discreetly nodded as he changed the subject. "Tell me about my grandmother, Maria Jewell."

I laughed as I shared a memory of her. "She was so full of life and joy," I said. "English was her second language, and as smart as she was, she would sometimes get things all twisted around. Like the night of my birthday dinner, she said, 'Just for you, Vonnie, I make birthday suit. *Si?*'"

Both Fred and David raised their eyebrows. "What had she meant to say?" David asked.

31

"Soup, she meant birthday soup!" I said, laughing.

David laughed while Fred shifted uneasily.

"That's really the first time I've heard you speak of your former mother-in-law," Fred said quietly. "I didn't realize how important she was to you."

My laughter stopped, and I changed the subject again. "So, David, you're going out with Donna for breakfast tomorrow?"

Fred shifted uneasily again. I inwardly threw my hands in the air. Was there no safe topic?

David nodded sheepishly. "Yeah, she's working the afternoon shift tomorrow, so we thought we'd do breakfast." He attempted another topic. "Vonnie, tell me more about your mother. Is she still living?"

This time, it was my turn to try to change the subject. "Mother? Yes, she lives not far from here, in Frisco."

"I'd love to meet her," David said. "If it would be okay."

I hopped up to scoop what was left of my pumpkin dessert into individual bowls.

"Wouldn't that be interesting," Fred said, then winked at me.

"That certainly would be," I agreed as I put a bowl before each of my men. "However, she might not be up for a visit."

David picked up his fork and dug into the rich dessert. "She's sick?"

Fred looked to me to see how I would answer. I nodded. "Yes, that's how I'd describe it," I said.

"That's too bad," David said between bites of the dessert. He smiled. "This is really good. Did you make this?"

"I did." I smiled at my husband. "It's one of Fred's favorites."

David looked wistful. "To think, all these years, I had a mom who could cook."

"Harmony didn't?" I asked, my own fork readied for my first bite.

David laughed. "No, she had employees who could cook, but she wouldn't go near the kitchen. She'd always give me 'what for' when she found me baking with her personal chef." He imitated Harmony's famous, sexy drawl. "My dear David, cooking is so beneath you. You're royalty."

32

I swallowed my bite. "Royalty?"

"Yeah, she meant Hollywood royalty. Not that any of those so-called 'royals' wanted anything to do with me." His voice rose an octave. "'Go to your room, dear, can't you see Mummy is busy with her leading man? We've got to practice our lines.'"

Fred looked at me then back at David. "So, I guess you're saying you didn't have much of a childhood, growing up in that mansion of yours."

"Childhood? No, you could say I missed that part of my life."

I reached for David's hand. "Fred and I missed it too, dear."

Fred looked at me with his eyebrows raised to question my meaning. "Come on," I said to my husband. "You know good and well you'd have been a father to this boy if the two of us had shown up in Summit View. Knowing you, you wouldn't have been able to resist us."

Fred looked as if he felt a bit ashamed of himself. "You're probably right. In some ways, this tragedy played out in a way that robbed me of the only son I'd ever have."

David stopped chewing and really looked at Fred. "Son?" He smiled. "Do you think it's too late for that—for us to be father and son, I mean?"

"We're practically strangers, you, me, and Vonnie," Fred said. "You were raised in a completely different world, ah, and lifestyle than ours."

David pushed his plate away. "I know that. I feel like I was cheated out of a real family. Not that Harmony wasn't good to me, in her own way; it's just she didn't know how to be a mother." He looked at Fred and then looked down at the table. "I know we can't really make up for all the lost years, but maybe, somehow, we could all become, you know, a family—especially since I'm moving here."

Fred's fork froze in midair.

"Sorry, I didn't mean to blurt it out like that," David said sheepishly. "I put the mansion on the market, and movers are already putting everything in storage. The contents of my apartment will be here in a couple of weeks. After breakfast with Donna tomorrow, I've got a date with a realtor so I can buy my own mountain

33

bungalow. Then I'm going to see about getting a job as a paramedic. I've loved my job in LA, but there's no reason I couldn't pick up here where I've left off there."

Fred's eyes widened. "You're moving here? Why—"

A pounding knock erupted at the front door. "Vonnie, Vonnie, open up!" a voice called.

I sprang from the table. "Daddy?"

"It's your mother, Vonnie, she needs you," he called from the other side of the door.

Fred and David followed as I flung open the front door while little Chucky performed his bark and dance routine.

There before me stood my mother, with my father by her side. She leaned on him like one would a cane. Then I noticed that her foot sported a brand new, rock hard, hot pink cast.

"She slipped on the ice outside our condo tonight and broke her ankle," Dad said. "We just left the ER, and she insisted I bring her here. She says she can't make it up and down our stairs, as steep as they are."

With Dad's help, Mother hopped on one foot, scootching her way toward me.

"It's only for a few weeks," she said. "I won't be a bother. Besides, I'll be much better able to navigate your place than ours."

I felt as if my feet were stuck to the floor. How presumptuous she was. She knew how angry I was at her, but no, never mind my feelings and never mind that she was interrupting one of the most sacred moments of my life, not that she'd noticed.

She hobbled over the threshold as Dad guided her by an elbow. "Your father will run home and pack some of my things for me. I think I'll manage fine in that guest bedroom of yours, even if it does need a good dusting."

"But Mother . . ."

David peeked around me. "Well, who do we have here?" he said.

Mother stared at him, then chirped at me, "You have company?" She looked back at David. "Or is this your handyman making a late-night repair? If that's the case, I'll want your number, young man."

34

"Mother!"

Her eyes locked to mine. "Yes, Vonnie?"

"Mother, I'd like to introduce you to David Harris." I detected a tremor in my voice as I announced, "Your grandson."

Mother's eyes widened in horror. David somehow ignored her reaction, and before she could protest, he gave her a quick hug, a hug that felt to me like sweet revenge. I tried not to smile as Mother stood stiff in his embrace, all the while her eyes locked with mine.

David pulled back and turned to my father. "And you would be?"

I said, "David, this is my father, your grandfather."

David reached out and shook his hand. "It's very nice to meet you, sir."

My father grinned. "I never thought I'd see this day," he said.

That was an understatement. I wanted to blurt out a laugh but somehow refrained. If it weren't for the announcement that Mother expected me to be her caregiver, the moment would have been perfect.

I mean, I hadn't spoken to Mother since I'd learned of her betrayal. And I probably would have slammed the door on her if David hadn't been watching my every move. But to tell the truth, my emotions were in such a jumble that it was hard to react with anything other than caution. I'd figure all this out later. All I knew was I was not going to let my mother upstage the miracle of my reunion with my son.

I found my voice. "Tonight, David, let's put you in the study on an air mattress. Dad, take Mother to the spare room."

As I watched everyone spring to action I inwardly turned to the Lord. *Now what?* I asked him. *How do you expect me to handle this?*

How indeed.

5

A Brand-New Me

Clay laid his head against the soft donut-shaped headrest and closed his eyes. From overhead the soothing sounds of Kenny G swept through the room. The scent of jasmine—or was that lavender—wafted from the flickering flames of nearby candles. His naked feet—which had experienced their first pedicure—stuck out from the stark white sheet covering him. They were cold, so he kicked a bit until the bottom of the sheet fell over his toes like a tent.

He breathed in. Breathed out. So this was what drew women in droves?

He heard a noise from beside him, and he peeped his eye to see the door open just enough to allow the petite Asian woman entrance. "You ready, Mr. Whitefield?" she said.

Clay closed his investigative eye and nodded.

Words were hardly necessary.

"I will begin by exfoliating your face," she said, and he felt her presence as she moved to his head. "Then the rest of your body," she continued.

"Will it hurt?" he asked, just above a whisper.

The girl giggled. "Not too much," she said. "That's the price of beauty, no?"

Goldie

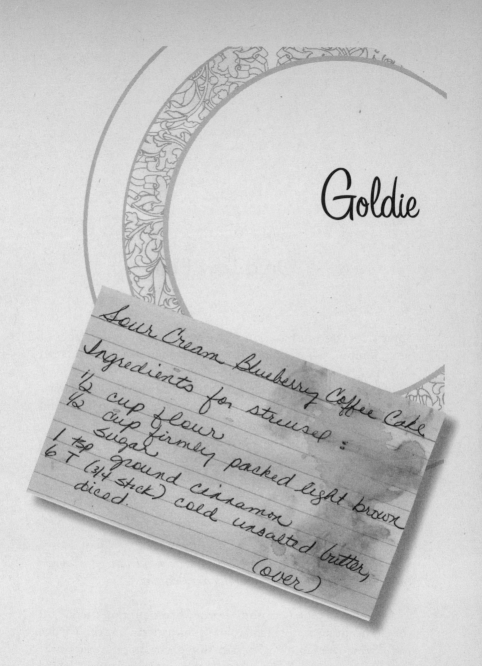

Sour Cream Blueberry Coffee Cake

Ingredients for streusel:

½ cup flour
½ cup firmly packed light brown sugar
1 tsp ground cinnamon
6 T (¾ stick) cold unsalted butter, diced.

(over)

6

On a Low Boil

Some days you'd just as soon wish away. Turn back the hands of time. Jump into bed, pull the covers over your head, and pretend they never happened. Such was this day.

It's not that I hadn't had bad days before. The good Lord knows I'd had some pretty bad ones. You can't be married to an unfaithful man for nearly thirty years and come away unscathed.

But this one . . . this one was the worst of all. This one was such a slap in the face, I thought I'd never recover. What had started out as a cold and crisp December morning touched with a hint of promise, followed by an evening of dining and laughter with one of my best girlfriends, had turned into a night filled with despair.

Despair and anger. Fury.

Remorse.

Oh, why did I ever say I'd go away for a weekend with my estranged husband, Lord? What in the world was I thinking?

I stood dead center before my opened bedroom closet, jerking at the clothes hung neatly and in color coordination along the wooden rod. "What was I thinking?" I said, ripping a maroon sweater away from its hanger and then shoving my arms into the sleeves. "Telling

Jack I'd go away with him to a mountain cabin up in Summit Ridge. For two days and two nights?" I wrestled out of the sweater and threw it toward the bed, where one of my oldest and dearest friends sat perched on the end as though she were modeling for a Sealy Posturepedic ad.

Lizzie Prattle caught it in midair. "Goodwill?" she asked.

I nodded, turning back to the closet. "You didn't answer my question."

"Well," she said with a purse of her lips. "Maybe deep down you really want to go."

My hand froze on a hanger draped with a long black velvet skirt and top I'd recently worn to a local church's early Christmas special with Jack. I'd bought it, wondering if Jack would notice the way it slenderized my hips and gave me an elegant flare. Though I'd kept him at arm's length the entire morning, the dress had certainly worked its magic. I felt beautiful, and Jack had barely been able to keep his eyes off me. Now the rhinestone buttons down the top's front winked at me, toying with my memories in the dim bedroom light of the "bachelorette" pad I'd been renting for the past couple of months, ever since I'd had my fill of my husband's cheating ways and, later, our daughter's overbearing will to see us reunited. It was not that I blamed Olivia. After all, we are her parents, and she loves us both. We did not raise her in a home of turmoil and calamity so that she might say, "Better separate than together." Instead, our memories are full of good times, of laughter around the dinner table as we readied ourselves for the next big high school sports game (Jack being the coach), where Jack would move beautifully across the field or the court and Olivia would stand proud in the center of the cheerleaders, kicking her legs, waving her pom-poms while I sat in the bleachers, sipping coffee and feeling content. We had memories that were good memories. Looking back on it, we—Jack and I—never really fought. But now that I know myself a bit better, I find that this was more my fault. I willingly allowed Jack to run over me in certain areas of our marriage, just as his mother had done with Jack's father. Like I said, I sat content in the bleachers. Not happy. Not unhappy. Just content. It wasn't until Olivia married and moved on with her life with her new family that I became sad. I was willing to continue to live as man and wife with Jack, reasoning that so many other wives out there had it worse. Besides all that, I did love Jack, and I knew that—in his own way—Jack loved me. He was a product of mimicking what his father had taught him. And now, since Jack had been in therapy, he seemed to understand that too, while I am learning things about myself and about my own role in the breakdown of our marriage and about my odd hopes of putting it back together.

I pulled the hanger holding the velvet frock from the rod, twisting around and displaying the outfit to Lizzie. "I looked right pretty in this, didn't I?" I asked, reverting back to my Southern "tongue."

She smiled at me, and for a moment I noticed how "handsome" she was. Silvery-gray hair worn short and always in place. Eyes that seem to dance even when she's sad or stressed. A face with so few wrinkles she'd have a hard time convincing anyone she's a grandmother. "You always do," she answered.

I returned the hanger. "That's not true." I threw up my arms as though I were a rag doll, then joined Lizzie by plopping down on the bed, my back bouncing just a bit on contact. "Until I left Jack, I'd pretty much let myself go."

Lizzie positioned herself alongside me. "Don't be ridiculous, Goldie."

I turned my head to look at her, then propped up on my elbows. "I'm not. Look at you. Your hair turned not gray, but silver. Your face barely has a wrinkle. You've had a houseful of children and your tummy is as flat as a sixteen-year-old's."

Lizzie laughed. "Genetics."

I had to laugh back. "Then I should be over two-hundred pounds and have hound dog jowls."

"Your mother is over two-hundred pounds and has hound dog jowls?"

I cut my eyes to her, running my fingers through my recently dyed red hair. "She deep fried everything," I said, and then the two of us laughed so hard that tears ran down our cheeks. I rolled over on my side and propped my head in the cup of my palm. "Lizzie, seriously. I can't believe I'm going away with Jack for a weekend. A month ago I was ready to divorce the man." My eyes widened. "And I could too. Legally and . . . you know . . . spiritually. He's had affairs on me since not too long after we married, and that was a long, long time ago."

"But he's getting help now. Meeting with Pastor Kevin."

I moaned. "I really don't know what he thinks we're going to accomplish in two days."

"And two nights." She grinned at me as though I were a virgin bride about to head off on a long-anticipated honeymoon.

"Separate bedrooms, I told him. No funny business."

Lizzie rolled over onto her stomach and gave me her serious look. "Goldie, I worry you won't last half a day. You're vulnerable right now, and you and Jack have history. It's not like a first date. You've been intimate for years." Her eyes softened. "Just promise me you'll be careful, okay?"

I held up my hand as though being sworn in before the judge. "I promise." I sat up straight and looked her dead in the eye. "I mean it, Lizzie," I said, then bounded off the bed. "And . . . you've got to help me find just the right clothes for keeping him at a safe distance. Nothing . . . sexy."

Lizzie rolled off the bed, leaving the sateen spread a mess of waves and ripples. She strolled over to the closet, reached in, and pulled my old and worn housecoat I'd owned since the late 1980s from a hook near the door. "Why don't you just wear this, then? And maybe we can head over to the thrift store on our lunch breaks and buy you some stained sweatpants a few sizes too big and some—"

"You are absolutely no help to me. No help at all." I feigned disgust as I brushed past her, walking out of the bedroom and into the kitchen. Lizzie followed. "Coffee?" I asked over my shoulder. "I made some coffee cake this morning, and there's still a bit left."

"Yum. Then I've got to get back home. Samuel will wonder what's keeping me so long."

After Lisa Leann's shower, Lizzie and I had met for dinner, and I assumed Samuel would know we'd be out late. I said so.

Lizzie sat at the table, folding her arms and resting them against the Formica of the table. "He misses me when I'm out too late." Her eyes scanned the room. "Do you ever get scared being here at night all by yourself?"

"Not really. No. Sometimes I'm a little lonely, but that passes after a phone call or two." I turned to prepare the coffee, my hands staying busy but my mind a hundred miles and a lifetime away. *Lord, where did it all go wrong?*

The coffee began to brew, and I joined Lizzie at the table. "Lizzie, can I ask you a question?"

"You know you can."

"You and Samuel . . . you've never really had any problems . . . I mean marital problems, have you?"

Lizzie gave her head a shake. "Not true."

"Really?"

"Of course." She leaned back. "You know about Michelle. Having a disabled child will put a strain on any marriage. Then, Tim . . . and his little upset in college."

"But having a child who's deaf or one who 'has to get married' in college isn't the end of the world."

Lizzie sighed. "Oh, but it felt like it at the time." She choked out a laugh. "When you don't really have anyone to blame, you tend to blame each other. Whew, those were bad days."

I raised my chin. "But you and Samuel. The way you love each other. You've always been like you are right now. Right?"

Lizzie stood and walked toward the coffeepot. "Don't be silly, Goldie. After all these years of marriage; are you kidding me?" She began pouring the coffee into two mugs I'd placed there moments earlier as I pulled the coffee cake from the cake pan in the corner of the countertop. "Oh, that does look good," she said.

"Thank you. How big a piece do you want?"

"Not very. If I eat too much this late, I'll have trouble falling asleep."

I chuckled. "We're getting old."

"Maybe you are," she said with a wink, carrying the mugs of coffee to the table, the steam from them emitting a most delicious aroma.

I joined her with two small plates, a couple of forks, and the coffee cake. As I sliced it, I said, "So tell me. I mean, if you don't mind being personal."

"Of course I don't mind." She took a sip from her mug, wrapping her slender fingers around it like a cozy. "In the early years . . . the really early years . . . Samuel was the moodiest man you'd ever want to meet."

"Really?"

She nodded. "Like you can't imagine."

"I can't imagine that," I said, repeating her words as I slid a plate topped with coffee cake toward her. "Not Samuel. He's the easiest-going man I think I've ever been around."

"That's what you see." She retrieved a fork from the tabletop and stabbed the coffee cake with it, then brought it to her mouth. "Mmm. This is good."

I took a bite of the cake for myself. "I did pretty good, didn't I?"

"You did."

"Okay, back to you and Samuel," I said, waving my fork at her.

She smiled. "That's about it, Goldie. He was very moody in those days and oftentimes difficult to live with. Back then, he was working his way up to being the president of the bank. It seemed to me that was all he had on his mind. Work, work, work. We'd come home from work—both of us—and I'd want to tell him all about my day. But he just wanted to sit in front of the television with the remote and watch the news or read the paper or whatever 'success' book he was reading at the time." For a moment Lizzie's eyes held a faraway look, then she shook her head and smiled at me. "He's a good man; don't get me wrong. And I love him dearly. Probably more than I let him know. But, that man can infuriate me like nobody's business."

I rested my fork against the side of my plate and picked up the coffee mug. "But, he's never . . . I mean, to your knowledge, he's never . . ."

Lizzie looked up at me sharply. "Had an affair on me? No. That much I'm certain of."

43

My shoulders drooped. "And I can't even count the number Jack has had."

Lizzie reached across the table, touching my arm with her fingertips. "He's getting help, Goldie."

"I know."

Lizzie paused for a moment, then spoke. "Goldie, tell me something. Do you still love Jack? Because if you don't, well, then, that's an issue unto itself. But, if you do . . ."

I didn't answer at first. Oh, sure, I knew the answer. The answer haunted me every single day of my life. But it was more complicated than just yes or no. There was a huge "but" at the end of the answer that muddied the waters, as my daddy always said.

"Well?" she asked.

"It's not as simple as a yes or no."

"Tell me."

I placed my coffee mug back on the table. "Lizzie, I know what everybody in this town has been saying about me. What kind of a fool woman stays with a man who runs around on her? And I honestly don't have an answer for that one. I don't. I could say that it was because I loved him or I hoped he would change or that I believe so strongly in my wedding vows I can't imagine ever divorcing. I could blame it on having Olivia and not wanting to bust up her little home. Or, I could just say that I was living a comfortable enough life—nice home, good friends, didn't have to work outside the home—or whatever. But, the fact of the matter is, I don't know why I stayed. It certainly wasn't because I was getting fine jewelry every time he ended one of his affairs. No matter what people might think."

Lizzie pressed her lips together. "The patience of Job, I always figured."

I humphed. "Job, nothing. The patience of Noah's wife is more like it."

Lizzie chuckled. "All right."

"Yes, I love Jack. I wouldn't have stayed married to him all these years if I'd merely liked the man. You know, Jack's not *all* bad." I peered at the ceiling for a moment, then back to my friend. "Oh,

Liz. If you could have known him when we first met. Before all this started. He was so suave. So adorable. And loving toward me? Please. It was as if the man absolutely worshiped me."

"When did it stop being that way?"

"Not even two years into the marriage. He still treated me well, and when we had Olivia he was a wonderful father to her."

Lizzie sighed. "What I don't understand, Goldie, is how he managed to make the rank of deacon in the church while all this was going on."

I shrugged my shoulders. "He was in church leadership before it really got out, I think. For the longest time—until this last one, really—he kept all his women to out of town. If he hadn't been buying me off with jewelry, I wouldn't have known it myself."

"What was it about the jewelry that—"

"His father did the same thing. To his mother. She warned me not too long after we'd married and . . . maybe that's why I stayed. His mother had stayed, and in the end she still had her home and her family. She seemed so content, and I loved her so much I—"

"Oh, dear. The sins of the father."

"Yep." I took a long sip of coffee. "In answer to your question, I don't know why the church allowed him to retain his position, but Pastor Kevin has removed him now. I think that Jack is glad of it, to be honest. It's a discipline he has to go through, and that'll only make him stronger. Better in the end." I sighed. "When Jack began having an affair with Charlene Hopefield, the Spanish teacher from Summit View high school, for crying out loud, I think . . . I think that . . . deep down, Jack wanted to be caught. He thinks so too. Or at least that's what he's said."

"Charlene Hopefield," Lizzie breathed out. "I don't know about that woman."

"Not to mention her age. Over twenty years difference between her and Jack."

"She's a flaunty one, and you know I don't like to talk ill of anyone."

I smiled at Lizzie. "Thank you. I needed that."

"Jack told Samuel that he ended it with Charlene right after you left."

My eyes widened. "Oh, yeah. He knew if he wanted to get me back . . . and Pastor Kevin told him that he wouldn't work with him at all if that wasn't the first step taken."

"Do you ever see her?"

I stood and walked toward the coffeepot on the other side of the room, bringing it back to the table with me before I answered. "Summit View, Colorado, isn't exactly New York or Chicago. Of course I see her." I topped off our coffee mugs. "I don't say anything to her. Not one word. If she walks into a store, I walk out. If she's coming down my side of the street, I cross it."

"But you didn't do anything wrong. She's the one who . . . well, it's your call." Lizzie took another bite of coffee cake before continuing. "I can't say I wouldn't do anything and everything to avoid her either. One thing's for sure; she's as far out of your life as she can get in little Summit View." She looked down at her watch. "I've got to get going. Samuel will get in one of his moods if I'm not home soon." She winked at me as she stood. "So, you leave tomorrow?" she asked, taking her plate to the sink. "For Summit Ridge?"

"I'll get that," I said, then added, "Tomorrow after church. Jack said he'd pick me up here in the afternoon and we'd go on up."

"Like I said before," Lizzie concluded, "just be careful."

"I will," I reassured her. "I promise."

"Charlene Hopefield is out of your life," Lizzie had said.

But she wasn't. Isn't. Not by a long shot.

Lizzie hadn't been gone five minutes when my doorbell rang. I'd already stepped into the small bath adjoining my bedroom and begun to scrub my face when I heard the gentle chime. Grabbing a hand towel, I patted my face dry as I moved toward the front of the condo, calling out, "I'm coming."

When I got to the front door, I switched on the porch light and peeked out the peephole. The hair on the back of my neck stood straight on end. It was Charlene Hopefield. *No store to walk out of or street to cross*, I thought as I drew back.

46

"What do you want?" I called through the closed door. I peeked through the hole again.

She wrapped her arms around herself as though she were freezing to death. "Goldie, I need to talk to you. Please. It's very important."

I stared at her for a long moment. What in the world did that woman have to say that would be of any interest to me?

"My name—as far as you're concerned—is Mrs. Dippel."

I watched her roll her eyes. Even in the dim overhead porch light, her disdain for me was evident. "Whatever. I need to speak with you. It's important. I'm being nice here. Nice enough to come to you instead of going over to Jack's and talking to him."

I flipped the lock and jerked the door open. "You stay away from my husband," I said.

She just stared at me. "May I come in or not?"

I stepped aside. "May as well." I looked down at her snow-covered boots. "But wipe your feet; I don't need your slushy mess on my carpet."

Charlene pounded her feet on the front mat for a few moments, then looked back up at me. "Will that do?" she asked, arching an eyebrow.

Cocky little thing.

"I guess."

She stepped over my threshold, pulling her long dark wool coat from her somewhat pudgy body. She held it toward me as though she actually expected me to take it, then threw it across the chair behind her. "Is that coffee I smell?" she asked. "Decaf? Because I can't have regular."

"It's stale," I answered, crossing my arms over my middle. "What do you want, Charlene?"

She turned toward the sofa and extended her arm a bit. "May I?" she asked.

I arched my brow. "May you what?"

"Sit? I'm exhausted." And then she sat down, in spite of the fact that I hadn't invited her to do so. "Not to mention I've been waiting across the street for your friend to leave. My gosh, what do you people have to talk about so long? My back end was going numb from sitting in my car that whole time." She paused. "Please sit, Goldie."

I coughed out a snicker. "I beg your pardon? I'll decide when or if I sit down. This is *my* home."

She nodded and looked around. "So it is. It's . . . nice. Certainly not the home you left, but it's . . . nice."

"You know nothing about my home." I sat in the nearest chair, one I'd picked up cheap at a thrift store down on Dyer Street.

She slid herself back on the sofa like a plump goddess, crossing one leg over the other. "Oh, Goldie, Goldie, Goldie." She laughed, sounding more like a cat than a woman. "Silly, silly Goldie."

I flushed red with a mixture of anger and embarrassment. If Jack had brought that woman into my home, he could take her and Summit Ridge and all the years we had between us, and choke on them as far as I was concerned.

"I hear you're going away for the weekend," she purred. When the question she clearly expected from me flashed in color on my face, she answered without my saying a word. "Oh, you know. One person tells one person and that person tells another. Eventually, it got to me. Summit Ridge, I understand?" I raised my chin before she went on. "Quaint. Not anywhere I'd want to be . . . least not with Jack . . . but for the two of you . . . well, I suppose it could be . . . quaint. Anyway," she said, stretching and draping her arms around her knees, "that's not why I'm here. I'm here because we have a bit of a problem."

"I can't imagine what," I said. "You are no longer a part of my husband's life and therefore no longer a part of mine." My heart began to pound as though it knew that life as I'd known it not ten minutes earlier was about to change forever.

Charlene looked down at her groomed fingernails, long and pointy and painted a frosty red. "How do I say this, Goldie? How do I put this delicately?"

"Mrs. Dippel," I corrected her in the firmest voice I could muster.

She looked up at me sharply. "Okay, then, *Mrs. Dippel.* Here's the deal: I'm pregnant, *Mrs. Dippel.* And the father of my child, *Mrs. Dippel,* is none other than your husband."

As soon as Charlene said the word *pregnant*, the blood rushed out of my head, past my heart, and out my toes. Lord have mercy, I'm surprised it didn't just pool right there on the dingy living room carpet of my condo, adding stain on top of stain. I'm also a little shocked I didn't have a heart attack and die right there on the spot. Somehow I managed to live. Somehow, after my vision had all but blacked completely out, it returned, bringing the blood back to my head, though I'm sure it was more like dishwater.

Charlene stood abruptly. "I see I've left you speechless," she said as she reached for her coat. "I'm sure you have a lot to think about, and I'll leave you to do so."

As she shoved her arms into the coat sleeves, I stood on legs made of jelly and said, "You can't just waltz in here and make a statement like that and then leave. I—I don't believe you. I don't. You're just upset because Jack and I are going away together."

Charlene spit out a cackle as she wrapped the sash of her coat around her waist. "Oh, please! Like I could care less at this point. Do you really think I was in love with that lug?"

I crossed my arms over my middle again, feeling a strange sense of protection for the lug. "So what you're saying is that you're the kind of woman who would just run off with anyone's husband? The kind of woman who would . . . who would . . ." I couldn't bring myself to say the words.

"Would sleep with just anybody?"

Apparently *she* could.

"I'm not like you, Goldie." She pulled her frizzy blonde hair out from under the collar of the coat. I watched as it lay in stark contrast to the dark wool, reminding me of a witch's broom against a midnight sky.

"What do you mean?" I choked out.

"I'm not Miss Goody-goody. Never have been. Never will be." She strolled toward the front door, then turned and peered at me over her shoulder. "Like I said, I just thought you should know."

I narrowed my eyes. "Does Jack . . . ?"

I heard the doorknob twisting open. "Does Jack know about the baby?" She pulled the door toward her, then turned back to me. "No. Not yet. I haven't decided what I'm going to do about all this." She cocked a brow. "Still, and like I've already said, I thought you should know."

And with that she walked out of the door without so much as bothering to close it. After a moment or two of standing there staring out at the bleak and the cold, I inched toward the door, pushed it shut, then turned and headed back to my bedroom. I stumbled as I neared the chair where I'd been sitting, falling to the floor in a heap. I attempted to pull myself up, albeit half-heartedly, then collapsed in a torrent of hot tears.

When I'd finally cried all I could cry, I rolled over then sat up on the floor, looking down toward my feet. There, wadded up and twisted, was the towel I'd had in my hands earlier. Apparently, I'd dropped it at some point between Charlene's swooping in and her life-altering announcement. I reached for it, threw it into the chair, then stood and hobbled back to my bedroom, where I stripped out of my clothes, donned the ratty housecoat Lizzie had teased me about earlier, then crawled into the bed, curling up like a baby.

Charlene's and Jack's baby.

I realized I was subconsciously holding my breath. When my chest began to tighten, I exhaled slowly and closed my eyes. *Why, Lord? Just when things were looking up.*

7

I Thought I 'Thaw a Puddy-Tat

Clay couldn't help it. With every chance he got, he stole a look at himself in the rearview mirror of his Jeep. Twice he stopped along the short road from Silverthorne to Summit View just to run inside a convenience store and head for the men's restroom so he could admire himself in the mirror.

He even flirted a bit with one of the salesclerks behind the counter.

"That's two-fourteen," she said as he paid for the bottled water flavored with only a hint of peach.

"And well worth it." He winked.

"You sure are a happy guy," she said, taking the two bills and change.

"Just had my first pedicure. My first facial. And my first massage. *What* is holding men back, I ask you. Why do we think this is just for women?" He ran his fingers through his hair. "What do you think of the highlights? Eh? Nice, right? For an Irish Native American? You think my ancestors are rolling over in their graves right now?"

The girl—her name tag dubbed her as Kristin—laughed. "You're right. Men should get prettied up too."

Clay frowned. "Well, let's not use words like *pretty*. But I did buy some pretty good-looking clothes over at the outlets."

He thought about it all the way home. His bad day—what with David Harris showing up—had turned out to be not so bad. He had a lead story, he was sporting a new look, and even the adorable Kristin from Rob's Pump-N-Go thought he was cute.

As he pulled into the city limits of Summit View, though, his mood changed. Passing by 6th Avenue off Main Street, he spotted Charlene Hopefield leaving the front door of Goldie Dippel's apartment.

No-good woman, he thought. He thought of another word too, but let it go. It didn't match his new look.

He slowed his Jeep enough to watch the blonde troublemaker scurry to her car parked on the other side of the road. She slid in with a look of . . . what was that . . . *triumph*? Nothing good, he thought, could come from her being over at Mrs. Dippel's. Nothing good at all.

"No-good woman," he said under his breath, then headed on toward his home. He needed to get writing on the article, get himself to bed, get plenty of sleep, so he would be well rested to do what he needed to do in the morning.

Donna

LARRY'S SPICE APPLE MUFFINS

2 CUPS FLOUR
1/2 CUP SUGAR
4 tSP BAKING POWDER
1/2 tSP SALT
CINNAMON

1 EGG BEATEN
1 CUP MILK
4 TBSP. MELTED BUTTER
1 CUP CHOPPED APPLES

SIFT FLOUR, 1/2 CUP SUGAR, BAKING POWDER,
SALT AND 1/2 TEASPOON CINNAMON —
(BACK)

8

Poached Paparazzi

On Sunday morning, I woke before my alarm sounded, even before the sun began to glide above the curtain of mountains that rose from my very yard. I sat up in bed and stretched, feeling somehow different, lighter. As a matter of fact, in the past few days it was as if I'd begun to awaken from a deep dream.

I rubbed my eyes at the thought. That was it. I hadn't had the dream about my failed rescue attempt since my baby's memorial service.

I swung my legs over the side of the bed then leaned forward and stared down at the floor.

What had Wade and I been, all of seventeen, eighteen? Too young to start a family, though I know Wade would have married me if I'd only said yes to his proposal. But after my pregnancy had . . . had ended, we'd drifted apart.

I turned to a career in law enforcement, and Wade turned to the bottle.

How many nights had I sat in my Bronco, waiting for Wade to stumble out of the Gold Rush Tavern so I could drop him off at his trailer?

Our routine never varied. "Sorry, Deputy Donna, I didn't mean to get drunk again," he'd slur as he'd stumble out of my truck and up the steps to his front door.

I'd roll down my window. "Want me to leave you a note to remind you where you left your truck?"

"Nah. I'll remember." He'd laugh. "It'll be where I always park it when you're on duty."

And so it went.

Lately, though, his truck hasn't been parked outside the tavern.

I figured he'd gotten behind on his bar bill again and taken to drinking alone, that is, till I discovered he'd been having dinner with Kevin Moore.

What an unlikely pairing, Wade and Pastor Kevin from Grace Church.

From what I'd gathered, they'd started sharing an evening meal down at the Higher Grounds Café after Moore's wife, Jan, had succumbed to cancer.

In fact, according to Wade, it had been the pastor's idea to hold the funeral for our long-lost baby. But as Vonnie later confessed, the funeral had been more of an "intervention" for me.

"Donna dear, you were so distraught, and with all your talk about dying, Fred and I were concerned. We had to take this course of action. We were trying to save your life."

Their action had been to invite me to dinner then surprise me with a drive to the graveyard.

I'd call it a kidnapping, really, though I wouldn't say so officially.

All I know is that when Wade, my dad, the Westbrooks, and the pastor had gathered around baby Jamie Lee's grave marker, I'd fallen to my knees, pounding my fists against the frozen ground as I wept.

Perhaps that was the reason I felt lighter: I'd finally acknowledged my secret grief and I'd wept until I'd felt God's presence.

I stood up and peeked out the blinds covering my bedroom window. It was still dark.

I laughed at myself. Me, feeling God's presence? I didn't even believe in the existence of God. (A little secret I kept from my Potluck Club friends.)

The thought of them made me stifle a laugh. What would they say if they knew?

I could hear Evie now. "I always knew that girl was a heathen." And Vonnie would counter, "Now, Evie, this just means we need to pray for her."

I snorted. Prayer. What good did it do to pray to a God who was such a cruel master? As far as I was concerned, if he existed at all, he existed as the author of all heartache. Who needed to serve a God like that?

My own heartache had started early, when I was only four. That's when the most important person in my life walked out on me. I'd watched, one Sunday morning, as my mother sang a duet with the church choir director. Their voices blended so perfectly that my toddler self sat beside my dad spellbound. But after the service, instead of heading for home, Mom hopped into the choir director's Volkswagen bug and headed for I-70 and a new life.

And me? That's what hurt the most. I wasn't a good enough reason for my mother to stay married much less stay around.

Dad did his best to raise me, but I'd wanted my mother. That is, until my fifth-grade Sunday school teacher stepped in. Vonnie Westbrook had reached out to me to become the mother figure I'd so desperately needed. We were now so close that strangers often mistook her for my mother. And as far as I was concerned, their misguided observation was truth.

Vonnie's motherly influence hadn't been enough to stop me from sleeping with my high school sweetheart. As latchkey teenagers, Wade and I had spent too many unsupervised hours alone in my bedroom.

That's how baby Jamie Lee came to be conceived.

I padded to the bathroom and switched on the light. When my eyes adjusted to the brightness of the room, I looked at myself in the mirror. It was a reflection I still hated. I hated it because of what I had done, for what I had become. I splashed cold water on my face, then patted it dry with a towel.

My constant guilt had somehow been relieved, if only temporarily, at the service as Pastor Kevin yammered on about God's love for me regardless.

Could what he said really be true?

Yeah, I wish.

I looked at the reflection of my eyes and saw the truth ignite in a flash of anger. I was too despicable for God to love. I knew it, and he knew it.

I hung my towel on the rack next to the sink. Even if there were a loving God, he had to know I was worse than my own mother. She'd only abandoned me, not terminated my existence.

I sighed deeply, trying to shake off the despair that had jolted me back to the past. I padded barefoot toward the kitchen to make a cup of joe.

If there was truth, I reasoned, I'd find it in a strong cup of coffee. I always said that if you drank enough of it no one would be able to tell you were dead.

Which was a good thing because since that failed rescue attempt up above Boulder, I had been dead. Vonnie had been right to be concerned for my life. When the Long baby was swept from my arms in those floodwaters, I'd finally come to understand the loss of my own baby. That loss had magnified, when, just a few days ago, I was served papers in infant Bailey Ann Long's wrongful death lawsuit. I wasn't sure what I'd have done if Clay hadn't been there to comfort me when I opened that envelope. Reading that letter made me feel as if my pretense at life was over. Suicide had seemed like a solid, logical solution to my pain.

But though my life was a lie, I'd decided to live. Maybe it was the presence of God that touched me or maybe it was something else. I don't know. All I know is I have to wait to see if there really is something called hope and if it can be applied to me.

Once in the kitchen, I poured ground coffee into the top of my coffeemaker and filled the reservoir with water and hit the start button. While the coffee brewed, I stared out my kitchen window and watched the first rays of sunlight turn the darkness into a pale blue that backlit the snow-covered peaks. Sunrise was another reason to live, I decided as the sun rose higher. It brightened as a long band of clouds striped the sky above the mountaintops with a bold pink. It looked as if Mother Nature was playing with her crayons.

I poured a cup of coffee into my mug, which was emblazoned with my favorite one-word description of me: "Dangerous." Some of the hot coffee splashed onto my new red flannel pajamas. Normally I sleep in my sweats, but Vonnie and Fred had given me the pj's as an early Christmas gift. I was surprised to find I liked the pj's, despite the fact they were covered in grinning snowmen. I grabbed a dishcloth from the sink and wiped the coffee off several of the snowmen's faces. "What do you have to smile about now?" I asked them out loud.

That's when I realized it. I was smiling too.

I took a swig of coffee, black and thick, just the way I liked it, and watched the ever-expanding rays of the sun pinken the snowcaps.

Come on, now, I chided myself. *What's the big deal?* Could it be that I was excited about my breakfast date with David?

That couldn't be it. I wasn't really all that interested in men. Okay, it's not that I preferred girls or anything like that. It's just that the truth, simply put, was I didn't think I deserved a guy.

I took another sip of my coffee. David, just like Wade and Clay, would have to settle for friendship. That was all I had to give.

With the sun spreading its glow over the morning, I decided to walk to the café, despite the bitter cold. Besides, in the warmth of my black down parka, only my nose and cheeks felt the sting of winter.

When I opened the door of the Higher Grounds Café, a community diner nestled inside a hundred-year-old schoolhouse, I realized it was still a bit early for David. But it wasn't too early for me to start on my second cup of joe.

I sat down at my usual spot and signaled Sal for a cup, which she immediately poured. As soon as she scurried to another table, I looked up to see Larry the cook standing in front of me. He was another one of the local clods who had asked me out following Lisa Leann's "dare to be brave in dating" column.

"Hi, Larry," I said without enthusiasm.

"Just stopped by your table to let you know I've enjoyed seeing you around here lately."

I felt my eyes narrow. "Thanks, Larry. I think. I guess it's good to see you too."

He looked goofy, with his netted hair slicked back, showing that gap-toothed grin of his. He continued in his politest of tones. "I wanted to tell you that I've noted and appreciate your improved attitude."

My sip of coffee almost spewed from my mouth. "Excuse me?"

Larry looked over his shoulder as Sal gave him the signal to get back to work. "Can't talk right now; the kitchen's calling. I just wanted you to know that red is definitely your color."

"I'm not wearing red," I said.

"You were last night."

I felt the color rise in my cheeks. "You were spying on me?"

He laughed and said, "You're really something, you know that?" as he scurried to the back. Just before he disappeared behind the counter he added, "Glad to see your sense of humor has improved too."

I blinked as he disappeared into the kitchen. Larry was a bit of a jerk, but I couldn't imagine him as a Peeping Tom. Well, whatever he was, I'd get to the bottom of it. No one was allowed to spy on me in my own home. I'm the law, after all.

The whole episode left me feeling off center until I thought of all the things I'd do to him if I caught him outside my house.

But first things first. Later today I'd run to the hardware store and order blinds for the kitchen and living room, a little chore I'd been putting off for ages. I already had blinds in the bedroom so I could sleep through the day when I was on the graveyard shift.

The door swung open, and Clay, looking as fashionable as a metrosexual, entered the room. Now I'd seen everything.

What had he done to himself? A haircut? An eyebrow wax? A new outfit consisting of a sleek gold-colored knit turtleneck with formfitting brown knit pants? I'd known he'd lost a lot of weight lately, but just who was he trying to impress? When he waved in my direction, my eyes widened. Tell me it isn't so—the man even sported a manicure.

I whistled. "That's some new look you got there, bud."

"Do you like it? I ran down to the Silverthorne outlets after the party yesterday and did a little shopping."

"What's going on?" I asked. "Are you filling in for Ryan Seacrest on *American Idol*?"

He pulled up a chair. "Just trying to change my image."

"What's wrong with your old image?"

Just then I caught that new waitress—Eleana, I think her name is—as she smiled in Clay's direction. I looked from her to him then said, "Whoa, hold on. Don't you think she's a little young for you?"

Clay looked confused, then caught my meaning. The man actually blushed. "No, no. It's not like that. I'm not interested in Eleana."

Then suddenly, pad and pen in hand, her long blonde hair swept up into a ponytail, she was standing next to our table. Was she batting her eyelashes?

"Hi, Clay!" she said in a voice that was three notches too perky. "What will it be?"

I rolled my eyes. The man was trying to impress a girl who looked like a teenager? Sick.

Clay pretended he hadn't noticed her enthusiasm. "Just coffee for now," he said without so much as a smile.

As soon as she turned to grab her coffeepot, I started scolding him. "Clay, Clay, Clay, I'd hate to have to arrest you for underage dating."

"I told you, I'm not interested in Eleana."

"Then what gives?" I asked. "There's definitely something going on here. Care to tell me?"

The man looked flustered as Eleana returned to pour him a cup of coffee. As soon as she left, he said, "Ah, well, Donna, to tell you the truth, I've been meaning to talk to you . . ."

The bell above the door sounded once again, and I looked up. "David," I called out. "Right on time."

David was looking good and, in fact, dressed much the same as Clay, except the turtleneck that peeked out of his black leather coat was also black, like mine.

Clay looked confused. "You're meeting David for breakfast?"

"Yeah, want to join us?"

Clay stood up so suddenly his chair teetered. "No, no. I'll catch you later."

"But you wanted to tell me something."

"Later," Clay said as he backed away.

I squinted at him. Clay had a scoop for me? Now, this was a reversal. He was the one always pestering me for the latest town gossip so he'd have something to print in that paper of his.

"All right," I said, watching him retreat to a table in the corner.

David sat down across from me, but I looked past him. Even though the morning glare was shining on the café windows, my "policed" eyes managed to capture a glimpse of Lizzie and her family drive past, probably on their way to church.

I turned my attention back to David and felt my heart skip a beat. He was looking at me so intensely.

"How are you?" I asked, hoping to break the moment.

"Has anyone ever told you how great you look? I mean, honestly, you look so normal."

"Is that supposed to be a compliment?"

David laughed. "Take it as one. The women of Hollywood are more about makeup and plastic surgery. They can't hold a candle to your natural beauty."

My cheeks burned at that remark. Natural beauty? I didn't know whether to laugh or to take him in for questioning. My eyes darted over to Clay to see if he'd noticed my blush. Our eyes locked, then he hid his face behind a menu as Eleana ran to take his order. Was she flirting with him? She was! She was even touching his shoulder, in a very friendly sort of way. From where I sat, it looked like the girl had it bad for him. Go figure.

After David and I had a breakfast of eggs, bacon, and Larry's spice apple muffins, David took a sip of his coffee then said, "I've been waiting till this moment to tell you my surprise."

I looked over to where Clay was sitting; he had finished his breakfast too. He stood up and flipped a dollar on the table before sliding into a new form-fitting leather jacket. Leather jacket? What was the deal with that?

I turned my attention back to David. "Surprise?" I asked.

Before he could make his announcement, the café door burst open and Lisa Leann rushed inside, stamping snow off the bottom of her furry snow boots, which perfectly matched her fur-trimmed, camel-colored suede jacket. I suppose she thought it complemented her red hair and all. Honestly, was color and fashion the only nonsense that woman kept in her head?

As soon as she saw Clay, she ran to him. "Clay, darlin', look at you. My, you are a handsome one." She looked at me out of the corner of her eye and spoke even louder. "The girls around here are starting to notice. Why, two of the single women in that Sunday school class I teach asked me about you just the other day."

David noticed my stare and turned to watch the exchange.

"I told them, the next time I see him, I'm inviting him to our class. It would make things a lot more interesting." She cackled. "Don't you think? I'm heading that way now, and I could give you a ride. Care to join me?"

Clay looked embarrassed, but he nodded his head. "Sure." He paused as if to make sure I was watching. "I guess. Yeah."

"Well, good. After all, there's not a finer bachelor in town than you."

She turned to leave then acted surprised to see me. "Donna, I hadn't realized you were sitting there."

"Ah, yeah."

Lisa Leann looked David up and down as if she thought he were a stale donut. Then in a fakely sweet voice said, "David, I guess you're about ready to head back for California."

"No, ma'am," David said with a twinkle in his eyes. "I'm glad you stopped by our table. I was just about to make an announcement."

Clay stepped closer. "What sort of announcement?"

David grinned at his audience. He looked at me. "Some of you knew this was coming, but today it's official. I'm here to stay." He paused, staring at me. "It seems I've fallen in love."

I stared back, not daring to blink. He continued. "Not only with this place but with the people. I said to myself, 'Summit View's the place you should be.' So here I am. My furniture is already en route and . . ." He craned his neck to look out the window. "There's my realtor pulling up to the café now."

He turned back to me. "Donna, would you help me look at houses this morning? You don't have to be at work for a while yet, do you? I could really use your advice."

All I could do was nod my head, while Lisa Leann said, "Honestly, David. Are you sure this is the wise thing for you to do?" She brightened. "Your girlfriend in LA, she's coming to join you?"

David winked at me then looked back at Lisa Leann. "I'm single and looking," he said with a grin. "I'm liking what I'm seeing right here in Summit View."

Lisa Leann, who looked less than amused, shot a quick glance back at Clay. "Oh, I see. Though I'm sure you'll get bored at our simple way of life and head back to Tinsel Town lickety-split."

"We'll see about that," David said, still grinning.

Lisa Leann's voice seemed to cool. "Well, we will, won't we?"

She turned to me as David's realtor, a Mrs. Wanda Whittman, walked up to the table. Wanda usually goes to Grace Church on Sunday mornings, that is, when she doesn't have a fish on the line. And David could be a whopper. By the gleam in her eye, I could see she thought so.

Mrs. Whittman paused, waiting for a break in the conversation. She was as much a fashion plate as Lisa Leann, dressed from head to toe in winter white cashmere, including her long flowing sweater jacket with fur trim. The posh black sunglasses she wore on top of her high-styled blonde hair were the crowning touch.

But Lisa Leann wasn't ready to let Wanda get in on the conversation yet. "Oh, Donna dear, good news from your soon-to-be stepmother, Miss Evangeline Benson."

I felt my eyebrows cock. What an unsettling thought to have that woman as my stepmother. I crossed my arms. "What did Miss Evangeline have to say?" I asked.

"Her wedding to your dad is going to be the event of the winter wedding season. And I'll tell you why: she's given me free rein in most areas of the planning, mainly because there's not much time, so she needs a professional to keep things on schedule."

This was news to me. "There's not much time?"

"Goodness, no. This thing's going to be a done deal by the end of January."

"What? Nobody told me that!"

"Well, consider yourself told. That's why I'll need you to drop by the shop tomorrow so I can take your measurements."

"For what?"

"Your bridesmaid dress. You must be excited to be the maid of honor."

I stood to my feet. "I'm the what?"

"The maid of honor. Who else did you think?"

"Vonnie," I stammered. "It should be her best friend, Vonnie."

"Well, she's got the matron of honor position all sewn up. Here's the exciting part, as all you girls in the Potluck Club are of so many different sizes and dimensions, and as there's so little time to pick just the right dress that will flatter everyone, I've been given the honor of picking out the design myself. Evie gave me her colors and cost guidelines. The rest is up to me."

"The potluck girls are Evangeline's bridesmaids?"

"Yes. All except me, as I'm the official wedding coordinator. Though I'm going to wear a matching gown because I'll stand in as an honorary bridesmaid."

"Evangeline asked you to be an honorary bridesmaid?"

"She didn't have to. I'm simply helping her make all the right decisions."

I was starting to like this woman. "Just let me know what I can do to help."

"Sure thing. Got to run. You'll drop by later, won't you?"

"Sure," I said to her back as she darted out the door.

The next hour turned into a blur, as David and Mrs. Whittman dragged me to mansion after mansion on isolated mountain ridges.

64

The latest house graced an upper ridge of Swan Mountain with a spectacular panoramic view.

Mrs. Whittman had stepped outside to take yet another call on her cell phone. I walked to the patio sliding glass door and looked out over the deck that seemed suspended on the side of the mountain. Just below us stretched a dark green pine forest, flocked in drapes of winter snow.

Honestly, it was breathtaking. David walked up behind me and put his hand on my shoulder as we looked at the view together.

"What do you think of this one?" he asked.

"It's a beauty. But a little rich for my blood," I admitted. "Though I'm sure you could be happy here. I mean, who wouldn't? But a sixty-two hundred square foot mansion on top of this mountain is not going to be cheap. Do you realize you could fit five or six duplicates of my little mountain bungalow in here?"

He squeezed my shoulder. "I'm not worried about the cost."

I turned and looked up at him. "You must be working with some budget."

David stepped closer and closed his eyes as if he were going to kiss me. I turned suddenly. "Did you see that?" I asked, pointing down the mountain.

"What?" he asked as he stepped closer to the window.

"That lone buck there."

This time, he placed a hand on either side of my shoulders. "Yes, I see it. Look, it's got a mate."

Before he could try to take advantage of the moment again, I darted to the counter to retrieve a color brochure of the house. "You may want this," I said. I looked at the price tag and gasped. "Five million dollars? You're prepared to spend five million dollars on this place?"

"Why not?" David said. "I'm thinking it might be a good investment. Don't you?"

"Not really." I plunged ahead, willing to break the intensity of the moment. "I mean, you gave up Harmony's home for an apartment. Why do you want a mansion now?"

David seemed to sense my unease and smiled at me in a way that, so help me, made me want to giggle. Though I hid my reaction with a scowl.

"You've got a good point," he said. "But I'm thinking I'll need the tax break after selling the LA home."

"But won't you be lonely in a big place?"

He looked at me with his puppy dog eyes. "Not with my family around. Besides, I'm not planning to be single forever. Are you?"

"Can't imagine why not," I said, folding my arms and leaning on the wall behind me.

He took a step toward me. "But don't you want to find someone special?"

I shrugged. "I've got my family."

"You're lucky." He walked across the floor till he stood before me, looking down into my upturned face. "Unless I leave LA, I'll never be able to escape Harmony's fame. I need to move somewhere where people don't get swept into all that Tinsel Town gossip. If I move here, I'd have family too. Family who'd see me for me without all the Hollywood hype."

I kept my arms folded. "Yeah. I get that."

David turned and walked to the patio window and looked down the mountainside. "Donna, I envy you. You've got your dad, and when it comes to your relationship with my mom, well, you're like a daughter to her."

I walked up behind him and hit him in the arm with my balled fist. "Then that would make me like your sister."

"Sister?" David laughed, rubbing his arm. He turned and looked down at me. "I'd like to be closer than that."

I took a deep breath. "David . . ."

"Let's just work at being friends," he said, "then we'll see from there, okay?"

"As long as you don't get the wrong idea."

"Who, me?"

I put my hands on my hips. "I'd hate to have to take you into custody." I felt my cheeks flame as I realized I'd just set myself up for a romantic play on words. I tried to backpedal. "I mean . . ."

"I'm already in your custody," David said as I grimaced.

"You are making me crazy," I protested.

"I know. Which is just another reason why I like you so much."

"Now, that's a feeling I'd like to arrest."

David grinned. "I know you think you mean that . . ."

"Just hush," I said. "You don't know who you're messing with."

"Don't be so sure."

Before I could continue the argument, Mrs. Whittman waltzed into the kitchen to join us. "Isn't it marvelous?" she asked David.

He looked smug. "Yes, as a matter of fact." He looked at me out of the corner of his eye. "It is."

An hour later, Mrs. Whittman had us tucked into her silver Escalade and was headed for town. "I think you'd be very happy at Swan Villa," she told David. "Do you want to drop by the office and make the owners an offer?"

"Let me think about it," David said.

"Wait a minute," I said. "The house has a name?"

"All houses in David's price range do," Wanda assured me.

"Oh."

At about four o'clock, Wanda drove the back roads into Summit View, then turned down Vonnie and Fred's street. The Westbrooks' front yard was full of vans and news trucks. "What's going on here?" I asked.

Mrs. Whittman slowed down. "It looks like a couple of camera and news teams are visiting the Westbrooks," she said.

David sighed. "They've found me already?"

A cluster of men and women with microphones turned to stare at us almost hungrily. David growled under his breath. "Well, that didn't take Clay long."

"What did he do?"

"Isn't it obvious? He put his story about Vonnie and me on the wire. Unfortunately, it looks like it made the headlines."

I felt my temperature rise. So that was Clay's little secret? He got a makeover so he could guest star on *Hollywood Nightly*?

"Stop the truck," I demanded as Mrs. Whittman pulled over to the side of the road. I turned to David. "Poor Vonnie and Fred, they weren't prepared for this."

David stepped out of the car beside me. "I was going to warn them tonight. The paparazzi arrived sooner than I anticipated." He looked back at Mrs. Whittman. "I've got to check this out. I'll call you later."

Mrs. Whittman leaned over the seat. "Is everything okay?"

"Peachy," he said in an exasperated tone. "Just peachy."

Before we could make it up the steps, Kendra Goodall, a face I recognized from *Hollywood Nightly*, stuck her microphone in David's face and said, "Mr. Harris, it was always rumored that you were the illegitimate son of the famed Hollywood actress, Harmony Harris, and one of her leading men. So, we can put those rumors to bed?"

I was surprised that David knew his way around a microphone. "Yes. Those rumors were false. Harmony's publicist has prepared a statement in the event this became known. But in the meantime, I can tell you that the late Harmony Harris was my mother by adoption."

"So, you've come to Summit View, Colorado, to meet your birth mother, Vonnie Westbrook? According to the news story that came across AP last night, there were mysterious circumstances surrounding your adoption. What can you tell us?"

David put on his sunshades. "No comment."

Out of the corner of my eye, I saw Wade Gage's truck come to a full stop as Wade swung open the door of his cab.

Kendra said, "So, David, is the rumor true that you're engaged to be married? Is this your fiancée?"

The camera focused on both of us as Wade stopped dead in his tracks and David slipped a protective arm around me. "I have no comment to make at this time."

"Then you're not denying the rumor?" The reporter shoved the microphone into my face. "Can you tell us your name and what it's like to be engaged to one of the most eligible bachelors in Hollywood?"

It was unlike me to freeze before a camera. How many times had I given a statement to the Denver TV news teams following a particularly spectacular automobile accident or rock slide? But this time, no words came from my mouth.

Wade, dressed in his cowboy boots, jeans, and fleece-lined denim jacket stomped toward the reporter and pointed at her cameraman. "Why don't you point that thing in another direction?"

Kendra quickly motioned for her cameraman to turn the camera in Wade's direction. "This is a free country, cowboy," she said. "I can point our camera where I please. And if you don't leave, I'm going to call in the local law."

Suddenly I found my voice as the camera whipped back to me. "That won't be necessary," I said as I flashed my badge, which I kept in my wallet. "I am the law, and you're trespassing on private property. I think it's time for you and your crew to leave before I call for backup."

9

Who's That Girl?

Clay would have tucked his tail between his legs and dragged himself home, but he needed to run to the office and handle some last minute details concerning the article he'd written and sent out the night before.

As soon as he arrived in the modernized building, he headed for his personal cubicle, sorted through the mail the receptionist had left stacked in a black-wired mail drop, tossed the junk, and returned the rest. It was a Sunday. He'd read it tomorrow.

He kicked back in his chair, turned on his computer, and deleted about a hundred forwarded emails. He skimmed the rest, grinning when he saw that he'd received an email from Britney, the new girl in town who worked at the Hallmark store. Her screen name was CardGirlBrit. Subject line read: Guess who?

It had been sent just before noon.

He opened it immediately.

> Hey, cutie. Bet you didn't think I was smart enough to figure out your email address over at the paper. But, I am. I haven't seen you in a while in the shop but caught a glimpse

of you heading down Main Street yesterday in your Jeep *and* in church today. So, what's up with that?

And, what gives? You don't have anyone to buy any more sweet gifts for anymore? Come to see me, okay? I'm working this afternoon from noon till five.

"Cutie," she'd called him.

He'd head over there soon. A sudden thought occurred to him. *Maybe two could dance to this tune, Miss Donna Vesey.* Maybe he'd ask Britney to dinner tonight, and make certain Donna found out about it. He grinned, then got busy with his work, grateful he was in the building alone.

A little while later, he went to the men's restroom to freshen up a bit. Happy with his appearance, he left the building and walked the five or six blocks to the card shop. A light snow was beginning to dance in the air; he'd read over the wire that an early blizzard was due to hit the area. He'd have to keep that in mind if Britney agreed to go out with him. He shook his head a bit. *When* she agreed to go out with him. He needed to stay positive, be confident. He was a man not used to dating. To be exact, he was a man not used to having women agree to go out with him. All that was about to change, he decided. He took a deep breath and sighed. He hoped it was, anyway.

About a half a block away he thought he saw Donna coming out of the card shop, but one look at the way this woman was dressed told him otherwise. Donna wouldn't be caught dead in attire like that. Still, the girl was about Donna's size. Had her hair color. Even had Donna's walk. Something in the way she moved . . .

He watched as she stepped toward a Nissan parked in front of the store. When she caught his stare, she smiled broadly at him and waved. No, definitely not Donna. Donna hadn't gotten that excited to see anyone in her life.

Still, he waved back, wondering who she might be.

Goldie

Hamburger Quiche for Real Men

1 unbaked 9" pie shell
½ cup chopped onion
¼ cup chopped green pepper
1 T. cooking oil
1 lb. lean ground beef
1 can condensed tomato soup
½ cup soft bread crumbs

(over)

10

Sweet Revenge

By Sunday morning, I had a plan. I was going to make Jack Dippel pay if it was the last thing I ever did. And I was going to stay strong through it all, even if it killed me. *Though, Lord, you know I didn't start out that way. Oh no. Last night I was a complete wreck.* Blessedly I didn't wake—not one time—during the night. When I woke it was because the alarm on my bedside clock was beeping at me, jarring me out of my deep slumber. I reached for it, pushing the "off" button, then rolled over on my back, aware that I'd not even moved in my sleep.

For a brief moment—only a second, really—the memories of the night before stayed locked deep within my mind's vault. That place where, while sleeping, humans put all the issues from the day before that they don't want to remember. It's almost like a gift from God himself. A fragment of time when, as far as we know, all is right with the world.

Then I remembered. It started out as a heaviness in my stomach, then pushed itself past my shattered heart and burst into my memory. *God . . .*

I sat up and held my head in my hands. *What am I going to do now?* I asked the One who knows me best.

But I didn't wait for an answer. Not really. I just kicked at the covers, padded over to the bathroom, and began getting ready for church and the rest of my day. A day, ironically, that would end with me and my skunk of a husband heading up to a mountain cabin for two miserable days and two unbearable nights.

It was sometime during church that my plan of action—of revenge—came to me.

Jack and I were sitting in our usual pew. I had placed my purse between us, just so he could not touch me in any way, shape, or form. During the sermon, I happened to glance over at Lisa Leann Lambert, Texan transplant and all-around busybody. (By the way, did my eyes deceive me or was she sitting with Clay Whitefield?) Well, anyway, that was when I remembered seeing an old Oprah (or was it Montel?) show in which women exacted what they called "legal revenge" on the men who had hurt them. One of the women (like Lisa Leann, hailing from Texas) had received a call from her soon-to-be ex-husband telling her he'd run off with his secretary (or was it her best friend?). He and the wife owned a brand-new BMW (or was it a Mercedes?). He instructed the wife to place an ad in the paper so as to sell the car, then to send him the money at "this address." Whatever else had been theirs was now hers. The other car, the house, the property, and the bank accounts. The now-jilted wife did exactly as he instructed. She placed an ad in the local paper and sold the car to the first respondent. As the new buyer handed her the check for $100, he said, "Why so cheap? This car is worth a fortune!" To which the woman replied, "He told me to sell it. He didn't say for how much."

By the time I got home from church—having heard not one word of the sermon, I am ashamed to say—my head was swimming with all the rotten things I could do to Jack during our time away in Summit Ridge. It would surely not be a time he would soon forget! Sure, this wasn't the Christian way to act, but right then, at that moment, as far as I was concerned, the Christian way just wasn't going to cut the mustard.

So to speak.

Jack arrived right on time, grinning like a schoolboy about to make his first conquest. When I opened the door, he stood on the porch, hands on his hips and feet spread wide. As the high school's head coach, he was most comfortable in this stance. "You ready?" he asked. He glanced upward. "It's supposed to start snowing again any minute. I'd like to beat it if we can."

December in Summit View almost guarantees daily snowfall, though we could go days without seeing so much as a flake. But the ground and surrounding mountains were always snow-topped, as pretty as a postcard. The past couple of days had seen clear skies, but the weatherman had promised that by early evening we'd start seeing the "white stuff" again.

"Come on in," I said to the snake, all the while giving him my bestest, most fakest smile. "I'm nearly ready."

As Jack stepped over the threshold, I pointed toward the kitchen, all the while heading back to the bedroom. "The groceries are already bagged up or in the cooler if you want to go ahead and load them."

I felt Jack's fingers wrap around my wrist. I stopped cold, a fraction of an inch from clobbering him with the fist of my other hand. He tugged a bit, turning me toward him, pulling me into his arms, kissing me gently on the cheek. "Here's to the start of a great weekend, Goldie," he whispered in my ear. I shivered. Not out of passion, but disgust. I had planned and plotted. I wasn't about to let a little thing like a kiss ruin my scheme.

I smiled at him, reaching over and giving him a quick kiss in return. "I can't wait," I said.

Well, at least that much was true.

We were halfway to Summit Ridge, which was about an hour's drive, when Jack declared that we needed to stop for gas. "Do you need to use the ladies' room?" he asked me as we pulled into one of those new, fancy-schmancy truck stops, complete with showers, restaurants, shops, and such.

I said that I could probably stand to stretch my legs.

76

That wasn't all I could stand to stretch. I'd like to stretch his neck from here to the maternity ward of Summit View Medical Center, but I didn't add that little bit of info into the conversation. Not yet, anyway. *That* would come soon enough.

It was all part of the plan.

As soon as Jack parked and we exited the car, I noted he'd left his cell phone sitting in the cup holder of the console. I smiled with evil delight.

"I'll pick up a few snacks for us. Want coffee?" Jack asked as we entered through the glass doors.

"You know how I like it," I said, making a beeline for the rest-rooms. I even managed to smile at him for good measure.

I have to say that the ladies' facility—though meant for women truck drivers, mainly—was fairly impressive. If I hadn't been in such a hurry to get back to the car, I would have taken the time to enjoy it. The wallpaper was feminine and completed with a matching border. The sinks and countertops were a nice faux marble, and there were little baskets filled with assorted lotions and soaps. Tiny paper cups were stacked near bottles of Scope, and there was even a cozy seating arrangement in one of the front corners of the room. The best part, though, were the electrically warmed toilet seats.

Now that's something worth coming home to!

But I didn't have time to linger, even on the warmth of a toasty toilet. I took care of Mother Nature's call, washed and dried my hands (and yes, I used some of the apple-scented lotion; I couldn't help myself!), and then went right back to the car. Jack, I saw, was still standing in line.

I hadn't counted on the car being locked, though. As soon as the door handle popped out and back, I grimaced. Drat. Didn't much matter, anyway. I looked toward the glass walls of the store and saw Jack making his way toward me, hands gripped around Styrofoam coffee cups and a small brown bag of goodies tucked under his arm.

He smiled at me as he exited, and I folded my arms across my middle. "You locked the car," I said.

Goldie

"Well, of course I did, Goldie," he said, making his way to me. He extended a hand, and I took my cup of coffee. "Just the way you like it, sweetheart," he said. "They were low on sugar, so I just stuck my finger in and stirred a bit."

Gag me. "Ha-ha," I said, pretending the man had made a charming remark. But my pretense didn't last long. "Could you hurry it up? It's freezing out here."

Jack unlocked my door with the remote, and I sat down in the already chilly car, wrapping my coat around my legs as Jack shut the door behind me. When he scurried around to the other side and slid in, he handed me his cup of coffee and set the bag on the back floorboard. "I'll just pull around and get gas. Boy, the prices are outrageous."

I just looked at him, then took a sip of my coffee. Darn Jack's hide, it was prepared exactly the way I like it. Nothing to complain about there.

"Coffee okay?" he asked me.

"It's alright," I lied. "For truck-stop coffee."

Jack drove the car alongside the pumps, got out, and began the task of putting gas into his car, his gaze continuously on the pump. I slyly reached over and picked up his cell phone, smiling when I saw that it was on. I dialed a number I'd memorized earlier in the day: Weather and Time of Day for Tokyo, Japan. As long as I kept the line open, the automated voice on the other end would keep repeating the information I cared nothing about. This call would cost the man a fortune. The less money he had in his bank account, I figured, the less Charlene and her baby could get a hold of.

I turned the volume down to zero and then slipped the phone under my seat.

When Jack entered the car I rubbed my free hand (the other still holding the coffee) against my leg and said, "It sure is cold. Turn the heat up, will you?"

Jack started the car and complied with my wish as we drove back onto the highway. "You'll be plenty warm when we get to the cabin," he said. "Pastor Kevin tells me there's a massive fireplace in the living room and smaller ones in each bedroom." He looked

78

over at me and winked. "But maybe we'll only need to build a fire in the master bedroom. You think?"

I sat up straight. "Jack Dippel, you promised no—"

Before I could finish my tirade he laughed. "I'm just teasing you a little, Goldie. Come on, now. I said I wouldn't push that issue, and I won't. But we are still married, you know. Won't be anything wrong if we pretend we're on our honeymoon again."

I pursed my lips together, looked straight ahead, and then took another long sip of coffee. Our honeymoon.

Jack and I had met in a hotel in Washington DC while I was on a senior class trip and he was there with some college buddies on a break from school. The attraction was both instant and explosive. When we married a couple of years later, we returned to the same hotel, this time completing what we'd only lusted for before.

We'd been married a year when Jack's mother warned me of the possibility that her son would not be faithful to our wedding vows. His father hadn't, she said. But, with each affair he bought her a lovely piece of jewelry to make up for it. I thought the woman had lost her mind, but a year later, she was proven to be correct in her assumptions. I'd been living with an unfaithful man ever since. Until a few months ago when I'd had enough and moved out.

Jack spoke up suddenly, as if reading my thoughts. "I see you're remembering those days," he said. "And nights." We hit a pothole, and I bounced a bit in my seat, raising my right arm, careful not to spill my coffee.

I looked at him hard. "For the record, I have no intention of sleeping with you until you've been tested for every venereal disease out there."

His head jerked toward me. "What brought that up?"

"Logic. It's probably a miracle you haven't been infected before now." I turned my gaze toward the stretch of highway before us.

He grew quiet. "I was always careful about things like that," he said finally.

I remained silent as I collected my thoughts. "You'll forgive me if your word isn't good enough."

He had turned back to face the road. "I've been tested. You want the medical report?"

I turned back to face him. "You have?"

"Every six months whether I thought I needed to or not. From the time this started."

I stiffened and returned my focus ahead. "I don't want to talk about it."

"You brought it up. Pastor says if we want this marriage to be saved, we've got to be honest. That's as honest as I can get. I'll have the reports sent to you so you can rest your mind."

"Rest my mind? *Rest* my mind? Oh my goodness, Jack. What do you know about my mind?"

He grinned. "I know your mind. Better than you know it yourself, I'd say."

I remembered the cell phone beneath my seat. "Maybe you don't know me at all," I said. "Maybe you only know the part of me I allow you to know."

"We're playing that game, are we?"

I crossed one leg over the other. "I don't know what you're talking about, Jack Dippel." I reached into my purse on the floorboard for the book I'd been reading over the past few days. "I'm going to read while you drive," I said, opening the pages. "I brought plenty of books to read, by the way. Don't know what you've got planned, but I thought this would be a good time for reading."

I sensed Jack's frown as I looked down to the pages of the book. "I'd like to do some ice fishing. Thought maybe the two of us could do some hiking. And, I brought a book—though only one—to read."

"Oh, yeah? What book? *Wild at Heart*?" I didn't bother to look at him, or the incredible scenery outside the car, for that matter. I just focused on a single word on page ninety-seven of the book, though I couldn't tell you what the word was.

Jack shifted a bit in his seat. "Actually, yeah."

Now I looked at him. "Really?"

"It's good. I'm learning a lot about myself."

I took a moment to study my husband. Though a bit stockier than when we married (back then it was all muscle and no pudge), he was still a good-looking man. He wore glasses now, but they only made him look more distinguished. His hair was a becoming shade of gray, and his face was naturally tan and slender with only a few character lines near his mouth and jaw. If I were to go blind tomorrow, I would carry his look in my memory forever, and it wouldn't be a bad thing either.

But inside . . . inside, Jack was a mystery. For years I'd known him only as the father of my child, the provider of my financial needs, and the thorn in my flesh. Now he was turning on me. He was changing. And I was not sure if I liked it or not. At least before, I knew what to expect from him. Now, every day was a mystery.

I shook my head a bit. *No, Goldie. Focus on the real issue here.* The man was about to be a father again. He didn't know it, but that didn't make him any less guilty.

Jack looked down to the console then. "Hmm."

"Hmm?" I repeated, glad for the change of subject.

"I could have sworn I left my cell phone in the cup holder there."

I put my cup of coffee in the second holder and pretended to look around. "Well . . . let me see. We hit a bump a ways back. Maybe it just fell out."

When did I become such a liar, Lord?

Staying in the character of a fraud, I reached under the seat and pretended to search. "Oh, here it is," I said, pulling it out and carefully ending the call. "Good as new," I said.

Jack took the phone from me and looked down at its face. "My battery is low. That's weird." He placed it back in the cup holder. "I probably need to buy a new one. This one's not holding a charge like it should."

I didn't respond. After that we continued toward Summit Ridge in silence.

Summit Ridge turned out to be everything Pastor Kevin had said it would be and more. My thoughts immediately went to his late wife, our beloved Jan, and remembrances of how much she loved coming here. "A home away from home," she'd said. "A place to unwind, reconnect to God and to each other."

Well, the God part sounded good, and even the unwinding. But right now the only connecting I wanted to do with Jack was my fist up against the side of his head. Still, I couldn't help but notice God's natural beauty as we drove through Gold Mine Pass, which Jack immediately pointed out as being haunted.

I gave him my best "give me a break" look.

"I'm serious," he countered from the driver's seat. "I saw a show about it on the History Channel. Old miners who got trapped up here when the snow banks collapsed from the weight of the snow. Sometimes they got trapped for months."

I jerked my head to look out the window and up the rising slopes of the pass. "I can see where that could happen," I said, then looked back to him. "Not the ghost part. But the snow causing a slide."

"They interviewed all these eyewitnesses. Said they occasionally see old miners walking up and down the road here." He winked at me. "Soon as they slow their cars down, the old miner turns and looks at them, then"—he lowered his voice to a whisper—"just disappears." His eyes grew wide.

"Jack, stop the nonsense."

He held up his right hand. "I'm serious," he said with a chuckle. "That's what they say." He jutted his neck out a bit. "I'll keep driving, and you can keep your eyes peeled for ghosts."

When we arrived in the actual "town" of Summit Ridge, located on an upper ridgeway between two passes, Jack slowed the car and parked it in front of the general store. "Need anything?" he asked me as he opened his door.

"Ah . . . no."

"I thought I'd pick up a few things. What groceries did you bring, by the way? Anything you might have forgotten?" He was now standing outside in the snow, with his head dipped down to look at me.

"Oh no. I think I remembered it all," I said with a nod. *Tonight, the chef is preparing your least favorite food in the world: hamburger quiche, a dish you had once claimed real men would never eat, even under the threat of starvation. Well, we'll just see about that, won't we?*

"Alrighty then. If you want to get out, stretch your legs, look around . . ." He shut his door, and I scrambled out of mine. With a single blink I could take in the whole town.

"What are you getting?" I asked. "I mean, I think I have everything."

"Firewood. Pastor Kevin said we'd need to stop here and get some firewood."

I felt a small sense of relief. "Oh." If Jack bought too much in the way of food, then part of my plan would backfire. And I couldn't have *that*.

I saw a small bookstore sitting alongside the general store and pointed to it. "I'll take a look inside there."

Jack nodded and then walked into the general store, bells tinkling as the door opened and closed. I had taken no more than two steps toward the bookstore when I felt a few flakes of snow on my face. I looked up then toward the way we'd come. A distant sheet of falling snow suddenly made the surrounding mountains indistinguishable. In mere minutes, the approaching whiteout would blanket this little burg.

I hurried inside the bookstore, hearing the same sound of chimes as when Jack had entered the general store.

When I say that the bookstore was small, I'm talking really small. A very studious-looking teenager sat in an old cushy chair next to a wood-burning stove, one leg tucked up under her and her nose pointed straight toward an open book that rested on the chair's arm. She was so engrossed, she didn't seem to realize that someone had walked in. I stood for a moment, watched her blow a bubble from the gum she chewed ever so slowly. She closed the book then looked up at me. "Oh, hi," she said. "Can I help you with anything?"

I smiled at her, then looked around the short, narrow room. Four long bookstands crowded the space. "What kind of books do you have?" I asked.

She shrugged. "All kinds, really. Used, all of them. People bring their books up to Summit Ridge, read them, then want something else, so they come here."

I took a few steps to the nearest stand, which was filled with thick romance novels. Even though there was no way I'd read one of these, I picked one up anyway and rummaged through its musty pages. "Do you live here?" I asked, then thought that to be a stupid question. "I mean, all the time?"

"Yeah. My parents own the general store. I'm Jenna, by the way."

I looked at her. "You're not in school, Jenna?"

"My mom homeschools me."

I replaced the book. "Does it get pretty lonely up here?"

She rolled her eyes, but not in a rude way. "I have a few friends, but, yeah. It can."

I pointed to her book. "So what are you reading?"

She looked at the book, then back to me. "It's about the old miners who died during the slides just on the other side of town. Back in the 1800s. There was a show on the other night about it, and I got sorta interested."

I crossed my arms. "My husband and I were just talking about that." I turned a bit to look out the windows and noticed that the snow was falling full force now. "The miners. And ghosts."

"Can't say I believe it for sure, but you never know. The ghost part. I mean, what do we really know about what happens after we die? Maybe if someone dies tragically like that, their souls really can't get to God." She shrugged again. "I dunno."

"I don't buy that," I said. "I think we either go to God or to the devil."

"You religious?"

I smiled at her. "I'd like to say I have a relationship more than a religion."

She smiled back. "I believe in God too. You can't live up around here and not believe in him. I'm young, but I know grandeur when I see it."

Grandeur. She was right about that. If God had left his fingerprint on anything on the whole planet, it was the Colorado Rockies.

Jenna laughed, then stood. "You want that book?" She pointed to it. "It's sleazy as all get out, but sorta well written."

I picked up the book again. "You've read it?" I asked. *And, why?*

"I've read every book in here," she answered, moving toward the L-shaped cashier's counter near the front door. "What else am I going to do with my days? Very few people actually live up here, and it's not like we have a mall or anything."

I took the book over to the counter. The price tag was only a dollar plus tax, and I figured it could be her only sale of the day. "Sure, why not," I said, feeling—in a way—sorry for a young girl who appeared to be about sixteen, trapped in a village comprised of a general store, a bookstore, a beyond-tiny post office and bank combination, a coffee shop, a motel, and a gas station.

She grinned at me. "Read this trash and you might actually learn something. My mom says if husbands were to read these books, wives wouldn't have to." She shook her head and giggled. "Cute, huh?"

The idea of Jack reading a book in which the cover is high-lighted by a chiseled and tanned man with hair flowing in the sea breeze, arms filled with the almost lifeless, barely dressed damsel in distress, and the pages filled with words like *loins* and *passion* was too much for me to imagine. I pulled two dollars from my purse and handed them to the girl. "I suppose you could call it cute."

"Well, you know what I mean," she said, slipping the book into a paper bag, then handing it across the counter to me. "Happy reading," she said and handed me my change.

I took the book and smiled at her. "Thank you," I said.

As I reached the door to leave, Jenna added, "How long you here for?"

"Just a couple of days," I said, turning back to her. "I can't believe that in all the years of living in the area, I've never come here."

She leaned across the counter, elbows and forearms resting on its unpolished surface. "Sometimes when something is so close, you don't pay it enough attention." She shrugged. "But two days for your first time? That's hardly long enough to enjoy the view."

"My husband and I both have jobs. We took tomorrow and Tuesday off, but we need to be back home by Wednesday."

She looked around the room, then back at me. "I know, right? Work. What a pain."

11

A New Detective in Town

It was becoming a new habit, running his fingers through his hair. And Clay was beginning to understand the power women had exercised over the years by the simple movement. And he liked it.

Sure enough, Britney noticed right away.

"Your hair," she said with a smile from the other side of the front counter. "Sharp look." Then she stopped. "Wait, there's something else too. What is it?"

Clay stepped up to the counter and returned her contagious smile. "Weight loss."

"I can see that."

"Had some highlights put in my hair."

She tilted her head, and the overhead fluorescent lights made her blonde hair shine all the more. "Nice touch."

Clay feigned a frown. "You don't think it's too much?"

"Not at all." She leaned over the counter, startling him by running her manicured nails through his hair. "Very good. Who did it for you?"

"Had it done over in Silverthorne. At a salon there."

Britney winked at him. "Next time, call me. I won't charge you half a week's salary. In fact, I wouldn't charge you at all."

"You can do this?"

She nodded. "Foils, right?"

Clay nodded back.

"Every girl worth her weight in high school and college has to learn how, don't you know that?"

He laughed. "I guess not." He turned slightly and looked toward the front door. "Say, who was that woman who just left? Maybe a minute before I walked in?"

Britney shrugged. "Don't know. I can check her credit card receipt."

"Would you?"

She wrinkled her nose. "For you? Sure."

Clay watched as she opened the cash register then pulled the one and only receipt from the drawer. "Says right here, Velvet James. Wow, what a name. Do you know her?"

Clay shook his head. "No, I don't. She must be new here."

"She bought a real pretty Christmas card and mother/daughter ornament for her mother."

"Oh, yeah?" Clay shifted his weight and leaned a hip against the counter and looked back to where the Nissan had been parked.

"Maybe she's here visiting her mother?" Britney speculated.

"Maybe. I'm pretty sure there aren't any Jameses living here, though." Then he turned his attention to the pretty woman on the other side of the counter, forgetting about the one who'd just left the store. "You really are quite the detective, aren't you?" He crossed his arms over his chest. "First you find my email address, then you get the scoop on the new girl in town."

Britney placed the receipt back in the drawer and pushed it shut. She laughed lightly and said, "Ask anybody in my family; they'll tell you. I know how to get what I want. That's all."

88

Lizzie

Million Dollar Pound Cake

Ingredients

3 C Sugar
2 C Butter
6 eggs (large)
4 C cake flour
3/4 C Milk
1 TB butter or Vanilla flav.
1/2 tsp almond flavoring

12

Family Upside-Down Turnovers

Immediately after church I'd hoisted myself into Samuel's black Lincoln Navigator and closed the door behind me, then looked out the windshield with eyes darting back and forth like a spy. Or a madwoman, perhaps. *Five minutes*, I thought. *I just need five minutes of quiet.*

Outside, on the snowy church grounds, my family was gathered in small clusters, talking to other church members. My son Tim, his wife Samantha, and Pastor Kevin were near the front steps, deep in discussion. I hoped—no, I prayed—it was about setting up marriage counseling appointments. I knew Kevin could help them, even for the short period of time they would be staying with us.

A month or so ago Tim had left his wife and children—Kaci, age ten, and Brent, age six—in Louisiana. When he'd arrived, it was with a cock-and-bull story that Samantha was demanding too much of him, both financially and materialistically. I was immediately suspicious. I may not know everything about my daughter-in-law, but I do know she is one of the least greedy people with whom I've made acquaintance. She's always been a loving wife and devoted mother. When she and Tim "had" to get married (as they say) while in college and were forced to live on a lean budget, she never once

90

complained. At least, not to me and—according to Tim—not to her husband or to anyone else that he knew of. When Kaci was born, she discovered the joys of shopping at second-hand stores and the humbling experience of filing for government assistance. Samantha always said these were her "Growing in Grace" years.

When Tim finished college and began working an entry-level job, they were able to let go of some things and grab hold of others, but I'd never seen even a hint of Samantha craving more than she could afford. She was always content.

My son, however, was another story. Tim was gung-ho on succeeding mightily in everything he did. He worked hard and climbed the corporate ladder at an impressive rate of speed. By the time Brent was a toddler, Tim's little family wanted for nothing. Still, Samantha volunteered at a homeless shelter once a week, and now that the children were both in school all day, two days a week. So, for Tim to tell me that Samantha had become materialistic was . . . well . . . just silly.

But Tim moved back to Summit View with his story, got a job at the same Breckenridge resort where our daughter Michelle works, and seemed to be settling in to the notion of living at home with Mommy and Daddy again. I was willing to be silent and prayerful and bide my time. But the night he proudly dressed for a date with one of Michelle's co-workers, I took immediate action. First by putting him in his place and then by calling his wife, insisting she and the children fly in for a surprise visit.

I'd picked Samantha and the children up from the airport last Thursday, but already it seems a lifetime ago. When Tim came home from work that evening—totally unsuspicious of his mother's plotting side—Samantha met him on the front lawn. When he saw her, he stopped. I watched from the living room window as they embraced and witnessed firsthand the power of prayer on my son's face. He was a young boy in love again, and I was the proud mother hen, clucking about in her roost.

I told Samuel later that evening that I suspected Tim & Co. would stay on through Christmas, then head back to Louisiana. Over Friday evening's dinner I asked Tim if he'd put in his notice at work. He looked up at me with a mouth full of spaghetti (albeit one stray noodle hanging from his pursed lips). His eyes registered surprise, then made their way over to where his wife was sitting, as though to say, "Not now, Mom . . . not in front of Samantha."

I dropped it. They have, after all, three weeks before the first of the year.

I sighed, closing my eyes. *Three weeks.*

It's not that I don't love my children. I do. I love them very much. It's just that for the past several years our house has been home to "just the three of us." Meaning Samuel, our daughter Michelle, who is twenty-five, and myself. With Michelle being deaf and Samuel and me being quiet by nature, our home had become a sort of silent retreat. I'd grown accustomed to it, eagerly anticipating coming home from my job as a high school librarian. I'd long ago forgotten the chaos children can bring into a house.

Later that night, as Samuel and I lay in bed together, holding hands and looking up at a ceiling shadowed by the moon and the evergreens outside our bedroom, I'd giggled a bit. "Remember the good ol' days?" I asked him.

I turned my head and watched in the moonlight as his smile spread across his still-handsome face. "You mean when the kids were little or when the kids were gone?"

I looked back to the ceiling and waited before I replied. "Good question."

We talked then about how it felt to have all the children, their spouses—or, in Michelle's case, boyfriend—and our grandchildren together for a meal. The night before we'd all gone out to Apple's, Summit View's best restaurant, for dinner. There were sixteen of us, total. Samuel and myself. Michelle and Adam, the new fellow in her life. Tim, Samantha, Kaci, and Brent. Sam Jr., his wife Mariah, and their children, Mia, Haley, and Julia. (The joke in the Samuel Prattle Jr. household is that Sam Jr. is so outnumbered, even the dog and cat are female.) Finally, there was our oldest daughter, Cindy (who we've always called "Sis"), her husband Isaac, and their son Elijah.

Too many for this old woman to keep up with.

Now, for the past hour or so, we'd occupied the better part of two pews at Grace Church. Samuel sat proud, and, I admit, I did too. It does a parent's heart good to know that all her children, children-in-law, and grandchildren love the Lord. It truly does.

I breathed in deeply, taking in the scent of the car's glove-soft leather. I shivered in the frosty air, knowing my time alone was about to come to an end. The cold would drive the entire crew—or, as many as would fit—within this vehicle in seconds.

Sure enough, it did. I sat passively and forced a smile as my brood turned from their various places on the church's front lawn and advanced toward me like a pack of hungry wolves wrapped in wool and leather.

I'd already begged Samuel to take us out for lunch, because I had not one single bit of energy for cooking for sixteen people.

"The café okay?" he asked me.

"Works for me," I said.

When we entered Higher Grounds we were greeted by the owner, Sally, who stood by Clay Whitefield's table, poised with a full pot of coffee.

"Table for sixteen," Samuel said with a grin.

I watched Sal blanch. Her eyes darted behind me, bouncing as she mentally counted the number of Prattles coming in behind us. One of Sally's servers, Eleana, stepped up.

"Eleana, put some tables together in the back, will ya?" she asked, though the question was more of a demand than a request.

Eleana, young and pretty, turned on her heel and moved to the back of the café. Within minutes, the Prattle family was sitting down, doing the two things they do best: eating and talking loudly.

Too loudly.

Just three more weeks, Lord. Just three more weeks. And then, back to what we call normal.

Tim and Samantha made the announcement in our family room over coffee and the cake I'd bought from the bakery counter at Higher Grounds. I was sitting in my favorite chair, legs crossed,

93

plate of cake in one hand, fork in another, ready to cut into the rich velvet of million dollar pound cake when my son barked out, "Mom, Dad, we've decided to stay."

Clusters of mini-conversation ceased. My mouth, opened and ready for its first bite of cake, froze. Samuel jutted forward in his recliner, and Sam Jr.—in his manner—snickered. "I knew it," he said. He looked over at Mariah, who swallowed hard, and said, "Didn't I tell you? Do I know my little brother or what?"

Mariah stood, placed her dessert plate of uneaten cake on the coffee table, then walked over to Samantha, reached down, and hugged her. "It'll be good to have my sister-in-law so close by."

Cindy pretended to be offended. "Hey, what am I? Chopped liver?"

Together the three young women embraced each other, no doubt envisioning days of shopping or skiing together, followed by dining out at Apple's or in Breckenridge. Fun-filled family outings that—God willing—would not include Samuel or me babysitting at every turn.

Michelle signed, *What is going on?*

Before I could answer, Tim signed back: *Samantha and I are staying in Summit View.*

Michelle clapped her hands together, leaping across the room and throwing herself into her older brother's arms. By this point, our grandchildren were skipping about, bouncing up and down, and squealing as though it were already Christmas morning and they'd actually managed to spot Santa coming down the chimney.

"Put your fork down, Lizzie," Samuel said, "before you poke your eye out."

I complied, then looked over at Tim. "What about your home in Baton Rouge? What about the kids? School?"

Tim's smile fell a bit, but he kept an arm looped around Michelle's waist as he said, "Mom? Are you upset with me? I thought you'd be happy."

I put my plate (with fork resting atop it) in my lap and pressed my fingertips to my chest. "I am happy. I'm just surprised, is all."

Tim nodded. "I guess it would be a bit of a shock, eh, Dad? You and Mom, here alone for so long, no telling what kinda wild things you two have been used to doing."

"Tim!" Samantha exclaimed, blushing for the both of us. "What a thing to say."

Tim released Michelle and came over to where I was sitting. He reached down and kissed me on the cheek. "Mom knows I'm kidding her."

"Does that mean," Samuel finally said, "that you are planning to stay *here*? In this house?"

Tim turned to him. "Well, just for the time being. We'll put our house in Baton Rouge on the market, and when it sells we'll buy something up here. In the meantime, I'm thinking this is plenty big for all of us."

He was thinking. How wonderful that my son had decided to start thinking.

I cleared my throat. "And how long do you think that will take, Tim?" I think I swallowed, but I could be wrong. I could have just lightly choked.

Tim squatted down, rested his elbows on his knees, and spread his hands wide. "Gee, Mom. I don't know. The market's pretty good right now. Seller's market, actually. I looked into it last night on the Internet. I also shot an email to our realtor and told her what we were planning to do."

"Have you heard anything back from her?" Samuel asked.

"Yeah, as a matter of fact I had an email this morning. I checked before we left for church. She said she could sell our house in a month, she thought. Maybe two. Maybe even less. It's new. It's in a nice neighborhood. Good school district for kids."

"And what about Kaci and Brent? What about school?" I looked over to where the kids had been jumping about just moments ago and noticed they'd all gathered around where Cindy and Samantha were still standing. They were glued to every word being said.

"It's probably going to be most difficult for Kaci here," Samantha said, reaching over to smooth Kaci's long dark hair.

95

"But I'll get over it," Kaci interjected. "I like it up here, MeMa." Her dark eyes grew wide. "I love the snow and the mountains and being near you and Grandpa. And I'm sure I'll make tons of new friends. Besides, I can email all my other friends."

I smiled at her. "It will be so nice to have you in Summit View, my love. To be able to watch you grow into a young lady." I looked back at Tim. "Well, it sounds like you've made up your minds. Thought it through. I don't mean to sound as though I don't want you to be here. It was just a bit of a shock for me." I touched my son's shoulder. "I love you and of course I want you to be nearby. And, you're right when you say that it's going to be a little different around here." I looked to Samuel. "But it's not forever, and in the end, we'll have all our children here. Right, Dad?"

Samuel, God love him, just laughed.

I was in the master bath brushing my teeth when Samuel came up behind me. I caught his reflection in the vanity mirror as he leaned against the door frame. He grinned at me for all he was worth. "Well, well," he said.

I turned, my mouth full of toothpaste and froth. "Well, well," I said back, albeit garbled. I resumed my brushing, rounding out my mouth to keep the toothpaste inside. "Life as we knew it," I said and spit.

"Over, babe." He took the necessary steps toward me and wrapped his arms around my waist. I continued to rinse, then dried my mouth on a nearby hand towel, came upright, and leaned against him. Even in his early sixties, he was still rock solid. "But, he's our son," he continued. "It's good that he and Samantha want to work through their problems."

I turned and draped my arms over his shoulders, leaning back so I could search his face. "Had he talked to you about this before?" I looked him dead in the eye. If he were lying, I'd know it.

"No. But we did talk a few minutes ago after the rest of the crew left. He and Samantha feel that they need a clean start. Apparently there were some very significant problems and for quite a while."

"Moving to Colorado won't solve old problems, Samuel."

"No. But Pastor Kevin has agreed to meet with them. He's doing a pretty good job on Jack and Goldie's marriage, after all."

"Jack and Goldie," I thought out loud. "They ought to be at Summit Ridge by now."

Samuel pulled me close and nuzzled my neck. "Wouldn't you love to be a fly on the wall at that cabin?"

"Like you don't know." I felt my legs go weak. "You'd better stop that. We have young children in the house now."

"Never stopped us when our kids were little," he said. Samuel stepped back, gave me a swat on my behind, and walked out of the room. I was on his heels. "Kaci and Brent really need separate bedrooms. Kaci is too old to share a room with a little brother."

"What do you suggest?"

"Well. We have three bedrooms up here. Two downstairs. Michelle, of course, has her room across the hall, and the other room has turned into a bit of a junk room, but I'm thinking we can clear that out—or, I can, I should say. Though I'm sure Samantha would be happy to help with that project. We can fix it up. You know, for a girl."

Samuel shook his head. "They're only going to be here for a couple of months. Tops."

"But I was thinking this would be a great time to fix up a room for all of our granddaughters—a place for them to call their own when they spend the night with us. Something pretty and . . . girly."

Samuel chuckled again. "Now that the shock has worn off, something tells me you're really going to enjoy this."

I shrugged a shoulder. "Maybe a little."

He touched the tip of my nose with his fingertip. "Maybe a lot." Then he kissed me lightly at the spot his fingertip had marked. "One good thing about this day being nearly over—nothing else can go wrong."

I was sitting cross-legged on the bed, talking on the phone with Evie and telling her the latest and listening to her go on and on about the Christmas tea and Lisa Leann, when call waiting interrupted.

97

Caller ID indicated it was my brother on the other end of the line. My brother, who rarely—if ever—calls.

"Evie," I said. "It's Charles. And he's calling from his cell phone. Let me call you back."

"Charles? Wonder what that's about."

"I don't know, but I'll be sure to let you know if something's wrong."

"So we can pray," Evangeline said, like the president of our prayer group that she is. Another beep came through the line.

"I have to go, Evie." I clicked over to the other line. "Charles?"

"Oh, Lizzie. Thank the good Lord you answered."

"What's going on?" I asked.

"It's Mom."

"Mom?" Our mother, who was in the beginning stages of Alzheimer's, had, for the past year or so, been living with Charles and his wife, Mildred, who is a retired registered nurse. They're only about a half hour's drive from here. Still, I don't see Mom (or them) as often as I should. "What about Mom?"

"Listen, Lizzie. I'm calling you from outside the hospital."

"The hospital?" I sat up straight, swinging my legs over the side of the bed. "Has she taken a turn for the worse?"

"No. No, but I need you to listen. You can't use a cell phone inside the hospital and I'm freezing to death standing out here. It's not Mom. Exactly. It's Mildred. She's had a heart attack, Liz."

My hand flew over my mouth. "Oh no. Oh, Charles. Is she . . ."

"No. But it's pretty serious, and she's going to be in the hospital for a while. Then she'll need to recoup. Doc says . . . well, the doctor says we need to do something about Mom. Mildred can't take care of her anymore, Liz, and I certainly can't. Not being a man, taking care of her personal needs. Not with my job and now having to take care of Mildred too."

"Oh, well, no, of course not. Of course not." Reality then hit me like a slap in the face. "Oh, dear. You mean you want Mom to come *here*?"

"I know it might be an imposition, Liz. I mean, if you have to put her in a nursing facility, I'd understand, but I just can't do any more than I'm doing right now. We've had Mom for over a year now. She's fairly lucid. Sometimes a little off." He chuckled. "She's still her old bossy self, so she must not be too bad, you know?"

My shoulders slumped. "Charles, Tim and Samantha and the kids are living here now."

"What? Why?"

I took a few minutes to explain, keeping it brief, aware that his teeth were chattering on the other end of the line.

When I was done he said, "Lizzie, I don't know what to say."

We were both silent for a few moments. "Shame Mom and Dad didn't have more kids," I finally interjected, and we laughed a bit.

"But you did say Samantha would be there during the day, right? I mean, fair exchange for Tim and his family living there rent free, don't you think?"

I frowned. That was really none of his business, but in a way, he was right. "I'll have to talk to Samuel. And to Tim and Saman-tha."

I heard a siren blaring in the background before Charles said, "Liz, I need to know something soon, okay? I've got our neighbor, Mrs. Hubble, watching Mom right now. But that won't last forever."

"Mrs. Hubble with her 101 cats?" I asked. "No, I imagine not." Mrs. Hubble was as known for taking in stray felines as she was for her lack of emotion toward human beings.

"She was my only option at the time. So you see what a bind I'm in."

"Yes, I see." I stood. "I'll call you in the morning," I said, then hung up the phone.

A minute later I stood over Samuel, who was stretched out on his recliner, watching a late afternoon football game. From the sound of things, Tim and family were on the ground level of our split-level home, watching *America's Funniest Home Videos* on the small television set in the little sitting room at the end of the hallway. "Samuel," I said.

He looked over his shoulder at me. "Hey, news brief just inter-rupted the game. Weather is turning nasty from the north and heading this way. We're in for a lot of snow. Schools will be closing, no doubt."

I sighed. Of course. That would leave me trapped in a house full of people all day. "I've got more bad news," I told him.

He shifted a bit. "What's that?"

"Remember what you said about nothing else going wrong?"

"Yeah," he said.

"Well . . . *wrong.*"

13

Move Over, John Grisham

Clay left the card shop with a box of overpriced Christmas cards, a light catcher for his mother, and a date with Britney that evening.

He'd spent over forty-seven dollars and nearly three hours in the store, moving aside when customers came in, allowing Britney to do her job, which she did with flair. He was fairly certain that girl could sell an ice cube to an Eskimo if one would just walk through the door.

Nearing his third hour there, he gathered up his nerve and asked her out. "Hey, I gotta get going," he began.

Britney pouted. "Do you have to? You make the time go by so much quicker."

Clay shuffled his feet a bit. "Hey, look. It's last minute, I know, but if you don't have anything going on for dinner, I'd like to take you out."

"Tonight?" she asked.

Clay frowned; he'd insulted her. "Like I said, last minute."

Britney held up her hand to stop him. "Oh no. No, no. That's not what I meant. And, yeah. I'd love to go out with you tonight."

"You get off at five?" he asked.

"Takes me till six to get home," she said by way of answer.

"So, then how about I pick you up at seven?"

"Seven is good. Do you know where I live?"

Clay grinned. He'd Yahooed her personal address earlier. Britney—though in her midtwenties, he'd been told—still lived with her mother, father, and brother, a young man named Adam who was dating Michelle Prattle. "You're not the only investigator in this town," he said with a wink. "I'll see you at seven."

As he was leaving, he saw the coach and Goldie Dippel driving toward the edge of town. For a moment his curiosity over their being together got the better of him. First, he'd seen Charlene Hopefield at Mrs. Dippel's the night before. Now this.

Something was stirring, and Clay suspected it was more than just the snow swirling over his head. He'd make his way on home and type some notes into the trusty file on his laptop.

One day, he decided, he'd write a bestselling novel. All about the girls of the Potluck Club.

Evangeline

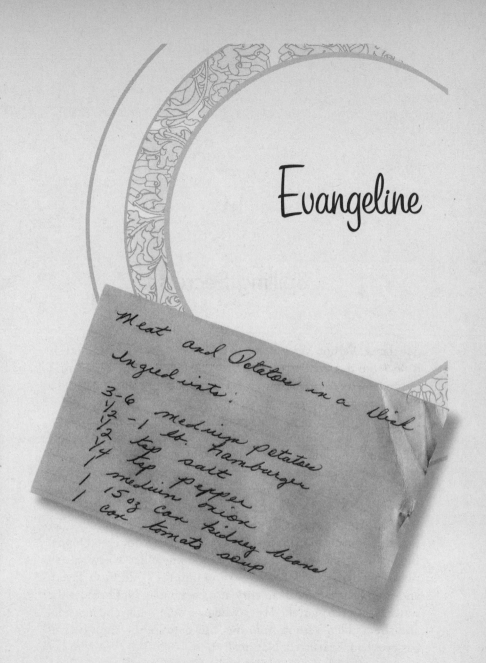

Meat and Potatoes in a dish

Ingredients:

3-6 medium potatoes
1/2 -1 lb. hamburger
1/2 tsp salt
1/4 tsp pepper
1 medium onion
1 15 oz can kidney beans
1 can tomato soup

14

Spilling Secrets

My fiancé, Vernon Vesey, was due to arrive at my house around six o'clock Sunday evening for dinner. We'd eat and then afterward, I figured, we'd talk about our upcoming wedding plans. That and a most pressing situation at hand.

As I put the finishing touches on what I call my "meat and potatoes in a dish," I thought about the sober conversation that must take place. And must take place that night. It should not and could not wait another minute. At least not as far as I was concerned.

Fact of the matter is, Vernon's ex-wife (and Donna Vesey's mother) was back in town in the worn-out person of Dee Dee McGurk. Since she had been gone for nearly thirty years, it was no wonder that most people didn't recognize her right away, not even Donna. But I sure as snowfall in the wintertime knew her. Knew her on sight the afternoon I followed Vernon into the Gold Rush Tavern and found the two of them cozy at a back table. Not because she was still the pretty girl she'd been when we were young and in school and she'd stolen Vernon from me, but because the emptiness in her eyes hadn't changed. Not in all those years. Not even with her running off with the choir director at Grace Church.

You'd think running off with a man practically a pastor, she would have had a good life. But she hadn't. Vernon had investigated and—as he told me later while I ate crow—found out that she'd been married six times altogether. Once to Vernon, once to the choir director (and we're all wondering whatever happened to that poor soul), and then four other times. Had three more children, Vernon said. One was taken by social services and the other two were raised by their father, who hadn't even bothered to marry Doreen, not that I can blame him. I mean, who wants a woman who has been around the block more times than a snowplow in a January blizzard?

So now Vernon was faced with Doreen wanting to see their daughter, and Vernon saying absolutely not. But if I know Doreen Roberts Vesey McGurk—and I do—she won't take no for an answer forever. She'll end up springing herself on Donna, and Donna would be hurt even more than she'd already been by that woman.

Her mother.

Now, for the most part, Donna and I get along about as well as two alley cats, but the fact of the matter is, she's Vernon's daughter and I love her. Okay, there. I said it. I love the girl. She could have been my daughter, but she is Vernon's, and what's Vernon's is nearly mine. After all, we'd be married in a little more than a month or so.

Married. White lace and throwing a bouquet and a honeymoon spent with the man I love. I trembled with excitement. I would be Mrs. Vernon Vesey. Evangeline Benson Vesey. Mrs. Sheriff Vernon Vesey. I giggled like a schoolgirl.

"Hello," I said out loud though all alone in my dining room, where I laid the silverware on the table. "Sheriff's office? This is Evangeline Vesey. May I speak to my husband, please?" No sooner were the words out of my mouth than Vernon was opening the front door.

The man didn't bother to knock anymore. And why should he? This would be his home soon enough. I shivered again.

"Vernon?" I called out, turning toward the front of the house.

"Hey, Evie-girl," he said. I reached the foyer in time to watch him peeling his way out of his leather sheriff's jacket and then hanging it on the foyer coatrack. His shoulders were covered in snow, thanks to the early blizzard we'd had starting late the afternoon before and pretty much continuing on all day. "Something smells good." He smiled at me, then took me in his arms and gave me a quick kiss. He lowered his voice and said, "And I don't mean what's on the stove."

I punched him playfully on the shoulder but smiled as I said, "Vernon, you are a sweet talker."

He patted his belly. "And a hungry one. We've had one emergency after another today, what with the blizzard, so I haven't had a chance to eat. What can I do to help?"

"I just put the silver on the table. Why don't you set everything up, and I'll bring in dinner. How's that?" I was already halfway to the kitchen.

"Sounds good."

As soon as we sat and said the blessing, Vernon dove right into his meal. I took a deep breath and began to say what was on my mind, not so much as even picking up my fork. "Vernon, we really need to talk."

Vernon stopped chewing long enough to take a drink of water. "What about?"

"About Doreen."

I watched as the color went out of his face and he grimaced. He shook his head. "What do you want to bring her up for when I'm sitting here with a near-empty stomach?"

"You have to tell Donna."

Vernon took another bite of food. "I will," he said, trying to eat and talk at the same time.

"Don't talk with your mouth full, Vernon."

He gave me a look and swallowed, then took another drink of water. "Listen here, Evangeline," he said. "Donna is my problem, not yours. And Doreen is my problem too. I can handle it."

I didn't say anything for a second or two, and Vernon went back to eating his dinner. I, too, picked up my fork and began to poke

106

at my food until I couldn't take it anymore. "But when?" I asked, leaning in.

Vernon dropped his fork with a loud clang. "For pity's sweet sake, woman. You aren't going to let this rest, are you?"

I pressed my hand against my breast. "I have waited my whole life, Vernon Vesey, to be your wife. My whole life! Or, near about. And I will not have Doreen Roberts messing things up for me."

"What makes you think—"

"We've got less than two months. And a lot can go wrong in two months. Or a lot can go right. Donna needs to know her mother is in town so she can go ahead and get whatever emotional upheaval she's going to have out of the way and be done with it before she walks down the aisle as my maid of honor."

Vernon opened his mouth, ready—no doubt—to argue, then closed it again. "Maid of honor?"

"That's what I said. Don't you think she ought to be?"

He shook his head. "I don't think I've bothered to think that far."

"Well, you must." I looked down at his plate. "Eat your supper before it gets cold." He dutifully obeyed. "We've got a lot to do and only a little time to do it in. I've already called Lisa Leann, darn her hide, and asked her to be the wedding coordinator."

"The what?"

"The wedding coordinator. Vernon, don't you know anything about weddings?"

"Well, yeah. I know how to say 'I do,' and I know all about cleaving only unto you," he said with a wink.

"Vern."

"I thought we'd just go to the church, have the preacher marry us." This time he leaned in. "Head out for a honeymoon."

I blushed, I'm just sure I did. "Vernon Vesey. You are changing the subject. And, no. I don't want that."

"You don't? No honeymoon for Mrs. Vesey?" He reached for my hand.

"Well, yes. I mean . . . what I'm trying to say is that I want a wedding. A real wedding. I've got the money set aside for it, and I want it. The dress, the girls, the groomsmen all dressed up in tuxes."

"You will not get me in a penguin suit."

I just stared at him for a moment, all the while wondering if I should give up and give in or use my womanly wiles, what few I had. I opted for using my womanly wiles. I stood and walked over to where he sat, pushed his chair back just enough so that I could drop into his lap. Wrapping my arms around his broad shoulders, I gave him the best kiss I dared give, then pouted and said, "You'd do it for me, wouldn't you, Vern?"

He turned bright pink, then sighed. "Yeah. For you I would."

I kissed him again. "And you'll talk to Donna?"

"Now that I don't know."

"You know you should," I said, running my fingers through the short curls at the nape of his neck.

"Evie."

"You should. You really, really should."

He sighed. "Alright. I will."

I sat up straight. "When?"

"This week."

I laughed, then stood and returned to my seat.

"You are a heartless woman, Evangeline Benson."

I grinned. "I know."

Vernon looked down at his watch, then pushed back from the table. "I've got to watch *Hollywood Nightly* tonight, and it's nearly seven o'clock now."

"*Hollywood Nightly?*" I asked, standing with him then reaching for our plates. "Since when do you watch *Hollywood Nightly?*"

"Since my daughter's face is going to be flashed across the country on it. She called earlier, nearly beside herself."

"Donna? Donna is going to be on *Hollywood Nightly?*"

I took the dishes into the kitchen, then followed Vernon into the family room, where he'd already turned on the television and stretched out in the recliner. With the remote in his hand, he kicked off his shoes, and they landed with a thud on the floor. I laughed to myself, thinking that the man was surely making himself right at home.

I sat on the sofa and curled my feet up under me. Within seconds the theme music to the gossip show started, and then the pretty

108

honey-toned face of Kendra Goodall filled the screen. Behind her, Main Street in a snowy Summit View filled the screen. Directly behind her, and across the street, Lisa Leann stood under the protective awning of her wedding shop and waved.

"Vernon, that's—"

"Shh," he said.

"Lisa Leann," I whispered. "That woman."

"Hello, everyone, and welcome to *Hollywood Nightly*." Kendra began her program, and Lisa Leann stopped her nonsensical waving. "We're broadcasting from Summit View, Colorado, where the snow has finally slacked off a bit and Hollywood has hit the high country."

Kendra's face was replaced by an old black and white of Harmony Harris. "The late Harmony Harris left Tinsel Town a mere six months ago. A woman of many secrets, she took to her grave the name of her illegitimate son's father."

Another picture swooped onto the screen, this one a color shot of Harmony and a very young David Harris. I estimated him to be about three years old.

I sucked in my breath. Vonnie's son. I wondered if she was watching.

"For years," the voiceover of Kendra continued, "it was rumored that Harmony Harris had affairs with nearly all of her leading men."

"Oh, my," I said.

"That's Hollywood for you," Vernon commented.

Photos of Harmony and male Hollywood legends shot across the screen, appearing to be tossed and fanned over. "But as David Harris matured to be the handsome, dark-skinned man he is today" —another photo, a more recent one, came into view—"it was more highly speculated that his father was Hollywood's notorious Latin lover, Eduardo Gonzales.

"But Harmony Harris never let on as to the paternity of her son. Instead she used him—and quite often—as a ploy for comebacks and speculation. The mark of a great Hollywood actress."

Video footage of Harmony came into view. She was lovely with her dark hair pulled sharply to the back of her head and large dark sunglasses shielding her eyes. Her bright smile flashed for the camera as she spoke, "Why, yes," she was saying, "it could have been Eduardo." Then she laughed. "But I never kiss and tell." She pursed her lips and kissed the air toward the camera.

"She's like a Marilyn Monroe," Vernon said. "My goodness above."

More footage replaced the old, this taken in front of Vonnie and Fred's house.

"That's Vonnie's!"

Kendra continued. "But all that's changed now, and the secret is finally out. David Harris is not the son of Eduardo Gonzales but of a man named Joseph Jewell."

A photo of Vonnie's first husband, dressed in his military best, flashed on the screen.

"How in the world did they get . . ."

The camera came back to Kendra and—lo and behold—Lisa Leann still in the background. By now Lisa Leann had put a fisted hand on one hip and was pointing to the sign above her shop. "*Hollywood Nightly* has the exclusive on the 1960s cross-cultural marriage of Miss Vonnie Swenson—now Mrs. Fred Westbrook of Summit View, Colorado—and the Mexican-American Joe Jewell, a man whose father was of German heritage, and who died while serving his country in Vietnam."

"Oh," I said. "I hope Vonnie's not watching this."

"Vonnie's mama came to stay with her; you know that?" Vernon said from the recliner.

"What?" I asked but kept my face glued to the television.

"I'll tell you in a minute."

Kendra's plastered smile turned sober. "It took this *Hollywood Nightly* reporter all day to get the real story, America. But I do have it . . ."

"Oh no," I whispered.

"And it will break your heart." For the next few minutes she told the story while life in Summit View passed behind her on camera. I sat transfixed as Clay Whitefield came to stand beside Lisa Leann then tugged her inside her shop. From beyond the glass doors there appeared to be a little tug of war going on between them, Lisa Leann clearly trying to get back onto the street. A few of the locals crossed the street, huddled under thick scarves and puffy jackets. Most didn't bother to look at the camera. Some did, starstruck. At one point I saw Donna dash across, head down, as though she were in a hurry to get to—no doubt—Higher Grounds.

"Was that it? Was that Donna's national debut?" I asked Vernon.

He frowned. "No, I don't think so. She said something about being at Vonnie's yesterday."

When the very personal story of Vonnie and her first husband was finally over, Kendra smiled broadly. "And now we know the truth, and from the son of Harmony himself."

Next on screen was video footage of Kendra shoving a microphone into David's face and saying, "Mr. Harris, it was always rumored that you were actually the illegitimate son of the famed Hollywood actress, Harmony Harris, and one of her leading men. So, we can put those rumors to bed?"

David smiled in the same manner his adopted mother had. "Yes. Those rumors were false. My mother's publicist has prepared a statement; in the meantime, I can tell you that the late Harmony Harris was my mother by adoption."

"So, you've come to Summit View, Colorado, to meet your birth mother, Vonnie Westbrook. According to the news story that came across AP last night, there were mysterious circumstances surrounding your adoption. What can you tell us?"

David put on his sunglasses and simply answered, "No comment."

In the background Wade Gage's truck came to a full stop.

"Oh, boy," Vernon commented. "No wonder Donna was beside herself."

Kendra continued, "So, David, is the rumor true that you're engaged to be married? Is this your fiancée?"

The camera lens panned and widened to show Vernon's daughter. My mouth fell open.

"Fiancée?" Vernon bolted upright.

"Vernon," I said, reaching a hand out to calm him. "Listen."

David slipped his arm around Donna. "I have no comment to make at this time."

"Then you're not denying the rumor?" Kendra went on, smiling all the while, turning her focus to Donna. "Can you tell us your name and what it's like to be engaged to one of the most eligible bachelors in Hollywood?"

Wade stepped up about that time. "Why don't you point that thing in another direction?"

With the cameras still rolling, but this time pointed at Wade, Kendra remarked, "This is a free country, cowboy. I can point our camera where I please. And if you don't leave, I'm going to call in the local law."

Vernon shook his head. "I do not believe this."

About that time the cell phone clipped to his belt rang. He jerked it from its holder and looked down. "It's Donna." I reached for the remote and turned down the volume as he flipped open the phone. "Hey, sweetheart. I just saw it." He paused for a minute. "Come again? Are you sure?" His tone was grim.

"What?" I asked, touching his arm. "What is it?"

He held up a hand to shush me. "Okay, here's what I'll need you to do; call Wade . . . yes, Wade. Call Wade and see if he'll let you borrow his snowmobile. He's got a fairly new one, and I don't want you out there on anything but the best. I'll put in a call to the sheriff out there and see what I can find out. I'll have one of his deputies meet you, go in with you. All right, sweetheart. And listen. You be careful, you hear me? Head on over there tonight, but don't try to do anything until the sun comes up, you hear me? . . . Do you hear me? That's an order, Deputy." He closed the phone and sighed deeply.

"What in the world was that about?" I asked.

"Sit down, Evie-girl," he said. He was so serious, I knew better than to argue. I sat on the sofa, and he sat beside me and took my hand. "There's been a snowslide at Jade Pass."

"Jade Pass? Where's that?"

"On the other side of Summit Ridge."

112

I felt the blood rush from my head. "That's where . . ."

He squeezed my hand. "I know. Goldie and Jack. Donna said everything from Jade Pass on is trapped behind the slide."

I looked from Vernon's face back to the flickering of the television, where Kendra Goodall continued in her exclusive, and Lisa Leann, who had escaped from Clay's clutches, was waving a sign, Wedding Helps.com, in the background. "Oh, Lord" was all I could say.

15

Between a Rock
and a Hollywood Place

Clay was in a bind. Torn between two lovers, so to speak.

His date with Britney had gone remarkably well. Just like his mother had always taught him, he arrived ten minutes early. Britney's father, a nice guy if Clay'd ever met one, welcomed him with an invitation to take a seat with the rest of the family while Britney finished getting ready. "We're just sitting here watching a little television," he said. "We understand that a local will be on *Hollywood Nightly*." And that's how he came to watch Donna Vesey on national television: surrounded by Britney & Family in the midst of a homey den (a far cry from his place). It was an odd moment if he'd ever had one.

Especially when he heard the reporter say the word *fiancée* when talking about Donna's relationship to Harris. "Oh, come on, now," Clay said, scooting himself up to the edge of the sofa. But when Wade suddenly showed up on the screen, he felt his eyes narrow and his cheeks grow warm.

"What's wrong?" Britney said, nudging his shoulder with her own. "Do you know that guy?"

Clay nodded. "Oh, yeah. I know him. Known him my whole life."

"Do you know her too? David Harris's fiancée?"

Clay swallowed hard. "They're not engaged" was all he could say.

Britney looked from him to the screen and back to him again. "I wouldn't be so sure about that," she said. "Looks like he's a man who knows what he wants."

Clay could only nod. He cracked his knuckles on both hands then stood and looked down at the pretty blonde before him. "You ready to go?" he asked. "I think I've seen enough here."

Goldie

Mexican Casserole

1½ lb. ground meat
1 T. chili powder or to taste
1 tsp. garlic powder
1 onion
Salt and Pepper
1 large can Ranch Style Beans
1 lb. velveeta cheese
1 can cream of chicken soup
1 can tomatoes
(over)

16

Honeymoon Chillers

I stood at the window of the cabin and stared out, not that I was actually looking at anything. Everything was the color of night. Not a star in the sky. No moon overhead. Certainly no streetlights. They'd gone out the same time as the electricity. But the snow was falling so hard it was driving itself sideways, white against the blue-black of the sky.

Behind me, Jack was tinkering with the battery-operated radio Pastor Kevin kept here for emergencies such as these. He sat hunched over the small dinette table in the combination living room/dining room, turning the dial this way and that, studying it all the while in the beam of the flashlight he'd found on the kitchen counter just after we'd come in.

But all he got was static.

"I don't get it," he said. "I don't understand why my cell phone battery went dead so fast. If I had *that* I could at least call someone and find out when they expect the electricity to come back on."

I turned from the window and moved toward him. "I'll start looking for candles."

"Good idea," he said, not looking up at me.

I shivered. "It's getting pretty cold. Don't you think you ought to go ahead and start the fire?"

He sighed heavily. "I left the firewood in the car. Let me make my way out there."

As mad as I was at the man, I didn't want him swept away in the snow. "It's snowing pretty hard out there, Jack."

Jack stood and adjusted his belt around his waist. "I'm an athlete. I can handle it."

I scoffed. "You're a coach and an overweight one at that."

He turned toward me—I was now standing at the edge of the kitchen countertop—and barked, "So what are you saying, Goldie? You don't think I can go out there and get the firewood? Don't think I can protect my wife?"

My eyes widened. I remembered how vociferous Jack could get. *Oh, Lord. If the man only knew the truth, that I'd called Time of Day in Japan and that's why his phone is dead. Goldie, what were you thinking?* "I didn't say that," I said, trying to remain calm. "But I certainly don't want anything to happen to you. You are, as you just pointed out, my husband."

Jack scanned the room with the light from the flashlight. "Let's see if we can find some rope," he said. "I'll tie one end to my waist and the other to the front door."

"There's a utility room just off the back of the kitchen," I said. "Washer and dryer back there. Maybe there's some rope too."

Jack moved purposefully toward the back door, leaving me to stand in the darkness. Still, I followed behind him, shuffling my feet so as not to fall over anything, lest there be something on the floor I'd not noted previously.

Inside the utility room, Jack rambled through boxes and the few cabinets inside while the wind whipped outside in fury. I felt my insides begin to quiver, fear taking over, though I didn't know why. It was, after all, just a power outage.

Jack reached his hand inside one of the cabinets. "Here we go," he said, pulling rope from within. He pushed past me and nearly stomped toward the front door, once again leaving me alone in the dark. "Get my coat, will you, Goldie? I'll go ahead and start tying this around my waist."

I shook my head. "I'm in the dark here, Jack." A light hit me squarely in the face, and I squinted. "Jack!"

"Well, come on," he said as though the whole situation were my fault.

I ground my back teeth in an effort to keep from blowing up. I pulled my arm up to shield the light from my eyes, then walked into the living room, where we'd dumped our coats before the power outage.

I retrieved his coat while he worked near the front door to tie off the rope. When I reached him, he'd gotten both ends tied off and was holding out his arms so I could slide the coat over them. "Just be careful," I said.

Jack sighed. "Look, Goldie," he said, resting a hand on my shoulder. "I don't mean to be cross with you. But this isn't going exactly as I planned."

I stepped back, and his hand dropped from my shoulder to his side. "I know" was all I could say.

I stood in the open doorway and watched as my husband pulled the jacket hood on, then plowed—head first—toward where we'd parked the car, which was all but buried by the blinding snow. "Jack!" I called out, though I knew he couldn't hear me. I watched the glow from the flashlight fade, swallowed up by the snowstorm. "Jack!" I yelled again. Still no answer. I stared at the line of rope as it pulled taut; then I wrapped my hand around it and tugged. It didn't give, not a bit. "Jack!" I screamed again. *Oh, Lord. Don't let him die. I need him here long enough to . . . beat him up for getting Charlene Hopefield pregnant. And to take care of me.*

I will admit, my prayers made no sense, not even to me.

The rope began to go slack in my hand; he was returning. Little by little the bouncing of light came toward me until a clear vision of my husband emerged, completely covered in snow, shivering in the frigid air, his arms wrapped around a bundle of wood.

"It's not very much, is it?" I asked as he dropped it near the front door.

120

He shot me a hard look. "When the lights come back on, I can go get more."

Minutes later Jack worked at building a fire while I lit the candles I'd found in one of the kitchen cabinets. The scent of warm vanilla filled the room.

I went to the table and began to fiddle with the radio. *"To-night . . ."* I caught the word, but it was replaced by more static. Jack turned toward me. "Keep doing that," he said. "Whatever it is you're doing, keep doing it."

I wiggled the knob back and forth. *". . . with a wind chill of . . ."* More static. I shifted closer to the table, as if my nearness would help. *". . . Jade Pass . . ."* More static. *". . . not expected for some time . . ."*

"What did they say about Jade Pass?" Jack stood at the fireplace now, which roared with light and heat.

"That's all I could catch."

Jack walked over, took the controls from my fingertips. *"One of the biggest avalanches to hit this area in more than fifty years,"* the reporter was saying before the static took over again.

I stood, grabbed Jack's shirtsleeve, and tugged.

"Avalanche?" I whispered. "Do you think there was an avalanche at Jade Pass? Was that the rumbling we heard earlier?"

Jack walked over to the window and stared out, leaving me to sit again. "Had to have been. I thought it was trucks from the highway, but . . . I cannot believe this," he said. "We're stuck here."

I felt my heart turn to bubblegum.

Jack began to get hungry. He'd gone out twice more to get two additional armloads of wood, using the same method as before. I'd stopped hollering his name after him, though. For the most part he'd just sat in front of the radio, still trying to get some news, barking at what little bit he managed to obtain. Clearly, we were in a rustic mountain cabin without electricity, behind a wall of snow, which was piling higher and higher around the cabin due to the snowdrifts. By morning we wouldn't be able to get out of the front door.

I stayed on the sofa and read by the light of the fire, keeping my distance.

But around eleven, he walked over to the refrigerator and began to poke around. "What is this?" I heard him ask.

"What is what?"

"Is this hamburger quiche?"

"It is." I didn't bother to move.

"Why do we have that mess? You know I hate that stuff. Where's the Mexican casserole I told you I was looking forward to having?" I listened—completely still—as the refrigerator door slammed shut and he stomped toward the living room area. "I'm starving here, Goldie."

"I clearly remember you saying to me once that real men wouldn't eat hamburger quiche unless they were under threat of starvation," I said, not so much as raising my chin to look at him.

"And your point?"

Now I cast him a sideward glance. "My point is: you say you're starving. Let's put your theory to the test, shall we?"

He took another step toward me. "Do you mean to tell me that knowing I hate that stuff, you brought it anyway?"

I just smiled at him. "I happen to like it. This is *my* vacation too, isn't it?"

Jack just turned and headed back to the kitchen. I held my breath as the refrigerator door opened again, then closed. The sound of the casserole dish being set on the countertop and the aluminum foil being peeled away reached me before another stomping of the feet toward where I sat. "You do know it's cold, don't you?"

"If you keep opening and closing that fridge door it won't be for long. We may want to see about putting some of the perishables in the snow just outside the door." I kept my tone very matter-of-fact.

Out of the corner of my eye I saw Jack shake his fist, though I knew he wasn't about to hit me. Jack had never sunk that low. *Low* but not that low.

"Will you put some on a plate for me too?" I asked sweetly. "Oh, and I also brought some homemade sweet tea."

"Well, at least you brought that," he said, turning again.

"Oh, you know what?" I called after him. "I forgot; I didn't bring tea. I brought Coke instead."

"I hate Coke," he barked. "You know I'm a Pepsi man."

"Oh, dear. It's been so long, I guess I forgot."

Jack stomped back in again. "You did this on purpose. You never once intended to try to make our relationship work, did you? You just intended to come up here and torture me."

I stood to attention. "You'd better believe I did."

"But why?" he asked, spreading his arms wide. "Am I not doing enough to make up for everything, Goldie? You have to kill me with food poisoning too?"

"Food poisoning?" I let my shoulders sink a bit. "I hadn't thought of that."

"I oughta . . ."

I placed my hands firmly on my hips. The fire crackled and popped as I spread my legs in my best defensive stance. I almost laughed at the thought of what I must look like. Wonder Goldie! "You oughta what? Are we back to playing *that* game again? You, the woolly-bully husband? Me, the dutiful, pitiful wife?"

The next thing I knew Jack had grabbed me, wrapped his arm around my waist, and pulled me down onto the floor, where a thick bearskin rug was spread romantically in wait. "Jack!" I shrieked, kicking my feet and pushing against the solidness of his shoulders. "Get off me! Get off of me!"

But Jack pinned my shoulders to the floor with the palms of his hands and smiled down at me in the same way he smiled at me all those years ago when we'd first met. For a moment I *almost* forgot all about Charlene Hopefield.

I wiggled again, trying to free myself. "Get off!"

Jack bent down and kissed me, a wet sloppy kiss, the kind he knows I can't stand. I turned my head away from him.

"I'll have you arrested, Jack Dippel."

"Arrested?" He laughed.

"I will!"

"For what? Loving on my wife?"

I took a deep breath and bolted as hard as I could, freeing myself from him, leaving him to fall on his face. In spite of my fury I burst out laughing. It was truly a funny sight; this grown ox of a man flat on his stomach as though he'd fallen from a thousand feet. Jack looked at me and began to laugh too, rolling over onto his back and spreading his arms wide. "Ah, Goldie," he said, and for a moment I saw the young man I'd fallen in love with. "You got me. If I know you, you've probably got some deal with God going. That's why the avalanche. You're gonna watch me starve to death for all my sins against you." His breathing was heavy and irregular, and for a moment I wondered if he were going to have a heart attack.

I stood over him, torn between dropping to my knees and wrapping my arms around him, and kicking him in the ribs. *Don't do it, Goldie,* a voice inside said. *Don't fall for his cuteness, no matter what. He may be your husband, but he's still the jerk who impregnated Charlene Hopefield.* A mental picture of her standing in my living room swooped in between us. I took a step backward.

"I'll see what I can find for us to eat," I said and turned toward the kitchen.

Just then, I heard another rumble, this one stronger than the one before. "Jack!" I screamed, then stumbled to the floor.

17

Are You Talkin' to Me?

His date with Britney had gone well, in spite of the blizzard swarming around them. They'd made a slow trek to Breck to eat at Bubba Gump's, had to wait nearly forty-five minutes for a table, and had not started back until about two hours later. But the good company and excellent food had made the dangerous drive worth it.

Britney had somehow managed to snuggle close to him across the console and in the cold of the Jeep. Clay was content. Britney wasn't Donna by any means, but she was sweet and funny and she smelled good.

Gracious, did she smell good.

He took her directly home, telling her that if he were her parents he'd be a nervous wreck. Like the gentleman he was, he walked her to the door but didn't kiss her. Kisses, he decided, shouldn't be thrown around willy-nilly, and he told Britney so as they walked toward her front door.

Oddly, she agreed with him. "Believe it or not," she told him, "I've never kissed a guy."

"You're kidding."

Britney shook her head. "No. I'm saving my kisses for the man I marry." Then she smiled up at him, and Clay swallowed hard.

Donna

SAL'S HOT TUNA MELT

SANDWICH:
UP TO 12 SLICES OF BREAD (BUTTERED)
UP TO 12 SLICES OF SWISS CHEESE
FILLING (SEE BELOW)

FILLING:
1 PKG. ONION SOUP MIX   SM. JAR CHOPPED
1 PINT SOUR CREAM   PIMENTO
2 CANS TUNA FISH DRAINED 2 TEAS. LEMON JUICE
- MIX ONION SOUP MIX AND SOUR CREAM
                        - BACK -

18

High Altitude Directions

I'd gotten the call from dispatch as I was watching *Hollywood Nightly* at the Gold Rush Tavern. I was on duty, of course, so I was the only one in the place without a beer in my hand.

I was surprised Wade wasn't perched on his normal stool. He was probably in his trailer, tilting back a cold one.

"Make yourself at home," the barmaid called out to me. What was her name . . . Dee Dee McGurk? She was carrying a heavy tray of beers. "What can I getcha?"

"I'm on duty," I replied, "but I'll take a 7Up."

"Coming right up."

I found a vacant bar stool just as *Hollywood Nightly*'s theme music began to play. The bar patrons whooped as Kendra Goodall appeared on the screen with . . . I squinted. Who was that behind her? Lisa Leann? I shook my head. *Oh, brother.*

Just then, my radio crackled. A voice asked, "Donna, you there?"

Why hadn't I thought to call in a 10-7 so I could sit back and watch the show?

I picked up the radio and walked to the bar entrance, where it was a little quieter.

"Dispatch, Donna here. What's up? Over."

I could hear Irene's voice crackle out of the radio. "Donna, I know this is out of our jurisdiction, but I thought you'd want to know. Over."

Behind me, the bar patrons hooted. I was too far away from the TV to hear Kendra's voice, but I could see Vonnie Westbrook's picture appear on the screen. I cringed at the display of my good friend on this national gossip show.

I spoke into the radio. "Know what? Over."

"An avalanche over at Summit Ridge. Isn't that where your friend Goldie Dippel and the coach went? Over."

I felt my blood run cold. "How bad is it? Over."

"They don't know yet, but Jade Pass is completely blocked. No one will be coming or going that way till spring. Over."

"Thanks for the heads-up. I'd better call her daughter to see if she's checked in with her mother. Over."

"I knew I could count on you," Irene said. "Got a pen? I've already looked up Olivia's number."

I wrote it down. Before I could put my pad away, someone tapped me on the shoulder. I turned around to look into Dee Dee's worried blue eyes as she handed me a cold glass of 7Up, served up with a straw. For a moment her eyes held mine. There was something familiar about them. But what?

Dee Dee said, "Donna, you'd better come inside. There's something on the program you need to see."

The bar was exploding with whistles and calls of "Hey, Donna, baby," as my image appeared on the TV screen holding my badge up to the camera. As if in a trance, I walked past Dee Dee so I could get close enough to hear Kendra.

"I *am* the law," I was saying as the patrons hooted. Allen, one of the locals, jeered, "And I've got the speeding tickets to prove it," while the room applauded him.

Kendra Goodall appeared on the screen, "And just who is this young deputy sheriff who's engaged to Hollywood royal David Harris?"

Suddenly Larry's image appeared in living color. He looked like a cartoon character still in his dirty apron and hairnet. "Deputy

129

Donna?" he said. "Yeah, we may have gone out. But she's a tough one. She even gave me a ticket, despite our, ah, affection for one another, if you know what I mean."

The patrons whooped and cheered.

I crossed my arms. *Affection?* Larry was a bigger creep than I'd realized.

Kendra asked, "But isn't there some mystery associated with the deputy?"

Larry lowered his voice, like he was betraying a confidence. "Yeah. I heard some kid died, and Donna had something to do with it."

My heart literally stopped as the noise level of the room dropped to dead quiet. Larry continued, "Clay, he's our local reporter, well, he won't report it, but I got my sources."

Kendra's face appeared on the screen. "Could it be that David Harris's Deputy Donna is a real killer? The fact is, we were able to confirm this report. According to the *Denver Post*, in an article that ran only a week ago, the deputy is being sued by the family of infant Bailey Ann Long for monetary damages in her death. You can be sure we will follow up on this story. Back to you, Alex."

Dee Dee was still standing by my side. "You okay, Donna?"

I turned away and tried to shrug off my shock. "I have to be. I've got to deal with what's looking like an emergency." Though my blood was boiling, I turned and walked back to the quiet entrance and pulled out my cell phone. I couldn't wait to get my hands on that Larry. First, he hangs outside my house to spy on me, though I never found any footprints in the snow to prove it; and now he defames me on national TV. I shook my head. I'd have to deal with him later, I decided as I dialed Olivia's number.

She answered on the second ring. "Hello?"

"Olivia, it's Donna."

"Hi, deputy, I just saw you on TV. I, uh, I guess congratulations are in order. You're really engaged to that Harris guy?"

"Do you really believe everything you hear on TV?"

"Oh. Guess not. Is that why you called?"

I cleared my throat. "I'm calling about your mom and dad," I said. "When's the last time you heard from them?"

I could hear *Hollywood Nightly*'s theme music coming through the phone. "Hang on," she said, "let me turn this down."

She came back a second later. "It's funny you should call and ask that. Mom left me the number of the cabin they're staying in, and Tony and I were going to let Brook call them after dinner tonight, but when we dialed the number, all we got was some sort of weird pulsating tone."

"Did you try their cell phones?"

"Mom doesn't have one. But it sounds like Dad's is either off or out of range."

"Not good," I said.

"Why? What's wrong?"

I grimaced. I hated this part of my job. Very quietly and steadily I said, "We've gotten a report of an avalanche in the area."

I could hear Olivia gasp.

"Now, there's probably nothing to be worried about, but I'm thinking of heading on up there, just to check things out."

"Oh, Donna. I think we'd better go to the Lord in prayer."

Like that will help. "I'll tell you what, Olivia. I can't take the time for that, but you and Tony should. Okay?"

She agreed, and I hung up.

I felt a tap on my shoulder again. I turned around to see Dee Dee looking at me. "Everything all right?"

"Swell," I said.

"Then, do you have a moment to talk? There's something I need to tell you."

Uh-oh. Whatever Dee Dee McGurk had to say, I had a feeling it couldn't be good.

I shook my head. "Sorry, maybe another time. I've got an emergency situation I need to deal with."

She nodded, looking so worn out I almost felt sorry for her.

I pushed open the glass door. "Catch you later."

Dee Dee walked to the door and watched me scurry through the whirling snow to my Bronco. She called after me, "Be careful."

131

I sent a wave in her direction as I got out my cell phone and called my dad. He told me that Wade owned a pretty good snowmobile. Maybe he'd let me use it. I gunned my truck out of the parking lot and raced to Wade's trailer.

I hurried over to the trailer park, just behind the Higher Grounds Café. I was a little surprised at the appearance of his trailer. It looked a lot neater than the last time I was here. Of course, this fresh snow covered all sins, like Wade's collection of beer bottles that always lined the yard. I bounded up his recently shoveled steps. *That's odd*, I thought. Wade usually waited a week to shovel his steps, and only did it if, in his own words, "they *really* need it."

I banged on the aluminum door. No telling what state of drunkenness I'd find the guy in. "Wade, open up. It's Donna!"

I heard the dead bolt click, and the door swung open. There was Wade, looking like the handsome cowboy he is, dressed in his black tee and denim jeans. His blond hair glowed under the lamplight.

He leaned onto the door frame. "What a coincidence," he said. "I was just watching you on TV."

"Never mind that," I said. "I've got a favor to ask of you."

"I've got something to ask you too," Wade said. "When's the wedding?"

I was confused for a moment, then remembered Evie and Dad. "Ah, at the end of next month. But that's not why I'm here."

Wade somehow looked disheartened. "I see," he said quietly. He took a deep breath. "So, what can I do for you, Deputy?"

"Your snowmobile. I need to borrow it."

"It's not really a good night to go for a ride," he said. "Or haven't you noticed."

"I need to borrow your snowmobile's trailer too. I gotta go up to Summit Ridge. There's been an avalanche."

"Isn't that out of your jurisdiction?" Wade asked.

"Yeah, but Goldie and Jack are up there, and Dad wants me to check things out. I thought I'd borrow your snowmobile and ride over to the cabin where they're staying."

Wade grabbed his down jacket from a hook near the door. "Then I'm going with you."

"Hold on, Wade. I don't need anyone else to worry about."

"Well, you can't rescue two people on the back of one snowmobile? Can you?"

"True. But I can hardly take a drunk along."

Wade, who was sliding his arms into his jacket, froze. "That's what you think of me? That I'm just some drunk?"

I wasn't about to fall for his act. "You're drunk now, right?"

He shook his head as he gave me a hard stare. "I've been sober for several weeks. Even joined AA."

I cocked my eyebrows then crossed my arms and for the first time in a very long time studied him. "You're on the level?"

"Of course."

I took a step closer and lifted my chin. "Then blow in my face."

He obeyed. I wrinkled my nose at the smell of liver and onions, Sally's special at the café tonight. "You've got nothing a breath mint won't cure."

He finished slipping his arms into his coat then began to pull on his gloves. "I may have done a lot of things in my time, Donna, but I've never lied. At least, not to you."

I turned on my official voice and said, "Call Brad and ask to borrow his machine. It looks like the two of us are going snowmobiling."

Later, with the snowmobiles filled with gas and fastened securely on the back of the trailer, I sped my Bronco up the freeway to Summit Ridge. We had two steaming coffees and two of Sally's hot tuna melt sandwiches wrapped in wax paper and tucked into a brown paper bag, complete with chips and her chewy peanut butter cookies.

I kept stealing glances at Wade. Normally, whenever he rode in my truck, he was in the backseat, behind the wire cage as I taxied him home from the Gold Rush. It was funny to see him up front with me.

"What's the latest report about the slide?" Wade asked.

I looked at him, glad for his concern and, I had to admit, for his companionship. This was going to be one long night, after all.

133

"I talked to the highway patrol, and they told me the slide blocked the entire Jade Pass into the valley where Goldie and Jack are. In fact, there's a chance that the old house they are staying in could be buried."

"Or crushed," Wade said.

"That's the fear. And since the weather hasn't let up yet, they haven't been able to get a chopper to fly over to assess the damage."

We rode in silence while the wipers swatted at the slush that continued to coat my windshield. Visibility was low as a wall of swirling white shone in the headlights, blotting out the road before us. I pushed the gas as hard as I dared, afraid we'd come to one of those blind curves this road was so famous for.

"So Goldie and Jack could be in real trouble," Wade finally said.

"Yes, they could."

The tires lost traction on a curve that loomed out of the darkness. We skidded briefly before the truck found its grip.

Wade looked over at me. "Deputy, you ever had an accident?"

He looked kind of scared, and I snorted a laugh. "What's the matter, Wade? I thought you liked living on the edge."

"Honestly, Donna, I've lived there too long. For the first time in a long time, I feel I've got something to live for."

"You mean like a woman?"

"I ain't had much luck with women, but you know that. I'm talking about something deeper."

I stole a glance at him. "What's deeper than love?"

"That's just it, there's nothing deeper than love. That's why I'm a changed man."

"You're starting to sound like the pastor there, Wade."

I slipped him another look and noticed his grin. He looked as if he were lit by an inner glow, like some of the folks down at the church. "You're sort of freaking me out."

He chuckled. "Just when you thought you knew me," he said.

"I know you, all right."

The truck slid around another hairpin curve.

134

"For gosh sakes, slow this baby down," Wade said. "There's nothing we can do until morning, anyway. And I for one see no need to go barreling off a cliff."

I let my foot ease a bit off the gas. "You're right."

Wade looked at me and grinned. "That's what I like about you, Deputy. You always were a woman who could be trusted to do the right thing."

"I don't know about that," I said. "I've made my share of mistakes."

Wade nodded his head. "True, and maybe I was one of them."

"Maybe," I said, more gruffly than I intended.

He turned and stared at me long and hard before he said, "Just the same, I've never regretted you."

I inwardly groaned. Now I'd gone and done it. I'd brought one of my lovesick pals out on a rescue.

Well, lovesick or not, when Wade was sober he was as capable as the next guy, and from what I'd heard, he was a mean machine on his snowmobile. Not that I'd ever gone riding with him. I was glad we had two machines so I wouldn't have to hang on the back of his.

An hour later, we approached Summit Ridge. The town was just a hole in the wall, really; nothing much to see. The town's main street was so short I could see the roadblock just ahead punctuated by the flashing lights of a parked highway patrol car. I drove up and circled so my window faced the officer's.

The grinning young highway patrolman said, "You're a long way from home tonight, aren't you, Deputy?"

I shrugged. "'Fraid so. I came out to assist with the rescue."

"There's no rescue in progress here," the officer said. "From what I understand, there's no one up in that high mountain valley to rescue, except two people possibly staying in one of the rentals up there."

"That would be the couple, two residents of Summit View who are reported to be in the Moore place. I just got off the phone with their daughter, and she hasn't heard from them. So they're definitely up there."

"Well, there's nothing you can do tonight. The blizzard's still raging and the snow's too unstable. Why don't you go on down to the motel and check in. Then come back here first thing in the morning for a briefing."

As I powered my window up, Wade said, "Told ya we'd have to wait."

"And that makes you smarter than me?"

"Among other things," Wade said with a grin.

I pulled into the motel parking lot, and Wade raised his brows.

"Don't get your hopes up," I said. "We're not sharing a room."

"Who says I wanted to room with you?" Wade shot back.

I found a place to park the parade I was pulling behind my Bronco and turned to Wade. "As long as we're clear."

"Yes, ma'am," Wade said. "Like you said on TV, you're the law."

19

What's Good for the Goose

Clay was busy feeding his furry little housemates, Woodward and Bernstein, when the call came from his boss about the snowslide at Jade Pass.

"And?" he asked, shrugging. "We have snowslides all the time. It's Colorado; or have you forgotten that?"

"You're getting a bit uppity, Whitefield. Must be all that weight loss."

That and a few other good things happening in my life, Clay thought. "Sorry about that, Chief."

"The point is," his boss continued, "is that Coach Dippel and his wife are up there. I got a call from Vernon Vesey that they could be trapped."

"No joke?"

"No joke."

Clay replaced the lid to the gerbils' cage while balancing his phone between his ear and shoulder. "Wow. Man. That's not good. Do you want me to head over there?"

"Not tonight. There are too many other things you need to deal with."

"Like?"

"Like a stack of work you seem to be neglecting lately over at the office. Oh, and by the way, call Donna Vesey on her cell tomorrow and get an update on the coach and Mrs. Dippel."

"Donna?" Clay stood a bit straighter as he said her name. "Did she go over there?"

"Sheriff said she and Wade Gage left right after he got word. They're using Gage's snowmobile and some other guy's . . . Brad somebody. See if you can't get the scoop."

Wade and Donna, Clay thought with a sigh. *Donna and David. Who next?*

"I'll call her first thing in the morning," he said. "I'll have the complete—and I do mean the complete—story for you as soon as it's ready."

"You're the man," his boss said. "That's why I keep you around."

Clay flipped his cell phone to cut it off then paced the floor of his little apartment for a few moments while Woodward and Bernstein scratched and scurried about in their cage like the two little furry rats they were. He stopped pacing long enough to look at them. They, in turn, stopped long enough to stare back, pink eyes bulging out in wonder.

"What are you looking at?" he asked them. "Haven't you ever seen a man nearing a breakdown?"

Clay walked over and sat at the desk chair, folded his arms over the scarred top of the desk, and rested his chin on his forearm. The gerbils repositioned themselves for a better look-see. "What I don't understand," Clay said to them, "is what she sees in him. Okay, so they were high school sweethearts. A lot of people have high school sweethearts, but that doesn't mean they still make goo-goo eyes at each other nearly twenty years later, does it?" The gerbils blinked back at him for several long moments. "I know, I know," he said. "I've got a beautiful girl interested in me. Move on with my life. But, I'm telling you guys, there's more to this than meets the eye. There's something more than the high school prom holding those two together; I just can't figure out what."

Clay sat upright. "But I will. One day." He frowned. "It just may not be today."

Vonnie

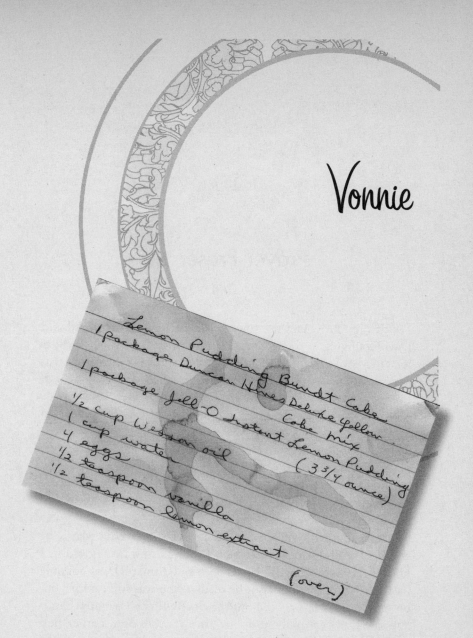

Lemon Pudding Bundt Cake
1 package Duncan Hines Deluxe Yellow
Cake Mix
1 package Jell-O Instant Lemon Pudding
(3 3/4 ounce)
1/2 cup Wesson oil
1 cup water
4 eggs
1/2 teaspoon vanilla
1/2 teaspoon lemon extract

(over)

20

Prayer Preserves

I wiped my brow and ran toward the kitchen, passing Fred and David lounging in the recliners in front of the television. Well, at least they looked happy, despite what we'd all just witnessed on that *Hollywood Nightly* program. I shivered in horror at the thought of such unwanted exposure of my private life. Not to mention Donna's. Poor girl. I should have called her to see how she was doing. I would have too if she hadn't been on duty.

I stole a look at my son. He was laughing with Fred at a *Malcolm in the Middle* rerun. It was like the boy didn't have a care in the world. Of course, he knew what they'd said about Donna was a lie, because we'd set him straight as soon as all those terrible words about her and Larry were broadcast.

I stole another look. How could he look so peaceful? Maybe he was used to the attention, though I didn't think he enjoyed it. I know I certainly didn't. This had been a nightmare. I was not only battling my mother but also the media, who was still camped out on my front lawn. I peeked out the closed kitchen window blinds and saw Dad's car pull out of our driveway. Oh dear. Earlier, he'd stopped over for dinner and had walked out the front door over fifteen minutes ago. That meant he must have granted a few interviews on the way to his car. How could he do that to me? And while we were at it, how could he leave me here with Mother *and* that brass bell of hers?

Ding! Ding! Ding! "Vonnie?"

I called over my shoulder, "Hang on, Mother. I'm making a phone call."

Her strong, determined voice called back, "Well, hurry up, I need you."

I closed my eyes and sighed. *Lord, if you get me through this, well, it will be a miracle. And Lord, you know I believe in miracles. I do! Can I please, please have one? Like right now?*

I thought back to last night when Mother had shown up on my doorstep, demanding I "stow" her in my home while her broken ankle healed. Maybe I was crazy, but whatever I was, I was still the ever-accommodating daughter.

Though I had to wonder why I'd let Mother's fractured ankle interrupt my reunion with David.

All I know is, under these circumstances, no court would convict me for what I'd do to her. No court would convict me, that is, as long as the paparazzi didn't capture her demise on film.

Kidding aside, the pastor always says we should forgive offenses, but I wonder. It's easier to forgive the kind of offenses you can justify. But what my mother had done to both my baby and me was unjustifiable. Which was probably why I was feeling such overwhelming disgust toward her now. But I would work hard to not let it show. I only hoped I could keep my act up until she went home.

The bell rang again.

"Just a minute, Mother."

Now, for my phone call, which would prove to be no easy trick. As my phone number was listed, the media had called nonstop, begging David for interviews. He seemed to take it all in stride, but the media circus was driving me crazy. Especially after I saw the photographer in the tree outside my bathroom window with what appeared to be a telephoto lens. Honestly! What publication did the man work for anyway? *Celebrity Bathroom Secrets?*

I looked at the phone before me. In an effort to stop our phones from ringing, Fred had turned them all off. "There," he'd said. "We can get a little peace."

"You're forgetting my mother is in the guest room," I said.

"I wish I could," he lamented.

I hesitated, then turned on the phone. *Ring!*

I had to get this caller off the line. I had to call Evie and Lizzie for some prayer support. *This is an emergency!*

I picked up the call. "You've got the wrong number," I said as sweetly as I could.

"Vonnie? What on earth?"

"Lizzie?"

"Vonnie, we've got a problem."

"You can say that again," I said with a sigh. "You tell me your problem, then I'll tell you mine."

"Oh, Vonnie, how are things going with Fred, your mother, and David?"

"Honestly? Not so good." I rolled my eyes and said, almost tongue in cheek, "So, can I come and live with you?"

Lizzie laughed. "I'm afraid I've got a full house too."

"Is that why you called, so we could pray for one another?"

"I'm afraid our problems pale compared to what I'm about to tell you."

I sat down. "Oh dear. What now?"

"Olivia just called."

"Goldie and Jack?"

"Yes, but it's not what you think. They're still on their 'weekend,' as you know, but it seems they may have been caught in an avalanche."

A little gasp escaped my throat.

"The operative words are *may have been*. We can't reach them by phone, and all we really know is there has been an avalanche at Jade Pass, just outside of Summit Ridge, a bad one. Apparently with all this new snowfall, the avalanche danger is extreme up in that mountain bowl they're in. They could be in real danger, if not from the Jade Pass avalanche then another one."

"Want me to start the potluck prayer chain?" I asked.

"Better yet, let's call an emergency prayer meeting."

"Your place or mine?" I teased.

"Shall we flip a coin?"

I laughed. "Let's do it at my place. I'd like to expose my son to a little prayer action, seeing as I know nothing yet about his spiritual upbringing or what he believes about God. Besides, it might even do Mom some good too."

"Excellent," Lizzie said. "Shall we say everyone at your place in a half hour? I know it's short notice."

"We'll make it work. Lizzie, could you make the phone calls and tell the girls not to talk to the paparazzi outside?"

Lizzie actually giggled. "I can vouch for everyone's good behavior except Lisa Leann's. I'm sure you saw her performance on TV tonight."

I rolled my eyes. "You tell Lisa Leann that if she talks to the press, I'll see that Evie takes her wedding business somewhere else."

"That will put the fear of the Lord in her."

"It'd better," I said, meaning it.

We hung up, and I unplugged the phone again as I appraised the state of my house. There were dirty dishes scattered about, newspapers, suitcases, shoes, and odds and ends strewn everywhere. In other words, the place was a wreck.

I sighed yet again.

Ding! Ding! Ding! "Vonnie, I've been waiting!"

A half hour later, the girls were pulling into the driveway. That is, all except Goldie and Donna.

Despite my mother's protest, I'd actually gotten her presentable in her fuchsia jogging suit and had her perched in my recliner, positioned so everyone would admire her cast. David and Fred had helped me spruce up the place and haul the kitchen chairs into the living room. I'd even managed to make a pot of coffee.

The first one through my front door was Lisa Leann, who came dressed in jeans and a long fringe-tipped sweater in teal. She was bearing a beautiful Bundt cake. As I took it from her, I realized it was still warm. "Don't worry, I didn't talk to the media," she said, as if she was proud of the fact.

"Good," I said. "How did you have time to bake a cake?"

"Oh. This is my lemon Bundt cake," Lisa Leann explained. "I keep an emergency supply of them in my freezer. All I had to do was defrost it in my microwave. Voila!"

I, who was almost speechless at the thought of having a stash of emergency lemon Bundt cakes in my freezer, could only say, "Oh, how nice."

"This cake has seen me through several seasons of emergency prayer meetings. Like this one time, when one of the ladies at my old church back in Houston found out her husband had been cheating on her, well—"

The doorbell rang. "Excuse me, Lisa Leann."

She followed me to the door and helped me usher in first Olivia, followed by Lizzie, then Evie through the door.

She hugged them, then hung their coats in my hall closet. "I'm so glad you could come," she told them.

She certainly has the gift of hospitality, I thought, *especially since this isn't even her house.*

Soon, we'd all settled in the living room. Fred and David pulled up a chair beside Mother, who looked like the queen of the world as she sat on her throne. "I do hope you'll pray for me tonight," she said. "Seeing as how I'm caught in this very difficult situation."

I looked at her and narrowed my eyes. "Now, Mother, of course we'll pray for you. But first we have an emergency on our hands. Olivia, do you know the latest?"

Poor pregnant Olivia. She looked absolutely frazzled with worry. She ran her fingers through her short red hair, which caused it to stick out at odd angles. She was wearing gray sweats, and that color seemed to wash out her usual ruddy complexion. She looked around the room at us. "Well, I've been in contact with Irene from dispatch, and she tells me that the first avalanche closed Jade Pass. The original assessment is it will be spring before they get the pass open again. Of course, they'll have to wait till morning's light to know more."

"Oh no!" Lisa Leann said. "Wouldn't it be awful if Goldie couldn't make it to Evie's wedding?"

"Honestly, Lisa Leann, is my wedding all you can think about? What does that matter now?" Evie snapped.

Lisa Leann said, "I'm sorry, but what if they can't get them out?"

"They'll get them out somehow," Evie said. "I mean, Donna and Wade are on their way now with snowmobiles."

David shifted in his seat. "Wade Gage is with Donna? Maybe we *should* pray."

"Amen to the prayer," I said. "But people, we're forgetting that we don't even know if Goldie and Jack are safe. After all, that little mountain valley is nothing but a bowl of potential avalanches. If one should come down above Pastor Moore's house, well . . ." I looked at Olivia's stricken face and stopped midsentence. I found my voice. "But that would be the worse case, and Olivia, well, we'll pray."

She nodded. "I appreciate that."

"I don't want Donna on a snowmobile if the avalanche danger is so high," David said.

I glanced over at my son. "That's one of the reasons we've called this prayer meeting, dear. We're all worried." I looked around the room. "Any other prayer requests before we get started?"

"My ankle," Mother chirped. "Pray for my ankle."

Lizzie spoke up. "And my mother. She's in early stage Alzheimer's, you know. My sister-in-law Mildred was taking care of her, but now she's in the hospital following a heart attack. So let's pray for Mildred too, and pray that we can find someplace for Mom—preferably an assisted living arrangement—by next week."

I nodded, wishing I had the guts to say, "And pray for me! My mother is driving me crazy, I hardly know my son, and the media won't leave us alone." Instead I said, "Anything else?"

Lizzie patted me on the leg. "And you, Vonnie. You've got a lot going on over here too. We'll pray for you."

Soon all heads were bowed.

One by one, we called out for heavenly help for Goldie and Jack, then for Donna and Wade. Lizzie spoke for all of us when she prayed, "Lord, turn this time of terror into a time of miracles, for both Goldie and Jack and for Donna and Wade. Use what seems like horrific circumstances to turn what the enemy meant for evil into good. We pray for the safety of our friends as we trust you with their very lives."

When it was David's turn, he prayed, "Protect Donna. Lord, save her for me."

The whole group peeked at the same time and caught the earnest look on his face. I saw Lizzie smile, but bless Lisa Leann if she didn't frown. *That's strange*, I thought. *You'd think she'd already be planning the wedding.*

It was finally my turn. "Dear Lord, we need a miracle, not only for Goldie and Jack but for Mandy, Donna, Wade, David, Fred, Lizzie, Lizzie's mother, and every person sitting in this circle. We pray to you for your miracles. And at the same time, we trust and believe you will make all these things come out for the good, as we are those who love you. In Jesus' name, amen."

My mother spoke up. "What about me?" she asked.

I bowed my head again. "Oh Lord, and please help my mother." *And me. Please help me get through these coming weeks. I don't think I can make it unless you give me the strength. So, please help me, dear Lord. Please.*

21

Apple's of Gold

Clay had decided to walk from his apartment and up the sidewalk to Apple's for a late-night cup of coffee, a decision that turned out to be most fortunate. As soon as he walked into the dimness of the restaurant where but a few patrons remained, he shook the dusting of snow from his coat and then shimmied out of it. After hanging it on the coatrack near the front door, he ambled over to the bar where a mounted TV was turned to the area news. The six or so customers nursing their drinks were completely oblivious to the breaking report of the snowslide at Jade Pass.

Brad Sumser stood behind the bar, pouring Jim Beam Black into a small glass as he rounded out the end of his shift. He glanced up at Clay, then turned his attention back to the drink preparation. "How's it going there, Clay?" he asked.

"It's going," Clay answered, sliding onto a bar stool.

"What can I get you?" he asked, then slid the glass of Beam to a waiting customer. "There ya go, brother," he said with a smile.

"Coffee," Clay answered.

"Straight up?" Brad asked with a dimpled grin.

"Nothing fancy," Clay answered. He pointed up to the television. "Can you turn that up just a bit?"

Brad poured a cup of coffee, placed it in front of Clay, and reached for the remote in one fluid movement. "Yeah, did you hear about that?" he asked as he leaned against the other side of the bar.

"My boss called me a while ago about it. I'll call Donna in the morning and see what's what. Coach and Mrs. Dippel are up there, you know." Clay blew at the hot coffee, watched it ripple across the mug.

Brad nodded. "Yeah, I know. Wade called me, asked for my snow-mobile. He and Donna ought to be there by now, toting his sled and mine. What a mess, huh? You think Coach will be alright?"

"Snowslides are dangerous." It was all Clay knew to say. He took a long swallow of the coffee, grateful that he could erase the picture of Donna with her arms wrapped around Wade Gage as they went into the dangers of a snowslide. "So what do you think about Donna and Wade going up there together?"

Brad shrugged his shoulders. "Wade knows his way when it comes to snowmobiling. Donna couldn't be in safer hands."

Clay frowned. He didn't like the picture that evoked. "Yeah." He took another swallow of coffee, cutting his eyes over the rim. "Those two, though. They go way back."

"Don't we all?" Brad answered, then pushed himself upright, grabbed a towel, and began to wipe up behind the bar. "But I know what you're saying. I kinda thought they'd end up married, you know?" Then he winked at Clay. "Not to say there's not still a chance, right?"

Clay set the mug down on the bar with a thud. "Right," he said. He sensed someone walking up behind him, and he shifted on his bar stool. His brow furrowed and his eyes narrowed.

"Hi," the pretty blonde said to him. "You waved at me the other day." She held out her hand. "I'm Velvet James." She smiled a "Donna" smile.

"Good gosh," he said. "Who *are* you?"

Donna

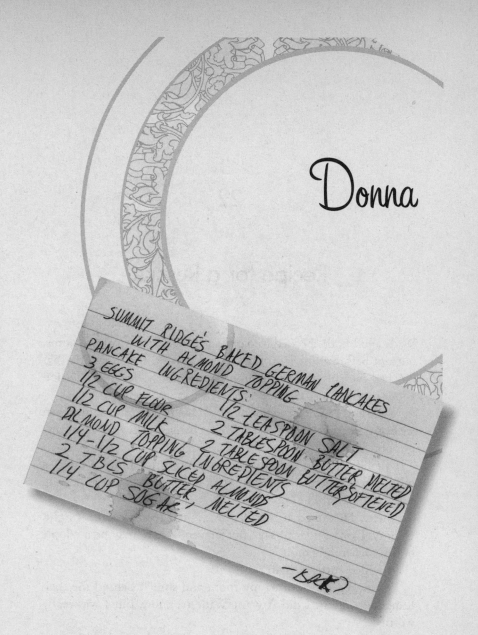

SUMMIT RIDGE'S BAKED GERMAN PANCAKES
WITH ALMOND TOPPING

PANCAKE INGREDIENTS:

3 EGGS

1/2 CUP FLOUR   1/2 TEASPOON SALT

1/2 CUP MILK   2 TABLESPOON BUTTER MELTED

ALMOND TOPPING 2 TABLESPOON BUTTER SOFTENED

INGREDIENTS

1/4-1/2 CUP SLICED ALMONDS

2 TBLS   BUTTER, MELTED

1/4 CUP SUGAR

—(BACK)

22

Recipe for a Rescue

Wade and I both checked into private, postage-stamp-sized rooms, but not before another rumble roared beyond the snowslide that blocked the entrance to the upper mountain valley. No question about it, it was a second avalanche.

Wade and I were just walking down the hall to our rooms when we heard the thundering crash. We exchanged glances. "That can't be good," he said.

I shook my head and turned to go into my room. "We're in a protected area here. So, grab some z's. We'll see what we're dealing with in the morning."

"Sure." He stared at me like he wanted to say more. "Night, Deputy. Don't forget to say your prayers. There may be a couple of lives depending on it."

I nodded curtly. "Right."

I unlocked the door to my room and shut it behind me then leaned against it. I didn't want Wade to know, but I was really worried.

I checked my cell phone. Sure enough, both Clay and Vonnie had tried to call while Wade and I were on the road. We must have been out of range, so the calls had gone to voice mail. I listened first to Vonnie's message: "Donna, dear, the Potluck girls met tonight, and we're all praying for you. Call me when you can. Love you."

Then Clay's message: "Donna, I'm worried. Could you call me and give me a report? Don't wait till morning, okay?"

I plopped back onto the bed as I punched in his number. He picked up on the first ring. "Donna! How are the Dippels?"

"I don't know. Won't know till morning. But Wade and I have made it to the hotel at least. We're spending the night."

"Oh? Well, you're both consenting adults, I guess."

I felt my eyebrows leap. "Consenting?"

"Ah, well, I mean, call me in the morning and let me know about the status."

"Of the snowslide, or how I'm getting on with Wade?"

The line went silent for so long I thought I'd lost the signal. Finally he said, "Why, Donna, I'm a reporter. You can tell me anything."

"Yeah, anything I want to read on the front page of the paper. I'll call you later. Night, Clay."

"Night."

I sat down on the bed and tugged off my shoes as I analyzed our situation. The local and state authorities weren't going to let us do anything until morning. All I could do for now was to try to get a good night's sleep, a task that soon proved almost impossible. First, my room was too cold, so I turned on the wall heating unit. It groaned and chugged until the room was absolutely boiling. Finally I turned the heater off and cracked a window to let in some cold air as I looked outside. I'd noted it was three in the morning, at least according to the red digits of the clock near the bed. So I wasn't happy to see thick snowflakes blowing sideways in the illumination of the streetlights. This blizzard was a bad one, and so far it showed no signs of letting up.

So much for Wade's prayers.

I tried to go back to sleep, but I tossed and turned for another two hours. At five I'd had it. I pulled my uniform back on over my underwear (as I had failed to pack for the trip) and strode down the hall. It was time for a cup of black coffee.

When I walked into the lobby, I saw that Wade had the same idea.

"Good morning, sleepyhead," he said and then took a sip of coffee. "You look terrible."

"Thanks," I said. "Nothing like a few minutes of beauty sleep."

I poured myself a cup from the courtesy pot, and Wade said, "Still snowing, though it may be letting up. I've already been outside and talked to the officer. He said the avalanche conditions in the upper valley are extreme. No one will be allowed to go into the area until they assess the danger."

"Great," I said, pointing toward the coffee shop next door, which was surprisingly open. Probably so they could serve the rescue and cleanup crews heading this way. "Might as well have breakfast while we wait."

An hour later, after we'd eaten a round of baked German pancakes with almond topping, the weather was still not cooperating.

Wade pulled on his coat and walked outside to the parking lot to talk to some of the county workers who'd started to gather. I watched the men while I made a few calls on my cell phone.

"Any word from the Dippels?" I asked Dad.

"No one's heard a thing," he told me. "How are things going up there?"

"Everything's shut down for now. Though I'm hoping to get going soon."

"We're praying for you, Donna."

"Uh, thanks, Dad." I shook my head. *Dad prays? This is news to me.*

After I hung up, I approached Wade, who looked like an iced version of himself, as his down parka sported a coating of snow.

"Any news?" he asked.

I shook my head. "I have to admit I'm worried."

"Have you talked to the local sheriff's department?" he asked.

"Yeah. They confirmed what we already knew. There was a second avalanche in the night. We won't be allowed in till the snow lets up and after they shoot off some of their avalanche cannons located on a few of the ridges in the area."

"Good idea. The sound waves will either bring down more slides or prove the snow's stable enough for our snowmobiles."

"Yeah, as long as it doesn't pull down a slide on the Dippels."

I rubbed my gloved hands together, feeling the icy pelts of snow on my face. "It's freezing out here, and we could be waiting for hours. I think I'll go inside."

"I'll join you," Wade said. He grinned down at me. "At least inside I can enjoy the view."

Like a lazy game of checkers, the day slowly played by. The snow didn't let up till noon, and even then the powers that be wouldn't give Wade and me the go-ahead to ride our snowmobiles into the upper valley until after three.

When we'd finally been given the green light, we only had a couple of daylight hours left. Wade unloaded the machines and checked our emergency supplies. He tossed me a helmet.

"As I'm a more experienced rider, I'll take lead. So stay close. There might be some tricky spots, and I don't want either one of us to get stuck, plus we don't want to trigger any more slides."

He tossed me an emergency beacon. "Turn this on. At least they'd know where to find us if we get buried." Then he grabbed my hand. "Let's pray first," he said, without giving me a chance to argue. I bowed my head as he said, "Father, guide us, keep us safe. Help us to lead the Dippels to safety. In the name of Jesus."

I couldn't argue with a prayer like that, so I said the only thing I could say. "Amen."

Wade grinned at me. "I'm one of the few people who knows you're a heathen, Donna. So I thank you for allowing me to pray. It makes me think there may be hope for you yet."

I put on my helmet in an effort to hide my irritation. "Ah, thanks, Wade."

"Ready to ride?"

"Let's go," I shouted as my motor roared to life.

With the sun out, the glare from the white snow was blinding. I was glad for the tinted ski goggles Wade had given me. They worked well to keep both the bitter wind as well as the bright sun out of my eyes.

The cold was going to be a problem, especially as the mountain shadows stretched between the patches of afternoon sun. How I wished for a pair of ski pants to slide over my uniform pants to cut the arctic air.

I decided to disregard the wind chill, which was probably hovering around ten below, as Wade and I raced out of the parking lot and onto the snow-covered road winding up toward the pass. Though the pass was completely blocked, we managed to shovel and pick our way through, around, and over the mounds of rocks and snow as our machines roared beneath us. I counted each dip and bounce through the wavy white ripples as a milestone bringing us closer to the Dippels.

The cold wind stung my cheeks and filled each breath with air so icy my chest literally ached. Still, the ride was exhilarating. Wade drove just ahead of me, creating a trail, a rut for my sled to follow. Periodically, he would turn back to check on me, and I'd wave to show I was fine. In fact, I was more than fine. Despite the danger and the cold, I was actually enjoying myself.

Soon, we'd made it through the slide area and tried to follow what should be the road, up the valley hill to the Moore cabin. I let out a whoop when I saw the bungalow.

We brought our machines to a halt and stared. Another slide, just to the west of the cabin, had come close to burying it.

I gazed at the second slide, not to mention the deep snow drifts, and realized Jack's car must be completely buried beneath the blanket that seemed to have knit the little house inside a winter's white turtleneck sweater. Only the tops of the windows peeked out, like eyes beneath a white cap.

Holy moly.

We parked the vehicles. If Goldie and Jack were in that cabin, they'd know help had arrived because of the sound of our motors droning up the valley.

"Goldie! Jack!" I called.

No answer.

Wade's voice joined with mine. "Goldie! Jack! Are you in there?"

The front door opened. The only reason we knew was because the snowdrift that nestled against the house shifted a bit then slid forward. We watched as Jack's head appeared as he climbed on top of the mountainous lump of snow that blocked his exit. He waved then helped Goldie as she scrambled up beside him. He slipped an arm around her and pulled her close. She didn't try to pull away, I noted.

I smiled with relief. It was good to see them looking so . . . so healthy. And not just healthy, those two looked . . . happy? Their cheeks glowed with excitement as they cheered our arrival.

I guess Wade and I were cheering too, because I was suddenly caught in Wade's warm embrace as he wrapped me in his arms. Our eyes locked, and my heart literally stopped as his breath mingled with mine.

For an instant, I felt all of seventeen.

Wade immediately let go, as if nothing had happened between us, and ran toward the Dippels. I soon followed, stepping into his footprints as he post-holed through waist-deep snow.

"Donna, Wade," Goldie called to us as she and Jack slid down the drift toward us. When we met, I gave her a hug. "I am so glad to see you two," I said as Wade and Jack shook hands and slapped each other on the back.

"You don't know how glad we are to see you too," Goldie responded.

I pulled back. "You and Jack ready to get out of here?"

Wade checked his watch. "It's time, folks. We only have half an hour of daylight left. Grab only what you need, wallet and coats, gloves, hats, and lock up. You can pick up everything else, including the car, after the spring thaw."

Jack climbed back inside the house and was soon back with the necessary items. Moments later, with Jack hanging on to Wade and Goldie clinging to me, we were off, racing against the darkness and the snowdrifts that blocked our path. We moved as fast as we dared. The last thing we needed was to get stuck on that avalanche field after dark.

Forty-five minutes later, the lights of the little town of Summit Ridge winked at us as we picked our way across the boulder field under a full moon that was just starting to rise.

When we pulled into the parking lot, I called Dad to report the good news. When I finished, I said, "Could you pass this report to both Vonnie and Clay?"

I handed Goldie my cell phone. "I imagine you have a couple of calls you'll want to make," I said.

She grinned. "How'd you know?" She turned her back to her husband, who was climbing off the back of Wade's snowmobile, and crossed her arms as if trying to size him up. "How'd you know?"

23

Business as Usual

Clay was hard at work, typing out the story as he knew it so far. The Dippels had gone away for a couple of days to sort out their marital problems. They were staying at the Moore cabin, and the snowslide had been caused by the unseasonably high snowfall.

He reached for the phone book buried under a stack of old papers in the far left corner of his office desk. Flipping a few pages he found the number he was looking for, then picked up the handset of the phone and dialed out. Seconds later, Goldie Dippel answered.

"Good morning, Chris Lowe's office," she said.

"Mrs. Dippel, Clay Whitefield. How are you this morning?"

"Grateful to be alive," she answered with a chuckle. "God is good."

Clay nodded. "That's what I keep hearing. Yes, ma'am."

"Did you need to speak with Mr. Lowe?"

"No. Ah, actually, I wanted to talk to you if you have time. Later on."

"Me?"

Clay smiled at her surprise. "Yes, ma'am," he repeated. "I'd like to talk to you about the snowslide. About how you and the coach survived it all. About the rescue."

"Only by the grace of God. We came awfully close to being completely snowed under. But I suppose you've talked to Donna," she said.

"She's next on my list," Clay answered, then closed his eyes momentarily. *Donna . . . if she only knew what I know.*

"How about tomorrow afternoon after work?" she asked. "I can meet you at Higher Grounds."

"You said the magic words," Clay said with a laugh. "I'll see you then."

He called Donna next. "Got a statement for me, Deputy?" he asked her when she answered.

"Good morning to you too," she said curtly.

"I was surprised not to see you at the café this morning."

"I'm a bit tired," she answered.

"So, when's a good time to talk?" he asked, pulling his PDA toward him, poised to enter in his appointment with Goldie Dippel and Donna.

"Can a girl have a day off?" she asked.

"Yes, you may," he said with a laugh. "I'm meeting Mrs. Dippel tomorrow afternoon. What if you both meet me at about five down at the café?"

He heard her groan, though a bit dramatically. "Fiiiiiiine."

He chuckled again. "You okay otherwise?" He entered the date.

"Why wouldn't I be okay?" she asked.

"Just asking." He slid the PDA across his desk.

"No, you aren't. You're up to something."

Don't ask, he thought.

"Is this about me and Wade? Because if it is, quite frankly, my friend, it really is none of your business. I'll tell you like I told him: separate rooms."

Clay closed his eyes and opened them quickly. "Ah, well . . . that's nice to know. Wasn't what I was getting at, but . . ."

He heard his computer "click," an indication he had a new email. With his free hand he shifted the mouse and glanced over at the screen. It was from Britney. He smiled.

What timing, he thought.

158

Lizzie

Spaghetti Pie

Ingredients

8 oz. spaghetti broken
into 2" pieces
2 TB. butter
1/3 C. grated Parmesan ch.
1/2 tsp. salt
1/4 tsp. pepper
1 egg, well-beaten
1 1/2 lbs. ground chuck

24

Dicey Discovery

I woke up with the knowledge that my friend Goldie was alive and well, a wonderful way to start any day. She and I had spoken on the phone just after eleven the night before, she and Jack having just arrived back in Summit View.

"Other than the avalanche, how'd it go?" I asked her, turning on my side so as not to bother Samuel too terribly much.

"Not so good," she said.

"Where are you?"

"Home. My home, not Jack's."

Jack's. For many years it had been *her* home. I sighed. I guess deep down I'd hoped for so much more. "So no reconciliation?"

She was quiet for a moment, then said, "No. We're moving toward it, though."

"That sounds good. It's a start, anyway."

She remained quiet, as though there was something pressing on her mind, something she wanted to say but wasn't sure how to say it. "Listen, Lizzie. I really need to talk to someone, and now's obviously not the time. I called you as soon as I got safely in the house, and now I need to shower. To wash the last couple of days off of me. Can you meet me after work tomorrow?"

I thought of the time. Goldie didn't get off until five o'clock. By then I'd really need to be home preparing dinner for the family. But Goldie sounded as though she really needed me, so I relented. "Sure. I won't have long, but maybe we can grab a cup of tea or some coffee over at Higher Grounds."

We ended the phone call with a "see you then." I replaced the phone's handset and then rolled over onto my back.

"They didn't get back together, did they?" Samuel asked from his side of the bed.

I patted his backside with my hand and closed my eyes. "No. They didn't."

Samuel let out a pent-up breath. "They've got a lot to get over, Liz. He's got to stay in therapy, and she's got to let go of the past."

I didn't say anything. I didn't have the right to; I'd never been through anything like what Goldie had been through. I patted Samuel's backside again and said, "Go to sleep. Tomorrow's another day, we've got to go to work, and somehow I still need to find a decent place for Mother to live before Mildred comes home from the hospital next week."

With the snowstorm over, school was now back in session, and I was glad for it. My work was becoming my refuge away from home rather than the other way around. I mentally pinched myself but hard for even having such a thought. Then I remembered the chaos in my home the day before. Tim and Michelle had managed to make it to work, but the bank had closed down and every last one of my grandchildren decided that a "snow day" meant a day at MeMa's drinking hot cocoa and playing video games.

I hate video games. I don't even know why my children allow their children to have them.

Samuel had spent the day in front of the television, watching shows like *Judge Judy* and *The People's Court*. *Where do they find these people?* I wondered.

When I arrived at work I was pleased to find that my library assistant, Ellie Brestin, was already sitting at her desk—a smaller version of mine—sipping on a cup of hot tea. "Yours is on your desk," she said, smiling.

I pulled my coat off and hung it on the metal coatrack in the corner of our little office. "Thank you," I said. Ellie was always good about preparing two cups when she arrived first, and I, in turn, did the same.

"How was your day yesterday?" she asked. "Because it could not possibly have been as insane as mine. What was I thinking when I had four children, I ask you. And Holly was about as premenstrual as they come. You've had daughters. How long does this last?"

I turned from the coatrack. "How old is she now?"

"Twelve."

"You've got a ways to go," I said with a smile as I reached my desk and began to prepare my tea. Ellie—always thoughtful—had left a small packet of honey and a stirrer on a cocktail napkin. Having Ellie as an assistant was not half bad, in spite of the disgruntled sigh she now emitted. "My home was pretty much insane too, though there weren't any premenstrual girls in the house." I giggled a bit. "I have to tell you I'm happy to be back at work."

"Well, you might not be when you hear about the meeting you're now scheduled for this morning."

My shoulders slumped. "What meeting?" I looked at my desk; I had so much work to do.

Ellie jerked her head toward her desktop PC and said, "Came in our email late Friday. Apparently some of the boys from one of Mr. Polsen's eleventh-grade poli sci classes got on a porn site sometime Thursday while they were in here doing some research." She used her index fingers to quote the word *research*.

I racked my brain trying to remember the class even coming into the library on Thursday. Already it seemed a lifetime ago. "And?" I asked, bringing the mug of hot tea to my lips and blowing.

Ellie's eyes widened as she continued. "And one of the mothers overheard her son talking to some of the other guys later that night—you have no idea the filth on the Internet—and she called Mr. Tobin demanding a meeting. He set it for ten o'clock this morning."

I buried my face in my hands, shaking my head ever so slightly. "I don't wanna go," I moaned. "And to think I was happy to be at work today."

Ellie stood from her desk and headed toward the office door. "Well, you *have* to be there. You have no choice. I, on the other hand, must stay behind and file books on overstuffed shelves and keep watch for hormonal students."

I peered up at her. She grinned, then added, "You know what they're going to say, don't you? They're going to say that you need to be up to date on the software filters."

I spread my hands in exasperation. "These kids today know how to break the filters, Ellie. Every time we add a new one or try out the latest, they break them in five minutes flat. Even I could break them, and I'm practically computer illiterate."

"I know that," she said, pointing first to herself and then pointing to me. "And you know that. Now all you have to do is see if you can get the parents to believe it."

With a wink she stepped into the library to begin her morning work. I took a sip of my now nearly tepid tea, booted up my computer, and went in search of the email that summoned me to a meeting I would dread from now until 10:00.

It was going to be a long day.

It was five o'clock on the nose when I entered Higher Grounds. Only a few of the locals were there, sipping on hot drinks, trying to ward off the cold. Clay was in his usual spot, of course. My eyes widened with a bit of maternal delight when I saw that he wasn't alone.

"Mrs. Prattle," he greeted me.

I walked over to his table, ignoring the "Please Wait to Be Seated" sign in the front. "Good afternoon, Clay."

He stood. The boy actually stood. "Would you care to join us?" he asked, sounding remarkably proper.

I looked from him to the pretty blonde I knew to be Adam Peterson's sister. "Hello, Britney," I said.

She smiled her million-dollar smile. "Hello, Mrs. Prattle. Michelle and Adam were over this past week. She's teaching me to sign," she said, then signed "Would you like a cup of coffee" to me.

"What'd you say?" Clay asked, beaming at her. *Good heavens*, I thought. *He's smitten.*

"I said," Britney began by signing as she spoke, "would you like a cup of coffee?"

"Oh." Clay looked to me. "Would you, Mrs. Prattle? You can join us . . . or are you meeting someone?"

I looked out the window and spotted Goldie dashing across the street as fast as her feet and the snow-slick streets would allow. "I'm meeting Goldie," I said. "But thank you."

Clay nodded. "I've got an interview set up with her for tomorrow. She and the coach barely survived that avalanche, I guess you know."

I shuddered. "I know. Prayer, Clay. Prayer saved them." I took a deep breath and exhaled. "Well, it was good to see you again, Britney." I placed a hand on Clay's shoulder. "And you, Mr. Whitefield. It was very good to see you in church on Sunday."

Clay pinked and said, "Yes, ma'am. I was somewhat roped in by Mrs. Lambert, but I have to say I enjoyed it."

Britney touched his arm lightly. "But you'll go again, won't you, Clay?" she asked.

Just then the front door opened and Goldie walked in. "That's my date," I said, then joined Goldie at the front. Within seconds we were seated and sipping on our hot drinks.

"So, tell me everything," I said. "And leave no detail out. No stone unturned. I want all the details, even the ones that'll make me blush."

Goldie cut her eyes from the left to the right, allowing them to settle halfway across the room on Clay. "I know you don't have a lot of time, and I don't really want to talk about the cabin experience. I want to talk to you about something else." She bit her lip. "Is that Britney with Clay Whitefield?"

I nodded. "Apparently, they're becoming a bit of an item."

"As long as she keeps him from eavesdropping on our conversation, I really don't care."

I was taken aback. "Goldie," I whispered. "What is it? What's wrong?"

She hunched over. "It's Charlene Hopefield."

I furrowed my brow. "What about her?"

Goldie blinked a few times before going on. "She's pregnant."

"What!"

Tears were forming in Goldie's eyes, and I reached for a napkin and handed it to her. "I don't know what I'm going to do," she said to me between dabs and a blowing of her nose.

"Is it—"

"Jack's? She says it is."

"Oh, Goldie."

Goldie blew her nose again, then rolled her eyes. "Lisa Leann once said she hoped Jack didn't bring home a venereal disease. What he's done is brought home a baby."

I pondered the idea for a minute. "Does Jack know?"

Goldie shook her head. "Not unless that woman has told him today." Her eyes jerked over to where Clay and Britney were sitting. "I don't know what to do," she said quietly.

I didn't say anything at first. I mean, what could I say? I've never been in Goldie's shoes. Never once even thought about or worried about my husband in the arms of another woman. Now, the thought and vision of Jack in the delivery room, coaching Charlene, holding his newborn, teaching him to play catch . . .

"You have to tell him," I said.

"Me?" Her eyes widened, and she lowered her voice another octave. "It's her baby. Not mine."

"I know, but he's *your* husband."

Goldie shook her head. "She can have him for all I care."

I leaned back in my chair. "When did you find out?"

"Charlene came over right after you left Saturday night."

"And still you went with him to Summit Ridge."

That's when I'm quite certain I saw the hint of a smile slide across her lips. "Only to torture him."

"Torture him?"

She waved the thought away. "Never mind. It's another story."

I leaned my forearms on the table. "I want you to answer this question. Don't think about the answer. Just answer it . . . Do you love Jack?"

Goldie didn't answer at first; she just looked at me. Looked through me, to be more precise. Then she nodded. "I do. He was so valiant while we were trapped in the cabin. Well, not at first. At first, when the lights had gone out and we didn't know about the first slide, he was acting like a real baby. Things were not going his way, and he was . . . testy. I wanted to strangle him. But after the second slide . . . Honestly, Lizzie, if it hadn't been for my knowing about Charlene, I would have . . . we could have . . . well, you know."

I knew.

I looked down at my watch. It was getting late, and this was no time to end the conversation. "Goldie, listen. I have to get going. Samantha is cooking spaghetti pie for dinner, and Samuel should be getting off any minute and heading home." I reached over and touched her arm. "I had the day from you-know-where and I really want to talk to Samuel about it before we get bombarded by the kids. Oh, and I think I may have found a place for Mother—"

"Your mother?"

"Ah. Another story, another cup of tea, another day. Okay?"

Goldie frowned. "I'm sorry, Lizzie. Here I am going on and on about my life, and you have your own problems too."

I patted her arm, then reached toward the back of the chair for my coat. "Go talk to Jack. Don't waste another minute. If you love him, be a team. Together you'll get through this a lot easier than alone. Either way, Charlene is going to have a baby. Together or alone, Goldie. It's up to you."

Goldie also reached for her coat, and we stood. "You're right. You're absolutely right." We both began to slip into our coats. "He's coming over tonight. I'll tell him then." She nodded. "I will."

"Good girl," I said, laying a five-dollar bill I'd earlier folded into my pants pocket on the table. "This is on me."

We headed for the front door. As we stepped onto the sidewalk in the dim light of early evening, I looked to the left and saw Donna walking toward us. "There's Donna," I said.

"My new best friend," Goldie said with a lilt.

"Oh, I'm sure of that. I want to ask her something about the Internet and some new filtering programs Mr. Tobin insists I look into."

"Oh?" Goldie remarked.

"Donna," I called out with a wave of my hand.

Donna continued to move toward us, waving back.

"Donna, you're just the one I need to talk to," I said as she neared. "What can you tell me about or what do you know about—"

The young woman in front of me stopped, cocked her scarf-covered head a bit, and smiled. "You must have me mistaken for someone else. My name's not Donna."

I was startled. "I am so sorry. I thought . . . well, my goodness, but you look just like her."

"No, I can see a difference," Goldie said. "Hello, I'm Goldie Dippel. Sorry if we scared you."

"You didn't," the girl said. "I've known for some time I look a lot like someone around here." She tilted her head a bit. "Donna, I think it is?"

"Donna Vesey," Goldie answered. "She's Sheriff Vernon Vesey's daughter."

"And a deputy herself," I added. "You may see her driving around here in her Bronco sometime. You'll see the resemblance."

The girl smiled broadly. *Good heavens*, I thought, *she even has Donna's teeth. Certainly has her eyes.* "Sheriff Vernon Vesey," she repeated. "I've heard of him." Then she nodded. "I surely have. How about that."

I frowned, wondering, *How about what?* But before I could ask, she said, "I'm Velvet James, by the way." She extended her gloved hand for a shake, and Goldie and I obliged her. "I'm new here, but so far I really like it."

"Did you move here alone?" Goldie asked, her Southern hospitality and curiosity spilling out. "Or with your family?"

"Well, sort of. My mama moved here a few months ago, and I followed her."

"Your mama?" I asked, wondering if she were someone we knew.

"Mmm-hmm. Dee Dee McGurk? Do you know her?"

We both shook our heads. "Not familiar with her," Goldie said. "Lizzie and I attend Grace Church just down the road. Perhaps the two of you can join us sometime. Very family oriented congregation."

"That might be nice," she answered. "I'll tell my mama. She's never been much of one to attend church, but she might go for it."

"It's never too late to start," I said.

Our newest town member nodded her pretty head. "Mama told me once that she used to sing in a church choir, but personally I find it difficult to believe. Not my mama, anyway." She placed her hand on her hip. "So, you know, it might be good for her to start going again."

"We could always use another voice in the choir," Goldie said.

I was just about to ask where her mother worked—thinking perhaps our paths might have crossed in that way—when my cell phone chirped from inside my purse. "Oh, I'm sorry."

As I dug around looking for it, Velvet said, "Well, I better get going. I'm heading toward the Gold Rush Tavern—that's where Mama works—to spend some time with her during happy hour." She smiled. "Like I said, Mama hasn't gone to church as long as I can remember. Anyway, the bus picks up just right over there."

Gold Rush Tavern? My question answered, I looked down at my cell phone ringing steady in my hand. The face showed that the call was from Samuel's bank. Just as I flipped the cover to say hello, I heard Goldie continue to speak with Velvet.

I stepped aside for privacy. "Hello?"

"Lizzie?" It was Samuel's secretary.

"Susan?"

"Lizzie, there's been an accident. Samuel fell on his way to the car, slipped on an icy patch, I think. Anyway, Curtis Murray got him in the back of his SUV, and they're heading toward the hospital now. I've called Dr. Walliston. He said he'd meet Samuel in the ER.

Lizzie, I think it's pretty bad. Samuel was hollering like a whipped dog, and you know he doesn't do that."

My shoulders squared. "No. No, he doesn't. Okay . . . let me think . . . okay. I'll head over to the hospital right now. Thank you, Susan. Thank you. I'll head right over."

"Keep me posted, will you?" she asked. "I really hated seeing him in that much pain."

"I will."

"And Lizzie, if you need anything, you call me. Anything. Anything at all."

I said I would, then flipped the top of the phone down. When I looked up, Velvet was halfway to the bus stop and Goldie was saying, "She's from Mississippi. I thought I recognized a Southern accent. I do know my people . . ." She paused long enough to look at me. "What's wrong?"

"It's Samuel," I said. "He's been hurt. I've got to . . . I've got to go." I began to flail my arms like a wounded bird. "I've got to go to the hospital." I felt myself begin to shake. *What now, Lord?*

Goldie grabbed my hand. "Come on," she said. "You're a bundle of nerves. I'll drive."

25

Coffee with a Mind Reader

Clay watched as the scene unfolded just outside Higher Grounds, and he frowned.

"What are you looking at?" Britney asked from beside him.

"Hmmm?" he said, not looking her way.

From the corner of his eye he saw Britney crane her neck to look out. "Is that . . . what was her name . . . Velvet James with Mrs. Dippel and Mrs. Prattle?"

Clay looked from Britney to the street and then back to Britney again. "Yeah."

"She looks an awful lot like that deputy sheriff, doesn't she?"

Clay looked back out the window. "You think?"

He felt Britney touch his arm, and he looked down to her hand. It was a pretty hand, soft and small and ornamented with but a single blue-stoned ring. He touched it lightly. "That's pretty. I don't think I've ever noticed you wearing it before."

"It was my grandmother's," she said.

"Pretty."

"Clay?"

He looked up at her. "Mmm?"

"What's really on your mind?"

Evangeline

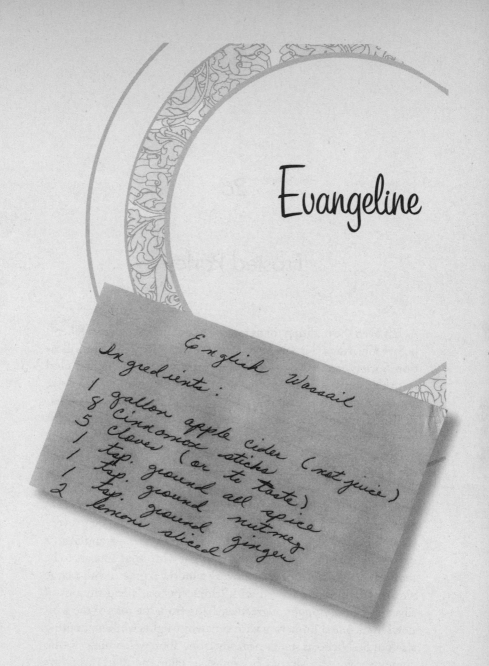

English Wassail

Ingredients:

1 gallon apple cider (not juice)
8 cinnamon sticks
5 cloves (or to taste)
1 tsp. ground all spice
1 tsp. ground nutmeg
1 tsp. ground ginger
2 lemons sliced

26

Frosted Parley

As has been the tradition for as long as I can remember, the weekend before Christmas a group known as the Summit View Beautification Society (started by my mother shortly after my father, God rest their souls, was elected mayor of our little town) takes a drive around Summit View for the sole purpose of determining who has the finest, most festive decorations on their property. There haven't been too many years in which I lost; not because my daddy was the mayor or because this was his home originally. And not because of the delightful English wassail I prepare and serve to them piping hot from my mother's milk glass punch set, although I do know for a fact that this is the very reason they save my street till last. I win because I bring a little Victorian England to Summit View every year by bringing an old sleigh—one from my great-grandfather's day—out from the back shed and filling it with what appears to be mounds of Christmas presents. Every window is graced with a large wreath wrapped and woven with iridescent pearls and ribbons of silver and gold. Boughs of greenery hang from the tops of the windows, each one shimmering with tiny white lights while an inviting six-foot St. Nicholas stands near my front door, welcoming all who come near with a "Merry Christmas!" It takes me all of three days total to get it done, but it's worth it. Not only for the joy it brings my neighbors but for the win it brings from the Society.

Now, I'm not saying I win *every* year because of my wassail or because of the lovely way I have of bringing the holiday season to my home. A newcomer (Rushies, we call them) won a couple of years ago, and one year—many years ago—Samuel Prattle built something akin to a real-life nativity scene and had his brood playing the parts of the essential characters, including Michelle Prattle as the Virgin Mary.

As I put the finishing touches on my front door wreath, fingers dancing lightly over it, I came to a sudden stop. *With all the people currently in the Prattle household, they could actually pull this off again.* I frowned at the thought.

I was headed inside to make a quick call to Vernon from the kitchen phone. What with him making his rounds, he would know if a barn-like thing had been erected in the front yard of the Prattle household.

"Evie, Samuel's in bed, remember? His back?"

"Oh, praise the good Lord," I said before I had a chance to think.

"Evangeline!" my future husband admonished from the other end of the phone line.

"I didn't mean it the way it sounded," I said just as quickly. I looked up at the clock. It was nearly ten o'clock on Saturday morning. Lizzie ought to be up by now. "As a matter of fact, I'll call Lizzie now. I haven't really spoken to her since Tuesday evening when she was at the hospital with Samuel."

"That surprises me," he said.

"Well, I've been busy, Vernon Vesey. What with Christmas right around the corner, the Christmas tea, making sure Lisa Leann doesn't ruin that, doing my own shopping, and keeping up the house. Not to mention all the things I've got to think about with our wedding."

"Ah. By the way, I ran into Lisa Leann the other day. She insists that the two of us get over there sometime this coming week to continue the process of planning for our wedding. She says we're way off schedule."

I frowned again. "If we were having a really big wedding, I couldn't agree more. But we aren't. Lisa Leann knows I want this to be lovely but simple."

"I just want this to be over," Vernon quipped.

I wasn't sure whether to be insulted or not. "I'll take that in a positive way," I told him.

He chuckled, giving me no indication as to how he meant it.

"I need to call Lizzie," I said. "So good-bye, Vernon Vesey."

"Goodbye, Evangeline Benson," he said with another laugh.

That man, I thought with a smile as I ended the call, then picked up the receiver and dialed Lizzie's number. Moments later the voice of a young child—no doubt one of her grandchildren, but God only knows which one—informed me that I had, indeed, reached the Prattle residence.

"Prattle residence and hospital," he (or she, I couldn't tell) giggled into the phone.

"Yes, this is Ms. Evangeline Benson. May I speak to your grandmother, please?"

"Meeeeeee-Maaaaaaa!" the child shouted.

I held the phone a good six inches from my ear and sighed deeply. Poor Lizzie.

"Hello?" I heard Lizzie say, followed by, "I have it, sweetheart. Hang up the phone." She sounded exhausted. Surely no nativity scene this year, I thought, then admonished myself in Vernon's absence.

"It's me, Evangeline," I said when the other phone had been set noisily down on its cradle.

"Oh, hello, Evie."

"Tell me what's going on with Samuel," I said, getting to the heart of the matter.

I think I may have heard her choke back a giggle . . . or a sob. I wasn't sure which.

"Let me close the bedroom door," she said. When she came back she continued, "Oh, Evie. This is just awful. I do mean awful."

I pulled a chair from the kitchen table toward me and sat down. "Talk to me, Liz. I'm listening."

174

"You can't imagine having all these people in your house at one time. The children are precious, of course, but I now know why we have them when we're young. And just when I think things are going well between Tim and Samantha, they break out in another argument . . ."

"Aren't they seeing Pastor Kevin?"

"That seems to be when they fight the most, after seeing him. Whatever he's doing, I'm sure it's working, but honestly! Samuel and I never spoke to each other like that and—"

"How is Samuel? What do the doctors say?" I didn't really want to hear about Tim and Samantha, though I didn't have the heart to just come right out and say it.

I heard Lizzie take in a deep breath, then let it out. "The doctor says he could be out of work for six weeks. He's going through some physical therapy over at the hospital, and praise God Samantha is here to take him. If I had to take him, I don't know what I'd do."

"God is good," I agreed with her. "He knows just what we need before we need it."

"That much is true. I'm not saying that God caused Samantha and Tim to have problems just for this, but I do know that he uses all things for good for those who love him and who are called according to his purpose."

"Preach it, sister," I said with a grin, enjoying my own humor. "So what's he doing with himself all day? Samuel, not God. I don't even want to think about what God's doing with himself all day."

Lizzie giggled. "Evie, you make me laugh. Thank you. I'll tell you what he's doing. We—unfortunately—have TiVo. So, he TiVo's what he calls 'judging shows' all day so he can watch them again and again or watch the ones he missed because he was watching another one or because his pain pills kicked in and he napped or because he had to go to physical therapy or—"

"Breathe, girl."

Lizzie took in another deep breath. "Whew," she said. "You have no idea how many of those shows are out there."

"Tell Samuel I said to watch *Fox and Friends*. It'll keep him righteously informed."

"I'll tell him." She paused for a minute. "I've never been a big fan of television, and now it's blaring all the time, and then with all the voices in the house too. Oh, Evie. I'm so tired." She paused again. "Not to mention Mother."

"How's that going?"

"Well, we found her a place. It took all of this week, but I'm lucky to have found a place even this quickly. Especially with Christmas only a few days away. Michelle and I are leaving in about an hour to go get Mother from my brother's and bring her to a nice facility I found in Silverthorne. We have nothing akin to it here in Summit View, and I don't want her in a nursing home."

"Just one more thing for you to do."

"Lisa Leann called me last night about the Christmas tea, wanting to know if I'm still planning to host a table. You know what, Evie? I told her no. Can you believe I told her no?"

What I could *not* believe was that Lisa Leann Lambert was running behind me when she knew good and well that I'd already taken care of the table hostessing. I ground my teeth together for a second, then said, "Good for you, Lizzie."

"How are things with you and Vernon?" she asked me. "Moving toward the big day?"

"Even with a small wedding, there's so much to do," I informed her. "I'm going to try to get Donna to look at some church decorations with me sometime soon. I've got a stack of bride magazines I bought over at Lisa Leann's."

"Speaking of Donna, have you seen the new girl—well, I call her a girl; she's really a woman—in town? Looks exactly like Donna."

"I don't think so, no."

"Well, you could have seen her and thought you were seeing Donna. I'm telling you, she's the spitting image of her. She said that people were always waving at her, so she knew she must look like someone."

"Who is she?" I asked. I didn't like the idea of someone new being in town and me not knowing about it. It wasn't right.

"Her name is . . . let me think . . . Velvet. Velvet James. What a name, huh?"

"I don't know any Jameses."

"Her mother is Dee Dee McGurk," Lizzie said. "You know who I'm talking about. The woman from the Gold Rush Tavern. Moved here a few months ago?"

The room began to spin around me. Literally. Things went black, then I saw little stars—brilliant and bursting before my eyes—and then, when all that had stopped, the room began to spin. The sound of rushing water filled my ears, replaced momentarily by Lizzie calling my name. "Evie? Evie? Evangeline?"

"I have to go," I whispered.

"Are you okay?" she asked.

I stood up and grabbed hold of the counter for support. "I'm okay," I said. "I just . . . I need to go, Lizzie. I need to go."

I'm not sure how I got to the car, or even how I got the car out of the garage and onto the street. My first fully conscious thought was that Vernon could have another daughter he didn't know about and that my world—my perfect little world of a handsome fiancé, good friends, and an upcoming award for my Christmas decorations—had come to an end. *Vernon could have another daughter. Oh, what will he think? What will he do? Does this mean that Doreen has a new magnet to draw him back to her? Or will this even matter?*

If I knew Vernon—and I most certainly do know Vernon—it would matter. He may even postpone our wedding to sort out his feelings. Dang that man! And dang Doreen for keeping this from him for all these years. Vernon had a right to know . . . a right to know that he has another child.

As I pointed my car toward the street leading to the Gold Rush Tavern I allowed my mind to figure the whole thing out: Doreen must have been pregnant when she'd left with the old choir director. Must have been carrying Vernon's child, though surely she didn't know it. Doreen Roberts, selfish woman that she was and is and always will be, would have waited until she gave birth, dumped both kids in Vernon's lap, and *then* taken off with . . . oh, what was that man's name?

I decided that I didn't even care to remember.

My cell phone, resting on the passenger's seat next to me, rang. I grabbed it as I slowed for a red light and looked at the face. It was Lizzie.

"Hello, Lizzie," I said.

"Evie," she said, sounding as though she'd just climbed Pike's Peak. "I'm getting ready to go get Mother, and it hit me. Dee Dee McGurk. Doreen Roberts. They're one in the same, aren't they?"

"How'd you know? How'd you figure it out?" I asked her. If Lizzie could figure it out, maybe others would too, and, oh Lord, what a mess that would be!

"Had to be the Lord. Had to be. I'm just standing in front of my closet, trying to decide what to wear, and it hit me. Hit me out of the blue. I remembered you telling me that Doreen was back, but I know *I* haven't seen her. But she's Dee Dee McGurk, isn't she?"

"You go to the head of the class," I said. "And I'm going to the tavern right now."

"Oh no. Evie. Wait. You should wait. Let's talk first."

"You have enough on your mind, Lizzie." The light turned green, and I gunned my accelerator with the toe of my boot. "I can handle this. If Doreen was pregnant when she left here, that means that Vernon has another daughter."

"I don't know about that, Evie, but what I do know is . . . wait a minute." Her voice became muffled. *"What? . . . I'm trying to get ready to go get Mother . . . I'll be there in a minute . . . In a minute!"* There was a break, then Lizzie said to me, "Lord help me, I've never sounded this much like a fishwife in my life."

I spied the Gold Rush Tavern in front of me. "I'm at the tavern," I said. "I'm going in, Lizzie. You can pray for me or you can just wish me well."

"Well, of course I'm going to pray for you," she said. "But I think you ought to talk to Vernon first, don't you?"

"Mr. Passive? No. He promised me he'd talk to Donna about Doreen being back in town, and he hasn't done that yet. No. I'm handling this one. That woman will *not* ruin my wedding day."

"Well, if you feel that way, Evie. Okay, Samuel is calling for me. I have to go. I'll pray for you, and you can pray for me, okay?"

I said I would and then hung up as I pulled into the parking lot of the tavern, sliding a bit in the icy slush left over by the week's snowfall. I got out of the car and stomped my way to the front entrance, swung it open, and stepped into its darkness. The lunch crowd had already gathered there, their silhouettes outlined in the smoky dimness. It took me a minute, but I finally spied Doreen carrying a tray of bottlenecks to a table in the back. She saw me too; her chin tilted in that way it always did when she was bracing herself for a fight.

Well, she was about to get one.

I headed straight for her and then stood nearby as she placed the beer bottles on the table. I crossed my arms, waiting for her to turn to me. She took her own sweet time, I'll give her that much. "Here you go, fellas" and "What else can I get for you?" and "You want an order of fries with that?"and "Chili on the fries?"

For heaven's sake, Doreen. Give 'em their food and hush with the small talk. But far be it from me to tell a barmaid how to do her job.

She finally turned my way. "Evangeline," she said, pursing her lips.

"We need to talk."

"We do?" She brushed past me. I turned and stayed on her heels.

"I need five minutes of your time, Doreen Roberts," I said.

She spun around. "I'm Doreen Vesey, remember?" she asked with a smirk.

"You are most assuredly not. I know about you, Dee Dee Mc-Gurk. I know about the marriages, the children, and I even know about your time in the . . . what do they call it? The pokey? I know about your time in the pokey for prostitution." My head was bobbing like one of those little dogs you see perched in the back of a tourist's car. Or, at least you used to see them. I haven't seen one in years.

Doreen's brow knit together, and even in the dim light I could see her turning red. "Shut up, Evangeline," she said, clenching her teeth. Then she jerked her head toward the kitchen. "Come on. We can talk in the office back there."

On our way through the grease-laden kitchen, Doreen yelled at the head cook, "Hey! Two number sixes, hold the pickle on one of them, and two number threes. Oh, and chili on the fries on all four. I'll be in the office with Miss Priss. I won't be more than a minute. I can promise you." She sashayed past all the men dressed in big white aprons, their hair held back with clear plastic caps and their hands shoved in clear plastic gloves. With all the grease dripping off the walls back here, I wondered what a little hair or fingernail dirt would hurt. But I wasn't here to inspect the kitchen. I had another mission.

When we reached the manager's office, a tiny little thing with what appeared to be a chain link fence for a back wall (and behind it all sorts of restaurant-size cans and boxes stacked on sagging shelves), an old metal desk, and a Playboy of the Month calendar—the only wall hanging—gracing the wall next to it, Doreen swung around and said, "I'd offer you a seat, but there ain't one."

"Ain't? Did you learn to speak like that in prison?" I cut my eyes over to the naked girl posed on the calendar. "Can you take that thing down long enough for me to talk to you?"

She pointed a sharply manicured finger at me, ignoring my request. "Look here, Evie. I haven't ever been in prison. I've been in jail, but that's nobody's business out there except the manager's. He knows my record, and he hired me, and I can't afford to lose this job. You got that? You make me lose this job, and you can be sure bettin' I'll see to it that you lose Vernon or half the hair on your head, whichever comes first. You get what I'm saying to you?" She took a step toward the calendar and jerked it off the wall, laying it face down on the desk. "Now, I *ain't* got no beef with you," she continued. "I'm not planning to do anything to upset your little wedding plans. I have no designs on Vernon Vesey. You can have him. My leftovers, anyway—"

"Hold on a minute," I said, taking a step forward.

"No. You hold on. I have caused you not one minute of trouble since I got here. You wouldn't have even known I was in town if you hadn't of busybodied yourself in here, snooping around after Vernon."

"That's none of your business. And Vernon is none of your business."

She planted her fisted hands on both hips. "Oh, but he is. He's the father of my child, lest you forget. We still have Donna between us—"

"Donna and Velvet?" I spouted back.

That got her. Her mouth clamped shut so fast, a fly could have been caught had it been buzzing by. Then it opened again, shut again, and opened one more time. "How do you know about Velvet?" she asked, her tone subdued.

"I know, that's all. One thing you don't know about me, Dee Dee McGurk, is that since you've been gone, I've pretty much run this town. I know everything that goes on around here."

Doreen stepped over to the desk and rested her scrawny rear end against one corner. She opened the middle drawer, and for a minute I wondered if a gun was inside. Maybe she'd pull out a .22; she'd shoot me dead and claim self-defense. "She went mad," she'd say to the authorities—ironically her ex-husband and her daughter. "I had to protect myself." Then she and Vernon would fall into each other's arms, make passionate love, and get married, and the four of them—Vernon, Doreen, Donna, and Velvet—would live happily ever after.

In my house. Wanda Whittman would be quick to put it on the market, and Doreen would be just as quick to buy it.

I shook my head, freeing the insane imaginings as I watched Doreen pull a pack of cigarettes and a Bic lighter from the drawer. She pulled a cigarette from the pack, squinted her eyes as she lit it, drew on it with lined lips, then blew the smoke in my direction. She studied me for a minute, taking in another draw, blowing it out again, this time toward the ceiling. "Well, apparently not," she finally said. "Apparently you don't know everything." She ran her tongue across her bottom lip.

My shoulders sagged. "Then, it's true. Vernon has another daughter."

She flicked the ashes from the cigarette to the stained concrete floor below.

I rubbed my hands up and down my arms. I was suddenly very cold. "When will you tell Vernon?" I asked.

"Why should I tell him? If Velvet wants to tell him, she can. She ain't had no real daddy since the day she was born. If she don't want Vernon to know, who am I to tell him?"

"But you have to. It's immoral."

Doreen coughed out a laugh. "Immoral? Like I've ever worried about immoral."

She was right about that. "You should stop smoking," I said. "You sound awful."

"Like you care," she said and drew on the cigarette again. "Look here, Evangeline," she continued, each word wrapped in a puff of gray smoke. "Leave my kid alone, you hear? I won't bother you, and you don't bother her, you got it? She's had it rough enough in life having me for a mama." She took another draw, then dropped the cigarette to her feet and ground it out under the sole of her black shoe. "I ain't much. But I'm all she's got."

Dear Lord, I was actually beginning to feel sorry for Doreen. I looked down, then back up. "What about Donna?" I asked, keeping my voice as tender as I could.

She pushed herself off the corner of the desk and took a step toward me. "I'd like to talk to her. Vernon won't like it, but . . . well, you've never been a mother, so you may not understand. I still love my baby girl. I don't want to do nothing that's gonna hurt her. I'd like to have something with her. Some kind of a relationship. Girls need their mamas. That's why Velvet followed me out here. Bad of a mama as I've been, she's still gotta be near me for some reason."

I nodded. "So, what do you want me to do, Doreen?" Lord have mercy, this was not going like I'd planned.

"Just leave me and mine to me, okay? And I'll leave you and yours to you. If Velvet wants to tell Vernon, that's for her to do. Deal?" She stuck out her hand for a shake, and I took it.

"Deal," I said.

27

A Plot Twist

Clay was on his way to the Hallmark store, hoping to surprise Britney with some takeout from MiZuppa, a small soup bar and bakery chain that made the absolute best homemade soup in the entire ski-resort area. Not to mention Denver. He'd ordered chicken 'n' dumplings for Britney and Indian mulligatawny for himself. But when he saw Evangeline Benson nearly speeding on the icy roads and headed toward the Gold Rush Tavern (talking on a cell phone, no less) he knew trouble was brewing and in a big way. He slowed his Jeep down, made an illegal U-turn, and then followed behind her. By the time he'd made it into the parking lot of the tavern, she was pulling the door open and stepping inside.

A sick feeling hit him in the pit of his stomach. He sat for a minute, trying to decide whether to go in or let it go. After all, it was none of his business. *But*, he thought, *very little about the Potluck Club is my business.*

Somehow he always managed to make it so.

He waited five minutes, then slipped out of his Jeep and quietly into the tavern. He scanned the room but could see neither Evangeline nor Dee Dee McGurk, who he assumed she'd come to see.

A Plot Twist

He'd known about Donna's mother's and Evangeline's feud since he was a boy. His mother had told him it was the stuff legends were made of. But this . . . this "legend" might hurt Donna in the long run. And *that* he didn't think he could stand. After all and no matter what, Donna was and always would be his good friend.

He took a seat in a dark corner and waited for several minutes. If his guess was correct, Evangeline was going at it nose-to-nose with Dee Dee in a back room somewhere. He pulled out his leather-bound notepad and began to hen scratch some notes. After a few minutes more of that, his face broke in a grin.

Yeah, Donna was his friend, but a good plot twist was still a good plot twist.

Lisa Leann

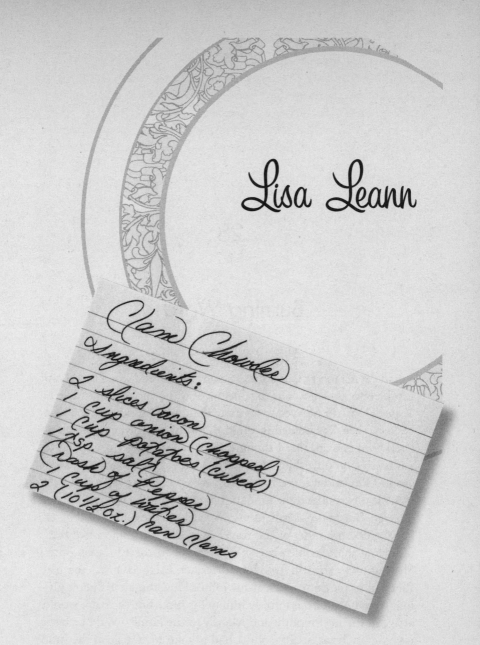

Clam Chowder

Ingredients:

2 slices bacon
1 cup onion (chopped)
1 cup potatoes (cubed)
1 tsp. salt
(dash of pepper)
1 cup of water
2 (10½ oz.) can clams

28

Burning Words

It had been a merry Christmas season. Henry and I had flown our son Nelson as well as our son-in-law, Ray, in on Christmas Eve as a special gift to our very pregnant daughter Mandy. When first Nelson, then Ray walked through the front door, Mandy had hollered loud enough that I thought Donna would be summoned to tell us to stop disturbing the peace. Mandy had thrown her arms around Ray and wept so hard she'd soaked his shirt clean through. It made me wonder if she thought her father and I were holding her hostage. But that was ridiculous. We weren't the ones who'd given her the doctor's order of "no travel" as well as "complete bed rest" following that terrible scare she'd given us in the ER last month. She was lucky she had us to look after her. I sighed. It was too bad Ray had to return to work at his job in Houston after Thanksgiving. Mandy had been terribly lonely for him. But the baby would arrive in the next month, and Mandy's little family would be back together in Texas lickety-split. I had to take advantage of the time we'd been given here and now. It would too soon be over.

I'd left Mandy, Ray, Henry, and Nelson back home with a pot of my clam chowder, a family favorite, while I busied myself getting ready for tonight's Christmas tea at the church.

I stood back to admire my handiwork. I'd just finished turning a large cardboard box into a festively wrapped present with an open top. My sign, "Place Toys for Toys for Tots Here," was prominently displayed. I sighed happily. I loved being in charge.

Okay, let Evie think she was Queen of the Tea; she didn't need to realize I'd succeeded in pulling off a coup. Though I couldn't gloat about it, as Evie was my oldest (and I mean that literally) and dearest wedding client. So my behind-the-scenes direction had to be not only friendly but subtle.

I'd easily figured out who Evie had called to be the table hostesses with a few well-placed phone calls. Then, in pleasant conversation, I'd gleaned the details of how each would decorate their tables. I'd also managed to discover who would join each hostess at their tables and how many of the seats would be available to open up to the community at large.

With this information, I'd even gone about town to individually invite the local women to join us. In my efforts to reach the locals, I'd called on barmaids and shop owners alike, finding a seat for everyone who'd accept my invitation, even that poor, haggard Dee Dee McGurk, who worked at the Gold Rush Tavern.

I must admit, I was pretty proud of myself. I'd managed, without Evie's help, mind you, to turn the annual Grace Church Christmas event into a community outreach. Evie'd never be able to argue about the good in that.

And, as the Toys for Tots auction had been put under my domain along with the special music, I had plans so rich they'd knock the socks off everyone. And again, I knew I had to be careful here as well. After all, the auction had always been under the special care of Jan Moore, our beloved pastor's wife who had recently passed away. So, I had to be especially sensitive to everyone's thoughts and feelings of loss.

I turned to admire my own decorated table from afar—a lovely affair with a two-foot tall, live pine tree on a revolving, motorized platform. To cover the base, I'd put twinkly white Christmas lights under fuzzy white bunting to create a sparkling snow effect. Of course, the tree, done in gold ribbon with glittering red edges, carried out the partridge and the pear tree theme in miniature. I'd placed my ivory cloth table napkins, each encircled with five gold napkin rings, next to my china plates.

As this was the table where I was personally hosting the women of the singles class, I'd also lovingly placed a carefully wrapped present, in gold foil, on top of each ivory plate. Every box contained a gift certificate for a complimentary makeover plus a free trial run of my new computerized dating service that I'd been advertising in the *Gold Rush News* since before Christmas. With that, and the fact that my wedding service had recently been on national television—and I had Vonnie to thank for that—business was booming.

I turned to help Vonnie, who was busily decorating her hostess table with a centerpiece of miniature rocking chairs crowned with some of her antique baby dolls dressed in their Christmas finest.

"How cute is that," I said to Vonnie, who gave me one of her sweet smiles.

"How's Mandy?" she asked as she finished placing her red cloth place mats then began to top them with large glass plates in opaque white. It was a pretty effect.

"She's good, though having to deal with a lot more Braxton Hicks contractions of late."

"That's to be expected. What is she, almost eight months?"

"That's right, eight months next week. She's looking forward to getting that baby home to her husband."

"I bet," Vonnie said. "How hard it must be to be in love but be separated by circumstances."

I nodded then sighed. "It is, I know. But this too shall pass." I laughed. "Someday, she may even be able to thank me for taking such good care of her."

Vonnie giggled as the door to the fellowship hall burst open and Donna Vesey, looking rather official in her sheriff's deputy uniform, blustered inside. She'd been baptized with a bit of fresh snow and looked right charming as she waved a fistful of gift certificates at me. "I got 'em," she said.

Vonnie waved too as I ran to greet her. "Donna, you're a peach. Thanks for picking up these gift certificates for me. Did you have any trouble at any of the stores?"

"Nope, just told everyone I was there to pick up their contribution for the Toys for Tots auction tonight. They all seemed to expect me."

I smiled and thumbed through the treasure of certificates for free manicures, custom framing, haircuts, fresh flowers, and so much more.

"I'll pick up the donated gift baskets during my afternoon break," she said.

"Great, and Donna, don't run off just yet, you're just in time."

"Not for decorating a table, I hope. That is, unless you want one decked out in personalized speeding tickets."

I laughed. Despite rumors to the contrary, this girl did have a sense of humor. There she stood, her blue eyes sparkling, her blonde curls gently framing her face, looking pretty. I was beginning to see what Clay saw in her. Now if she'd only let me apply a dash of pink blush and a bit of mascara. But that would come with Evie's bridesmaids' makeover party next month. I'd just have to be patient for now.

"No, you're off the hook," I said. "It's just that Clay was about to stop over to take some photos of the Grace ladies getting ready for tonight." I swept my hands dramatically as if showcasing the number of women gathered over each table, busy with their decorations.

"You don't need me for that," Donna said. "Besides, I'm late for a lunch date with David."

"Tell me, darling, you're *not* seeing David after he falsely announced your engagement on national TV?"

Donna crossed her arms over her black leather jacket and frowned. "David and me? Well, our relationship is complicated, though I don't see it as any concern of yours."

"But sweetie, is he really your type? I would have thought someone more down to earth, someone like Clay, for instance, would have more appeal."

The door pushed open again, and a chilly breeze swept over us. Donna cocked her head. "He's got a girlfriend, or haven't you heard?"

"Well, Donna, he's a handsome man. I'm sure a lot of girls are attracted to him. Including you, perhaps?"

A deep voice spoke up from behind me. "Ah, this is an interesting conversation, and I hate to interrupt, but . . ."

I turned suddenly. Why, if it wasn't that handsome devil himself. "Clay! I'm so glad you're here. Donna and I were just talking about you."

Clay looked from Donna to me and grinned. "So I gathered." He patted his camera case that was slung across one shoulder. "So, where should we start shooting, at one of the tables?"

I gave him one of my winning smiles. "How about starting by telling me if the rumor's true that you're dating someone?"

Clay turned red and stared hard at Donna. "Well, ah, maybe as a friend."

Donna laughed. "Friend, my eye, Clay. I've seen you and what's-her-name. Britney? I've seen the two of you around town, looking, let's say, very cozy."

Clay shrugged, looking awkward. "No, no, it's not like that. We're friends, that's all."

Another voice, one from just behind us, said, "Friends? Clay!"

So help me if we didn't turn around to see Miss Britney herself standing there, looking pretty in her pink leather coat with the faux fur hood that framed her sweet little face. She was holding a box of Christmas party supplies that included festive paper plates and napkins. *For one of our tables?* I thought. *How tacky!* But I tried to sound sweet when I said, "Britney, honey, is there something I can help you with?"

"I came in the back way as I was running these items down from the card shop, for Goldie. I guess she's decorating a table here today?" She tossed her head in a way to direct a look at me but at the same time to exclude Clay from the conversation. "Where do you want these?"

I put my arm around her and led her away from the couple I was trying to match. We didn't need any competition, if you know what I mean. "Honey, be a dear and put those things on the far table in the corner. Would you?"

When I turned around, I almost ran into Clay, who was close on our heels. "I'm sorry, Britney," he said. "It's not what you think."

I turned to see Donna offer a wave as she headed out the door. Britney put her hands on her hips. "I guess not," she said, slamming the box onto the table before pushing past him.

"Wait up," Clay called after her.

"What about the interview?" I called behind him.

He pushed open the double doors just as Britney disappeared into the cold. "Uh, there's something I've gotta do. I'll be back later."

For heaven's sake! How could I fix him up with Donna when he was chasing another woman down the sidewalk? This could be one match I was going to lose, and not through any fault of my own.

I frowned. I'd get to the bottom of this later. In the meantime, Evie was waving at me from across the room.

I approached and took in her table. She had quite the thing going with a bead-decked pine wreath centerpiece that was filled with red and gold candles on long brass candlesticks. She'd carefully placed dark green ceramic plates with matching green stemware at each place setting. On top of each plate sat a lovely red-wrapped gift tied in gold string.

"That's lovely, Evie. What's in the gift boxes?"

She looked down at them absentmindedly. "Oh, they're empty. Just props."

I cocked my eyebrows. "Oh. Well. It's a lovely effect."

"You really like it?"

"I do," I said with a grin. "The gold foil place mats are a nice touch."

"Are you all set for the auction tonight?"

"Yep. I've got a bumper crop of gift certificates and gift baskets, plus several women will be bringing homemade craft items to auction off too. I've got a place set up in the back."

Evie looked at me thoughtfully. "That's nice. Do you have the special music covered?"

"Oh yes, it will be quite the surprise."

"Oh?" A shadow seemed to fall across her face, but then she brightened. "Well, you've certainly been a good sport about taking my direction. And to tell you the truth, Lisa Leann, I didn't realize it, but I really needed your help."

What an admission! But I didn't make a big production out of it; I simply smiled and said, "We all really do need one another, don't we?"

She nodded. "So tomorrow, you and I will get back to work on the wedding plans?"

"Drop by the shop," I said. "I've got some pictures of flower arrangements to show you. And I want to go over my ideas for the church."

"Okay."

As I walked back to the kitchen to see how the food prep was coming, I couldn't help but smile. Who'd have thought it would be the Christmas tea that would bring Evie and me together. I checked my watch. Oh my, it was only a few hours away.

But no worries. What could go wrong?

29

Death of a Salesman

Clay rushed out the doors of the Grace Church fellowship hall.

"Britney, will you wait up?"

Britney was at a standstill in the middle of the parking lot, and Clay thanked his lucky stars she'd come in the back way and couldn't easily jump in her car and drive away. She could walk away, alright, but she'd be knee deep in snow before she hit the road.

"I have nothing to say to you right now." Britney turned away from him and walked toward a row of parked cars and to where his Jeep was parked.

Clay reached her, having jogged toward her as carefully as he could manipulate the camera slung over his shoulder and the snow beneath his feet. "Would you listen then?" He glanced around. Fortunately there weren't any nosy women lurking about, including Donna, who'd apparently managed to get going before Britney had stormed out of the church.

Britney lifted her pretty chin and closed her eyes, the perfect martyr. He couldn't help but smile.

"Do you want to get in the Jeep or stand out here and freeze to death?" he asked.

"I'll stand right here." She paused. "And I'm listening," she said, opening her eyes to him then. He saw the beginnings of tears forming.

"Now, don't start the crying thing. Look, I asked Lisa Leann to help me get Donna's attention weeks and weeks ago." He put his hand on her shoulder. "But that was before *you* got *my* attention." He watched as her shoulders squared. "Donna is a friend. She'll always be a friend. We go way back. And I don't want anything bad to happen to her, but . . . I realize now that we're just going to be friends."

A tear escaped Britney's eye, and she pushed it away with her leather-gloved hand. "Then why did that woman in there seem to be so excited about you and Donna?"

"That's just Lisa Leann, Britney. She fancies herself a bit of a *yenta*."

She had begun to shiver. "She was practically giddy, Clay."

Clay took a deep breath and sighed. "Okay," he said. "There was a time when Donna could have been . . . well, in my mind anyway . . . could have been more than a friend. But a friend is all she is. I swear." He opened his arms, and she stepped in. Wrapping his arms around her, he kissed the top of her head. "I haven't told Lisa Leann to back off yet. She doesn't mean any harm to us, Britney. If you're going to be mad at anyone, be mad at me."

"Oh, I'm mad all right," she said, though to his ears she wasn't convincing. "So why haven't you told her?" Her voice was muffled as she spoke into his shirt.

"There hasn't been time. Work is crazy, you and I have been seeing each other nearly nonstop, Christmas, and . . . there's been some other stuff I've been looking into."

She raised her head. "Like what?"

"Like . . . I . . . I can't talk about it right now. Let's just say I'm investigating something. Something important."

She smiled up at him, and he kissed the tip of her nose. They still had the "no kissing" rule, so this was as close as he would get. "Really important?"

"Really, very important. It could turn this whole club upside down."

"The Potluck Club?" She looked toward the church.

He nodded. It was all he wanted to say right then. After all, Britney already knew a hint of what he knew; she'd met Velvet James before he did. She just didn't know what he knew. "Ready to go back inside and help me take pictures?"

Britney turned and linked her arm with his. "I'll be your assistant," she said proudly.

"And such a pretty one too," he said, glad to have his world righted again.

Goldie

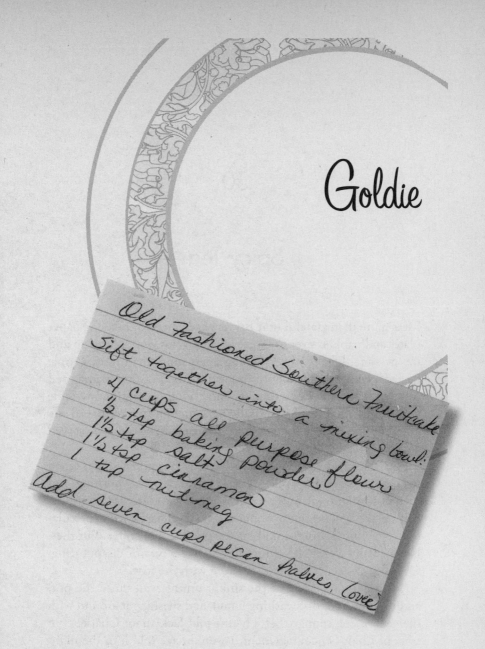

Old Fashioned Southern Fruitcake

Sift together into a mixing bowl:
4 cups all purpose flour
½ tsp baking powder
1½ tsp salt
1½ tsp cinnamon
1 tsp nutmeg

Add seven cups pecan halves, cover

30

Spicy Tea

I was more than grateful that Britney had agreed to take the paper plates and napkins over to Grace for me. With work piling up and my personal life seemingly falling apart more than most people realized, I hadn't had time to "put on the dog" as my mama used to say. There would be no china and crystal decorating my table at the Christmas tea. I was doing well enough to have baked my grandmother's recipe for Southern fruitcake that was to be served as one of the desserts.

As five o'clock neared, I shut down my computer, straightened my desk into neat little piles of work to attack in the morning, and then walked into the break room. I pulled the coffeepot out of the coffeemaker and fleetingly wondered whatever happened to percolators. Now those things could make a good cup of coffee. But they, like so many wonderful things in life, had a way of disappearing. Or becoming relics. The old replaced with the new.

I shivered as I stood at the sink, running water into the pot, adding a squirt of dishwashing liquid, and swishing it around with the yellow sink sponge. I still hadn't told Jack about Charlene, in spite of Lizzie's encouragement. I would have told him the night Lizzie and I had met for coffee had it not been for Samuel's accident.

Then the following night Charlene showed up at my place again, wanting to know my opinion on how we were all going to live with this new addition to the Dippel bloodline in Summit View. And did I have any thoughts on how she should tell Jack.

"I've thought about telling him myself," I told her. I squared my chin. After all, he was my husband. I still had some rights.

Charlene prowled around my living room like a caged tiger waiting for its steak dinner while I stood near the front door with my arms crossed.

"But you haven't," she said, stopping.

"Not yet. Lizzie Prattle's husband hurt his—"

She raised her hand. "I don't really care, Goldie. Oh, excuse me, *Mrs. Dippel.* What I do care about is how we are all going to handle this. Personally, I haven't said a word to Jack yet. I want to know first what *you* are going to do. Have you told Olivia? After all, she'll be my baby's older sister." She placed her hand on her stomach. Charlene wasn't thin by any means, so it was difficult to see if she was showing yet or not. Still, I stared, which caused Charlene to say, "I'm not showing yet, if you're wondering. My doctor says that first babies don't usually cause their mothers to show right away."

Not to mention the extra padding, I thought but said nothing in response. Rather, I addressed my daughter's relationship to this unborn child. "My daughter doesn't know. She's pregnant herself and—"

"Isn't that wild?" she said with a laugh. "Jack's daughter and Jack's mistress pregnant at the same time." She took a step toward me. "Here's what I'm thinking: you and Jack will get a divorce and that will allow Jack to move in with me so he can help me take care of Little Junior here." She patted her tummy again.

"Move in with you?" I was stunned by this new revelation, let me just say.

She curled her lip. "I told you before. I don't want to marry him, but I'm certainly not up for doing the diaper and bottle thing on my own."

Well, bless her heart.

I had to tell Jack. I just had to. But how? And when?

I dried the coffeepot and the four or five mugs dirtied during the day and placed them in their rightful places. I dried my hands on the dishcloth, retrieved my coat from the coatrack, and headed down the hall toward my desk and purse. Chris was there, slipping his arms into his coat.

"Is your wife going to the tea tonight?" I asked.

He smiled at me. "She wouldn't miss it. Lisa Leann and Evie have her hosting a table. What about you?"

"Oh, yeah." I smiled. "I wouldn't miss it, either. I made fruitcake from an old Southern recipe my grandmother had since I can't remember when."

"I love fruitcake. Weird, I know. Most folks don't. But I do." He helped me into my coat.

I reached for my purse, which I'd left on my desk. "I know. Have you ever heard of the Claxton Fruitcake Company?"

"No," he said as he led me out the door then locked it behind us.

"Claxton, Georgia, isn't far from where I grew up. Remind me to tell you about it one day." We took the stairs slowly, with Chris in front of me.

"How's it going with Jack?" he asked.

"Christmas was . . . strange," I said. "But Jack was smart enough not to give me jewelry, considering that had always been his atonement gift after each and every affair."

"No jewelry?" Chris asked as we reached the bottom of the steps. "Smart man."

I laughed as we made our way through the card shop. "His gift to me was a footed treasure chest for my living room."

"But no efforts of reconciliation since the trip to Summit Ridge?" he asked, looking down at me. Chris Lowe is evermore a tall man. I'd suspect six-foot-six.

I shook my head no. "There's a complication," I said. Chris opened the outside door for me, and we stepped into the frigid evening air. The street lamps and holiday decorations up and down Main Street were beginning to flicker on, bringing a postcard atmosphere to the night. I glanced down the street and focused on the rocky, snow-covered mountain that rose proudly behind the row of businesses along the town's main thoroughfare. "A big complication."

"Do you want to talk about it?" he asked, pushing his hands into thick gloves.

I thought about it. Seriously thought about it. Then decided against it. "No," I answered after a moment. I pointed toward 6th Avenue. "I'll just head on home. There's still a bit to do before I get to the tea."

Chris nodded. "Let me know if I can help you in any way, Goldie."

I told him I would, then began walking home, keeping my arms wrapped around my middle. It was getting colder by the second.

When my apartment was in view, I noticed Jack's car pulling into the driveway. I paused, and he waved at me from the driver's seat. *What is he doing here?*

My question was answered as soon as he stepped out of the car. "Hey!" he hollered. "Thought you could use a ride to the tea."

I made my way to the driveway, and he met me, looking quite pleased with himself for having thought to be so gallant as to drive me to a social tea. Something I knew Jack thought was quite frivolous.

"You shouldn't be walking in the cold, Goldie," he said, taking my shoulders in his hands and planting a kiss on my cheek. "You'll catch your death out here."

"It's only a couple of blocks," I said. "And I like the walk. It gives my head a chance to clear."

He wrapped his arm around me and guided me toward the front door. "I hate it that you have to clear your head at all. I'm to blame for part of that . . . okay, all of that. If it weren't for my wrongdoing, you wouldn't even have to work at all."

I know he was trying . . . but he was missing the mark. "I do enjoy myself at work, Jack," I told him. I opened my purse and removed the house key then jabbed it into the brass lock. "And I don't intend to leave." I pushed the door open and walked through.

201

Jack was right behind me. He pointed to the treasure chest and said, "I really like the looks of the chest in here, Goldie. Like the way you angled it near the fireplace."

I took off my coat and threw it over a nearby chair. "I have to get ready for the tea now."

"Is that your grandmother's fruitcake I smell?" he asked, ignoring me.

"Yes. I need a quick bath and—"

Jack grinned. "Want me to scrub your back?"

I frowned. "I do not. I want you to just sit down and . . ."—I looked around—"watch TV or something." I started toward my bedroom.

"What about a cup of tea? Would you like a cup of tea? I can make it for you while you're getting ready."

I stopped and glanced over my shoulder at him. He hadn't been this attentive since *I* was pregnant. "Sure," I said. "I won't be but a minute or two."

I struggled all the way to the church, with Jack sitting next to me. Should I give him a hint? Should I say, "We need to talk?" But the opportunity never came, what with Jack talking nonstop about his plans for us, about his continued sessions with Pastor Kevin, about Olivia's baby and the start of a new life with this new addition to our family.

Yeah, well . . . Lord, just wait till I tell him about the other new addition to our family . . .

When we arrived at the church, Jack pulled right up to the fellowship hall door and ran around to my side of the car to help me out. I cradled in my arms the fruitcake wrapped in plastic wrap and resting on an old cake plate I've had since I was a bride.

I sighed heavily. Jack shut the door behind me and guided me to the door as though I were an invalid. "I'll pick you up when it's all over," he said. "Livvy coming?" he asked, using a nickname for our daughter he hadn't used in years. "I didn't even think to ask if she needed a ride."

"Tony is bringing her," I said, ready to get inside and get the whole evening over with.

Jack kissed me on the cheek again as he opened the door for me. "You have a good time, and I'll see you shortly. Save me a piece of that cake." He patted me on my backside and chuckled.

I turned sharply. "Jack, we have to talk," I blurted out.

He leaned in close with a grin. "Sorry about the patting thing. I forgot where I was."

I shook my head. "That's not it. Entirely. We have to talk about something else."

Jack sobered. "Don't tell me you want a divorce. Not here. Not now. We're making headway, Goldie. We're going to make it. I know we are."

"It's not that, Jack. We'll . . . we'll talk later tonight, okay?"

He didn't say anything for a minute. "We're letting the cold air in and the hot air out," he said quietly. "I'll see you in a couple of hours."

Lizzie met me at my table, which was so far in the back of the room it was practically in another state. "Lisa Leann," Lizzie whispered in my ear with a giggle. "She doesn't like your paper products."

"Well, pooh on her," I said.

Lizzie nodded toward my set table. "I went ahead and set everything up for you."

"Thanks," I responded, casting my gaze across the room. It was lovely. Truly lovely. Every table was highly decorated in the personal theme of the hostess. The overhead lights and the lit candles atop each table cast shimmering lights across the crystal and china and the glass Christmas ornaments. "I see she's got herself front and center."

"Don't let it bother you," Lizzie said. She reached for the fruitcake. "I'll take this to the serving table. You mingle." She started away from me, then turned back. "You and Jack talk yet?"

I shook my head no. "Not yet. I told him I want to talk to him tonight." I took in a deep breath, then let it out.

"Good girl," Lizzie said, then walked away, leaving me to mingle with the other women who were hostessing tables.

I went to Evie's table first, a lovely Victorian setting, her mother's china and silver resting beautifully on damask linen. I touched it with my fingertips. "This is lovely, Evie," I said. "Was this one of your mother's? I've never seen it before."

Evie smiled at me as she adjusted one of the candles of her centerpiece. "Believe it or not, it's a piece of a bedsheet. I thought it was so pretty, I bought it, took it down to the Sew and Stitch, and had Dora make it into a tablecloth."

"You are very wise," I said with a wink. "Are you counting down the days till the wedding?"

Evie sighed. "I'm trying not to think about how far behind I am on everything." She inched closer to me. "And with the Queen Wedding Bee over there trying to run everything . . . well . . . I'm just letting her. She's having so much fun, and quite frankly it keeps her out of everything else that's going on around here, so . . ."

"What do you mean? What else is going on around here?"

Lizzie joined us just then. "Are you telling her?" Lizzie asked.

"Telling me what?" I looked from one to the other.

Evie's shoulders seemed to drop a bit. She stopped in her table primping and crossed her arms. The three of us formed an awkward circle. "Okay. You'll have to promise not to say anything, though."

I raised my chest and held up my hand as though I were taking a pledge. "Girl Scout's honor."

"Doreen Roberts is back in town," Evie whispered.

I couldn't believe what I was hearing. "Doreen Roberts? Doreen Roberts Vesey?"

Evie scowled at me. "Yes, Doreen Roberts Vesey. Do you have to remind me?"

"Sorry."

Lizzie touched my arm with her hand, bringing my attention to her. "She's Dee Dee McGurk. That name sound familiar?"

I had to think for a minute. "The barmaid? The one that . . ." My hand flew over my mouth. "Oh, dear Lord. That *is* her. I thought she looked familiar." I widened my eyes at them. "Does Donna—"

"Know?" Evie asked. "Not yet. Though Vernon and Doreen have gone round and round about it. Personally, I think Vernon ought to tell Donna. Now, before we get any closer to our wedding. But, like a typical man, he's putting it off."

"Men," I said. "And women too, I suppose. I have my own secret I'm holding on to."

Evie turned fully to me. "Well, you know my secret. What's yours?"

I looked from Evie to Lizzie and back to Evie again. "Charlene Hopefield is pregnant."

Evie rolled her eyes. "I should have known it could come to this. Jack's I assume."

"She says it is."

Evie pointed a finger at me. "I'd have a paternity test done. That woman has been around more tracks than a Derby horse."

Lizzie and I burst out in laughter. Evie just has a way of putting things. "I hadn't thought about a paternity test. I just assumed it really is his."

"Never assume," Evie said. "You know what they say about assuming."

Lizzie laughed again. "Don't say it, Evie. Not in God's house."

"Well, I wasn't going to say it," she said, then looked around. "Speaking of assumptions, here comes Lisa Leann. Act normal. Or natural. Whichever you are most comfortable with." And we burst out laughing again.

"Girls, girls! What is so funny over here? We can hear the laughter clear across the room," Lisa Leann said. She touched the sleeve of my Christmas-green suit and said, "Don't you look lovely, Miss Goldie. Did I see the coach with you at the door? Should I go ahead and book the chapel for you?"

"Not just yet, Lisa Leann," I said.

"Darlin', don't waste time. It won't wait for any of us, you know. I had really hoped the time at the cabin would—"

"The time at the cabin was good. I mean, except for the whole avalanche thing and nearly getting ourselves killed. And trust me, we're working on it. Not the killing . . . the getting back together."

Lisa Leann turned her head toward the front door as it opened. "Oh my! They *did* come, after all!" she exclaimed.

Evie, Lizzie, and I gawked. Simply gawked. "Dee Dee McGurk?" I finally squeaked out.

Lisa Leann practically bounced like a jumping bean. "Yes, indeed. This event is supposed to be about reaching out to the lost, my sisters. And believe me, no one is more lost than that poor woman and her adorable daughter." She turned back to the group of us. "Besides, I understand they have lovely singing voices, and I've asked that they bless us with a tune. By the way, have you all noticed how much that young woman looks like our Donna?"

I stole a glance over at Evie, who had turned so pale I thought we were going to have to call for an ambulance. Lizzie reached for her. "Do you need a drink of water, Evangeline?" she asked.

Evie took a deep breath. "No, thank you. I can handle this."

"What is there to handle?" Lisa Leann asked. "You girls are acting very strange. Even for you."

It was about that time that Vonnie joined the group, coming up from behind us. "What's going on around here?" she asked. "Can't a girl work in the kitchen without you gals causing such an uproar?"

Lisa Leann turned to Vonnie. "This tea is supposed to be an outreach, isn't it?"

"Of course it is," Vonnie assured her. "Who says it isn't?"

I glanced again to the front of the fellowship hall, where Doreen and her daughter were standing. *Is that the girl Lizzie and I met on the sidewalk?* I wondered. Which is, of course, when it all hit me. *Velvet James is the daughter of Dee Dee McGurk. Dee Dee McGurk is . . . or was . . . Doreen Roberts.* "Well, no wonder she looks like Donna," I said out loud without meaning to.

"Who looks like Donna?" Vonnie asked, then parted the cluster of us a bit. "Good heavens, who is that? Is that . . . oh my goodness. Is that . . . Doreen Roberts?"

"I'm afraid so," Evie said. Then she turned to Vonnie. "Donna's not here, is she?"

"Talk to me, people," Lisa Leann said.

"No," Vonnie answered Evie. "She said she wasn't coming."

"Which brings me to my next point," Lisa Leann continued, totally oblivious to what was going on—or coming down—around her.

"Never mind, Lisa Leann," I said.

Vonnie wrapped her arms around Evie from behind. "Oh, dear girl. How long has she been here?"

"Long enough."

"Somebody better talk to me. After all, I'm part of the planning committee here," Lisa Leann sang. "Who is Doreen Roberts?"

"Dee Dee McGurk," I said. "Dee Dee McGurk is Doreen Roberts."

"And Doreen Roberts is Donna Vesey's mother," Lizzie finished.

"Donna's mother?" Lisa Leann stammered, then closed her tiny, pink-lined lips.

There was really nothing left to say, though I was sure someone would. After all, Doreen Roberts and Velvet James—both dressed in flashy red and now sporting "Hello, My Name Is—" stickers over their right breasts—were heading straight for us.

31

Here Comes Trouble

Clay stood in the back of the room, photographing the lineup of good food displayed on the serving tables. The sound of laughter skipped across the room, and he turned. *The ladies of the Potluck Club sure are having a good time*, he thought as he watched a small cluster of them standing shoulder to shoulder and giggling like schoolgirls.

For a moment he wondered what secrets they collectively held, then he turned back to the spread his camera lens was focused on.

The table before him held every delectable food a man could possibly think of, and his mouth watered from wanting to dig into each and every dish. Not that he *would*, but he surely wanted to.

He heard laughter again, then felt Britney's tiny hand as it touched the small of his back. "They sure have a good time," she said. "Wonder what it's like to have such history with a bunch of friends."

Clay smiled down at her. "I was just thinking the same thing."

"You were?"

"Yep. Sure was."

Britney looked up and furrowed her brow ever so slightly, then relaxed. "Why do they call themselves the Potluck Club?"

Clay turned a bit. "It started years ago. Evangeline Benson and her childhood friend Ruth Ann McDonald got together once a month, had some coffee cake and coffee and a little prayer too, I'm told, and it sort of went from there."

"Ruth Ann McDonald? Why don't I know her?"

"She died a long time ago. Died young. Cancer, I think it was."

"That's so sad," Britney said, looking back over at the women. Clay followed her gaze and noted that Evie, Lizzie, and Goldie were now joined by Lisa Leann, who seemed even more animated than usual.

"When did the others join?"

Clay shrugged. "One by one, they just joined." He chuckled. "Then, just a few months ago, Lisa Leann practically swooped in on the group. Invited herself without so much as a nod from Evangeline Benson." Clay chuckled again, and Britney laughed with him. "Best get back to taking the pictures," he said. "Can a man gain weight just by standing so close, do you think?"

Britney pointed to the collection of desserts. "Have you ever in your life seen so many homemade goodies?" she asked by way of answering his question. "I mean, couldn't you just die?"

"I would if I ate all this. See that? That's a Lisa Leann concoction if I ever saw one. And that," he said, pointing to Goldie's fruitcake and putting on a Southern accent. "Miz Goldie Dippel from Alma, Georgia, baked that. You should not leave this room today until you've tried some of it. Better'n fried chicken smothered in thick gravy."

Britney laughed again and slapped him on the arm. "You are so funny, Clay Whitefield."

Clay winked. "Sometimes I think the ladies of the Potluck should start a catering service."

"It would certainly go well with Lisa Leann's wedding boutique," she said.

"That it would." Clay hunkered down a bit. He was leaning just so as to get a long shot of the dessert table when he heard another commotion coming from the ladies of the club. He stood upright and turned to see two women dressed in red standing just inside the outside doors. "Oh no," he said under his breath.

"What is it, Clay? What's wrong?" Britney asked, peering around him.

"Tell you what, honey," he answered. "Do me a favor and go sit at Goldie's table, will you? Just trust me on this one."

"Sure, but . . . why?"

"Don't look now," he answered, "but here comes trouble."

Vonnie

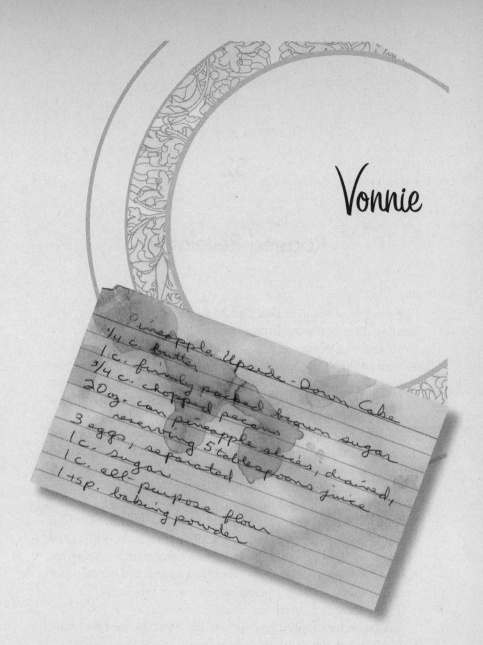

Pineapple Upside-Down Cake

¼ c. butter
1 c. firmly packed brown sugar
¾ c. chopped pecans
20 oz. can pineapple slices, drained,
    reserving 5 tablespoons juice
3 eggs, separated
1 c. sugar
1 c. all-purpose flour
1 tsp. baking powder

32

Roasted Revelation

I blinked. Sure enough, Dee Dee McGurk and Velvet James were heading directly for our little cluster of potluck ladies. Velvet's resemblance to Donna was uncanny enough to make me question if Vernon could be her father as well. But it was Doreen herself who caused me to gasp. The morning she ran away with our former choir director almost three decades ago, she'd stood at the front of the church as her sweet face radiated joy. It was only later we realized her glow came from the thrill of planned deceit and betrayal against her husband and child. But in no way did her later actions tarnish the purity of her song. The words of "Amazing Grace" had flowed from her like the sweet swells of the violin.

Could the meaning of those words have been lost to her? Could it be that the deep lines that mapped her face traced her fall from grace? It was apparent that these past thirty years had been unkind. No wonder she'd been able to waltz into town without being recognized. Her once-glowing eyes had grown hard, and her once-soft skin had leathered with a permanent scowl of bitterness.

It was enough to break my heart.

We potluckers looked from one to the other. It was Lisa Leann, God bless her, who first recovered from the shock of facing our difficult past, probably because she didn't share it with us.

Lisa Leann gave the newcomers a big Texas welcome as Clay snapped pictures. I'd seen him earlier, hovering about the card-shop girl, Britney, who was now seated at Goldie's table.

He exchanged a look with me as if to say he understood the drama of the situation and felt he had to record it. I hoped to no end Clay wouldn't run this picture or any mention of these particular guests as front page news.

"Ladies, I'm so glad you could make it," Lisa Leann said. "And Dee Dee, I hear tell that you know my friends? Are introductions in order?"

Clay snapped one more picture before stepping back to photograph the decorations and people at the table behind us. I knew he only turned his back on us so he could stay within earshot.

So help me if Dee Dee didn't look us up and down and say, as cool as you like, "Yes, I know these girls."

Her daughter looked confused. "Some of your regulars?"

"No, honey, they're part of a past I've tried to forget."

Those words seemed to break the spell that had made Evie's mouth gap open. As if magically given a voice, Evie said, "If a person is trying to forget the dead, why would they take a shovel to the cemetery?"

Dee Dee crossed her arms over her simple red knit pantsuit that looked as if it had seen too many wash days, pilled and faded as it was. "Why, honey, some corpses have a few valuables left to pick through. I've just come to claim what's mine."

Evie made a kind of shocked squeak while Dee Dee turned to Lisa Leann. "I see you've put place cards at all the tables. Can you tell me where Velvet and me are to sit?"

Lisa Leann checked her list. "You've drawn Vonnie's table, near the back."

"My mother's joining us," I explained, like that put a clear spin on the why of our faraway location.

Just then, my handsome son David, who had just wheeled Mother through the foyer, caught my eye from the back of the room. Mother was holding my pineapple upside-down cake, one of my specialties. Velvet gave David a big grin and waved. Surely

213

David realized Velvet was not Donna. But from the look on his face, I didn't think so.

I motioned to my family to stay where they were. "There's Mother now," I said to Dee Dee and Velvet, leading them to my table where they sat. "Welcome," I said, more grimly than I'd intended. "I'll be right back."

Just as I was heading back to Mother and David, Lisa Leann pulled me aside. "Oh, Vonnie. I'm so sorry. I had no idea Dee Dee was Donna's mother. I've heard all about that mess. Leave it to me to pull something like this. Do you think the girls will ever forgive me?"

I looked at Lisa Leann hard, surprised to see she had tears gathering in the corners of her eyes. "I've tried so hard to fit into our group, and all I do is stir things up," she said.

I reached for her then and gave her a hug. While I held her in my arms, I whispered into her ear, "It's okay, Lisa Leann. You didn't know. I know you didn't."

I pulled back and looked her in the eye and said, "Now, you've got a tea to run, dear. Things have a way of working out. You'll see."

Lisa Leann looked unconvinced and pointed at a guitar on the stage. "But you don't know what I've gone and done . . ."

The shrill voice of my elderly mother interrupted. "Vonnie, Vonnie?"

I turned toward her. "Just a moment, Mother."

Mother crossed her arms over her dark green pantsuit that clashed with her hot pink cast held high by the leg brace of the wheelchair. "Vonnie, I need you now," she said.

"Sorry, Lisa Leann. We'll talk later, okay?"

She nodded, and I turned to my mother. "Mother, what is it?"

"I need you to help me lower the leg rest on my chair so I can pull up to the table."

David said, "Gram, I can help you with that."

Mother looked unhappy. "But Vonnie, I need you to . . ."

"Let him help," I said with a bit too much irritation in my voice.

214

I watched David as he kneeled down to make the adjustment then looked back at the sour face of my mother. So help me, if she didn't stop pushing her grandson away I was going to push both her and her chair off a cliff.

Be nice, I told myself for the millionth time. *God will get you through this; he will.*

When David stood, Mother asked, "Vonnie, where would you have me sit? Surely, not here by these doors that keep blowing cold air at me every time someone opens them?"

I turned to David, to dismiss him. I couldn't have him wheel Mother to the table, at least not while Donna's sister sat there grinning at him like the Cheshire cat.

I took the cake from Mother and handed it to David before grasping the handlebars of Mother's chair. "David, be a dear and run my dessert to the kitchen. I'll take over from here."

David kept his eyes on Velvet. "It's no trouble. Let me wheel Gram to your table. That is your table with your white plates on it, right?"

I put my hands on my hips and more harshly than I intended said, "Never mind that, son. Take this to the kitchen. I'll call you to pick up Gram later."

"Okay." He gave one last wave to Velvet. "See you," he called.

She nodded and waved back.

I pushed Mother to the table. As I got her settled, her eyes turned first to Doreen then to Velvet. Mother eyed Velvet's name tag sitting by her plate. When Velvet followed her gaze, she quickly tucked the tag into her purse. Mother said, "Young lady, I thought you were the deputy. You're not, are you?"

Velvet grinned. "Donna Vesey? Nope, never met her."

"But you know my grandson? You waved at him."

"You mean David Harris? I've seen him on TV." She giggled. "He probably thinks I'm Donna too."

"I wouldn't fool around like that, pretending to be someone you're not."

Velvet laughed, sounding much like Donna when *she* laughed. "I'm only having a bit of fun. Besides, Donna, it seems to me, has more than enough guys."

I joined the conversation. "But surely the men around here know you're not her."

She smiled. "As far as I can tell, Donna's got them under some sort of spell. All I have to do is wear black, keep my mouth shut, and smile and wave, and . . . Well, let me put it this way—it doesn't take too much for the guys around here to think she's finally noticing them."

"You're kidding me," Mother said. "You pretend to be Donna?"

Velvet shrugged.

"But you can't get away with that," I said.

"You'd think so, but as most people don't know Donna has a sister, you'd be surprised what I *can* get away with."

I must have gasped, because Mother patted my hand and said, "Let me handle this. Young lady, you will certainly not be going out with my grandson. I simply won't allow it."

"What makes you think we haven't already gone out?" she asked coyly.

Dee Dee said, "Settle down, Velvet. We're here to build bridges tonight, not make things worse."

Velvet looked miffed. "I'm your daughter too, you know. I'm the one who's been there for you. Not Donna."

"Let's not talk about that now, Velvet. Just help me reach out. That's all I want to do."

Velvet sighed and rolled her eyes, much the same way Donna did. "Mom, if you'd already approached her to tell her you were in town, like I told you to—"

"I've told you, I've tried, but this way, well, it might be easier."

"Did you consider she might not even be here tonight?" She turned to me. "Where is she?"

I shook my head. "Had to work," I said.

Dee Dee looked crestfallen. "Just my luck." She leaned into Velvet with a playful nudge of her elbow. "Behave anyway. I want to make a good impression as I reenter this community."

"Mom, I'm telling you, you're going about it the wrong way. These people are nothing but a bunch of hypocrites."

216

That pushed my button. I wanted to say something, but I didn't know what. I pushed my chair back and stood up, then I sat down just as my other table guests arrived.

"Hello, Vonnie, good to see you," Dora Watkins said. Dora, the proprietor of the local Sew and Stitch, stood before me, along with her thirty-something daughters Paige and Mrs. Ellen Allen, the wife of Terry Allen, the publisher of the *Gold Rush News*.

I tried not to grimace at the realization that the trio would get a front row seat to the drama that was unfolding before me. Oh brother! This would be all over Summit View by tomorrow afternoon. Everyone but Donna would know her mother and sister were in town.

My heart skipped a beat. I nodded at Dora and her girls. "Welcome, make yourselves at home," I said.

I looked at Velvet again. Somebody had to tell Donna about Dee Dee and Velvet, and soon, I realized.

But what if Donna dropped in at the church for dessert? She was on duty, of course, but that never stopped her from sampling home-baked goodies. I felt my eyes widen. *Oh boy. This could get interesting.*

This was all Donna needed, what with the depositions for the lawsuit starting. People wouldn't know if they were describing Donna or her sister to the gathering attorneys. I felt my stomach churn.

"Well, we didn't know if we could make it," Dora was saying. "But with this being the first women's event without our dear Jan Moore, we felt we had to come. To support her memory, you know."

She turned and looked at Doreen and her daughter for the first time. "Oh dear," she said to Velvet. "Did you know you look just like Donna Vesey? I almost thought you were her."

Velvet grinned. "You don't say?"

Dee Dee extended her hand. "Dora Watkins, long time no see," she said. Dora's eyes went to Dee Dee's name tag, then back to her face. "Do I know you? Oh my sweet red calico. Doreen? Doreen Vesey?" Her eyes darted from Dee Dee to Velvet, and she let out a little gasp. "Oh! You're Donna's sister?"

217

Suddenly the lights dimmed, and Evie and Lisa Leann were up in front of the room, sharing the microphone. Their voices chimed a welcome as the group applauded politely while Clay snapped their picture. Next, Lisa Leann and the choir director, Pastor Hal, did a lovely duet of "Away in a Manger." Dee Dee and Velvet rose from their seats and began to walk toward the front of the room. Now, where were they off to? Before I could ask, Mother leaned over to whisper, a bit too loudly because of her hearing loss, "Vonnie, take me to the bathroom please."

I stood and pushed Mother back through the foyer doors to the ladies' room. I got her situated, then decided to step outside the bathroom just in time to see Donna breeze through the outside door. I scurried to head her off, but before I could, I could hear Lisa Leann and Hal finish their song. Hal took the microphone and said, "Tonight we have a special treat for you. Lisa Leann introduced me a few days ago to a former church choir member from thirty years back, Doreen Roberts Vesey, who is here with her daughter Velvet. They've asked to sing for us tonight, and after hearing them, I couldn't say no."

A collective gasp escaped the Grace ladies, the loudest of which I'm sure came from Evie, who was probably about to have a coronary.

Donna stopped in her tracks and stared at me first and then at the door of the fellowship hall.

"My mom?" she mouthed as she walked to the fellowship hall entrance. I stepped behind her just as Doreen's eyes fastened on Donna.

Through the doorway, I could see Evie, who sat at a table near the front, shift her body so she could follow the path of Doreen's stare. As Evie's gaze came to rest on Donna, a look of horror rose with her arched eyebrows.

Clay snapped a picture.

Doreen had the microphone in her hand now. "The last time you saw me, I was singing, so it's appropriate that as we meet again the microphone is back in my hand. As I'm not very good with words, I thought I'd use a song to express my regret and to let you

218

know, well, that I'm ready for a fresh start and I hope to put the past behind me. This is my way of saying hello. Tonight, I'm going to sing a Christmas favorite of my daughter Velvet and myself. It's not a song from your hymnal, but it's a special song that I want to sing in honor of my daughter Donna Vesey." She gave a shy smile. "I've missed you, honey."

The crowd gasped again as Velvet, who'd been strapping on her guitar that had been placed at the side of the stage, began to strum the first few notes of "Please Come Home for Christmas," a song recorded by the Eagles that one of the local stations always played this time of year.

Mother began to call me from the bathroom. "Vonnie? Vonnie! Are you going to let me sit here all day?"

I was caught. Should I let Mother wail loud enough to disrupt the group or should I stand with the daughter of my heart as she listened to her natural mother plead in song about coming home?

Donna and her frown were frozen in the moment as her mother sang and my mother continued to wail. "Vonnie, come and get me, will you?"

33

A Million Little Pieces

Clay had been unable to help himself; the opportunity for picture-taking had been too much of a temptation for him to stop. He was sure the ladies thought he would use them for tomorrow's paper, but he had not a single intention of that. These were going in his personal file. Or, he should say, his personal file of the ladies of the Potluck Club.

He'd thought ever so fleetingly about something his boss had said to him earlier in the week. "Whitefield," he'd said, "I'm having lunch today with an old college buddy of mine; we studied journalism together. He's a big-time editor now of some big-time publishing house in New York."

Clay had been sitting at his desk, his boss standing over him, and he peered up. "Really?"

"You've no doubt heard of it," he said, then spouted off the name of one of the top publishing houses in the country. No, make that the world.

"Really?" Clay repeated.

"He's over in Breck skiing and looked me up." Clay's boss smiled wryly. "Yes, really." He stepped away then looked back. "Hold down the fort for me, will you?"

"Sure, sure," Clay had said then. Now his mind whirled with thoughts of contacting his boss's old friend . . . of talking about acquisitions and such . . . talking about fiction. Or, would it be . . . what were they calling it these days? Creative nonfiction? Either way, he could easily turn this chaos into fame and fortune.

But that was before Donna walked in.

Before he saw the look on her face.

The look on Dee Dee McGurk's.

Before he watched Donna's world shatter into a million little pieces.

Donna

LARRY'S FUDGE BAR COOKIES

1/2 CUP BUTTER
1 EGG YOLK
1 1/4 C. SIFTED FLOUR
SUGAR (SEE RECIPE)
2 C CHOCOLATE PIECES

2 EGGS
MELTED BUTTER
2 TSP VANILLA
2 C. FINELY CUT NUTS

BEAT 1/2 CUP BUTTER WITH 1 EGG YOLK AND 2
TABLESPOON WATER SIFT FLOUR, 1 TEASPOON
-BACK-

34

Digesting the News

When I stepped into the foyer of the fellowship hall I felt like I'd entered the twilight zone. In the dim light, the building seemed to echo a sort of shocked hush. I walked to the entrance, where I saw two women glowing in the spotlight on the platform at the front of the room. Something struck me about the pair. For one thing, the younger woman, especially from this distance, could have been my twin, and the older woman looked familiar. Was it Dee Dee McGurk, the barmaid from the Gold Rush Tavern?

Then the woman held her eyes with mine as she announced, in front of God and all the world, that she was my mother.

I mouthed the words "My mom?" then stared at a ghostly image of Vonnie as she glided toward me through the darkened hall. She nodded, confirming this nightmare was not a dream.

I couldn't believe this. The entertainment at tonight's Christmas tea was my Benedict Arnold mother and some long-lost sister singing a song about coming home, in dedication to me?

That just tore it. Wasn't it enough that my privacy had been exposed on national television with Mr. Hollywood himself and that I was being sued in the baby Long case? Now this?

If I could have stepped outside of myself to view this fiasco from a different perspective—like maybe as someone from Mars—I might have found it somewhat amusing. But there was my mother, the mother who had abandoned me to raise yet another daughter, singing me a song. I blinked then stared at my sister. She appeared to be a younger, kinder version of myself. This was not what I needed.

If Vonnie hadn't put her arm around me when she did, I think I would have sunk to the floor in a puddle of humiliation.

I pulled my eyes from the horrific vision before me and looked at Vonnie.

"My mother?" I mouthed again.

Vonnie leaned to whisper in my ear. "I'm afraid so, dear. I only realized moments ago that she was in town."

Somewhere in the background, I could hear a voice crying above the strains of the Christmas song that seemed to hold the women of Grace Church captive.

The voice sounded like Vonnie's mother. "Vonnie! Come get me now!"

Vonnie gave me one last squeeze. "Donna, I've got to get Mother out of the bathroom. But I don't want to leave you like this."

"Go," I said, my focus on the apparition before me.

I'd known that old woman from the Gold Rush Tavern was up to something, but I'd never have guessed this. How dare she make a mockery of how she'd rejected me and my dad, all to music, no less?

The last strains of the song faded, yet the women in the room sat as if they were held in a trance. That is, all except Evie, who was craning her neck at me as if she was afraid she'd lost her mind and I knew where she'd put it.

Dee Dee, or I guess I should say, my mother—or at least the woman who had given birth to me—spoke into the microphone again, her eyes still holding me prisoner. "Donna, I'm glad you're here. I'm glad you're here so I can tell you how sorry I am. Could you ever find it in your heart to forgive me? To let me be your mother again?"

225

Suddenly, the women of the room shifted and turned, all eyes on me, waiting for my response.

They wouldn't get one.

I slowly turned and walked back toward the outside doors, my steps echoing across the foyer.

"Donna?" Dee Dee called out after me.

I didn't turn around. After all, what did she expect? For me to run to her as if in a slow-motion moment of ecstasy, butterflies fluttering as I leap through flowering gardens while violins crescendo in joy? *Oh, Mother dear, thanks for coming home after thirty years of abandonment. Wanna bake cookies?*

I snorted. That kind of reconciliation would never happen. Not here, not now, not ever.

I pushed open the double doors and felt the stinging cold slap me in the face. I swatted at a stray tear, disgusted by my emotional response. I wanted to feel nothing. But instead, my stomach flipped as the stars overhead blinked out of focus. I reached for my keys from my pocket. Was my hand shaking?

Vonnie's Taurus turned into the parking lot and pulled up next to me. David Harris powered down his window.

"Is the party over already?"

When I didn't respond, he stared at me. "You're certainly a quick change artist," he said. "Weren't you just wearing red?"

I stopped dead in my tracks. He'd thought my sister, what was her name—Velvet?—was me. Actually, that explained a lot of the strange comments I'd gotten in the past few weeks. I stared through David and kept walking. He parked, then popped out of the car. "Donna? Is everything okay?"

I shook my head. "Later," I said before climbing into my Bronco. He walked in my direction. In response, I turned on the motor and prepared to steer out of the parking lot.

The lights of a Jeep sliced through the darkness.

Clay. Had he been inside to witness yet another humiliation? Sure he had. He'd probably even recorded the whole thing with his trusty camera. Hey, with my luck, this could make front page news in the morning. "Deputy Publicly Spurns Apology from Mother." Maybe even *Hollywood Nightly* would pick it up.

Hey, maybe Baby Bailey Ann's mother would even see it and add it to her "Why I should sue Donna's pants off" file.

Perfect.

I pulled out of the parking lot, as did Clay's Jeep. I guess he had to hurry back to the paper if he was going to make tomorrow's edition with his scoop.

Me? I'd drown my sorrows in a cup of joe at Sally's. It should be quiet there.

Moments later, I pushed through the jangling door and sat down at my usual table. I signaled Sally for a cup then slid into a chair, not bothering to look up when the door jangled again.

"Donna? Are you okay?" Clay dropped into a chair across from me.

"Nope."

"You mean you didn't know Dee Dee was your mother?"

"No!" I blurted. "Did you?"

"Well, I'd hoped your dad or Miss Evie would have told you by now."

I felt my jaw set. "So, the three of you were just going to keep this a secret? Or were you all in on the great revelation tonight?"

Clay reached for my hand. "I swear, Donna, I didn't know about that. I don't think anyone did."

"Well, I for one can't wait to see it in the paper."

"I wouldn't!"

"Your publisher's wife was there. I saw her sitting near the back. I'd wager this will make the paper whether you write it up or not. Don't you think?"

Clay blanched. "Um, I don't know. I'll see what I can do."

"You've certainly done a lot, Clay. You leaked the story about David Harris to the national media, and now you're going to paint me as the bitter woman I'm fast becoming."

"Bitter? No, Donna, that's not how I see you."

I stared at his hand over mine, then looked him in the eye. "Aren't you afraid your girlfriend is going to see us together?"

227

"I . . . uh . . ." He stood up. "I gotta go. I'm going to call my publisher to see what I can do about the story I have to file tonight."

"You do that, Clay."

He leaned over and hugged me. "Donna, you know I care about you. I'll see what I can do to make this all go away. Who knows? Maybe I can turn this around to paint you in a positive light."

He turned to leave, but I called out to him. "Clay, I appreciate you trying, anyway. With the depositions starting, tonight's little show is the last thing I need. As it stands now, the judge and jury are going to see me as a high profile fiancée of a Hollywood prince and a spoiled woman who hates her mother. You just can't get better publicity than that, at least not when you're being sued in the death of a baby."

Clay seemed to shrink into his jacket. "So, it's official, you and Harris are engaged?"

I stared at him before I answered, "I'm just quoting *Hollywood Nightly*, so it must be true, right?"

Sally arrived with my coffee just as Clay nodded his good-bye then stepped into the evening.

Sally scurried back behind the counter, and I sat there watching the steam rise from my cup. I was alone, truly alone. My best pal Clay had a girlfriend, and my entire family had in one way or another betrayed me. Sure, there were a couple of other guys I could count as wannabe boyfriends, but who was I fooling? No one was going to want me, not now anyway. If they didn't realize it already, they soon would. I was nothing but a reject, rejected by my own mother, by Clay, and soon, the world.

I closed my eyes. *God, even if I could believe in you, I could never trust you. Life's been nothing but one big joke, and the joke's on me. I hope you're amused.*

I looked up as Larry stepped out of the kitchen and made a beeline for me. He looked like a man who was gloating over a terrible secret. Word must travel fast. The tea hadn't even broken up yet, and here came my first so-called friend to rub in my humiliation. I took a long sip of my coffee and averted my eyes.

"Why, what a pleasure to have you drop in to see me," Larry said.

I groused over my hot coffee. "Yeah. You're the big attraction, all right."

He rumbled a purr like a sexy kitten and winked as he handed me a plate. "I love a girl in uniform, and I want you to be the first to try my new recipe for fudge bars, on the house."

I stood up. "Larry, what's wrong with you?"

He set the platter on the table. "Well, I'm on break. I thought we'd have a little moment to ourselves, just you and me."

"Yeah, sure. You, me, and a nasty little migraine." I averted my eyes and hunkered back over my coffee in an effort to end this weird conversation.

Larry looked confused. "Why, Donna, you've been waving and winking at me all week, ever since our national TV debut."

I felt my face burn as I slapped my payment down on the table and stood up. "I have not been flirting with you, and after your TV stunt, well, you're lucky to be alive." I let my hand rest on my holster. "Understand?"

Larry stepped back and watched as I slammed through the front door and stalked back to my truck, shivering at the thought of Larry and me as a couple. "Ewww!"

Then it hit me. *Velvet. He'd mistaken my sister for me. That's probably what happened that night when I thought he'd seen me in my pj's.*

It all made sense. I hesitated before I swung open my door. This was a disaster.

As I slid into the seat, my cell rang. I picked it up without looking at my caller ID.

"Donna, thank God I've reached you."

I could hear Lisa Leann auctioning off a basket of books and scented soaps and candles in the background. "Going, going, gone!" she whooped.

"Evangeline? Is that you? You've got a lot of explaining to do."

"I do. The auction has just started, and I'm making my way to the parking lot. Can you meet me back over here? I want to talk to you."

I pulled my Bronco onto the street. "This ought to be good," I said, heading back to the church.

Evie was standing at the door of the activities center when I arrived; she hurried to my truck and slipped in. She reached out to hug me. "Oh Donna!" she cried. "Oh, I'm so horribly embarrassed about this, for you, for all of us."

I accepted her quick hug but didn't return it. I pulled back to watch her dab her eyes with a soggy tissue.

Was she hoping I'd forgive her for this? I folded my arms. "I've got a few questions. For starters, you knew? You knew that Dee Dee was my mother and you didn't tell me? Plus, you gave her the microphone at your tea? Why would you do that?"

I looked out my side window and waited for an answer.

Evie's voice sounded tired. "I deserve that, Donna, I know I do. But you've got to believe me when I tell you I didn't know that Dee Dee and Velvet were coming tonight, and I certainly didn't know that they had arranged with the choir director and Lisa Leann to sing. It was an innocent mistake, I assure you. No one meant to hurt you. You've got to believe that."

I turned and looked at her. "But why didn't you tell me who Dee Dee was?"

"Your father wanted to do it."

I stared back out the window. "How long has he known?"

"A while now. But with all you've gone through of late, he didn't have the heart to tell you. Then, when he discovered what kind of person your mother had become . . ."

I felt myself stiffen. "Okay, I get the picture. But it would have been nice if one of you had told me. Can you imagine how I felt to be surprised like that?"

I looked back at Evie who was staring at the back of her hands, her head down. "I saw it on your face. Oh Donna! I'm so, so sorry."

Was she genuinely repentant? I narrowed my eyes.

Evie looked up at me. "Don't you see what she was doing?"

"What's that?"

"Both your father and I had told her to leave you alone. She laughed at us. So, she's taken her revenge out on you and us, trying to create a scandal such a short time before the wedding." Evie dabbed the tissue at her eyes again. "How could she?"

"Ah, so this turns out to be all about you and your many grudges."

"Donna, no. Why would you say a thing like that to me?"

"Simply an observation."

"Donna, we'll talk about it later, when you're not so upset. Why don't we meet over at your father's house? Let him know what happened." She pushed the door open and slid out. "I'll meet you over there, okay?"

I looked at her bundled in her beige wool coat, her mascara smudged at the corners of her eyes. Since when did she start wearing makeup?

"I don't think so," I said. "I'm on duty, you know."

"Okay, but before we meet at Lisa Leann's shop next week for my shower and fitting for the bridesmaids' gowns, okay?"

I nodded.

The door of the church opened, and Dee Dee and Velvet scurried out, with Velvet lugging her guitar, which she slid into the backseat of a red, older-model Toyota.

Evie called out to the women. "Doreen, Velvet, may I have a word with you?"

I called after her. "Evie, just walk away."

Evie turned and flashed her eyes in my direction. "This is for our honor, our family."

"As an officer of the peace, Evie, I'm telling you this is not the time."

Evie ignored me and made her approach. My two blood relatives looked up as if ready for battle. "What do you want, Evangeline?" Dee Dee hissed between clenched teeth.

Uh-oh. Looks like I could have a catfight on my hands. Quietly, I slipped out of the Bronco and walked toward my so-called family. As I was still on duty, I tried to act official.

"Ladies, is there a problem?" I asked.

Velvet turned and looked at me. "Why, if it isn't Miss High and Mighty herself."

I folded my arms. "Pardon me, but I don't even know you."

"Well, I know you," Velvet charged. "You're all the men in this town ever talk about."

I sighed slowly but deeply. Was this sister-intruder jealous of me? I tried not to smirk.

Suddenly, Dee Dee McGurk turned on me, full of rage. "Your father certainly did a poor job of raising you, I'd say."

"What are you talking about?" I asked.

"Here I was, taking a risk, seeking you out like that. I put it all on the line, honey. All. Velvet told me not to, she told me I'd just end up embarrassing myself. And she was right. But I've been watching you, Donna. I never dreamed you'd be the kind of woman who'd let her mother down, to embarrass her by walking out on her in front of the whole town."

"Isn't that what you did to me and Daddy?" I charged. "Walk out on us, in front of the whole town?"

Suddenly I realized my voice was as loud as hers.

"I didn't have a choice," Dee Dee said. "I was alone in a loveless marriage. When I got a chance for love with Harvey, well, I took it."

I stared at her hard. "You weren't alone. Daddy loved you. It almost broke his heart when you left. I know I was only four, but I heard him crying, so many nights. You almost destroyed that man. Not to mention the child you left behind."

"But don't you see, I was no good for you the way I was. Depressed, bored in my marriage. You were better off without me."

"If that's what you think, why didn't you do me the favor of staying away?"

"Why, you little brat!"

Evie joined the fray. "How dare you call her that? Donna is a fine young woman that you threw away. As for you, I've seen your record, I know all about you, and soon Vernon will show Donna your arrest record for prostitution and the like."

"How dare you talk about my private business in front of my daughters!" Doreen shouted, shoving Evie hard.

Evie stumbled backward, then walked forward and shoved Dee Dee back. "Keep your hands to yourself, you dried-up old prune."

The voice of dispatch suddenly screeched out of my radio, which I had fastened to my belt.

"Donna, be advised of a 10-100. You're needed in the Grace Church parking lot. We've had a call of some sort of altercation in progress."

"Ten-four," I said. "I'm already on it."

That's when I noticed the crowd of Christmas tea partygoers that was gathering around us. Some of the ladies had cell phones in their hands. Just then, the pastor stepped out of his office located across the parking lot. Wade tagged at his heels.

"Deputy, what's going on out here?" the pastor asked.

"I've got it under control," I said. I turned to Evie. "You get in your car and drive to Dad's." I turned to my mother and sister. "We've got a lot to talk about, but here and now's not the time. Understand?"

The women nodded.

"Go home," I said. "We'll talk later."

As the cars in the parking lot began to empty into the street, I pulled out my flashlight as if to direct traffic.

"Donna, what are you doing?" a familiar voice asked. "What happened here tonight?"

I turned around, surprised to see Wade was standing beside me. He was dressed in jeans and a fleece-lined denim jacket over one of his favorite black tees. "That woman"—my voice began to tremble—"that woman arguing with Evie? That was my mother."

"What?" Suddenly Wade was helping me into my truck. "I need to get you out of here, Donna."

I nodded. "How about to Jupiter? That might be far enough away."

Wade walked around to the passenger's seat, then swung the door open and climbed inside. "I'm done with my meeting with the pastor, so that means I'm available for you."

I stared at him. "I'm on duty."

233

Wade snapped on his seat belt and gave me a grin. "Good thing, because I'm your ride-along. Would that be alright? We can go by the station, and I'll sign the necessary paperwork. Okay?"

I nodded then started my Bronco. Wade let the silence thicken as I prepared to follow the flow of traffic out of the parking lot. "You don't have to tell me anything if you don't want to," he finally said.

I nodded again, then turned briefly to study his eyes. When he wasn't drinking, they were the clearest blue, like they were right now. I fought back a tear that threatened to slip from my lashes and tried to smile. Wade smiled back as I merged with traffic. My mind formed a new and startling thought. Maybe, just maybe, I had a friend after all. And with all I was going through, I needed all the friends I could get, even if that friend was an old flame who happened to be a recovering alcoholic.

35

The Great American Novelist

A week to the day had passed since the tea.

And what a week it had been.

Clay had gotten busy working on the book proposal he hoped
to somehow get into the hands of a man he now knew was named
Mr. Thomas Jean, whose father had been a French winemaker and
whose name was therefore pronounced "John," with a little "ja" in
the "john."

Clay had spent a great deal of time practicing saying, "My editor,
Mr. Thomas Jean . . ." as he pecked away at his laptop keyboard
while Woodward and Bernstein watched from their cage. "Be good,
boys," he said to them, "and when Daddy sells this book idea and
gets a six-figure advance he'll buy you a nice new cage. A big one.
Big, big, big."

The only downside in the whole week had been Donna. He
couldn't seem to keep up with her . . . or her boyfriends. At times,
he'd spot her with David Harris. At other times with Wade Gage.
Clay wasn't concerned she'd had some kind of moral breakdown;
he knew that there wasn't anything immoral going on. But he was
concerned about her nonetheless.

Clay had done some other writing too, besides that which he hoped would be the story of his life. The Great American Novel, as some said. He'd begun writing editorial pieces about Donna, hoping to help some with her legal case. He'd written about the good she'd done over the years, both as a friend and as a deputy. About cases she'd solved and even how she'd saved Coach and Goldie Dippel in the snowslide a few weeks back.

The thought of Coach and Goldie caused a frown to form on his lips and a crease to wrinkle his brow. He'd seen them in the parking lot at the tea. Coach was helping her into his car. She seemed . . . tense. Jerked the car handle away from his grip and shut the door herself. Something in that scenario wasn't right. But what?

"Clay, my boy," he said aloud, "it's your business to find out." He looked at the gerbils. "Sorry, guys. I've gotta go do what they call investigating."

Lizzie

Tiramisu

Ingredients

1 lb. (16 oz) Mascarpone Cheese
3 TB. Sugar
4 TB Coffee extract
1 c Heavy Cream whipped
24 Ladyfingers, split
1 1/2 Cups cold Espresso or
strong coffee

36

Fresh-Brewed Day

By Thursday, Summit County public schools had been back in session from Christmas break for two days, and I had already asked for a day off.

I'll admit, this did not endear me any to our school principal, but I didn't care. When he asked me why, after two weeks paid vacation, I needed another day off, I simply told him the truth and let the chips fall where they may, as they say.

And I hate clichés. But there you have it. My life has disintegrated to the point where I am using clichés.

So, I called my principal, Mr. Tobin, on Wednesday night after church services and said, "Mr. Tobin, here's the deal. My husband, as you know, is home with an injured back. What you don't know is that the man has become a slave to court TV. You name it, he's watching it. Judge Judy, Judge Alex, Judge Mathis, some judge from Texas, and—I'm not sure, but I'm fairly certain—Judge Roy Bean."

"Isn't he dead?" Mr. Tobin asked, his voice as expressionless as a corpse.

"That's the thing," I answered. "He's back. He's back from the dead, and I'm listening to him hand down sentences left and right all day long." I took a deep breath and sighed. "By the way, did you happen to see the segment on *The People's Court* where—"

"Which judge is that?" Mr. Tobin interrupted.

"The pretty one. Judge Milliron or Milrod. Wait a minute . . ." I paused long enough to hear the voice of the announcer. "Judge Marilyn Milian!" I exclaimed as happily as a kid who just discovered that Santa brought the one thing on her list that she really, really, really wanted.

"Lizzie, are you alright?"

I rolled my eyes. Did the man not listen? "No, I'm not alright. I'm going slap crazy. My husband watches too much television, my son and his wife and their kids are living here, my daughter and her boyfriend are, seemingly, always here, and my mother is now in an assisted-living facility nearby. I have not one second of private time anymore, I haven't read my Bible other than at church in I don't know how long, and the laundry is piled so high I'm thinking about building on an extra room for it."

Another long pause. I tapped my foot to its rhythm.

"So, you need a day to do laundry?" he asked.

I pressed a fingertip against one temple. "No. I need a day to just *be*."

"But your husband will still be home, right?"

"Yes."

"And your daughter-in-law? Why isn't she helping?"

"Because she now has a job to help pay the bills of a mortgage in Baton Rouge while they're looking for a house here, which doesn't really seem to be happening, or at the very least does not seem to be happening quickly enough."

"You sound like you're having a nervous breakdown."

I jerked a bit. What was the name of that singer from way back when? The one who jerked? Joe Cocker, wasn't it? That's who I looked like for all of ten seconds before I said, "Look, Mr. Tobin. I don't ask for anything really. I'm easygoing, and I never take personal time off. Well, I'm taking personal time off. It's mine to take, and I'm taking it."

"That's fine," he muttered.

"It is?"

"Sure. You don't owe me any detailed explanations."

I threw my head back and stared at the cobwebs forming on the ceiling. "Then why did you ask why I need a day off?"

"Well, Lizzie, I was curious, seeing as you just had two weeks, but I wasn't really expecting such a long justification. What I mean to say is, that's a lot of personal information I simply didn't need."

I did the Joe Cocker thing again and then said, "I'll see you Friday, Mr. Tobin. Unless I take another day off. Then I'll see you Monday."

I think he snickered, but I'm not sure. "Why don't we just say Monday? I think you need more than just one day, Lizzie."

I straightened. "Monday it is, then."

"Take care," he said, then snickered—or something close to it—again and hung up.

Thursday morning I helped Samuel get settled in his recliner, gave him his medication, fluffed his pillows, positioned the TV remote, and then helped Samantha get the children ready for school. I waved as they climbed on the school bus, shoved a cup of coffee-to-go into the hands of both of my children, and ran them out to the car, where they climbed in, looking somewhat perplexed, and drove toward Breckenridge. I stood guard as Samantha got ready for her job, and I walked her to her car as well (which a friend of theirs had brought up from Louisiana during Christmas vacation for the small price of five-hundred dollars). She winked at me as she slid behind the driver's wheel and then drove away.

I was alone.

Sort of. By this time one of the judge shows was up and going—Milian, I think—but I paid it no mind. I called out to Samuel, asking if he needed anything. He said he'd like a cup of coffee, so I poured him a fresh cup, took it to him, then literally ran up the stairs to our bedroom, where I shut the door and climbed onto our bed, pushing the pillows toward the headboard at the same time. I pulled my Bible from the bedside table and opened it to anything, then read for the next thirty minutes.

After that I took a nap for about fifteen minutes. A more glorious fifteen minutes has never been spent, though I dreamed the entire time about baking . . . stuff. I was standing in a large kitchen—a baker's kitchen, they call it—and I was putting food dishes together like the pros one sees on the Food Channel when one's husband was not watching judges with stage makeup wield their power. I was wearing a pretty dress and an even prettier chef's apron with this nice design on it, though I couldn't tell what it was. But it was pink. Lisa Leann pink, to be honest with you. And I was baking and baking and baking. At the end of the dream I pulled what appeared to be tiramisu out of a stainless steel refrigerator.

Then I woke up, sat up, and called the facility where my mother was staying so I could check up on her.

"You might want to come see her today," the charge nurse said. "She's a little feisty."

"My mother is always feisty, but I'll come," I told her. "I'll be there around lunch so we can eat together."

"I'll let her know," the nurse said.

I took a shower. A long, hot shower, and then I took my time slathering my body with lotion and body spray, and I played around with my makeup and thought that Lisa Leann would be so proud of me. I fluffed my hair a bit more than usual, and I put on a pair of black jeans and a pretty blue sweater and some funky earrings Michelle had given me for Christmas that are so not me, but who cared.

Then I went downstairs to check on Samuel, whose meds had kicked in. He snored and drooled—a blessing considering he was in constant pain when awake—while Judge Mathis sat with his chin propped in the palm of his hand listening to the defendant explain why it was not her fault. I smiled, turned the volume down just a bit, then went into the laundry room and started a load. After that I cleaned the kitchen, and after that I went back into the family room to tell Samuel—who was now awake and

241

trying to find a comfortable position—that I was going to see my mother.

"So much for your day off," he said.

I laughed. "So far, I'm not complaining."

Mother was her usual bossy self, fussy because she didn't like the way the kitchen personnel prepared the English peas. "Not enough pepper," she was saying.

I reached for the pepper packet on the tray that had been delivered moments earlier and said, "Pepper, Mother?" Without invitation I tore at it and began to sprinkle the spice onto the vegetable.

"Well, why didn't they just do that for me?"

"What if you didn't like pepper on your peas?"

"Who wouldn't like pepper on their peas?" she asked.

After lunch I helped Mother into a lounging chair and styled her cottony white hair and smiled at her while she looked at me as though I had three heads. "What are you looking at, Mother?" I asked.

She chuckled a bit. "Who did your makeup today? Dolly Parton?"

I continued to smile. "No, Mother. I did. Now hush your fuss and enjoy having someone play with your hair. Do you remember when you used to style my hair?"

"Unruly hair," she said.

"Yes, but you styled it just so."

"What I remember is the time you cut it all off so you'd look like . . . who was that?"

"Peter Tork."

"A man. My daughter cut off her hair to look like a man."

"I thought he had a nice haircut."

"But he was a man," she said, shifting in the chair as though indignant.

"Yes, but he had long hair," I reminded her.

"Wasn't he a Beatle?" she asked, suddenly spry.

I smiled at her and shook my head. "No. He was a Monkee."

"Beatles and Monkees. No wonder your generation has problems."

242

My generation has problems, I thought later. *Yes, indeed.* Well, at least one member of my generation did—me—and for once, I was stumped as to how to fix her.

As I drove down Main Street toward home I spied Lisa Leann walking into her shop, laden with what appeared to be magazines, so I stopped and followed her inside.

"Lizzie, what brings you here?" she asked, pulling herself out of her thick mink coat. "Why aren't you at school?"

I smiled at her as I unzipped my parka. "I took the day off." Lisa Leann had walked behind the L-shaped counter near the front of her shop, where she dropped the stack of bridal magazines. "I had the most interesting dream about something this morning," I told her. "It reminded me of you."

"Was John Tesh involved?" she asked, pulling a CD case sporting the entertainer's face off the back shelf and popping its top.

"Ah . . . no."

"Drat. I can't seem to get him into my dreams either." She laughed and added, "At least not those I dream at night."

She came around the counter and walked over to a built-in stereo system where she popped John Tesh in. Seconds later, an inspiring and romantic melody filled the room.

"Lovely," I mused, pulling my parka off and hanging it on a coat tree near the door.

Lisa Leann crossed her arms and studied me for a minute. "What have you done to yourself, Miss Lizzie? Makeup? Hair?"

"I know. I got creative."

Lisa Leann gestured to the Victorian seating arrangement. "Care to sit for a minute? I can get us some tea."

"Tea sounds wonderful."

Lisa Leann headed toward the back, calling over her shoulder while I took a seat. "Good," she was saying. "I want to talk to you about the makeover and shower I'm having for Evangeline." Her voice faded momentarily, but minutes later she came waltzing back, carrying a silver tea service and two bone china cups and saucers atop an ornate and heavy silver tray.

I stood. "Let me help you."

243

"Oh, posh. This is my job," she said.

I sat again.

"Cream or lemon?"

"Cream," I answered, pushing myself back against the velvety softness of the settee and then reaching for the cup she'd prepared for me. "This is nice, Lisa Leann. Thank you."

"I just wish more of the girls would come by." She sat down. "So, let's talk about the shower, shall we?"

"Have you run it by Evie?"

Lisa Leann's eyes danced with delight. "Evangeline has placed her entire wedding, reception, and anything to do with it, completely in my hands. Except for her gown. She has chosen her own gown . . . not that I've seen it. Oh, goodness, I do hope it's appropriate for a golden girl wedding." She paused long enough to ponder. "I'm just dying to know if it will be white. Do you know? Because, I'm just *sure* Evangeline is still a virgin and so, naturally, she should wear white; not that it seems to make a bit of difference these days, but I was just wondering."

"I don't know," I said, somewhat stunned.

Lisa Leann continued as though I'd said nothing. "The wedding is the 28th and the club meets this Saturday for prayer, so I was thinking the 14th or the 21st. If we wait until the 21st, of course, we'll have the altered dresses, and we can have a fitting party too. I just hope Mandy's baby doesn't arrive at the same time, and I do surely hope Donna will attend the party." Lisa Leann shook her head sadly. "Other than church, have you seen hide or hair of her since that awful thing that happened at the Christmas tea? I take total responsibility, of course. Then again, if someone had just *told* me that Dee Dee McGurk was actually Donna's mother . . ."

"None of us knew," I said. "Except Evie. She and Vernon knew, of course."

Lisa Leann shook her head and sipped at her tea. "Poor Evangeline. Bless her heart, bless her heart. What it must be like to have waited your whole life to marry the man of your dreams, the love of your life, your childhood sweetheart, only to have his first wife swoop into town and try to break things up."

I was a little stunned and wondered if Lisa Leann knew something I didn't. "Has Doreen done that?"

"No. But I'm sure she will. Did you see the look on her face when she and Evie were fighting out there in the parking lot? My lands, I thought we were going to have a catfight."

I set my cup and saucer on the antique coffee table before me and said, "We did have a catfight."

"Have you spoken to Evangeline since then?" Lisa Leann asked, crossing her short legs.

"Only at church, and she and Vernon seemed to be handling things okay. I guess you saw that Donna was there too."

Lisa Leann cocked an eyebrow. "With Wade Gage on one side and David Harris on the other, no less. And Clay Whitefield with that card shop girl."

"Britney."

Lisa Leann waved her hand. "Whomever. All I know to say is, they're putting the mojo on the dating service I've been trying to get up and running."

I giggled, but Lisa Leann frowned.

"To answer your question," I continued, "I've seen Donna a few times. She came out to the high school on Tuesday to talk to the kids about drugs and—"

"How'd she look?"

I thought for a moment. "She looked good." I looked down at my hands for a minute. "The depositions have started. I guess you know that."

"That poor darlin', that poor darlin'. She does not deserve any of this. I understand from our illustrious Mr. Whitefield that he is developing a campaign to help Save the Donna. He'll have something about it in this week's paper, so be sure to read it."

I scooted up a bit and stood. "I will. I really should go," I said. "Thank you for the tea."

Lisa Leann scampered up and said, "But we haven't decided on the date for the party!"

"I should think you'd do better to talk to Evie about that. But my money is on the 21st."

Lisa Leann pointed upward. "I'll make a note of it," she said and then escorted me toward the coat tree, where I retrieved my parka and put it on.

"By the way, how is your dating service going?" I asked.

Lisa Leann beamed. "Thanks to me, there are three new couples in Summit View."

I had to smile back. "Who otherwise might never have found each other," I said. "Thank you again for the tea."

I headed out the door, but before I reached my parked car I spied Goldie going into Higher Grounds, so rather than leaving just yet, I crossed Main and followed behind her.

She was standing at the counter, purchasing two cups of Sally's special hot cocoa.

"Yum," I said from behind her.

She jumped and then smiled. "What are you doing here?" she asked.

"Following you," I said. I looked around at the near-empty restaurant. "Want to sit while we wait for your hot cocoa?"

"Sure," she said.

We sat at a nearby two-seater. I leaned over the table a bit. "So? Have you told Jack yet?"

She shook her head. "I was going to the night of the tea, but then . . . well, you know. The fight."

"I saw the two of you getting into his car."

Goldie chuckled. "I was actually angry with him over the whole situation."

"You mean the situation with Doreen and Velvet?"

Goldie nodded. "Not that he had anything to do with it, but he just seemed like a good target. Doreen had an affair and caused all this hurt. Jack has had multiple affairs and caused all this hurt. I just . . . got mad at him."

I frowned. "But you haven't told him about Charlene?"

"No."

I rearranged the novelty salt and pepper shakers on the table between us. "I saw Charlene the other day at school. I tried to see if she's showing, but . . ."

"It's difficult to tell. I know." Goldie looked toward the counter, and I followed her gaze. Sally was moving toward us, carrying two hot drinks to go. "Thank you, Miss Sally," Goldie said in that Southern way she still has, even after all these years in Colorado.

"Tell Chris I added some extra whipped cream on his," Sally said with a laugh.

"He'll love you for it," Goldie commented as Sally walked away. Then she looked at me. "I'd best get these back across the street," she said, cupping the two Styrofoam cups in her mittened hands.

We stood together. "Goldie," I said. "Tell him. Get it over with, girl."

Goldie nodded. "I will. Soon." She licked her lips. "I'll know when the time is right, and it just hasn't been yet."

We walked out of Higher Grounds and straight into Clay, who was coming in.

"Ladies," he said.

"Clay," we said together.

"I understand you've begun a campaign to help Donna," I said.

Clay gripped the handle of the door but didn't open it. "Yes, I have. You can read the start of it in today's paper," he said.

"We certainly will," I replied, then watched as he walked in. I looked back to Goldie. "I'd better get home," I said. "Samuel's probably in need of something by now, and there's more laundry to do." I winked. "Call me and give me all the details once you tell Jack, you hear me?" I said more than asked.

"I will," she said, then shivered in the cold. "Gotta go. See you at the potluck?"

"See you then," I said, then crossed the street to where my car waited to take me back to reality.

37

The Good Egg

Clay ambled into Higher Grounds and immediately went to the
newspaper stand, pushed in a dollar's worth of quarters, and then
pulled open the door. He swiped the top paper toward him, then
let the metal door bam shut before heading toward his table.

Sure, he could get his papers for free at the office, but Clay liked
the sensation he felt whenever he bought a copy. It was the same
stir of emotions he'd felt the first time one of his articles ran and
he'd rushed down to the corner store right after school to buy his
personal copy. He'd been a boy of thirteen then, but he still had
the same feeling when, on Thursdays, he came into the café and
purchased a paper.

Today he was particularly anxious to read his editorial. He'd spent
hours longer than usual working on it. He'd interviewed anyone
and everyone he could think of—from Vonnie Westbrook, Donna's
childhood Sunday school teacher, to Betty Yancy, the housebound
woman Donna drove up Snake Mountain once a week to bring
groceries, prescriptions, and mail to. He'd ended with the story of
her rescue efforts in Summit Ridge and how she'd practically dug
the Dippels out of the snowslide. Enough was being said to destroy

his friend, and he'd interviewed more than a dozen people who couldn't say enough good about her.

He opened the paper to the second page and sat in his usual chair in one fluid movement, then looked toward the counter so as to catch Sally's attention. "Cup of coffee," he said easily.

"Coming right up," Sally said, then ambled over with a mug and a pot of fresh coffee. The aroma of it reached Clay before she did, and he smiled.

As Sally poured the black gold into the mug she'd placed on the table, she ran her free hand over his shoulder and said, "You did a good thing for Donna there."

Clay looked up but not at Sally. "Thanks. I just hope it helps."

Sally patted him. "Front page article about how Donna saved that baby's mother was good too."

Clay shrugged as he pinked. "That part is just reporting. The editorial came from here," he said, pointing to his heart.

Sally patted him again. "But how are you going to make sure it gets into the right hands? I mean, we all love Donna, but those folks who are suing her—"

"It's been handled" was all he said.

Sally tugged at a lock of his red hair before moving away. "You're a good egg, Clay Whitefield. I've always said that, and I always will."

He smiled after her, then went back to reading his editorial.

Goldie

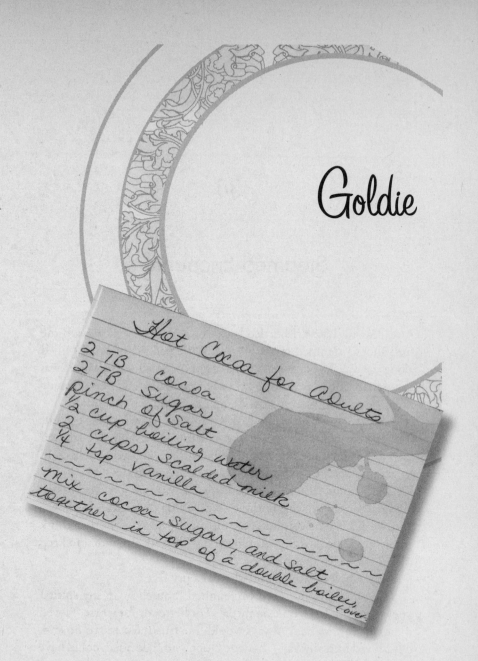

Hot Cocoa for Adults

2 TB   cocoa
2 TB   sugar
pinch of salt
1/2 cup boiling water
2 cups scalded milk
1/4 tsp vanilla

~ ~ ~ ~ ~ ~ ~ ~ ~ ~ ~ ~ ~ ~ ~

Mix cocoa, sugar, and salt
together in top of a double boiler,
(over

38

Steamed Encounters

After leaving Lizzie, I hurried back down the sidewalk toward the card shop. I stamped my boots free of the packed snow I'd gained along the way. The delicious aroma of hot cocoa wafted upward; I was more than a little anxious to get back upstairs so that I could enjoy the little mid-afternoon pick-me-up Chris had sent me out for.

This was but one of the many things I'd grown to love about working for Chris Lowe. He was generous to a fault. He allowed for my personal life. He listened when I just needed to talk. And he often treated us to something wonderful from the café.

If Jack thought for one second that I was going to go back to being a housewife with nothing to do all day but clean his house and wash his clothes and cook his meals, he had another think coming, I reminded myself. I loved my job and I intended to keep it even when we reunited.

I felt a look of surprise splash across my face.

There. I'd said it. *When* we reunited. Somehow in my spirit I knew we would. In time. Some day. For better or for worse, I loved the man. Always had. Always would. He frustrated me to no end, but I loved him anyway. Charlene Hopefield, I decided, could have his baby. We'd deal with it. But the daddy was mine. All mine. I had managed to make a couple of counseling sessions with him over the past month, and we'd had a marvelous Christmas together with our extended family. I wasn't ready to throw in the towel, to give up totally. Somehow, we'd make it work.

I squared my shoulders.

"Can I help you with that?" I heard a voice behind me say, just as I realized that I had but two hands and they were both full and that the door before me wouldn't open on its own.

I turned to see Van Lauer—my friend from last year—standing behind me. He smiled, and for a moment I forgot where I was.

My, how that man could smile.

I naturally smiled back. "Van! What are you doing here?"

He reached around me, and I caught a whiff of his cologne, masculine and expensive. "I came into town to open this door for you; didn't you know?" He pulled the door toward us, and I stepped into the card shop, stammering out a thank-you. "Chris didn't tell you I was coming?" he asked. "That surprises me."

I looked up at him and shook my head as we took a few steps into the store, then stopped. One thing hadn't changed about Van in the month or so since I'd seen him last. He was still incredibly good looking. Six and a half feet of toned flesh—even for a man working on the last half of his life—crystal blue eyes, and a golden tan that didn't seem to know it should go away in the cold of winter. I wondered for a fleeting moment if it were one of those airbrushed numbers I'd heard about.

"No, he didn't. And it doesn't surprise me." I looked down at the hot cocoa. "Somehow I think he sent me across the street for a reason other than these."

Van put his hand on the small of my back and guided me toward the back of the store. I felt a tingle rush down my spine; it settled behind both knees, and I wondered if I could even make the stairs. "You're wrong. I'm here because of the Vesey case. I understand Donna Vesey is to be deposed tomorrow."

I nodded. "She is. Nine o'clock. All the hotshot lawyers from out of town will be here too. The family of the baby. I don't know how Donna is dealing with all this, but personally it makes me sick.

253

There's no finer deputy out there than Donna Vesey. She wouldn't hurt a bug, let alone a child."

We reached the stairwell, and Van opened the door for me. As I went before him he said, "That's why I'm here. Van Lauer, Hotshot Lawyer."

I stopped on one of the stairs and turned sharply. "You're here against Donna?"

Van's head jerked a bit. "No. I'm here to help Chris. Didn't I say that?"

I paused. "I don't think so." I sighed in relief. "I don't think I could stand it if you were here to hurt Donna."

Van looked down with hooded eyes. "Still married?" he asked out of the blue.

"Mmm-hmm," I said because all other words were stuck in my throat.

"Darn my luck."

I cocked my head a bit. "That's sweet of you to say."

"It's honest of me to say," he replied, then nodded toward the top of the stairs. "Your cocoa is getting cold."

I turned and began taking the stairs again, evermore aware of Van's presence behind me and my rear end not far from his gaze.

"Life can be full of regrets," he crooned.

I stopped and turned again, forcing the smile from my lips. "Van . . ."

"But, then again, full of good things . . . great things . . . wild and marvelous things."

He sounded for all the world like Frank Sinatra. I bit my lip, then said, "Thank you for that."

He nodded. "You're welcome. I think."

As soon as Van and Chris were settled behind closed doors, I called Jack on his cell phone. He didn't answer, and I didn't leave a voice mail. But a few minutes later my desk phone rang, and it was him calling me back.

"You called?" he asked. "Sorry. I was putting away some gear from practice."

254

"That's okay," I told him.

"How are you on this blustery day?" he asked, and his carefree tone reminded me of the young man I'd fallen in love with so long ago.

"Cold," I said. "But Chris sent me out for some of Sally's hot cocoa, and it's doing the trick of warming my insides."

"If you'd like, I can come over and warm your outsides," he said with enough mischief to warm me all over.

I looked toward the back of the office to the closed door where Van Lauer no doubt sat, looking tan and wonderful. A man who was more than a little interested in me. A man who had never cheated on me. A man who didn't have an ex-mistress about to swell in the belly with child.

But a man to whom I wasn't married, nonetheless.

"I'd like that," I said softly.

There was a pause. "Hello?" Jack finally said. "Is this the party to whom I am speaking?"

I giggled. "It is."

"Goldie?"

"Yes."

"This is Goldie? My wife, Goldie?"

I giggled again. "It is." Another pause. I'd say it was a pregnant pause, but . . . "I love you, Jack," I finally said.

"Goldie, don't mess with my mind, woman."

"I'm not." I took a deep breath. "We have some things to talk about."

"I know."

"You know?" *You know about Charlene?*

"I know we have some things to talk about."

"Oh. For a moment there, I thought . . ." I leaned back in my chair.

"Thought what?"

"Nothing."

Another pause. "Goldie?"

"Jack, can I come over tonight? To our home? I'll bring dinner. And, we'll talk. We'll figure this thing out. Okay?"

"I have my meeting with the pastor tonight," he reminded me.

I raised my chin. "Cancel it," I said, my voice firm.

"Yes, ma'am," he returned, and with that I ended the call.

When five o'clock came, Van and Chris were still in the conference room. I shut the office down without saying good-bye, closing the door with a click behind me. I took the stairs quietly and hurried toward the outside door of the card shop.

"Good night, Mrs. Dippel," Britney called from behind a glass shelf of what-nots.

"Good night, Britney," I said, smiling at her.

"You sure are in a hurry there," she said, picking up a Hallmark figurine and dusting under it with a white cloth I now spotted in her hand.

"Tonight's a big night," I said, then continued on, wondering just which way that door might swing.

Before the door closed behind me I heard her say, "My best to Mr. Dippel!"

I shivered in the freezing temperature before heading toward Higher Grounds, where I ordered dinner for two. To go.

As I left the café I spied Velvet James at the bus stop, and I wondered for a moment what trouble she was stirring up. I kept my eyes on the building just over her shoulder as I made my way to where Sixth intersects with Main. I hoped she wouldn't see me, but I had no such luck.

"Hello, Goldie," she said as I came near enough for her to be heard without yelling. "That is your name, isn't it? Goldie?"

I stopped. "Yes, it is. How are you, Velvet?" My voice was terse, no doubt.

"I'm doing wonderfully, thank you." She grinned at me, but it wasn't genuine. *My lands, but she looks like Donna. If that poor girl doesn't have enough to deal with, now this . . .*

"That's nice." I continued on.

"My mother is doing well too," she said.

I continued on. "That is also nice."

256

"How's your husband?" she asked, lifting her chin just enough that she no longer looked like Donna to me, but more like Doreen Vesey thirty years ago.

This time I stopped. "Why do you ask about my husband?" I asked, an old fear washing over me.

She turned a bit and leaned against the lamppost that marked the bus stop while shoving her hands into the pockets of her long, deep blue coat. "Mama says that at one time your husband was quite the lady's man. Why, she told me she imagines there's not a bed in Colorado he hasn't warmed."

I felt my chest tighten. *Had Jack and Doreen . . . ?* "That's really none of your business," I said firmly, though I know my face reddened.

"Mama says," she continued as though I'd said nothing, "that the two of you haven't been living together for some time, and that by this time he ought to be fair game." Then she laughed. "But I told her that he's too old, even for me."

I stepped closer to her. "What are you doing here, Velvet James? What are your intentions? Don't you think it's enough that Donna is having to deal with Doreen being back in town? What's *your* purpose?"

"Maybe I just think it's time I got to know what it was like being my sister. Having Vernon Vesey for a father. She lived one life, I lived another." She looked around her. "Summit View is a beautiful place. Why should she be the only one of Doreen's children to get to live in it?"

"Oh, so that's it?" I asked. "You want to make Donna miserable because you think she got the life you never had?"

She just stared at me.

"That's what I thought," I said.

Velvet raised a brow at me and growled. Actually growled.

I took a step back. "You don't scare me," I said anyway, then pointed my finger at her. "You hurt Donna, and I'll be on you like white on rice. You hear me? Donna is not only the daughter of a friend—and I do *not* mean your mother—but she is a fellow potlucker."

"A what?"

"Never you mind," I said. "You just heed my words. Everyone knows who you are now. If you want to be the next big floozy around here, then you just have at it, but don't you for one second do it in Donna's good name. Donna may not be perfect, but she's a good girl. And that's a whole lot more than I can say for you right now." I nodded my head once. "My supper's getting cold, and I don't have time to waste on this conversation," I finished, then started to walk away.

"Oh sure!" I heard Velvet bark behind me. "Just walk away!"

I stopped for a moment, then continued on.

"I wonder what she meant by that," I said to Evie on the phone not ten minutes later.

"I don't know. There's probably a lot we don't know about Doreen and the children she had after leaving Summit View. By the way, have you told Donna?"

"No," I said, then cradled the phone between my ear and shoulder blade as I shucked out of my clothes. I was standing in the chill of my bedroom. "And I don't know if I will. Actually, I was calling to ask you to pray about something."

"What's that?" she asked.

I leaned over and picked up my clothes from the floor and laid them haphazardly across my bed. "Will you pray for me tonight? I'm going over to Jack's to talk to him . . . to tell him about Charlene."

"I was wondering if you'd done that yet."

I stepped into the adjoining bathroom. "No. I was going to talk to him after the tea but then . . ." I burst out laughing as I turned on the water for my bath. "Then you . . . you and . . . you and Doreen . . . put out your claws . . ."

"It's not funny," Evie said, but she was laughing too. "I had . . . I had scratches for days that I thought would . . . would never . . . would never heal!"

And we laughed all the harder as I added lavender bath salts to the water.

Then Evie sobered as I turned off the water and stepped into the warmth of the tub. "Let me ask you a question, Goldie," she

258

said. "Do you think you stood up to Velvet on behalf of Donna out there at the bus stop or do you think you were really thinking about someone else?"

I sat up straight and extended my legs to immersion. "What do you mean?"

"Like Charlene Hopefield, for instance."

I wiggled my toes, and the burnt orange polish on my toenails winked at me as the scent of lavender reached my nostrils. "You are a wise woman, Evangeline Benson," I said. "A very wise woman."

Jack opened the door to our home before I even had a chance to knock. As soon as I took three steps over the threshold he took me in his arms and held me for a moment.

And I allowed it, nearly oblivious to the sack of food—and the news I had for him—pressed between us.

"Welcome," he said when he'd finally released me and taken a step back.

"Thank you," I said. I looked down. "I think we've crushed our dinner."

"Who needs food?" he asked, then reached for me again.

This time I took a step back and said, "But we have to talk, Jack."

He showed his disappointment. "Can't we talk later?"

I shook my head and pulled away, knowing I had to keep my wits about me. "No. We really have to talk."

I walked around him and into the kitchen with him following on my heels. "Do you want to try to salvage that?" he asked, pointing to the wrapped and crumbled food I placed on the table.

"Not right now, no." I pulled out a chair and sat down, and Jack did the same, sitting directly across from me.

"So, let's talk," he said.

I took a deep breath and sighed. "We need to talk about Charlene Hopefield."

Jack dipped his head, and it came back up again. "Oh, for crying out loud, Goldie. I haven't seen that woman other than at school since I don't know when. Since right before you found out."

259

I reached over and took one of his hands in mine. "Which was how long ago?"

He looked down at our hands as I wove my fingers with his, then back up at me. "Months."

"How many months, Jack?"

"I don't know. Since . . . what . . . September? October? I didn't exactly keep a calendar. That's not the kind of thing a man does."

"So at least three or four months?"

"If you say so."

I thought for a moment. "It seems like it's been longer than that."

Jack gave me a look and said, "Tell me about it." He winked.

"I need for you to be serious here."

"Sorry," he said, then shifted a bit in his chair. "So, what's this about? You want to talk about Charlene? We'll talk about Charlene. She was pushy and brazen and was like a woman obsessed where I was concerned. Honest to Pete, Goldie, and I'm coming clean here. I've had affairs, yes. And you've known that."

I pulled my hand away, but he caught it and returned it to his.

"You've known that," he repeated as he continued. "But never with anyone you might . . . might run into."

"How gracious of you."

"Don't do that, now," he said, squeezing my hand. "If we're going to get through this, you can't be snide."

He was right about that. "Sorry."

"But here she came, wearing her low-cut outfits and sexy perfumes—"

I raised my free hand. "Don't say it, Jack. Please. I can only take so much."

"Now I'm sorry," he said, and I felt the pressure from his hand relax a bit.

I took another deep breath and nodded. "Charlene Hopefield can be malicious and underhanded when she wants to be," I said.

"You have no idea," Jack said, I'm sure without thinking.

I swallowed. "No, *you* have no idea."

He looked at me for a long moment. "What are you talking about, Goldie? What's your point? Charlene Hopefield was but a moment in my life. But you *are* my life. It's over with Charlene, and I swear to you before God that I will never, ever break our marriage vows again. If you'll just move back home and let me be your husband again, I'm sure I can prove to you that I've changed, Goldie." He honestly looked pitiful. "I have."

"But it's *not* over, Jack," I said, barely above a whisper.

"Now, wait a minute." This time he pulled his hand away from mine. "Yes, it is. Yes, ma'am, it is."

I clasped my hands together. "No. No, Jack. Charlene Hopefield is pregnant."

I stared into my husband's eyes and watched them grow wide. "She's what?" he said as though he didn't believe a word of what he'd just heard.

"She told me the night before we went up to Summit Ridge."

Jack stood, walked a few steps away, then turned back to me. "She told you she was pregnant?"

"Yes."

He placed his hands on his hips. "And that's why you acted the way you did the day we went up to the cabin?"

"I admit that, yes."

He walked back over to the table, placed his palms flat on its surface, and leaned toward me. "I got my cell phone bill, by the way."

I shifted a bit but said nothing.

"Japan? Japan, Goldie? I hope you know I had to take money out of our savings to cover it."

"I was angry," I said. "I was angry with you that you had gotten Charlene Hopefield pregnant and that we'd never be able to fully put this behind us."

Jack stood straight again. "And coming to me and just telling me never occurred to you?"

I smiled wryly. "I wanted you to suffer first."

He nodded. "Mmmm," he said, then crossed his arms and spread his legs wide in that "coach" stand I'd come to know over the years.

261

"Are you just going to stare at me or are we going to talk about how we're going to deal with Charlene and her baby?" I asked.

He didn't move. Not even a muscle. "I have no intention of dealing with her or her baby," he said, keeping his eyes on me.

"But, Jack!"

Then he returned to his seat. He leaned over a bit, taking both my hands in his. "Goldie, Charlene Hopefield took eight weeks off from teaching last year. Do you want to know why?"

I'm sure I looked puzzled. "She needed a long vacation?" I asked.

"No. She was getting a full-blown hysterectomy."

I felt my jaw drop. "A full-blown—"

"Charlene Hopefield is no more pregnant than you are." He raised his brow. "Unless there's something about you that I don't know."

I closed my eyes against the absurdity of it all. "Why that little . . ." I began, opening my eyes again. Jack was grinning at me, and I began to laugh and cry all at the same time. "I ought to call Japan on her phone," I said, pulling my hands from his and wiping the tears from my cheeks.

"Mmm-hmm," he said, pursing his lips together. He folded his arms across his chest again and leaned back in his chair as though God was in his heaven and all was right with the world.

I crossed my legs and leaned back in my chair, keeping my focus on my husband and his adorable face. "Jack," I said finally.

"Goldie," he toyed.

"Why don't you go look in the backseat of my car?" I asked, keeping my words to more of a suggestion than a question.

He nodded toward the crumpled bag from Higher Grounds. "Did you bring more food?" he asked.

I gave him a half smile. "No," I answered, shameless. "I brought an overnight bag."

Jack leaned toward me. "Well, now. You don't say?"

I kept my eyes on his before answering, "I will agree to come home but on certain conditions."

"Which are?"

"I'll stay in Olivia's old room. We keep going to counseling and . . . we talk. No more secrets. None."

He stared at me for another long moment before leaning over the table and extending his right hand. I took it in mine, and we shook on it. "Deal," he said.

"Deal," I said. Then I added, "It won't be easy."

"Nothing worth having ever is."

He stood then and gave me a quick wink before walking away. I heard the front door open and close. My cue, I thought.

I pushed myself away from the table, then stood and walked purposefully toward Olivia's old bedroom.

I had come home.

39

Going Home

Somehow—though he wasn't exactly sure how—Britney had talked Clay into joining her and her family for a weekly Bible study they held in their home.

"I don't know," Clay had stalled, standing on the other side of the card shop counter from her earlier in the day. "Bible study . . ."

But then Britney smiled her radiant smile, and he felt his knees go weak. "I promise you not many people are there," she told him. "So if you think you might be put on the spot in front of a bunch of folks . . ."

Clay nodded his head. "So, like, who will be there? Is it the same people every week? You don't handle snakes or anything, do you?"

Britney laughed at his humor, endearing her to him all the more. "No, nothing like that, but if you want, maybe we can fly some in from . . . where? Alabama or somewhere like that?"

Clay crossed his arms over his chest. "Okay, so give me a roll call."

"I'm there, of course. Mom and Dad. My brother and Michelle Prattle." Britney grinned and wiggled her shoulders a bit. "Don't tell," she said in a near whisper, "but I think Adam is going to . . . you know . . . pop the question pretty soon."

"Really? To Michelle?"

"No, to Velvet James. Of course to Michelle!" She wiggled her shoulders again like a child in front of a toy store window. "Isn't that awesome?"

Clay agreed it was. "Okay, so who else?"

Britney had run down a list of about four more names, pouted, then smiled, and he had acquiesced.

Hours later, he was leaving his first honest-to-goodness "home group." Britney's father had led a study and discussion on Genesis 31. Jacob leaving the "world" behind and "going home." Something stirred inside him . . . something strangely familiar and unfamiliar at the same time. Something he'd felt years ago while sitting in Vonnie's Sunday school class. What was it?

On his way home he drove down the street where the Dippels lived. Way past dark, he noted, and Goldie's car was parked in the driveway.

Her car was in the driveway, and all the house lights were out.

It looked, Clay surmised, as if Mrs. D. had gone home too. He slowed his Jeep until it came to a stop at the stop sign. Though no traffic was heading his way, he remained where he was. And he wondered what it would be like to have someone to go home to . . .

Donna

DONNA'S EASY BISCUITS

2 C. SIFTED FLOUR   1 TSP. SUGAR
4 TSP. BAKING POWDER   1/4 C. SHORTENING
1 TSP. SALT   1 C. MILK

SIFT DRY INGREDIENTS TOGETHER THEN
MAKE A WELL (OR HOLE) IN THE CENTER
PLACE SHORTENING AND MILK INTO THE
WELL. MIX WITH WOODEN SPOON UNTIL
                                - BACK -

40

On the Lunch Menu

When had Clay taken this picture? I wondered as I sipped my first cup of joe with a copy of yesterday's *Gold Rush News* spread before me. There I was on the front page in an article entitled "Hero of Summit View."

I was backdropped by the majestic mountains and dressed in my uniform, with my arms folded across my chest. It looked as though I was contemplating the future as the wind blew through my curls.

Clay. He was always snapping photos, but this one looked like it was from the *Mayberry RFD Gazette*. All it lacked was an American flag and Andy Taylor's grin.

The subheading read "Local Hero Saves Summit View Couple." Goldie and Jack were pictured in a small photo below mine. The article went on to describe how I'd rescued Tina Long and risked my life to save her baby.

Another article authored by Clay was on the front page of the living section. It featured a picture of Lisa Leann with her Christmas tree tea table, along with a story about the Christmas tea. The article had even contained a write-up about the shenanigans of my mother and sister. I don't know how Clay had done it, but I'd come out smelling like a rose.

Then there was Clay's editorial on the second page of the paper. It told about the civil lawsuit I was facing. Clay had even managed to dig up the one witness to the tragedy, a Mr. Leonard Davidson, who was pictured leaning against his Jeep. He was quoted as saying, "I served in 'Nam, and I can tell you that officer's actions were the bravest I've ever seen. Not only did she single-handedly rescue that mom, but she then risked her life to save the baby. That officer deserves a medal, not a lawsuit."

I looked back at the paper. Normally, I detested reading about myself, but now, fighting the legal battle of my life, the articles were a godsend, perfectly timed with my hour of need.

The phone rang. I picked it up.

"Hello, Donna?"

"Vonnie!" I looked at the white kitchen clock that hung above my refrigerator. It was 8:30. "I don't normally hear from you so early in the a.m."

"I knew you'd be up, getting ready for your deposition. And I wanted to see if you saw yesterday's paper."

I wiped a few crumbs from my honey-coated biscuits off the article I'd been reading. "Yeah, I was just looking at it."

Vonnie proudly read, "Donna Vesey, who teamed with snow-mobile expert Wade Gage, was the first officer on the scene of the massive snowslide to help rescue a local couple, Jack and Goldie Dippel. From the safety of her Summit View home, Goldie Dippel later said, 'If it weren't for Donna, Jack and I would still be snowed in at Summit Ridge. Donna risked her life to save ours.'"

I felt a blush burn beneath my coating of makeup that Lisa Leann had shown me how to apply just the day before. I took another sip of my coffee and told Vonnie, "Clay's been a pal to write this. Maybe it will even help, but I'm not holding my breath."

"What I don't get," Vonnie said, "is you saved that woman's life and in the process almost lost your own. I mean, it's very sad about her losing her baby, but you weren't the one who drove her car off the road and into the river. You did everything possible to help."

"God knows I tried." I looked at the clock again. "Oh, it's getting late, and I still have to figure out how to apply Lisa Leann's mascara without poking my eye out."

"Oh dear, how did your makeover go?" Vonnie asked.

"Fine, as long as I don't mind my new industrial strength glow," I said.

Vonnie giggled. "Before you go, I wanted you to know that the whole family prayed for you this morning: Fred, Mom, me, and David."

"That's sweet," I said.

"David says you two are doing lunch today. I think he has a surprise for you."

"Really? Did he get that job with the Summit View paramedics?"

"I'm not spoiling his good news. Call me later, okay?"

We'd said our good-byes, and I soon found myself standing in front of my bathroom mirror trying to wipe a mascara smudge off my cheek with my finger. This makeup stuff was harder than it looked. Of course, it would help if my palms weren't so sweaty and my hands weren't trembling. I took a deep breath. I didn't know how I'd make it through this day.

I stood back and tried to look at the makeup's effect. Not as good as Lisa Leann's job, but passable.

I looked at my watch then grabbed my jacket and hurried to the Bronco.

As I drove toward my attorney's office I decided it felt pretty good to know that Vonnie and her family were praying for me. Not that I deserved it. I still wasn't on speaking terms with God, though I sat in church when I wasn't sleeping off a night shift. I'd been surprised to see Wade there lately too, sitting right next to me as David sat between Vonnie and me.

"We all need a higher power, meaning God," Wade had told me one night as he'd gone on another ride-along with me. "At least, that's what I've been learning in AA."

"How's that going for you?" I'd asked.

"Been sober for several weeks now, though I don't think I could have made it if Pastor Moore hadn't helped me."

"He's not your sponsor, is he?"

Wade shook his head. "Nice try. But you know I can't talk about that stuff, Donna. I can tell you that Moore has been counseling me, first down at the café and now at his office. Moore's shown me that the power of God is a very real thing."

"So you're putting it on God and not just a higher power, huh?" I asked, thinking on the language of what was probably the most famous twelve-step program out there.

"You should try it sometime," Wade answered.

I gave him a look, and he smiled at me.

"Yeah, well . . ."

Wade gave me a sideways glance and grinned. "They say alcoholism is a disease, but as Pastor Kevin says, with God's help, people can change."

I only nodded. I hadn't known a lot of recovered alcoholics, but maybe Wade could recover. At least I hoped so. There were so many things I could forgive him for, but I wasn't sure I could forgive him for being a drunk. And even though he'd spent these last few weeks sober, his wasted years still stood between us.

I found a parking space near the card shop. I still had a few minutes before I had to go in, so I sat in the cab of my truck, trying to build up my nerve. I watched a dark green SUV pull into a spot near mine. A small dark-haired woman climbed out of the passenger's side. It was the Long woman, Tina, and her tall but thin husband, Errol. They were early.

She saw my sheriff's Bronco and shot me a cross look as Errol scowled. Their faces told me their motivation for the lawsuit. Apparently it had been easier for them to deal with their grief by blaming me. Now, three years later, they were ready to make me pay.

I shook my head. How could I follow that angry couple up the stairs? How could I face their wrath, their loss, a loss I understood more than anyone realized?

I closed my eyes. *God, I can't go in there. I can't.* I took a deep breath. *If you're really there, please help me.*

It was ironic, me praying to God. We hadn't been on speaking terms in years. It wasn't that I didn't believe in him; it was just I didn't think he believed in me.

Do you care about me? I asked. *Because if you do, I need to know. If I believed you loved me, I think it would make a difference; it would give me a reason to trust in you.*

I sighed. What a dumb prayer. I checked my makeup in my rear-view mirror then got out of my truck, feeling heavy with dread.

It was time to face the past.

As I stood at the top of the stairs, I hesitated, knowing that when I pushed open the office door, my life would never be the same.

When I reached for the doorknob, the door swung open, and there was Goldie. She silently greeted me with a hug then ushered me inside, past the angry eyes in the waiting room, and into the conference room where a court reporter, as well as Chris and his friend, Van Lauer, shuffled through papers and conferred in low voices.

Goldie, who looked most professional—and different some-how—in her smart red business suit, settled me into a gray leather chair at a large mahogany table before disappearing to return with a steaming cup of coffee. "Black. Just the way you like it," she said with a smile.

Van, who I'd learned in recent days was the attorney who'd been hired as a legal consultant to represent the interests of the Boulder County Sheriff's department, turned to me. He was handsome with his gray hair combed back from his tanned face. "Now, Donna, as you know, in a few moments the other legal team, as well as the Longs, will be invited in. Their attorney will have a chance to ask you a lot of questions about the details of the accident and rescue. A lot of the questions will be routine, but some of them will be rather pointed and meant to trip you up. But even so, don't forget this is a fact-finding mission. Though the other side hopes they can trip up your testimony so they either settle out of court or contradict your testimony at trial. But try not to worry. We have truth on our side. Just don't allow your sorrow over the death of the baby to lead you into any kind of false confessions of guilt. Okay?"

I nodded as Chris stood up. He wore a dark blue suit and maroon tie and reeked of hometown charm tinged with sophistication. He walked over to where I sat then bent down to give me a hug of encouragement. "It's going to be okay, Donna."

I nodded.

"Did I tell you we'll have a special assistant in the room today?" He motioned to Goldie, who said, "I'm in charge of filling the water pitcher, refilling the coffee cups, and praying for you," she said.

I smiled weakly.

Too soon the Longs and their legal counsel faced us at the conference table. After a lot of preliminary questions about who I was, how long I'd been a sheriff's deputy, and the details of my career and marital status, as well as the date, time, and circumstances of the accident, Mr. Lauer said to me, "Donna, in your own words"—he gave a stern look at the balding Long attorney, a Mr. Anderson—"tell us what happened on the night of March the 15th, three years ago."

I'd admired the effect his glare had on Mr. Anderson, who suddenly seemed subdued. *So, that's why they pay Lauer the big bucks—his commanding presence.*

Time passed as I relived the horror of being flagged down by Leonard Davidson during a torrential rainstorm. That's when I discovered a sedan beneath the flooded canyon river, a river yawning past its banks.

I described how Leonard had helped me tie myself to a nearby pine tree with a long piece of rope I kept in the back of my Bronco. I explained how I'd braved the frigid waters, alone; how I'd pulled Tina Long from the hood of the car; how she'd grabbed me, pulling the both of us beneath the debris-filled current and how I'd fought to turn her around so I could safely pull through the wild current, using the rescuer's hold. I told how I'd managed to pull her to the bank only to have her tell me that her baby was still in the car.

The faces in the room were replaced by the drama as it swam before me. I quietly told of going back into the floodwaters; of becoming trapped beneath the water when the roof of the car had lodged against my foot; of finally breaking free to the surface for a breath. I told how I pulled myself down to the window of the car by the door handle, then entered the car, freeing the baby from her car seat.

The tears came as I told how I'd been struck by the log as I neared the safety of the bank and described the moment when I'd realized little Bailey Ann had been ripped from my grasp.

I could hear the soft sounds of weeping, and I realized the sounds came from both Tina Long and from me.

I took a sip of water and tried to recover my composure.

After a few more clarifying questions about my testimony from Chris, it was Mr. Anderson's turn to cross-examine me. "You didn't have a proper grip on the baby, did you?"

"Proper grip?"

"You let go of Bailey Ann Long, and that is in fact why she drowned. Correct?"

"Let go? Well, I . . ."

"You've already admitted to letting go in your earlier testimony. Now for the sake of clarification, tell us again. You let go of the baby, correct?"

"I did, but—"

"So in other words, the baby was not secured? You had not secured the baby with a rope or tie or other means of restraint. Correct?"

"Well, yes, but—"

"So, because of your actions, you failed to bring the baby to safety. Is that correct? Please answer yes or no."

I felt my face burn. "Failed? Yes, I . . ."

"Then, Deputy, let me get this straight. Are you agreeing that it was your actions or failure to act that led to baby Bailey Ann Long's death?"

I looked up, and my eyes met Tina's brown ones. She looked absolutely stricken. I answered steadily, "I've replayed the scene, in my mind, time and time again . . ."

The Long attorney spoke as if rebuking me. "I'm sure you have. Deputy, you've already admitted to letting go of the baby, you've admitted to failing to secure the baby to yourself. So, you're saying

274

it was your negligence that cause baby Bailey Ann's death? Is that correct?"

"No. I did everything possible to save her."

"Did you? But you let go, you failed to secure the child. Let's stop playing games. You and your actions caused the drowning death of Bailey Ann Long. Correct?"

My eyes held Tina's. "I would have done anything to save your baby."

Anderson interrupted. "But you didn't save her, did you? I need a yes or a no."

"Well, no. But Tina, I would have traded my life for the life of your daughter, if it had been possible."

Before Anderson could strike back, my spirit warmed and flooded with peace as a still small voice whispered to my soul, *"That, my child, is what I did for you. My son exchanged his life for yours."*

I was so startled I sat speechless.

Anderson barked, "Deputy, by your answers we could summarize that it was in fact your negligence that led to baby Bailey Ann Long's death. Am I correct? We're still waiting for your answer."

I blinked, in awe of the sweet presence I felt.

"Answer the question, Deputy."

Before I could regain my composure, there was a commotion across the table from me as Tina shook her head then whispered to her husband. Errol signaled their attorney, who leaned into a hushed conversation between the three of them.

Their attorney looked up and said to Chris and Mr. Lauer, "My clients have requested a short break from these proceedings. Let's say we reconvene in about twenty minutes."

Mr. Lauer stood, looking as if he had received some sort of secret signal. "Take all the time you need," he said.

Chris stood too. "We'll step out of the conference room and let you confer together."

Mr. Anderson nodded.

Once Chris, Mr. Lauer, and I were in the safety of Chris's office, I asked, "What's going on?"

275

Chris smiled then stretched. "I'm not making any promises, but Tina's interference with the proceedings could be a good sign."

Mr. Lauer nodded in agreement and flashed me a winning smile. "Let's not get our hopes up, but this could be a promising develop-ment."

Goldie, who'd stayed behind in the conference room to refill coffee cups, rushed through the office door, looking like she'd just discovered the legendary bandit gold, rumored to still be hidden in these parts.

"Did you overhear anything?" Chris asked her.

"I certainly did," she said. "As I was walking out the door, Mrs. Long was pleading with her attorney to stop the proceedings. Don-na's emotional testimony about her valiant rescue attempt really shook her up."

I felt my mouth drop open. "Then all this could be over?"

Van winked at me. "Depends on how greedy and persuasive their attorney is. But let's remain hopeful."

Goldie rushed at me with a box of tissues. "For heaven's sake!" she cried. "Why didn't Lisa Leann sell you a tube of *waterproof* mascara? You look like a panda!"

Chris laughed. "Better take this opportunity to freshen up," he told me.

I scurried out of the office and into the bathroom. There on the sink was a copy of Clay's "Local Hero" article perched in a prominent place on the counter, no doubt for Tina to see. It was a certainty that she had. *That Goldie.* I grinned at my mottled reflection in the mirror, suddenly feeling loved, not just by Goldie, but by . . . by God himself.

For the first time since the early days of my childhood I felt God's presence. It was as if he was wrapping me in a glow of love from the inside out. In the depths of my heart, I quietly whispered to him, *Lord, I do believe. I believe in you, in the work of your son dying for my sins. I trust you with my life, regardless of what happens next.*

When I walked back into the waiting room, the Longs' attorney was saying his good-bye to Chris and Mr. Lauer. As Tina passed me, her eyes held mine for an instant, as if she was releasing some deep anguish from her inner being. Then she and Errol were gone.

My attorneys and I waited until we heard Goldie lead the group down the stairs. It was only when they were safely out of hearing distance that Chris let out a whoop. "You did it, Donna! It was the power of your testimony that sent them running."

Mr. Lauer gave me a hug. "It's over; go home and celebrate."

When Goldie returned she encircled me in her arms. "Girl, you're finally free of this nightmare. Oh, I can't wait till you tell the pot-luckers! This is an answer to prayer!"

My eyes flooded, and I could feel what was left of my mascara melt down my cheeks. I couldn't help but laugh. "It was Lisa Leann's makeup that did it. How could they war against someone who looked as pitiful as me?"

Goldie pulled back from yet another hug and watched me wipe another streak across my face with the back of my hand. "Oh dear, you are a mess" was all she could say, laughing and crying at the same time.

It was only twenty or so minutes later when I slid into one of the corner tables at Apple's with David. By now, most of my makeup had been wiped off.

"You look like you've been through the wringer," David said.

"You can say that again," I agreed. "But the news is good. The Longs have dropped their lawsuit against me."

"That's great!"

He reached for my hand. "I have some news too."

"You got the paramedic job?"

David grinned. "Sure did. Now all I need is a place to live. I can't stay with Vonnie forever."

"Then you're going to put an offer on Swan Villa?"

"I've got some time to decide yet, but I'm thinking about getting a month-to-month lease on a condo Mrs. Whittman showed me last week."

A young man with a goggle tan from his recent skiing adventures placed glasses of ice water in front of us then handed us our menus. "Your server will be here shortly to take your order," he told us.

David nodded. As I scanned the selections, he said, "This is a great day for us."

There was something about the way he said "us" that made me look up. "What do you mean?"

"I mean, we've spent most of our Sundays at Vonnie's and, well, we've connected. Am I right? You feel the same thing, right?"

"David . . ."

"Let me finish." He reached for my hand again. "I don't want this time we've had to end."

"But why should it? I mean, we'll always have Vonnie, and—"

"I want more." His voice dropped to a whisper. "I want you."

I pulled my hand away. "But . . ."

David dropped to one knee beside my chair. "This may be a little premature . . ."

"David, don't you dare."

I stood up—to do what, I wasn't sure. A moment later I realized my hand was resting on my holster. Surely I wasn't thinking to shoot the man. Though from the lovesick look on his face it might put him out of his misery.

I sat down again. "David, stop it. Get back in your chair. Now!"

I don't know if it was my commanding voice or the fact that I'd been ready to draw my weapon, but he obliged as the sound of the conversations around us hushed, robbing us of any pretense of privacy. I looked up to see all eyes on us. Leave it to me to make a scene. I fumed as I lowered my voice. "What are you thinking, David?"

The conversations, though softer, started again as the people in the restaurant continued to glance in our direction.

David looked stunned, then hesitant. "The future."

"But we can't have a future unless we have a past."

He almost whispered, "You mean like you have with Wade?"

I scooted my chair away from the table. "What do you know about that?" I said, my voice unsteady.

"I'm sorry. That didn't come out right."

278

"Then why bring it up?"

"It's just . . . I know we don't have a history, but I'd like to make one. You'd said we could take things slow."

"What does *slow* mean to you? To pop the question on our first official lunch date?"

"Okay, I'll give you that. That was stupid. But, I want you to know that I'm hoping the two of us will—"

"Don't, David. My emotions are too raw, too worn to know anything but this: if you ever try that kneeling stunt again I'll make sure the safety is off my gun."

He blinked once, then twice. "Whatever you say, Deputy."

The waiter, a tall man in his twenties, interrupted us. He looked both amused and alarmed, which made me wonder how much he'd heard. *Wait. Was that one of those tiny digital cameras hidden in his hand?*

He said, "Have you had a chance to look over the menu?"

I shut mine. "I don't think I want anything," I said as I stood up to leave. "Sorry, David, but I can't stay. Catch you later, okay?"

He nodded, and without another word, I was out the door and scurrying down the sidewalk. I'd go to Vonnie's house, but that's where David was sure to head. So I climbed into the Bronco and headed for home. Maybe I'd call the girls later and give them a report about the lawsuit and thank them for their prayers. And maybe they'd hear my voice and realize how desperately I still needed them. David's speech had moved me, but to what? Insanity?

I needed time to process not just what happened today, but all that had happened in recent days. And David? He needed to understand I wasn't like the members of Harmony's fan club. He couldn't drop on one knee and expect me to swoon. Poor man. I mean, he was sweet. Had been sweet. But now, at least, he knew whom he was dealing with.

I shook my head. I may have a better understanding of both God and his Son, but that didn't seem to change the fact that I was still a crazy woman with a gun.

41

As He Sat Typing

Clay had just finished what he now knew novelists referred to as a "plotline," a timetable, really, that graphed out the dates of incidents and scenes the writer intended to include in his or her work. This one began with the very first potluck meeting between Evangeline Benson and Ruth Ann McDonald and ended in the present with Evangeline becoming a bride on her long-awaited wedding day.

Of course, he'd changed the names and places. He had five members rather than six; a tropical beachfront setting rather than the mountains. The women were younger in the opening chapters, older in the closing ones. He'd combined some of their stories, changed a few genders of folks along the way. But, for the most part, the six women of the Potluck Club had inspired him to a work he was sure he'd been born to write.

He was a fan of Faulkner—a big fan—and especially loved *As I Lay Dying*, so he thought he'd write the novel with Faulkner's style: multiple viewpoints and rich descriptions. He opened five blank documents on his laptop, labeled each one with a different name—first, middle, and last—and then began working on a list of character descriptions and traits. He was halfway through the second one when his phone rang. Woodward and Bernstein scampered a bit in their cage, and he eyed them first, then the phone, vacillating between answering and continuing in his work. The work won, and the phone stopped ringing.

But no sooner had he begun to peck out the words than the phone rang once more. This time he answered it.

"Clay Whitefield," he said, momentarily forgetting he was at home.

"Clay?" A man's voice came from the other end.

"Yes." Clay struggled to recognize the caller.

"It's Brad, man. Brad Sumser."

"Hey, what's up?"

There was a chuckle before an answer. "How fast can you get down to Apple's?"

Clay raised a brow. "About a minute or two. What's going on down there?"

Brad chuckled. "I'm standing behind the bar, right?"

"Okay."

"And Donna and Mr. Hollywood are over in the corner having lunch, right?"

Clay felt himself pink. "Yeah?"

"Well, you might want to get down here for this, my friend. Our Miss Deputy just got herself proposed to!"

Clay heard a swell of laughter in the background. At least he thought it was. There was every possibility his ears were merely ringing.

"Clay?"

Clay took in a deep breath, then let it out. "What does this have to do with me?"

"You don't want to miss this," Brad said. "And I gotta go. Sheriff Vernon Vesey just walked in. Man! And I was gonna call in sick today!"

Evangeline

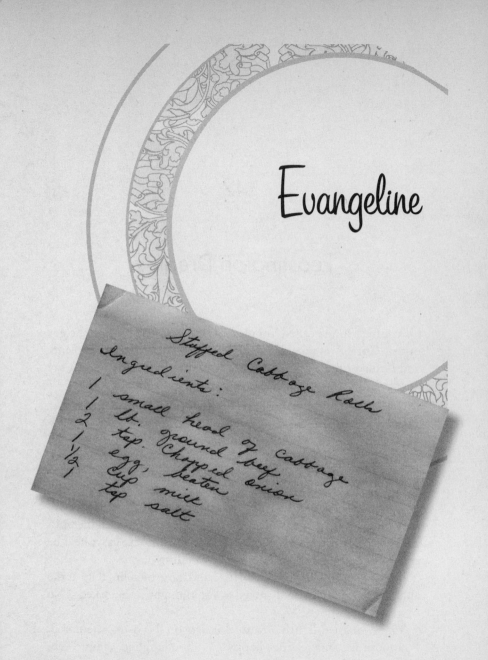

Stuffed Cabbage Rolls

Ingredients:

1 small head of cabbage
1 lb. ground beef
2 tsp. chopped onion
1 egg, beaten
½ cup milk
1 tsp. salt

42

Feasting on Dreams

Of course, Donna called Vonnie first, the absolute minute she got out of Chris Lowe's office, I'm certain. Vonnie then called me, and I called Lizzie. Goldie already knew but by ethics couldn't say anything, so she called no one and no one called her.

It was a morning for phone calls, that much was for sure.

When Vonnie called me, I told her I'd call Lizzie and Lisa Leann. I had business with both of them, after all, and I might as well kill two birds with one stone, as the old cliché goes.

I called Lizzie first, knowing my call with Lisa Leann would last the longest. Lizzie was at work. She sounded tired, and I said so.

"I am tired," she replied. "But the good news is that Samuel will soon be heading back to work. The doctor and the physical therapist are very pleased with his progress. And you can rest easy; he'll be able to stand next to Vernon on your wedding day."

"That does sound good. So many handsome men lined up at the altar of Grace Church." I smiled at the thought, then asked, "No more judging shows?"

Lizzie laughed lightly. "Samuel insists on TiVo-ing them still. I suppose if it makes him happy . . ." She laughed again. "Oh, Evangeline. I've been such a bear."

"I'm sure you haven't."

"Oh, believe me. I have. But Tim and Samantha are doing so much better—thanks to their counseling sessions—and Samantha has a job now. They're hoping to sell the house in Louisiana, and as soon as they do, they'll start to look here."

I took the cordless phone into the family room and curled up on the sofa. "I don't mean to put my two cents into business that's not my own—"

"Since when?" Lizzie threw in.

"Ha-ha," I said with a feigned frown. "Anyway, they might want to look into something that's called a bridge loan. I'm surprised Samuel doesn't know about it."

"Real estate isn't his forte."

"Several of my clients have it. It allows you to buy one house while you're selling another. Tell Tim to look into it."

"Evie, you're a dream. I'll do it tonight." She paused for a moment. "Have we heard anything from Donna yet? Have you gotten a call from Vernon?"

"Not Vernon. Vonnie. And the lawsuit was dropped."

"Dropped? You're kidding! Just like that?"

"Just like that," I repeated. "I'm sure we'll hear all about it at the next meeting. You'll be here, won't you?"

"Of course. I'm bringing stuffed cabbage rolls."

I licked my lips in anticipation. "Oh, I do dearly love it when you bring that dish."

Lizzie laughed again. "Do you need for me to call anyone? To give them the praise report on Donna?"

"No," I said. "I've only got to call Lisa Leann, and I need to talk to her anyway."

We hung up, and I called Lisa Leann, giving her the news straight up. She said her glory hallelujahs, and then we talked about the wedding plans, about fittings, the shower, and everything else in between. I felt myself getting all goose-bumpy and excited. Before we hung up she said, "Oh, Evie. One more thing. I just want you to know how very upset I am about what happened at the tea. And I do apologize. Again."

"Think nothing of it," I said to her. "What's done is done. You had no way of knowing who Dee Dee McGurk is."

"Well, that much is true, but still . . ."

"Still nothing. You're one of the girls now."

Lisa Leann was quiet before she said, "I appreciate that more than you can know, Evangeline."

I felt warm and tingly inside. It was a good feeling, but one that wouldn't last long. My husband-to-be would soon be arriving, I noted, checking my watch, and he and I had one final issue left to talk about. One big final issue.

Vernon arrived an hour or so later looking flustered beyond words. I thought perhaps he'd heard that I'd decided most definitely on the style tux I wanted him and his men to wear and hoped against hope I was wrong.

I was wrong.

He kissed me at the door and then took me by the hand and said, "You won't believe what just happened." He led me into the kitchen, where he opened the refrigerator door and took out a bottle of water. I heard the cracking of the top as it was being opened and watched as Vernon took a hearty chug. When he was breathing again he said, "David Harris just proposed to my daughter."

My mouth fell open. I said not one single word. Far be it from me to say anything at a time like this.

"Are you just going to stare at me or are you going to say something?" he asked before taking another, slower sip of water.

"Donna?"

Vernon jerked his head back a bit. "Well, of course Donna. What other daughter do I have?"

Velvet, I thought. I hadn't been able to tell him about Velvet as of yet. This was the big issue we needed to discuss, and I thought this was as good an opening as any. "Vernon, do you think Velvet James could be your daughter?" I asked, just blurting it right out.

Vernon had the water bottle halfway to his mouth, and he stopped. He didn't lower it or raise it; he just kept it right there in place. "Say that again?"

"Do you think Velvet James could be your daughter?" I asked again.

"No." He took another sip.

I took a step toward him. "Vernon, think about it . . ."

"I don't have to think about it, Evangeline. There's no way she's my daughter."

"But how can you be so sure?"

He finished the water and set the empty bottle on the kitchen counter. "Because I've already put her name in with NCIC. She wasn't born until two years after Doreen left."

I crossed my arms over my middle. "That Doreen." I shook my head lightly.

Vernon laughed at me. "What? Did she tell you that? That Velvet was mine?" He pointed to his chest.

I nodded, blushing to beat the band, I'm sure. "That stinker." I held up a hand, then let it drop. "Though I have to admit, she didn't really tell me. She just hinted at it. I guess I had that coming."

"When did you talk to her?"

I fanned my hand at the air. "It's not worth talking about, Vernon. It's just Doreen trying to get my goat."

Vernon stepped toward me and wrapped me in his strong arms. I felt him kiss the side of my head. "Well, don't let her do that again, you hear me?"

I nodded in agreement.

"Pretty soon," he continued, "you and I will be husband and wife. You and me, Evie-girl, after all these years."

I leaned back, supported by his arms. "After all these years," I whispered.

And then he kissed me again.

"But what about Donna?" I asked when we broke for air. "Did she say yes?"

Vernon shook his head. "That girl of mine flew past me so fast she was no more than a blur. All I heard was 'I don't want to talk about it,' and she was gone. Harris was left standing there looking a bit embarrassed."

"Where were they?"

"Apple's."

"Apple's? He proposed in Apple's in the middle of a Friday afternoon?"

Vernon kissed the tip of my nose. "He did. Can you imagine?"

I hugged Vernon tight. "And they say Hollywood is romantic."

I called my sister Peggy, who lives on the East Coast, later that evening so we could talk about the wedding, her and her family's arrival for it, and just about anything else. It was reminiscent of so many, many years ago when she and I had burrowed under the thick comforter of her bed, plotting and planning *her* wedding.

"Do you remember the night before your wedding?" I asked now. "When we cuddled together in your bed and spoke of the wonders of love and marriage?"

"Oh, I certainly do, Evangeline."

"Do you remember telling me that my Prince Charming would come soon enough?" I said. I was propped up in my bed. As I said the words, I slid to my back, turned off the bedside lamp, and then turned on my side, facing the other pillow. I drew it sideways and pretended it was Peggy and that she was lying beside me, as I had laid beside her all those years ago.

Peggy laughed from the other end. "It sure took him long enough," she said.

"But I'm glad I waited for Vernon," I said. "I'm glad I did."

"I know you are." Her voice was warm in the moonlight's glow that bathed my room in a shimmering gray. "I'm just thanking God you're marrying Vernon and not that Bob Barnett you were engaged to for all of five minutes a month or so ago."

"Oh, please. Let's not go there." I was quick to change the subject. "Leigh and Gary are still coming, aren't they?" I asked, speaking of my niece and her husband.

"Yes. With the baby, of course. They said they'd fly in on Saturday and stay at one of the inns in town. Matthew and I will arrive on Wednesday, and the boys will fly in with Leigh and Gary. We're getting the boys a room at the inn too."

I hadn't seen my nephews in years, but I knew they were hardly boys. "Any special loves in their lives?"

Peggy sighed deeply. "They say not. They're more interested in getting their individual medical degrees, and then they'll talk about settling down."

"Doctors, just like their father," I said, sleepy but proud.

"So tell me about your dress, your bridesmaids, and all that fun stuff."

"I feel bad that you aren't going to be one of my attendants, Margaret," I said.

I filled her in on all the details followed by, "Matthew ready to give me away?" I teased.

Peggy giggled. "Matthew said he was more than happy to give you away—and I quote—'at long last.'"

I closed my eyes. "That stinker."

"What about you and Vernon? What are your honeymoon plans?"

I blushed, I just know I did. "Vernon won't tell. He says to think tropical and pack for warm weather."

"Sounds like heaven."

"I can hardly wait," I said and wiggled a bit, thinking of palm trees and coconut-flavored drinks.

"And how about your maids?" Peggy asked, bringing me back to Colorado and the chill.

"Donna has finally acquiesced to be the maid of honor, Vonnie the matron of honor."

"How nice."

"Lizzie and Goldie will be bridesmaids, and Lisa Leann is our wedding coordinator. When you're here, remind me to sit down over a cup of coffee and tell you all about Lisa Leann and her plans for this wedding. She's having so much fun I can hardly say no to anything she comes up with."

"Like what?"

"Like everything!" I yawned. "I'm so tired, Peg. I'm going to sleep now."

"You do that, Evangeline, and I'll call you tomorrow. We have a lot to talk about."

I smiled. "Mmmm. Yes, we do," I said, then hung up the phone and fell right to sleep.

Sometime during the night, I dreamed of white lace and satin, tulle and taffeta, of bridesmaids in georgette dresses a shade Lisa Leann called "rose petal" but which I called "a pretty pink." I watched blissfully as Donna and Vonnie stepped in rhythm to "The Bridal March" before me, both draped in flowing dresses in "azalea." Through tear-filled eyes I saw Vernon, dressed so handsome in what Lisa Leann had described as an Oleg Cassini three-button peak tuxedo. Next to him were his groomsmen.

I stepped down the aisle, my arm linked with Matthew's. He whispered something endearing in my ear, and I giggled like a bride of twenty.

Then, a movement from the left of the church—the bride's side. I turned my gaze from my bridegroom to the distraction, and in my dream I saw myself as though I were having some sort of out-of-body experience.

I first frowned, then began to wail as Doreen Vesey stood up and began to laugh. She laughed and laughed and laughed that echoing kind of laugh you hear so often in old movies. And when she was done laughing, the man beside her laughed as well. I shifted my attention from her to him. It was Bob Barnett, my ex-fiancé. The man I'd almost married over Vernon.

My dream had become a nightmare.

I awoke with a start.

43

Wonder Where . . .
Wonder Who . . .

Early on Sunday morning—a little more than a week after Donna's victory and subsequent marriage proposal—Clay sat alone in his usual spot at Higher Grounds and nursed a hot cup of coffee.

When he'd come in at such an early hour, Sally had commented on the time. "You're here practically before Larry," she said. "Certainly before anyone else. What's got you out of bed so early?" Then she eyed him. "And dressed so smart?"

Clay had blushed. "I'm going to church," he said.

"With Britney?" Sally asked.

Clay merely nodded.

Now he sat sipping coffee and staring across the street to where Lisa Leann's bridal shop was located. Just looking at it gave a man a lot to think about. He wondered where Donna was . . . what she was thinking about . . . why he hadn't seen much of her lately.

It was then that Velvet James walked in, looking more like her sister than she ever had before. As she pulled herself out of her coat, she looked over at him, the lone patron of the restaurant.

"Yeah, it's me. Velvet," she said, as though to quell any question as to identity.

"I know," he said. She was wearing skintight, hot pink jeans and an even tighter matching sweater.

She joined him without invitation, called out to Sally, "Hot tea, please," then laid her forearms on the table and leaned in. "So, what do you think of my sister's marriage proposal?"

"I try not to think of it at all," he said and set his coffee cup on the table with a little too much force.

She smiled a half smile. "Touchy subject?"

"Donna is really none of your never-mind," he answered.

Velvet sat back in her chair, crossing her legs as she did so. "Really? She is my sister, after all."

Clay picked up the coffee mug and took a long sip. "Only because you share the same mother." He stood and set the mug down again. "And the way I see it, that's not much to share."

Lisa Leann

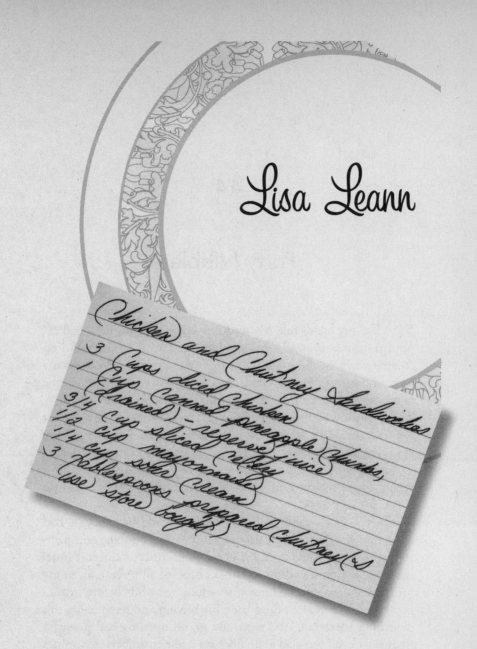

Chicken and Chutney Sandwiches

3 cups diced chicken
1 cup canned pineapple chunks,
(drained) - reserve juice
3/4 cup sliced celery
1/2 cup mayonnaise
1/4 cup sour cream
3 tablespoons prepared chutney (or
use store bought)

44

Party Nibbles

My, I had my hands full. My wedding consulting business had exploded since *Hollywood Nightly* had featured my shop as a backdrop to their newscast about Vonnie's son. It was a smart move to get my web address on camera. I still don't know why Henry pulled me away from my once-in-a-lifetime public service announcement.

"What do you think you're doing?" he'd asked me once he got me back inside my shop. How strange he looked. Though it was a cold day, beads of sweat were popping out all over his forehead.

I put my hands on my hips and gave it to him straight. "Just trying to get a return on some of this money we've poured into this place."

My TV spot—though shorter than it could have been—had done the trick. Since my national debut, I was booking and planning weddings down at the church, in exclusive ski resort hotel conference rooms, and on top of ski lifts (of all places), all to my little heart's content. I'd known it would be awhile before I could pay Henry's retirement fund back for buying and remodeling this charming Victorian. And since my grand opening had proved a financial bust, I was glad to finally have a few customers. Yes, things were looking up.

The only thing missing in this one-horse town was a good catering service. As it was now, I was one-stop shopping all by myself, including the food for today's bridal shower for Evangeline.

So, early this morning, after waving to my husband, who was headed out for a ski day, I'd kissed my very pregnant daughter goodbye, then hightailed it down to my bridal boutique and my state-of-the art, commercial-grade, stainless steel kitchen.

A little ditty played in my head as I arranged stuffed mushrooms and Irish and French cheeses onto silver platters.

Something old.

Something new.

Someone to wed in Summit View.

A girl could put something like that to music and upload it into an mp3 file on her website. I'd have to call Nelson. He'd know how to make it happen.

I laughed as I opened the door to one of my two double refrigerators and reached for a tray of my chicken and chutney sandwiches.

"Looking good, girlfriend," I said to myself as I admired my handiwork. Today, the girls were in for a treat as they were going to get a sample of the wedding fare at our "multipurpose" shower, makeover, and bridal gown fitting.

I heard the door of my bridal boutique jingle. "I'm back in the kitchen," I called out.

Just as I'd hoped, it was Vonnie. She was dressed in one of her best appliquéd sweatshirts, featuring a bluebird on a picket fence. She'd coupled it with a pair of black slacks. I handed her one of my pink aprons embroidered with "Lisa Leann's High Country Weddings" in white thread, just like the one I was wearing. Dora at Sew and Stitch had whipped them up for me on one of her prized embroidery machines.

Vonnie slipped the apron over her head and surveyed my trays. "Wow, this is some spread."

"Remind me to give you the recipe for these stuffed mushrooms before you leave," I said.

"Is there anything else I can do to help you get ready for Evangeline's big day?"

295

I looked up at her. "You mean besides stuffing mushrooms and keeping the bride happy? How's that going, by the way?"

Vonnie giggled then helped me set the trays around the sitting room of my boutique, which sparkled in marble countertops and oak woodwork. "You know Evie; it's one crisis after the other with her." She put a tray of sandwiches on my marble-topped coffee table then looked up. "Did you know I make a mean potato salad?"

"Really! We'll have to talk about that," I said as the door jingled again. I peeked out to see Goldie and Lizzie making their entrance. Through my romantically chiffon-draped front window, I could see Evangeline scurrying toward my front door. I rushed out the back of the kitchen then up the back staircase as I told Vonnie, "Could you greet everyone? I'll be down in just a sec."

Once upstairs, I slipped into the floor-length bridesmaid's dress I'd ordered for me. It was a chic satin number in rose petal pink with a golden blush, Evie's favorite color. It was shockingly strapless and bare shouldered, a design that was all the rage in wedding wear. I'd been lucky to get five, one for me and for each of the Potluck bridesmaids.

I stepped back and looked in the mirror. I looked stunning in this $4,000 Vera Wang knockoff. Who would ever know, except the girls who'd have to pay for them, that I'd gotten them for the rock-bottom bargain price of $165 apiece?

I hovered at the top of the staircase that wound down into my sitting room, where all but Donna had gathered. I waited till the women were done hugging and congratulating Evangeline, then I slowly began to glide down the stairs.

"My lands!" Goldie exclaimed. "Lisa Leann, what is that you're wearing?"

I batted my eyes appropriately. "You like? You have one just like it upstairs in the dressing room, to try on later."

Gasps filled the room. Vonnie said, "Are all the dresses so . . . so bare? I'd hate to think of the whole town watching my arms jiggle."

I smiled and stopped midway on the staircase. "I totally understand your concern, Vonnie. That's why . . ." I slipped into the matching shrug jacket that looked as though it were a satin wrap

Party Nibbles

gathered at the breast with a gold and rhinestone pin. "See how the jacket just kisses the shoulders but hides the upper arms?"

"And extra cleavage," Goldie said as though relieved.

"I'm too thin to have to worry about that," I said breezily as I finished my descent.

Evangeline looked, I don't know, speechless at my performance, though I'm sure it was in admiration of my ability to steal the show. But what was I thinking? This was her show. One I had to get on the road if we were to get everything done before five o'clock.

"Where's Donna?" I asked no one in particular.

"She'll be here in a bit," Vonnie answered. "She said to go ahead and start."

I turned to Vonnie and lowered my voice. "How is she doing?"

Vonnie shook her head. "I'm not sure."

Lizzie stepped forward about that time and threw in, "Has she given any indication as to—"

Before she could finish her sentence, Vonnie raised a hand to shush her and said, "No. Nothing. Not a word. David is just as mum."

I crossed my arms, no easy feat in the dress, and said, "Lizzie, speaking of how-do-you-do . . . how are you?"

Lizzie coughed out a laugh and said, "Stressed." Then she smiled cheerily. "But this too shall pass, no?" Without waiting for me to give her my best advice, she turned to Goldie. "This woman, my friends, is a fine specimen of God answering prayers." She pinched Goldie's cheek, and Goldie turned the most lovely shade of pink. "Look at that face," Lizzie teased, sounding more like she was talking to a baby than a grown woman who'd just gotten back with her husband.

"Life is good," Goldie said. "I'm still working for Chris, of course. I told Jack I wasn't going back to being a housewife, no way, no how, and he said it was fine with him as long as I gave him another chance."

"A chance to get you back in bed, but then the marriage bed can be a wonderful thing," I announced with all the authority of a woman who had been married long enough to know, at which point Evie said, "Oh my sweet Aunt Bessie."

297

I honestly thought the girl was going to faint right there in the center of my shop. It would most certainly ruin my party, so I caught her by the elbow and ushered her to the sofa. "Here you go, Evie. It's time to eat, then you can open your presents!"

I waved my arm like Vanna White toward the small table topped with white and silver gifts in sparkling silver ribbons before walking to the counter where I'd placed my crystal tray plates and punch bowl. I topped a plate with nuts, mints, stuffed mushrooms, and my chicken and chutney finger sandwiches. I poured a cup of my red velvet punch into a crystal cup and picked up a white napkin that proclaimed in silver script "Vernon and Evangeline" along with their January wedding date.

I brought the plate to Evie, then returned to fill the awaiting crystal cups with punch.

"Really, this is lovely," Lizzie said as she sat down with her feast in one of the Victorian chairs I had pulled out of my shop's nooks so as to help the girls encircle Evie.

It didn't take long to polish off the finger foods, and soon Evie sat opening her presents as we Potluck women ooohed and aaahed. She looked like a queen, with us, her loyal subjects, gathered around. She was dressed very fashionably in a rich raspberry kimono jacket, done in a swirling burned-out velvet pattern. She repeated the color in a matching scooped-neck shirt and pant. She was radiant, especially as she'd applied a hint of blush. Just think, in a few minutes, I'd lead her to my vanity and show her how to enhance what she'd already started.

But for now, I was curious to see what the girls had thought to give her, seeing that she and Vernon already had two of everything.

Much to my delight, Evie unwrapped scented body soaps and lotions, gift certificates for local furniture boutiques and knickknack shops, as well as restaurant certificates for date nights, and there was even a certificate for a wonderful overnight stay, for two, at a Vail resort and spa.

But my favorite gift was one that I'd selected and wrapped myself. A scandalous, sheer baby doll in black with hidden snaps, of course.

Watching her blush the shade of her outfit was a lovely payoff.

Just as we women were lost in peals of laughter, the door jingled open, revealing poor little Donna dressed in her old black sweats. Her face was pale, and she looked as though she hadn't slept for days. I jumped up to greet her. "Donna, welcome to the party. Here, let me help you get a plate of food."

I busied myself while she took a seat and added a present to the diminishing gift pile.

Vonnie turned to her. "Are you okay, dear?"

I turned back in time to see Donna's face blanch even paler. She shook her head. "Not really."

"I would have thought you'd still be celebrating your victory," Goldie said.

Donna nodded then shrugged. "You'd think."

"Is this about David's proposal at Apple's?" I asked, wanting to get to the heart of the matter. "So, the rumors have been flying. Are you engaged or not?"

"Not."

It was Goldie who first found her voice. "Well, good for you. I mean, you hardly know the man."

Vonnie said, "Well, they have been spending a lot of time playing cards with my mother."

We all looked back at Donna, who continued to look miserable. I said, "How do you feel about David?"

Donna buried her face in her hands. "I don't know. I wasn't expecting a proposal," she said. "One of the reasons I agreed to have lunch with him was to find out if he'd been dating my sister."

Vonnie gasped. "Oh dear!"

"Had he?" I demanded.

"I don't think so, though I saw them sitting together at Higher Grounds yesterday morning."

I put my hand to my heart. "Then he hasn't called you?"

"You could say I haven't been available," she said.

Vonnie said, "I've missed you at the house."

"I know. Honestly, I don't know what to do about that. Though I'm glad to know he's moving into his own place soon."

"Back to this proposal," Lizzie said. "What happened exactly?"

"One minute, David and I were making light conversation, and the next he was on one knee asking me to marry him, in front of everyone. I was stunned, until I saw the cameras come out. That place was filled with paparazzi."

I felt the hair on the back of my neck stand on end. "The paparazzi are here in Summit View?"

"You bet they are," Lizzie said. "They probably got wind that he'd made a major jewelry purchase from one of the Hollywood jewelers."

Donna sounded surprised. "He had a ring?"

"Didn't he show you?"

She shook her head.

Lizzie continued, "At least according to this article. It's pictured on the second page of the story." She opened her leather purse that doubled as a satchel and pulled out a copy of *Entertainment Everyday*, a slick gossip magazine. "This came into the library yesterday. I'm surprised none of you saw it."

And there it was, in living color. A cover shot of David kneeling before Donna as she stood with her hand on her holster. "Deputy Shoots Down Hollywood Proposal," the caption read.

Donna made a choking sound. "Oh no."

Before I could blink, Donna had darted through the swinging kitchen door.

I turned and looked at Evangeline, who asked in a small voice, "I'm as upset as anyone about Donna's love life, but I have to know, is my bridal shower over?"

Oh dear. This was supposed to be Evangeline's day. "Hang on, girlfriend. Let's all take a break. Everyone, why don't you help yourself to a slice of my daffodil cake?"

I rushed after Donna and found her crying at the back door of the kitchen.

I pulled her into my arms. "Sweetie, it's going to be okay. It is."

The swinging kitchen door banged open, and Evangeline stormed through. "Begging your pardon," she told me, "but Donna is my

300

future stepdaughter. Thank you for trying to help, but this is my responsibility."

She replaced my nearly bare arms with her own raspberry-clad ones as she held the sobbing girl. "There, there," she said. "Tell me all about it."

I popped on an apron then pretended to busy myself in the kitchen.

The two pulled up kitchen stools, and Donna spoke in hushed tones, revealing the confusion of her heart. As she talked and as Evie listened, it was like rays of love, straight from heaven, parted the storm clouds to shine down on those two. This had to be the first heart-to-heart these two women had ever experienced. And it was happening right here in my little wedding shop. I tried not to break into song.

As I walked by the pair on the way to the refrigerator, I discreetly handed Donna a tissue. She wiped her eyes and continued what she was saying. "I guess I haven't returned David's phone calls because I don't know *what* I feel for him. I really don't."

Evangeline patted her arm. "Then there's someone else? Someone like Wade?"

I stole a peek and saw Donna with that deer caught in the head-lights look. "Why would you ask about Wade?"

"We all know you two have a past. So, is it true? You still feel something for Wade?"

Donna bit her lip. "I can't say."

"Can't say or won't?"

Donna shook her head. "It's complicated. I . . . I just don't know."

Evangeline took Donna's hands and held them in her own. "Let me give you a piece of advice. I've loved your father since I was twelve. It was hard when he married another woman. Then Doreen left him. I had opportunities with him, time and time again, but I'd always let foolish things like hurt from the past as well as my own stupid pride stand between us. As I look back on all those wasted years, I realize my mistake. Donna, if you're like me, then you know in your heart whom you love. Don't do what I did. Face

301

it. Don't let that love slip through your fingers. Who's to say you'll ever get a second chance?"

I'd slowly been creeping toward the private conversation as I wiped down my stainless steel countertops, so I'd be available if they needed me to put in my two cents. I saw my chance to speak up and took it. "Well, Donna, I hope it's not Clay who's in your heart. He'd asked me to play matchmaker for him and get the two of you together, but my makeover attracted more than flies to that honey. Thanks to my help, he's dating that Britney girl. I'm so sorry about that, sweetie."

Donna looked hard at me and then smiled. "Don't worry, Lisa Leann, I don't have a history with Clay other than friendship."

I smiled to myself, knowing I'd been given a big hint as to the nature of Donna's heart.

I walked to the kitchen door, then hesitated. "Well, girls, it's time to try on the bridesmaids dresses, when you're ready, that is."

When I walked out to the girls gathered in my sitting room, they all looked more than a little worried.

"It won't be long now," I said. "And here's the good news. These past few minutes have been a time of intense healing between two soon-to-be family members." I grinned and gestured widely. "Things are looking up for those two."

Vonnie finally said the words that were bursting in my heart. "Well, glory hallelujah!"

45

Ice Castles

Clay was party to the ploy, the great plan of proposal between Adam and Michelle.

Britney had roped him in, or so she thought. What he knew that she didn't was that there were more surprises in this evening than just the one designed for Michelle.

The plan was as follows: the four of them were set to double date. They'd have dinner at Apple's, then head over to Ice Castles, an indoor skating rink. Once there, they'd do a little skating, then take off their skates and go into the café for cappuccinos and cheesecake. After the late-night treat, Clay and Britney would excuse themselves, both saying they had to use the restroom, and head out to the Jeep to retrieve Clay's camera equipment. They'd sneak back inside and hide in a corner booth—perfect for Britney getting video footage and Clay snapping still shots. Adam would then retrieve their skates, slipping the ring into one of Michelle's skates. As soon as she slipped her foot in, she would know something wasn't quite right. A little dip of the fingertips and . . .

"Adam has been practicing signing 'Will you marry me' for days," Britney whispered to Clay from the horseshoe-shaped booth where they waited patiently.

Clay had only nodded.

Mere moments later, they watched as Adam gave the signal to start the video. "There's my cue," Britney half-squealed, half-whispered.

"Why are you whispering?" Clay teased her.

"So she won't hear me," she answered, then blushed. "Oh." Her tone returned to normal. "Oh yeah." Then she frowned. "Very funny, Mr. Whitefield."

The proposal went as planned, with Michelle leaping up and down, patrons applauding, and Clay and Britney recording the moment. They both giggled as Adam signed, "I asked your father first," and Michelle burst into tears.

When there was nothing left to photograph or film, Clay nudged Britney and asked, "Can you get that little lens case out of my bag for me?" He indicated his camera bag lying near her feet.

"Oh. Oh, sure," she said, bending over to retrieve the case.

Clay pretended to fiddle with his camera as he said, "Get the lens in there for me, okay? I need to change this one out."

With a sideward glance he watched as she unscrewed the top of the case, then gasped at what was inside. Nestled in deep blue velvet was an antique ring of diamonds and sapphires set high on ornate platinum.

"Oh my gosh," Britney breathed out, reaching for the ring with trembling fingers.

Clay set his camera aside and draped the arm nearest her along the back of the booth's padded seat. With his other hand, he took the ring from her. "It was my grandmother's," he said softly. "And her grandmother's before her."

Britney looked up at him with shimmering eyes. "It was?"

He nodded. "Forty diamonds, twenty sapphires." He chuckled a bit. "I could never afford anything like this on my salary, and it may be the most extravagant thing you get from me, but . . ." He swallowed hard. "If you will . . . will marry me, Britney . . . I promise to be the best husband you could ask for."

She didn't answer right away. A few tears slipped from her eyes and cascaded down her cheeks. "We've hardly known each other—"

He shushed her. "I know. But how much time does a man need to know he's in love before he decides to marry the girl of his dreams?"

"You love me?" she choked out.

"With all my heart," he said. "And you?"

"I love you too." Then she smiled at him and extended her left ring finger. "And the answer is yes."

Evangeline

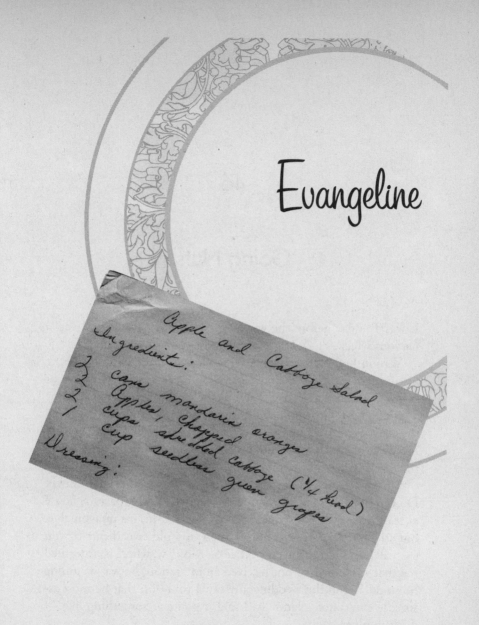

Apple and Cabbage Salad

Ingredients:

2   cans mandarin oranges
2   apples, chopped
2   cups shredded cabbage (1/4 head)
1   cup seedless green grapes

Dressing:

46

Going Nuts

It was Tuesday before the wedding. With just days to go I was a nervous wreck.

Vernon had pretty much steered clear of me, saying he'd have his dinners for the remainder of the week at Higher Grounds or Apple's. Alone. I can't say that I blame him much. I had become a bit of a bear. Growling about this. Snarling about that. Showing my claws every time I passed a calendar. It was a good thing Vernon loved me as much as he did, otherwise I'd be a lonely bride come the last Saturday of the month.

Of course, the characters of Summit View didn't help much. Doreen Roberts and her daughter Velvet had to drive past my house at least once a day—with me living where I do, it's unavoidable, but still—and I ran into Bob Barnett, my old sweetheart (if you can call him that) at the post office on Monday, where he informed me that while he had not received an invitation, he was assuming he could attend the wedding anyway. I told him that he most assuredly could not. Naturally, I said it politely. Something like, "I don't think so, Bob."

To which he replied, "Well, I don't see why not. After all, we've been friends for nearly sixty years."

"Thank you kindly, Mr. Barnett, for reminding me of my age."

I immediately went home and called Vonnie. "What am I thinking? Marrying a man at nearly sixty! What in the world am I thinking?"

Vonnie giggled in that little-girl way she laughs and said, "So what, Evie? If you both died at eighty, that would be twenty years together. Do you know how many couples would be thrilled to make it to twenty years?"

She had a point. "You're right. You're absolutely right."

"Do you know what I think?" she asked without waiting for an answer. "I think you've got a bad case of cold feet. That's what I think."

I decided to change the subject. "So what's new with David?" The whole David-Donna issue was too strange for me, but it was a fact of life in Summit View.

Vonnie was quiet for a moment before she answered. "He's been . . . sullen."

"Sullen?"

"Gloomy. Depressed."

"Ah. Do you think he really loves her? I mean, really?"

Again, Vonnie was quiet. Then she answered, "I have to be honest, Evangeline, and say I'm not sure. Maybe he's in love with her. Maybe he's in love with the idea of her. Donna is a fine young woman. She's spunky. She's got her own career going. She's brainy and gutsy and—"

"And possibly in love with someone else."

"Do you have any idea who?"

I smiled. "Don't you?"

"I have some thoughts on the subject. What about Vernon? Has he talked with her?"

I shook my head as though she could see me, then said, "He hasn't said. Vernon doesn't talk a lot about things like that."

"I see."

I decided to change the subject again. "Peggy will be here tomorrow," I said. "She and Matthew."

309

"Oh, how fun! How fun! I can't wait to see her again. What a blessing for you, Evie. To have your sister here."

I couldn't agree more.

The following day my anxiety had given way to something akin to a nervous breakdown. As soon as Peggy and Matthew arrived and all hugs and kisses were exchanged and the luggage put away, I said quite frankly, "I really need a prescription or I'm going to fret myself to death."

Matthew just smiled in what I'm sure he calls a part of his bedside manner, but I wasn't kidding. "You want me to write you a prescription for some Prozac, Evangeline?" he asked, though I wasn't sure if he was serious.

I plopped in one of the Victorian chairs in my living room. It was nearly noon, and I hadn't even run a comb through my hair. "Do you think it will help?" I asked.

Matthew merely walked over and patted me on the hand. "I was only teasing you. What I think you need is to take a few deep breaths and try to enjoy the moment. You'll only pass through these doors once, you know." He stood erect, looked at his wife, and said, "I'm going to go lie down." Then he bobbed his head, said, "Ladies," and walked out of the living room.

Peggy watched him go, then grinned at me. "I see I got here just in time. You look absolutely awful." She took a seat in a nearby chair, crossed her legs, and leaned toward me.

"You don't," I said. "You look wonderful."

She ran her fingers through her silver hair, cut short enough to be a man's, and said, "I'm sure I look a fright. What with traveling since the light of day."

"No. You look marvelous. You really do. I like your hair like that, by the way."

"My friends say it's chic."

I stared at her for a few minutes and drank her in. Peggy and I don't look a thing alike. Never have. She was always more stylish and . . . almost handsome. She should have been a model. Tall, thin, large blue eyes, and a natural rose to her complexion that girls of sixteen would give anything for. Of course, being married to a doctor didn't hurt. She'd spend days lounging around the pool or hitting a fuzzy yellow ball at their country club's tennis courts. She had a maid and a cook. She went once a week for manicures and pedicures and to get her hair trimmed. There wasn't a month that went by that she wasn't at a day spa somewhere.

I finally nodded at her. "It is."

The next thing I knew she was leaping out of her chair, grabbing me by the hands, and yanking me out of my chair. With a quick glance at her watch she said, "Oh, gosh! Look at the time. Come on, sister dear. Have I got plans for us!"

Peggy's plans had obviously been made long before she arrived. After she dragged me upstairs and practically dressed me herself, she pushed me outside to where her rental car—a BMW, naturally—was waiting. "Hop in," she said, rounding the car toward the driver's side. "This thing has got heated seats so we'll have warm fannies in no time." She laughed lightly as I slid into the car. She pulled out of my driveway and then zoomed through the streets, pointing out first one thing she'd forgotten about and then another. "My goodness. Is Higher Grounds still in business?" she asked.

"Where are you taking me?" I asked her.

"Oh, you'll see."

Fifteen minutes later, Peggy and I arrived in Breckenridge, where she'd previously scheduled appointments at a day spa. We spent the next several hours being pampered beyond my wildest imaginings.

The spa itself was really quite something. Hardwood floors polished to a shine, muted colored walls, lots of plants, therapeutic music, and scented candles filled the rooms. We were ushered from the entrance down a wide hallway and then to the back, where large tubs filled with hot water and sea minerals awaited us. After a half-hour soak, we were massaged with fragrant scrubs, followed by oils. Then we had facials and hot stone therapy until I do believe my brain became bubble gum. Following all that, we had pedicures, then manicures (both with paraffin treatments). As though that were not enough, Peggy had made an appointment for me with a man named Jacques, who ran his fingers through my hair, pulling at it from root to tip, and then studied my face and declared, "You really deserve something more modish, like your sister. Look at those cheeks! That bone structure! I'm going to give you the look of Dame Judi Dench!"

Hours later—having been shampooed and my hair razor cut and highlighted—I hardly recognized the woman in the mirror. Peggy stood behind me, expressing over and over, "It's you, it's you, it's so absolutely you!"

"This is the easiest style in the world," Jacques said.

I sincerely hoped so.

A makeup expert came in and tried to sell me on all sorts of cosmetics, but I knew that Lisa Leann would have my hide if I dared buy any other products than the ones I'd already purchased from her.

When all was said and done, it was after eight o'clock in the evening and I was famished. Absolutely stunning to behold, but famished.

"Not to worry," Peggy said. "Matthew is meeting us shortly at Wasabi's. We have reservations."

I'm sure I looked stunned. "How is he getting here," I asked, "seeing as we have your car?"

She grinned at me. "Vernon is bringing him."

I had been missing Vernon very much. Still . . . "Oh, Peggy," I said, running my fingers along the base of my very short hairline. "I don't know if I want him to see me just yet."

She draped her arm around my shoulder and led me toward the exit door. "You look marvelous, you smell divine, and you know you want to see him."

I smiled at her. "I have so missed having you here. I don't think I realized how much until today."

She squeezed me. "I've missed you too."

The following morning I was more than certain I wanted to call the whole thing off. Twice I picked up the phone to call Lisa Leann— to tell her to stop baking the cake and to put the floral arrangements on ice (or whatever they do). Twice, Peggy took the phone out of my hand and said, "You just calm down, Evangeline."

Matthew sat in my father's old chair in the living room and read a book he couldn't seem to get his nose out of. Occasionally he would look up at us and chuckle.

"You're a fine specimen of brotherly help," I said to him once, but he replied only with a wink.

Thursday afternoon Vernon called and asked if he could take the four of us to dinner. "After all, Matthew paid for that rather extravagant meal last night."

He was right about that. It was expensive. It was also delicious, and I ate entirely too much. "No," I said. "For one thing, I think we should stay apart for the next few days. It will make the wedding day all the more special."

"Not to mention the wedding night," he teased.

I broke out in a sweat, handed the phone over to Peggy, who was standing nearby, and then collapsed onto the sofa.

"Vernon?" I heard Peggy say through a tunnel. "Vernon, no . . . no, no. She's fine." Then she giggled, and I decided that I would kill her just as soon as she got off the phone. "She's just a bit nervous."

"I'll give you nervous," I said weakly from beside her. Minutes later I was moaning, "Oh, Peggy. I can't do this, I can't do this, I just can't do this."

Peggy sat down on the sofa beside me. "Yes, you can, Evie." Then she propped her elbows up on her knees. "Evangeline, let me ask you a question."

"What?"

"Is it marriage that makes you nervous or the wedding? Let me rephrase that. Is it marriage that makes you nervous or the wedding *night?*"

I turned three shades of pink. "Well, it's not something I've ever experienced before."

Peggy laughed lightly. "I suppose I should now give you the same speech our mother gave me not five minutes before I walked down the aisle."

313

I cut my eyes over at her as the memory of our mother on Peggy's wedding day washed over me. She'd been so pretty, dressed smartly in a bright yellow satin dress with white lace overlay. She'd worn white gloves and a hat made of yellow and white daisies that encircled her head like a crown, white high-heeled pumps, and a yellow and white large bead necklace and earring set. She'd been nearly as lovely as the bride. I took a deep breath and sighed. "What'd she say to you?" I asked in a whisper.

Peggy leaned back and wrapped her arms around her middle as she gave me Mama's "wedding night" speech. By the time she was done, we were both wiping tears of laughter from our eyes. "Mama sure was something," Peggy ended. "She just had a way with words."

"She obviously loved our father very much."

Peggy nodded. "I have the notion there were things going on you and I wouldn't have ever imagined." Again we laughed. Peggy wrapped my chin in the cup of her hand and squeezed. "Don't worry about the wedding night, Evangeline. I'm sure you'll be just fine."

I nodded.

"Are you going to be alright, then?"

I nodded again.

Peggy squeezed one more time. "Good. Now, you take a nap," she said as she got up. "I'm going to make a cabbage and apple salad to go with our dinner tonight."

I watched as she walked over to the quilt stand, pulled a throw from one of its rungs, and then walked back to where I lay. Draping it over me, she added, "How's that sound?"

"Divine," I said, closing my eyes.

47

Her Good Side

It seemed to Clay that life had taken on a whole new feel in Summit View.

He was certain it had more to do with Sheriff Vesey and Evangeline Benson's upcoming nuptials than anything else, but there was no doubt that a lot of love was in the air. Of course, news had spread about the marriage proposal of Adam to Michelle, followed by the—he was sure—shocking report of his own engagement.

He spent a lot of time hearing "congratulations" and "well done." He relished them all. Yes, he would say to them, he was getting a great girl. No, he'd answer, they hadn't set a date yet.

It had been hard facing Donna, though. She'd come into the newspaper office to drop off some reports just as he was descending the steps leading to the upstairs offices.

"What's this I hear?" she'd asked him, adjusting her gun belt around her tiny waist. "You? Engaged?"

He felt himself go red in the face, then he changed the subject ever so slightly. "What about you? I hear someone had a rock the size of LA presented to her."

She shrugged. "Yeah, well . . . who knows? You don't see a ring on my finger, do you?"

He looked down at her gloved hands. "Not when they're wrapped in thick leather, no."

She followed his eyes and smiled. "Oh, yeah. Well, you won't see a ring. Not right now. I uh . . . I have some thinking to do, and then I'll . . . uh . . ." She turned her head and looked away momentarily. "You're going to the wedding, right?" she asked.

"I'm the photographer," he said, jutting his chest out in mock pride.

Donna reached out and patted him on the arm. "Well, don't take any photos of my bad side," she said, then turned and walked away with a "See ya."

Clay stood still for a moment and watched her leave. When she was clear out of earshot he said, "My friend, you don't have a bad side."

Lisa Leann

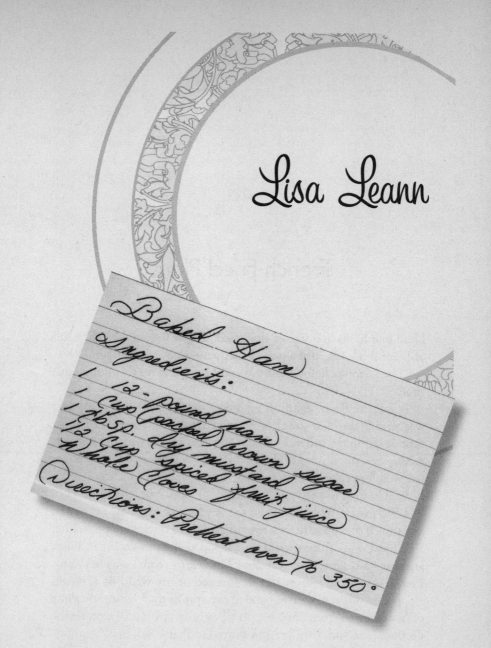

Baked Ham

Ingredients:

1 12-pound ham
1 Cup (packed) brown sugar
1 Tbsp. dry mustard
1/2 Cup spices fruit juice
   Whole cloves

Directions: Preheat oven to 350°

48

French-Fried Plans

I had four hams in my oven that needed to be basted, a kitchen full of helpful friends, and a phone that would not stop ringing.

"Lisa Leann's High Country Weddings," I said for the thousandth time.

It was the florist again. It seemed a delivery van full of flowers was already down at the church, and there was no one there to accept or set up the order. I rolled my eyes as I dealt with yet another crisis. "Yes, my husband Henry is on the way there now to deliver the wedding cake. He's got a diagram of where to put the flowers so he'll be able to help you . . . Yes . . . Thank you."

I laid my portable phone on the counter, then opened the oven and pulled the top wire rack toward me with a thick pink potholder. I grabbed one of my spoons and scooped the brown sugar, juice, and mustard sauce over the top. The warm aroma was heavenly. Lizzie, who would soon also be in need of my wedding services, stepped beside me, wearing one of my aprons over yet another one of her cute velveteen pantsuits in a bright navy blue. "Here, let me do that," she said. I smiled and started to thank her, but the phone rang again and Lizzie knowingly smiled at me.

It was Henry. "Yes, dear, put the cake in the church kitchen . . . Right on top of the cabinet by the sink . . . I'll be down in a few minutes to put out the tablecloths, and we'll move the cake into the reception room then."

I hung up, and Vonnie tapped me on the shoulder. "You've got a delivery out front."

I ran to the sitting room to see the FedEx man. I hoped beyond hope he had Evangeline's veil. The first one I'd ordered had been all wrong for her, what with her stunning new hairdo and all.

I checked the packaging label. "Hooray! I won't have a bare-headed bride after all," I crowed, signing on the driver's electronic form.

With a jingle of the door, he was gone. I sat on the velvet sofa and opened the package. I pulled out a lovely pearl bejeweled comb that would slip into Evangeline's new hairdo like a tiara. Fastened to the comb was a spray of knee-length organza that was edged with tiny seed pearls and rhinestones. Perfect!

The phone rang again, and I ran back toward the kitchen to catch it. This time Donna, who'd been sitting on a stool and peeling hardboiled eggs for Vonnie's potato salad, wiped her hands on a towel and grabbed it for me. Would I ever be able to get her out of those black sweats and into something pretty, like a fashionable pale aqua top? I smiled to myself. In a matter of hours, though, she'd be transformed in her bridesmaid dress in a shade of pink that would pull out her natural beauty.

It was Henry on the phone again. "What do you mean there aren't any daisies in the bridal bouquet?" I squealed. "I promised Evangeline daisies."

I heard another phone ring. This time, the phone belonged to Donna. She unfastened it from her waistband and held it to her ear. "Hello?"

I continued my conversation. "Uh-huh . . . yes."

Donna tapped me on the shoulder. "Lisa Leann?"

"Just a minute," I said, slightly turning my back on her. "Okay, tell the delivery guy he's got to take the bouquet back to his shop. It's got to have daisies mixed with the roses."

Lisa Leann

Donna tapped me on the shoulder, holding up her own cell phone. "I think you'll want to take this. It's an emergency."

I held my phone away from me. "Honey, everything is an emergency on the day of a wedding. Hang on." I finished my call with Henry. "You got that? . . . Good. Gotta run."

I turned to Donna, who was standing looking at me with wide blue eyes. "What's wrong now?" I asked, with only half a smile.

"It's Wade."

"Oh. He's over at the house fixing the leak in my dishwasher. Can't this wait?"

"Ah, I don't think so. He's been trying to call you here at the shop, and when he couldn't reach you, he called me."

I must have looked confused, because Donna held her phone higher and said, "It's Mandy. I think she's in labor."

"My lands!" I snatched Donna's phone. "Wade, is Mandy okay?"

I heard Wade's warm voice. "Now, Lisa Leann, don't panic. But it's a good thing I was here at your place today. Mandy's water broke, and we've got to get her to the hospital. Soon, I'd say."

I froze and looked at the beehive of activity around me. "Oh! Did you call an ambulance?"

"Yes, but there's an hour wait. Seems there was a big car accident down on the interstate, and all available trucks are out there."

"Oh no! An hour's wait?"

Donna stepped closer. "You want me to go pick her up in the Bronco?"

I nodded.

Donna put her hand on my arm. "Meet us at the hospital, okay?"

"Donna's coming," I said into the phone as I watched my friend dive into her leather jacket.

I hung up and returned Donna's phone to her just before she ran out the door.

When I turned around, the Potluck girls, minus Evangeline and of course Donna, had encircled me.

Lizzie said, "We'll pray, of course, but how else can we help?"

320

I handed her a checklist of things to do, the one that I'd hung from my clipboard on a nail on the wall. "Follow this list. Oh, and the hams need to be sliced. They'll be ready in another twenty. Vonnie can finish her potato salad, and then you'll need to deliver all the food to the church. See, I've listed everything I was going to bring, right here. Oh, and make sure the flowers look good. Someone . . . Vonnie . . . needs to deliver the new veil to Evangeline, and the reception hall needs to be set up with the linens and flowers and cake, and the silverware, plates, and napkins, of course."

"Got it," Lizzie said, making a few notes with the pen I kept fastened to the top of the clipboard.

I pulled my apron off over my head and hung it on the pegboard by the back door. I turned to address the group. "It's eleven now, and we have till five this afternoon. Come dressed and ready at four, in case the photographer needs to snap a few poses of you with Evangeline."

"Don't worry about anything; we'll take care of it," Vonnie said. "Did Wade say how far apart Mandy's contractions are?"

"Three to five minutes."

"How long has she been in labor?"

"I don't know. She's two weeks from her due date. She complained of a backache this morning, but she thought it wasn't anything that a hot water bottle couldn't handle."

I slipped into my coat.

"Ever hear of back labor?" Vonnie asked.

I felt a heavy cloak of guilt engulf me. "Oh dear, I was so busy I'd missed that. How could I miss that?"

I had my keys and purse by this time, and Lizzie held open the back door, toward the parking lot where my car was. "Don't worry about that now," she said. "Just go. Mandy needs you. We can keep things running while you're gone."

And run I did, slipping and sliding through last night's inch of snowfall, all the way to my car.

Then it hit me. It was as if a ray of sunshine sliced through the midmorning chill to ignite my soul with joy. "The baby! I'm going to be a grandmother!"

49

All in All a Good Day

As Clay busied himself with the preparations for the wedding later in the evening, Woodward and Bernstein scampered and scraped in their nearby cage.

"You boys had better cut that out before I get married," he said. "My bride may not like all the noise you make. Do you know what that means for you? Tiny little fur rugs for my new house, that's what."

The gerbils stopped and stared at him as though they understood. Just then, his cell phone rang.

"Whitefield."

It was his boss.

"Don't tell me you want me to go out and report on some news story. I'm getting my equipment ready for the Benson-Vesey wedding."

"Well, take a breather. There's been a pretty bad accident out on the highway. Head over to the hospital and see what you can find out."

Clay's shoulders slumped. "Will do. But I'm not staying forever."

"Not asking you to." There was a brief pause. "Oh, and White-field . . ."

"Yes?"

"My friend Mr. Jean called last night. He's seen your proposal. Likes what he sees. He's asked to meet you next week when he comes into town."

Clay felt his shoulders straighten. "Are you serious?"

"As a heart attack. Now get down to the hospital as quickly as you can."

Clay said he would. Yes sir, he surely would.

"Clay Whitefield," he said to the boys. "Novelist."

Donna

EASY OATMEAL CRISPIES

½ CUP BUTTER
½ CUP MARGARINE
½ CUP SUGAR

1 CUP FLOUR
1 ½ CUP QUICK OATS

WITH ELECTRIC MIXER, CREAM BUTTER AND MARGARINE. NEXT, ADD SUGAR, FLOUR AND OATMEAL, ONE AT A TIME, INTO MIXING BOWL AND BLEND. CHILL DOUGH FOR 1 to 3

50

Plum Amazing

I flipped on my siren and took off in the direction of Lisa Leann's condo. As I whipped around the cars that were pulling off the side of the road so I could pass, I called dispatch to inform them of my off-duty adventure. Then I slipped my hand in the brown bag nestled in the front seat and pulled out an oatmeal crispy cookie and popped it into my mouth. It tasted good—crunchy and sweet. The way things were going, this cookie might be the only lunch I'd get.

I turned into the Gold Rush subdivision with its posh condos and pulled in behind Wade's pickup.

I looked up to see him waving from the top of the stairs of one of the units. He was dressed in his denim jeans and work shirt. "Hurry!" he called to me as I ran across the lawn. Wow, I'd never noticed how steep those stairs were until just now. When I reached the top landing I asked, "Where is she?"

Wade, who was looking a bit stressed, pushed his fingers through his blond hair, making it stand out in different directions. "I have her lying on the sofa. But I'm not sure we can move her."

"We're only five minutes away from the hospital. We've got to move her. Unless you want to help me perform a delivery."

Wade paled. "No, I . . . ah . . . seems that, like the rest of the locals, I've got a wedding to attend."

I felt my eyebrows flex as I stared back at him. "That makes two of us."

Wade opened the door, and I could hear Mandy as she cried out. I rushed to find her panting a practiced breathing routine, full of hu hu hus. She was dressed in cute blue maternity pj's covered in dancing white bunnies and pink hearts with the message "Some bunny loves you."

Her head was propped on the armrest of the couch, and it appeared Wade had bolstered her with a few pillows behind her back. I was dismayed to see that her knees were bent and her legs were spread.

Bad sign. "You're not trying to push, are you?" I asked her.

Mandy's splash of tiny freckles popped across her pale face. She looked guilty but didn't answer my question. "It hurts, it hurts," she moaned between her breathing exercises.

"That's normal," I said. "Can you stand up?" I looked over my shoulder. "Wade, help me."

With Mandy's arms around our necks, we managed to get her to the front door, where her knees buckled. "I don't think I can make it down."

"Sure you can," I encouraged. "Just take it one step at a time."

By the time we got her to the bottom, I knew I'd made a mistake. She was just too far along to make it to the hospital. Her arm slipped from our necks, and she crumpled onto her hands and knees onto a carpet of thick snow. She gasped. "It's coming. It's coming!"

I grabbed her by the elbow. "Help me get her into the backseat of my truck," I ordered Wade.

Just as we stretched her out, Mandy started her breathing routine again. "I've got to push, I've got to . . ." she said, instinctively pulling her pajama bottoms down to her ankles. I rushed to check between her thighs. "The baby is crowning." I turned to Wade. "How fast can you run inside to bring me some clean towels and a shower curtain?"

327

Donna

He instantly disappeared up the stairs. "Hold on," I told Mandy. "It's going to be okay."

Moments later, Wade was back with the necessities. I spread the shower curtain beneath Mandy and covered it with a fresh towel. I put on a fresh pair of latex gloves that I kept in my emergency supplies.

The poor girl was in excruciating pain. Her little face was squished, and her eyes were mere slits, and she was coated in sweat.

"Open the door of the Bronco and stand behind her," I told Wade. He did and let her lean against him. I said with as much assurance as I could, "Mandy, it looks like I'm going to deliver your baby. Is there anything I need to know?"

She shook her head, her eyes squeezed tight. Wade pulled her strawberry-blonde bangs out of her eyes. "It's going to be okay," he told her gently as he cradled her. His eyes met mine, and he smiled. "Donna knows what she's doing."

I felt a warm glow from his confidence. I looked back into Mandy's face; her eyes were closed against the pain. "You're not carrying twins, are you?"

She shook her head again then moaned, "I've got to push."

Before I could ask or say anything else, she did.

I put my hands on the baby's head and pushed back to gently control its glide into the world. The last thing I wanted to do was to let it get away from me or drop it. Lisa Leann would kill me, that's for sure.

I gently held the crowning head. Then, there in my hands, was a face, shoulders, an arm that broke free, and a little hand that quivered a wave. Next, the tummy and finally the legs and feet.

I held the squirming baby in my hands. "It's a boy," I cheered, looking up at Mandy.

I caught a glimpse of the expression on Wade's face. He was enraptured. "He's beautiful," he said with awe in his voice.

Mandy tilted her head so she could see him. "My baby," she cried.

"Are you going to cut the cord?" Wade asked.

I shook my head. "No, I'll let the doctor do it. Hand me a couple of those towels."

While he did so, I carefully checked the baby's airways for mucus and was relieved that the passages were clear, as I didn't have a bulb syringe. Then I wiped the baby clean as best I could before wrapping him in another fresh towel. The red-faced infant howled as I handed him to his mother, who cooed to him. The sound of her voice seemed to soothe him, and she held him close.

I watched the happy pair for a moment, then began to clean up the backseat so Wade would have a place to sit.

"We're going to the hospital now. Wade, you ride in the back. Let me know if she delivers the placenta."

"The what?"

"Don't worry, you'll know it if you see it."

Five minutes later, I pulled up next to an ambulance that was parked at the emergency room entrance.

We were met in the parking lot of the hospital by a wild-eyed Lisa Leann. "What took you so long?" she cried.

Instead of answering her, I swung open the back door and said, "Congratulations, Grandma. You've got yourself a little grandson."

Upon seeing her Mandy holding the baby, Lisa Leann screamed, though I couldn't tell if it was from sheer shock or from joy. Probably both. Wade ran inside to get a gurney. The three of us helped Mandy onto it, while Lisa Leann held the baby close to Mandy, seeing as he was still attached to his mother.

"Oh my! Oh my, little one," she crooned. She looked up at me and said, "Oh my."

Wade and I pushed the pair inside, and our entrance generated quite a commotion. Nurses and doctors rushed the mother, child, and grandmother back to the ER.

Suddenly, I felt a bit light-headed and sat down in a waiting room chair. Wade sat beside me.

He flopped his head against the wall. "Wow."

Staring straight ahead, I nodded. "Wow."

He put his hand over mine. "That was mighty good work you did there, Deputy. Do you deliver many babies?"

Something peaceful stirred in my heart at his touch. I slumped back and gave him a sideways look. "My first one," I admitted sheepishly.

Wade nodded then squeezed my hand. "Mine too." He sat silently for a moment. "Seeing that new life come into the world makes me think of all that the two of us have lost."

I nodded, unable to look at him, afraid if I blinked I'd free the tears gathering in my lashes. "I know," I said, squeezing his hand back. "Not a day has gone by that I—"

A door banged open, and I looked up to see David dressed in his new dark blue paramedic's uniform and looking rather handsome as he rushed into the waiting room. He must have come in earlier with the accident victims. Wade leaned over and whispered in my ear, "Here comes your boyfriend," as he stood up and stepped to one side.

David was all smiles. "Donna, Wade. Congratulations on the baby."

Wade and I looked at one other, and we both suppressed a laugh. "Word travels fast," I said.

David grinned. "Especially when it travels by Lisa Leann."

The guys shook hands like old pals. Wade said, "There's a rumor you two might be engaged." He swallowed hard. "So, have you set a date?"

I sat up straight in the chair. "We're not . . ."

David finished for me. "Engaged *yet*. We talked on the phone late into the night and we've decided to take it slow."

David sat down in the chair next to mine and attempted to put his arm around me. I stood and wrapped my arms around myself and said, "I've got a lot of things from my past that I've yet to work out."

I shot a look at Wade, who looked back at me hard. "What would it take for you to say good-bye to your past?" he asked.

My voice dropped to almost a whisper. "Don't know that I want to."

David stood up. "Look, I was born at night, but it wasn't *last* night. Is there something going on between you two? Something I need to know?"

I shrugged. "You yourself said you know that Wade and I have a history," I responded.

David folded his arms. "But your history is in the *distant* past. Right?"

Wade stepped closer. "Donna?"

My breath caught in my chest. "What?"

"Am I?"

"Are you what?" I felt sweat begin to bead across my forehead.

"Just your past?"

I stared at Wade, then David. "Nothing like being put on the spot," I managed to stammer.

Wade dropped his voice. "Donna, you've got to make a choice. Which of us is it going to be?"

My heart began to hammer in my chest and I felt dizzy. I felt the blood rush to my head, and I looked at the spectacle of the two men standing before me. Heat began to rise from my neck and into my cheeks. I lifted my hands as if to keep my cheeks from sliding off my face.

My voice sounded broken. "Don't either of you realize how painful this is for me?" I turned to David. "This is not the place for this conversation. We'll . . . we'll talk later."

I turned to Wade. "And that goes for you too."

With that, I turned on my heels and stalked out of the waiting room into the chilly afternoon.

"Donna, wait!"

I turned and saw Wade running after me.

"Not now, not here," I said, feeling the tip of my nose sting from both emotion and the cold. I opened the door of my Bronco and climbed inside. Before I could slam the door shut, Wade gripped it with his hand.

"Donna? You're my ride, remember?"

"Oh. Oh yeah. Get in; I'll drive you back to your pickup."

I caught a glimpse of David watching from the glassed-in entryway. He stared for a moment, then turned away as Wade climbed into the front seat next to me. I put my key into the ignition.

"Donna, can I . . ."

I hesitated then looked at him.

Wade reached into his back pocket and pulled out a bandana. "Can I . . . I mean, you look like you could use this."

331

I took the bandana then dabbed at my eyes. "Thanks," I said before handing it back.

"Here." He leaned over and wiped my cheek. "You had blood on your cheek . . . from the birth. That's better." He gently wiped it away. "I'm sorry," he finally said, "if I hurt you back there."

I took a deep breath and held on to the steering wheel as I studied it. I shook my head. "Wade, it's not you. So much has happened these past few weeks, my head is spinning. Jan Moore's and the baby's funerals, the lawsuit, my mother coming back practically from the dead, my dad getting married, Vonnie and her birth son, not to mention the paparazzi, and now this baby." My voice dropped to a whisper. "And then there's you."

He sounded almost hopeful. "Me? What did I do?"

I looked at him then. "You surprised me. You got back on your feet, and you . . ."

"Got sober and found the Lord," Wade supplied.

I gave him a little grin. "Yeah, that and . . . well, all this has stirred up a lot of the old feelings and . . ." I looked back at the steering wheel. "I don't know what to do with those feelings, Wade. I don't know if I can trust them or you."

I looked up, then tried to look away again, but the spark in his eyes held me captive. "You're pretty much describing my feelings too." He looked bashful. "It's no secret that I never got over you. But I can't live my life on hold, not anymore. I've got to settle this with you, or I've got to let you go."

My insides went from warm to hot, to cold, and back to warm again.

"I'm afraid of us," I finally said.

Wade nodded. "I'm afraid too." He reached across the console and pulled me toward him, then wrapped me in his arms. I relaxed into his embrace as I inhaled the scent of him, both familiar and comforting.

"But we're not those frightened little high school kids anymore," he murmured. "We're adults. We can figure this out together, one day at a time."

51

Reporter's Eye View

Clay had arrived in the parking lot just in time to see the commotion. First, Donna had stormed out of the ER, Wade on her heels. Then the couple did a little tug of war at the driver's door. When Wade moved to the passenger's side, Clay noted movement from the ER entrance. David Harris turning away.

"What did I just miss?" Clay said out loud, mentally kicking himself for not arriving five minutes earlier.

Later, when the Bronco pulled out of the parking lot, Clay slipped out of his Jeep and sauntered into the building. He looked first to the reception area then to the waiting area, which would have been empty had it not been for the lone figure sitting in the far right corner, his head in his hands, his elbows on his knees.

"Harris," Clay said, approaching.

David looked up.

Clay gave him a wry smile, sat next to him, and patted him hard on the back, the manly equivalent to a woman's hug to another woman in need.

"Ah, my man," he said. "I understand."

"Do you?" David asked.

Clay couldn't help but notice that David's voice quivered just a bit.

Clay nodded. "Yeah. I do." He stood. "Come on. What's say you and I go have a cup of coffee and talk about this? Anything you want to know about the deputy, ol' Wade out there, whatever. I'm your source for information."

David also nodded as he stood. "I could use a friend right about now," he said.

Evangeline

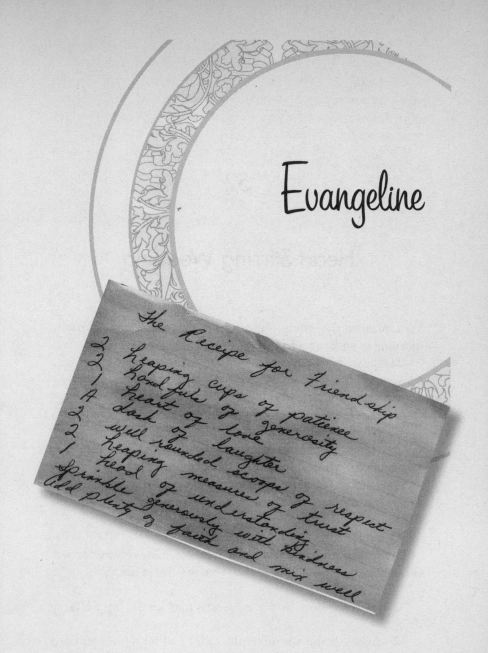

The Recipe for Friendship

2 heaping cups of patience
2 handfuls of generosity
1 heart of love
A dash of laughter
2 well rounded scoops of respect
2 heaping measures of trust
1 head of understanding
   Sprinkle generously with kindness
   Add plenty of faith and mix well

52

Heart-Stirring Wedding

Vernon called first thing—and I do mean first thing—Saturday morning to wish me a happy wedding day.

"Happy wedding day to you too," I mumbled, caught somewhere between sleep and dreams.

"This time tomorrow, you'll be Mrs. Vernon Vesey."

I smiled, my eyes still closed, and stretched under the mounds of covers on my bed. "Long live the queen," I said.

"And king," he reminded me. "Are you packed?"

I nodded. "Mmm-hmm."

"You packed for warm weather, right?"

Peggy and I had spent all day Thursday at the Silverthorne outlets shopping for my honeymoon trousseau. "I did."

"Did you pack a bikini?" he teased.

I pulled the cover over my head. "I did not." The very notion was enough to upset my sensibilities. "Vernon?" I said finally.

"Yes, Mrs. Vesey?"

"I have to go now. Today is, as you may know, my wedding day."

He chuckled, and we ended the call. I had no sooner replaced the phone to its receiver than Peggy bustled into my room, looking radiant for so early in the day. I peeked one eye at her. "Good morning, sister dear," I said.

Peggy waltzed to a nearby window and jerked open the thick chenille drapes. A ray of sunshine, muted by the sheers behind the draperies, shot through the room. "Happy is the bride the sun shines on," she sang.

I pushed myself up in the bed as Matthew came in, dressed in his pj's and a maroon satin robe and carrying a heavy silver tray laden with Mama's silver coffee service and two bone china cups and saucers. "For the bride and her sister," he announced.

Peggy turned from the window. "Put it on the dresser, Matthew."

Matthew was obedient as a butler. I giggled.

Peggy waved him out of the room. "I can handle it from here," she said, then began to pour our coffee.

I smiled at her. "Thank you, Peggy," I said. "You are making this day all the more special."

She presented me with my cup of coffee. "We've got until this afternoon before we have to start getting you dressed and ready. With that new haircut you only have to shampoo and gel." She turned toward the closet, where my gown hung on an outside hook from the top of the door. "Oh, Evangeline. You are going to be the most stunning bride."

I took a sip of my coffee. "I have to admit, I did a good job picking this out." I widened my eyes. "I went out all by myself and bought it. I want it to be a surprise for everyone."

Peggy turned and smiled at me, then walked over to the dresser and prepared her own cup of coffee. "So, what do you want to do as we ready ourselves for this day of days?"

I set my coffee cup and saucer on my bedside table and swung my legs over the side of the bed. "There's something I need to take care of first thing. Then, I suppose . . . relax until time to panic."

Peggy took a sip of her coffee. "What do you need to do?"

I slipped into my terry robe as I shook my head. "I'm going to shower and get dressed now."

337

Peggy was on my heels as I made my way into the bathroom. "What do you need to do?" she repeated.

I stopped and turned to face her. "It's just something I need to do, Peggy." I smiled at her. "Don't fret. I won't be gone long, and I promise I'm not going to see Vernon."

She narrowed her eyes at me but didn't push any further. Peggy was older, but at least she knew when to leave her little sister alone.

I pulled my car into the trailer park behind the Gold Rush Tavern, guiding it toward the trailer I knew belonged to Doreen and her daughter Velvet. I shut off the engine, then exited the car quietly but with an air of assurance that came from who knows where. God above, no doubt.

I knocked on the door and waited for the minute or two it took Doreen to answer the door. It was after ten o'clock, but I'd obviously roused her from her slumber. She was wearing an oversized, long-sleeved T-shirt and a pair of thick socks, and her scraggly hair was pulled back in what at one time might have been a ponytail.

"Good gosh," she growled. A wave of morning breath tinged with ashtray breath met me full force. "Don't you have anything better to do this morning? Aren't you getting married in a few hours?"

I kept my eyes on her bloodshot ones. "May I come in?"

She put one fist on a hip and said, "What for?"

I sighed. "Doreen, it's cold out here. May I come in? Now, the proper thing for you to do is step aside and allow me entrance."

She complied but not without muttering, "Hoity-toity."

I ignored the jab. I stepped into the tiny living room with its secondhand furniture and stained carpet and said, "Is your daughter here?"

Doreen walked over to the bar separating the kitchen from the living room and retrieved a pack of cigarettes and a lighter. "How should I know?" she asked, pulling a cigarette from the pack. "She's a grown woman. We don't keep tabs on each other."

I watched as she lit her cigarette, then glanced over to the sofa. I'd thought to suggest we sit down, then decided against it. I would say what I had to say standing right where I was. "Look, Doreen,"

I began. "I just wanted to come by and say that . . . you and I . . . you and I used to be friends . . ."

Doreen coughed out a laugh. "Oh yeah? When was that?" She drew on her cigarette and blew the smoke upward.

"When we were children. I know that was a long time ago, but . . . what I'm trying to say is . . . I forgive you, Doreen."

Doreen stared at me for a full minute before saying, "You forgive me? You *forgive* me?"

I raised my chin. "Yes, I do."

"For what?"

I pressed my lips together before answering. "For taking Vernon from me when we were younger."

"We were twelve," she barked. She turned and paraded around the room in an obvious search for an ashtray. Finding one overflowing with old butts jutting out every which way, she flicked her ashes on their remains as she shook her head. "You are really something, Evangeline Benson. Coming here with your forgiveness for something that happened when we were knee high to grasshoppers." She took another draw. "Well, I don't need your forgiveness."

I took a deep breath and exhaled slowly. "I'm not forgiving you for you," I said, about as meek as I'd ever been. "I'm doing it for me." Before she could speak I said, "And I want you to know that I will do my part to help you with your daughter. With Donna. She's got a lot of healing to do . . . and I want to help her with that. For both of you."

Doreen blinked at me. "You'd do that for me?"

"I would. But more for Donna than for you. The way I see it, we only get one mother and father, Doreen. And you're it for Donna when it comes to mothers." I took a step toward the door. "That's all I came to say."

Doreen took one step toward me, then stopped. "Thank you for that," she said. "I'd give you a hug but . . ."

I gave her a weak smile. "Let's not get carried away." I didn't want to embarrass her, so I winked.

She looked down at her feet, and I took my leave from the same door by which I'd entered.

Lizzie called some time after lunch to see how I was doing.

"I'm okay," I said. I had my hand pressed against the kitchen table where Peggy was applying another layer of clear topcoat to my painted nails. "Peggy's doing a touch-up on my manicure."

"So, have you heard the news?" she asked from the other end of the line.

"About Michelle and Adam? Of course. Who hasn't? Pretty soon you'll be the mother of the bride, sitting pretty on the front row of Grace Church."

"Another thing for my already overfilled plate," she said. "But they want a year to plan the wedding, so . . . But that's not what I meant. Lisa Leann's daughter just had a baby."

"You're kidding!"

"A boy."

"A boy," I echoed. "How precious. I'm sure Lisa Leann is beside herself . . . Wait a minute. Lisa Leann! What about my wedding?" I jerked my hand away from Peggy's ministrations.

"Evangeline!" she snapped.

"Sorry," I said and laid my hand back against the tabletop. "What about my wedding?" I asked Lizzie again.

"Don't fret. The Potluck Club Catering Party is at your service."

"The what?"

I could practically hear Lizzie smiling. "That's what we've been calling ourselves all morning. When Lisa Leann and Donna flew out of here—oh, and Donna birthed the baby, but I'll tell you more about that later—Lisa Leann left us with a flurry of instructions. Vonnie, Goldie, and I have had a blast all morning. The food. The floral arrangements. The musicians. The nonstop ringing of the phone. Oh, and your veil arrived. Wait till you see it, Evangeline." She took a breath. "Well, anyway . . . I don't know when I've had so much fun and worked so hard at the same time."

I frowned. "Will Lisa Leann make it back in time for the wedding? I don't want to sound selfish or anything, but I'm not sure I can do this without her." I gulped. "Oh dear Lord, what did I just say?"

Lizzie called out, "Vonnie! Goldie! You won't believe what Evangeline just told me." I heard the "whats" in the background, but Lizzie didn't answer them. "Okay, sweet bride. I'm going to say good-bye for now. We'll see you in the bride's room of the church in a little bit."

I hung up the phone and shook my head. *Oh Lord*, I prayed. *Not that I want to be selfish, but . . . I need Lisa Leann!*

Oh, dear Lord, what did I just pray?

I stood in the bride's room at Grace Church, staring into the full-length mirror before me.

"You look wonderful," Vonnie said from behind me, giving my shoulders a squeeze.

"I do, don't I?" I whispered back.

"Your gown is exquisite," Goldie commented from the other side of the room, where she was applying a last-minute touch-up of lipstick in front of a small table mirror.

"It's called 'Grace Kelly,'" I said. I had chosen for my wedding gown a lovely one-piece, lace over satin A-line gown with a satin sash, which accented the empire waistline and wrapped to the corset back, finishing the gown with cascading streamers.

"Oh, now there was a bride," Lizzie said. "When she married Prince Rainier, what a fairytale that was." In my mirror I could see her reflection behind me. She was slipping her feet into the shoes Lisa Leann had dyed to match the color of the bridesmaids dresses.

The door opened, and Peggy stuck her head in. I turned in her direction as she said, "Never fear. Lisa Leann has just arrived. And, might I say, she looks no worse for the wear."

I smiled. "Of course she doesn't. She wouldn't have it any other way." I took a deep breath. "Are you going to come in or just your head?"

Peggy stuck her tongue out at me playfully. "I'll be back in a second. I'm scoping everything out." Her head disappeared, then reappeared. "Oh, girls. You should see Vernon Vesey in his penguin suit." The door closed, and I made a sound that reminded me somewhat of a drowning woman taking her last breath.

341

Next to me, Donna sat in a chair positioned against the wall. "My father. In a tux. Who'd-a-thunk-it?"

We all laughed. Well, all but me. I was too nervous to think about Vernon in a tux. I turned from the mirror and walked over to the table where our bouquets of roses and daisies awaited us. "Perfect," I said to no one.

Peggy walked back through the door. "Ladies, if you're ready, Clay is here to photograph the bride's side." She smiled at me. "You look beautiful, baby sister," she said. "If only Mama . . ."

I pressed my lips together. *I will not cry . . . I will not cry . . .* "Let's get this show on the road, shall we?" I said, then jutted out my chin and walked toward the door.

I stood at the side of the vestibule and listened as the bridal march played. First Goldie walked down the aisle, then Lizzie. Lisa Leann, standing near the doorway, was ordering their steps. "One-two-three-four-one-two-three-four . . . glide . . . glide . . ." she whispered. "Oh, perfect. Perfect."

After Lizzie, Donna took her place at the door's entrance. I saw her breath catch in her chest. She turned and looked at me, mouthing "He's so handsome. My daddy . . ." and then she began her march down the aisle.

Vonnie followed behind her, taking her position. She, too, turned her head toward where I stood waiting alongside Matthew. She smiled, and I blinked. When she'd disappeared from my view, Lisa Leann stepped over and closed the double swinging doors. She motioned to me. Matthew and I moved toward her as the music from within changed and the rustling of people standing followed.

Matthew and I took our positions as Lisa Leann fluttered over my gown.

"Are you ready?" Matthew asked, extending his arm.

I placed my gloved hand on top of his forearm as Lisa Leann had instructed I do. "It's more formal," she'd said.

I looked up at him and whispered, "I am."

I turned my gaze back to the closed doors.

342

"Here we go," Lisa Leann practically sang.

She opened the doors in one swift, melodramatic moment. Through the shimmer of my veil I saw Vernon standing at the end of the aisle beside our pastor and alongside his groomsmen. He pressed his hand to his chest, and I took one final deep breath.

At Lisa Leann's lead, I took my first step toward my future.

53

What the Journalist Saw

With Britney beside him, Clay had snapped about eight rolls of film. As he removed each roll from his camera and handed them back to her, he'd say, "These are all going to be great. Just great." He carried a digital camera, taking first one shot with it, then the final shot with his trusty 35mm, which allowed him more options for effect.

At the reception, he'd snapped pictures of the bride and groom dancing, the guests who followed them on the dance floor, and the clusters of well-wishers who waved or raised their toast glasses. He'd shot an entire roll of casual poses, catching the guests when they least expected it.

At her command, he'd taken several pictures of Lisa Leann as she "did her thing" so she could blow them up and have them matted and framed for the wall behind the counter of her shop. She was as big a ham as the pork she'd glazed and garnished and placed on one of the food tables.

Two days after the wedding, Clay and Britney worked with the photographs at her family dining room table, separating them by time sequence, placing the "good shots" in one pile and the few "not-so-good shots" in another.

"Eyes are closed," Britney said from beside him, placing another in the latter pile.

He glanced over, then pulled the photo toward him for a look-see. It was a photo of Peggy and Matthew with all their children and their grandchild. Leigh's eyes were closed tight as a drum, and she looked as though she were about to sneeze. He pulled the picture toward him, remembering the excitement from just a few months ago when she'd shown up pregnant and unmarried. It seemed like a lifetime ago. Now, there she stood, next to her husband.

"Fortunately, you took two," Britney interrupted his thoughts. "And this one of the whole family is perfect."

Clay went to place the picture back in its proper pile when something caught his eye. Something in the background. "Well, would you look at that," he said.

"What?" Britney looked over.

Clay pointed to two figures in the background of the shot. "Right there."

"My, my," Britney said. "My, my, my."

Donna and Wade, hands locked together, her head on his shoulder, his lips pressed against the top of her head.

"Well, would you look at that," Clay repeated.

"I wonder what it means," Britney said.

Clay pursed his lips, then smiled. "I have no idea."

The Potluck Club Recipes

Crushed Pineapple Fruitcake

¾ cup butter
1 cup white sugar
2 eggs
1 teaspoon almond extract
2 cups all purpose flour
2 teaspoons baking powder
1 teaspoon salt
3 cups golden raisins
½ cup red candied cherries
1 (20 ounce) can crushed pineapple with juice
1 cup candied mixed fruit peel
3 tablespoons (melted) butter for later

Line the bottom of your angel food pan with parchment paper then spray pan and paper with Pam.

Cream butter then beat in sugar. Beat in eggs one at a time, beating well after each addition. Stir in extract. Mix in flour, baking powder, and salt. Stir in raisins, cherries, pineapple, and mixed peel. Allow dough to sit in covered bowl overnight.

Bake at 300 degrees for 2½ hours. Place a pan of hot water on the lowest rack of your oven during baking. Remove cake from oven then brush with melted butter.

Lisa Leann's Cook's Notes
This fruitcake recipe has a little something extra, with the crushed pineapple. My mother used to make it every Christmas, and I don't think I could go through the season without doing one up myself.

347

Pumpkin Dessert

> 36 large marshmallows
> 1 cup pumpkin (cooked or canned)
> ½ teaspoon cinnamon
> ⅛ teaspoon salt
> 1 cup cream (whipped)
> 1½ cups vanilla wafer crumbs (crushed)
> ½ cup brown sugar
> ⅓ cup butter (melted)
> whipped cream for topping (optional)
> 6–8 candied or fresh cherries (optional)

Melt in a double boiler: marshmallows, canned pumpkin, cinnamon, salt. Mix thoroughly and let cool for 1 hour. Add 1 cup cream, whipped, and put the mixture in the refrigerator.

In separate bowl, mix vanilla wafer crumbs, brown sugar, and melted butter together. Put half of crumb mixture in bottom of 9-by-9 pan.

Pour pumpkin filling over crust and cover with remaining crumbs. Chill until firm (overnight). Garnish each serving with whipped cream (sweetened) and top with a cherry.

Serves 6 to 8.

Vonnie's Cook's Notes
If you like pumpkin like I do but want to do something a little more creative than your average pumpkin pie, this dessert is for you. Now that I'm building memories with David, I think this is fast becoming one of his favorite homemade desserts.

Sour Cream Blueberry Coffee Cake

INGREDIENTS FOR STREUSEL
½ cup flour
½ cup firmly packed light brown sugar
1 teaspoon ground cinnamon
6 tablespoons (¾ stick) cold unsalted butter, diced

INGREDIENTS FOR COFFEE CAKE

2½ cups flour
2 teaspoons baking
     powder
1 teaspoon baking soda
1 teaspoon salt
1 cup (2 sticks) unsalted
     butter, softened

1 cup sugar
3 large eggs
1 cup sour cream
1 tablespoon vanilla
     extract
2 cups blueberries

Directions for Streusel: Combine flour, brown sugar, and cinnamon in a bowl. Add diced butter and blend with your fingertips until crumbly. Set aside.

Directions for Coffee Cake: Preheat oven to 350 degrees. Grease a 9-by-13 baking pan. In a bowl, sift flour, baking powder, baking soda, and salt. Set aside. With an electric mixer, cream butter and sugar together until fluffy. Add one egg at a time, beating well each time. Mix in sour cream and vanilla. Add the sifted dry ingredients and mix just until blended. Fold in blueberries gently with a rubber spatula to create this very thick batter.

Scrape batter into greased pan. Spread batter evenly with the spatula. Sprinkle the streusel mixture over the top.

Bake until the top of the cake is golden brown and a toothpick inserted into the center comes out clean, about 45–50 minutes. Allow the cake to cool in the pan about 10–15 minutes. Serve.

Goldie's Cook's Notes
This takes a little time to prepare, but it's worth it in the end!

Larry's Spice Apple Muffins

    2 cups flour
    ½ cup sugar
    4 teaspoons baking powder
    ½ teaspoon salt
    ½ teaspoon cinnamon
    1 egg, beaten
    1 cup milk
    4 tablespoons melted butter
    1 cup chopped apples

    TOPPING
    2 tablespoons sugar
    ½ teaspoon cinnamon

Sift flour, ½ cup sugar, baking powder, salt, and ½ teaspoon cinnamon together. Combine egg, milk, and melted butter in a separate bowl. Add dry ingredients to the egg mixture. Beat well; fold in apples. Drop batter by spoonfuls into greased muffin tins, filling ⅔ full. Combine 2 tablespoons sugar and ½ teaspoon cinnamon; sprinkle over muffin batter. Bake at 425 degrees for 15–18 minutes.
    Yield: 12 muffins.

Donna's Cook's Notes
I got this recipe out of Larry, and I have to admit I make it from time to time. If you like muffins as much as I do, give it a try.

Hamburger Quiche for Real Men

    1 unbaked 9-inch pie shell
    ½ cup chopped onion
    ¼ cup chopped green pepper
    1 tablespoon cooking oil
    1 pound lean ground beef
    1 can condensed tomato soup
    ½ cup soft bread crumbs
    1 cup grated cheddar cheese
    1 egg, beaten
    ½ teaspoon salt
    ¼ teaspoon pepper
    1 large fresh tomato, peeled

Sauté onion and green pepper in oil until soft. Add beef and brown well. Remove pan from heat. Combine soup, bread crumbs, ½ cup cheese, egg, salt, and pepper. Add to meat and stir until well blended. Pour mixture into pie crust.

Bake at 375 degrees for 30–40 minutes or until crust is golden brown. Cut tomato in eighths and arrange in circle on top of pie. Sprinkle remaining cheese on top and return to oven for 3–5 minutes.

Yield: 6–8 servings.

Goldie's Cook's Notes
Though Jack hates this (he says real men don't eat quiche) I am here to tell you that it's a wonderful feast for the mouth!

Million Dollar Pound Cake

2 cups butter
3 cups sugar
6 eggs (large)
4 cups cake flour
¾ cup milk
1 tablespoon butter or vanilla flavoring
½ teaspoon almond flavoring

Cream butter and sugar well. Add eggs one at a time, beating well after each addition. Add flour alternately with milk. Add flavorings. Beat well. Bake in 10-inch greased and floured tube pan, in preheated oven at 275 degrees for 2–2½ hours or until done.

Lizzie's Cook's Notes
If this were any easier you'd have gone down to the bakery to purchase it! I've used this recipe for years as a quick dessert that's delicious, and there's never a crumb left over.

Meat and Potatoes in a Dish

3–6 medium potatoes
1½ pounds hamburger, cooked
½ teaspoon salt
¼ teaspoon pepper
1 medium onion
1 15-ounce can kidney beans, drained and rinsed
1 can tomato soup

Slice the potatoes in a greased 2-quart casserole dish and crumble hamburger on top. Sprinkle on half the salt and pepper. Slice onion and spread over hamburger. Spread kidney beans over onion. Cover all with the undiluted tomato soup. Add remaining salt and pepper. Bake for 1½ hour in 375-degree oven.

Yield: 6 servings.

Evangeline's Cook's Notes
Everyone in Summit View knows I hate to cook, but they also know how much I love this dish. Why? It's simple and easy, that's why. And it has everything in one dish!

Coach Dippel's Favorite Mexican Casserole

1 onion, chopped
1 tablespoon butter
1½ pounds ground beef
1 tablespoon chili powder or to taste
1 teaspoon garlic powder
salt
pepper
1 large can ranch style beans
1 pound Velveeta cheese
1 can cream of chicken soup
1 can diced tomatoes
12 soft tortillas

Sauté onion in butter. Add ground meat and brown. Season with chili powder, garlic powder, salt, and pepper. Line 9-by-13 casserole dish with about 8 tortillas. Top with meat mixture, then beans. Slice cheese and lay on top of meat and beans. Mix soup and tomatoes and pour over mixture. Top with remaining tortillas. Cover and bake at 350 degrees for 1 hour. Uncover and bake 15 minutes more.

Serves 8.

Goldie's Cook's Notes
Okay, this one my husband loves. And I'll admit that I love it too. It's the perfect simple meal, whether you're living through cold weather or having a summer's picnic.

Sal's Hot Tuna Melt

SANDWICH
Up to 12 slices of bread (buttered)
Up to 12 slices of Swiss cheese
Filling (see below)

FILLING
1 package onion soup mix
1 pint sour cream
2 teaspoons lemon juice
2 cans tuna fish, drained
small jar chopped pimento

Mix onion soup mix and sour cream together. Sprinkle lemon juice over drained tuna fish. Combine all ingredients. Spread on sandwiches. Add one slice of cheese on each sandwich. Toast sandwich with buttered side out in pan on medium heat. Flip sandwiches until both sides are browned and cheese is melted. Slice and serve warm.
   Yield: 5–6 sandwiches.

Donna's Cook's Notes
No wonder this tastes so good. It's loaded with fat. Though, unless you're on a diet, I think it's worth the calories. I think this would be good at parties, or even as a potato chip dip.

Lemon Pudding Bundt Cake

1 package Duncan Hines Deluxe Yellow Cake Mix
1 package Jell-O Instant Lemon Pudding (3¾ ounce)
½ cup Wesson oil
1 cup water
4 eggs
½ teaspoon vanilla
½ teaspoon lemon extract

Put all ingredients in large mixing bowl and beat all together. (Use electric mixer and beat 5 minutes.) Put in well-greased and floured Bundt pan or in 2 loaf pans and bake for 1 hour at 350 degrees. Cool in pan 15 minutes. Sprinkle cake with powdered sugar after cake has cooled. (High altitude adjustment: add 3 tablespoons flour to mix and increase water to 1½ cup + 2 tablespoons. Bake at 375 degrees about 45 minutes or until done. Cool in pan 20 minutes.)

Vonnie's Cook's Notes
I was taken aback that Lisa Leann keeps a stash of emergency Lemon Pudding Bundt Cakes in her freezer, but I was so impressed with the flavor that I got her to give me the recipe. But a few words of advice: if you freeze this cake, use it within a couple of months. I don't think it would taste nearly as good with freezer burn.

Summit Ridge's Baked German Pancakes with Almond Topping

PANCAKE INGREDIENTS
3 eggs
½ cup flour
½ teaspoon salt
½ cup milk
2 tablespoons butter, melted
2 tablespoons butter, softened

ALMOND TOPPING INGREDIENTS
¼–½ cup sliced almonds
2 tablespoons butter, melted
¼ cup sugar

With wire whisk or fork, beat eggs until blended. Sift flour, measure, and sift again with salt. Slowly add flour mixture to beaten eggs, beating constantly. Beat until mixture is smooth.

Next, add milk (¼ cup at a time), beating slightly after each addition. Gently beat in 2 tablespoons melted butter.

With 2 tablespoons softened butter, butter bottom and sides of a 9- or 10-inch heavy skillet. Pour batter into skillet and bake at 450 degrees for 20 minutes. When pancake has baked 15 minutes, quickly sprinkle center with almonds, drizzle with melted butter, and sprinkle generously with sugar. Return to oven and bake remaining 5 minutes.

Serve immediately with (optional) syrup of your choice.

Donna's Cook's Notes
This is exactly why I like coffee shops in remote places. You never know when one is going to have a specialty that made your visit worth the trip. If I'm ever out this way again, I'll be sure to have seconds.

Spaghetti Pie

    8 ounces spaghetti, broken into 2-inch pieces
    2 tablespoons melted butter
    ⅓ cup grated Parmesan cheese
    ½ teaspoon salt
    ¼ teaspoon pepper
    1 egg, well beaten
    1½ pounds ground chuck
    1 medium onion, chopped
    ¼ cup chopped green pepper
    2 tablespoons vegetable oil
    1 jar (15½ ounces) thick spaghetti sauce
    1 teaspoon sugar
    ½ teaspoon leaf oregano, crumbled
    ½ teaspoon garlic salt
    1 cup cottage cheese
    4 ounces mozzarella cheese, shredded

Cook spaghetti in boiling water following label directions; drain.
Place in 9-by-13 baking dish. Stir in next five ingredients until
thoroughly combined. Spread mixture evenly in pan. Sauté chuck,
onion, and green pepper in oil in large skillet until meat is brown;
drain. Stir in spaghetti sauce, sugar, oregano, and garlic salt. Spread
cottage cheese over spaghetti layer and top with meat mixture. Bake
at 350 degrees for half hour. Sprinkle mozzarella cheese over top
and bake an additional 10 minutes or until cheese is melted and
just begins to brown. Let stand 15 minutes before cutting.
    Serves 6.

Lizzie's Cook's Notes
This recipe has been a favorite in my daughter-in-law's kitchen
from the early days of her marriage to my son. When she wants to
prepare a hearty meal in a short period of time, this is her recipe
of choice.

English Wassail

   1 gallon apple cider (not juice)
   8 cinnamon sticks
   5 cloves (or to taste)
   1 teaspoon ground allspice
   1 teaspoon ground nutmeg
   1 teaspoon ground ginger
   2 lemons, sliced
   1 orange, sliced

Mix together, bring to a boil, then reduce heat and let simmer for an hour before serving.

Evangeline's Cook's Notes
Nothing says Christmas like the scent of wassail simmering on the stovetop. Try it and I promise you won't be sorry.

Clam Chowder

2 slices bacon
1 cup onion, chopped
1 cup potatoes, cubed
1 teaspoon salt
dash of pepper
1 cup water
2 10½-ounce cans of clams (minced)
2 cups half and half or evaporated milk
2 tablespoons butter

Chop and sauté bacon. In large saucepan, add onions and cook for 5 minutes. Next, add potatoes, salt, pepper, and water. Cook 15 minutes.

Add clams, clam juice, milk, and butter to larger soup pot. Add ingredients from saucepan. Mix well, don't boil.

Serves 4–5.

Lisa Leann's Cook's Notes
I like to make a double recipe. This is perfect for cold evenings when your family is gathered around.

Old-Fashioned Southern Fruitcake

> 4 cups all-purpose flour
> ½ teaspoon baking powder
> 1½ teaspoons salt
> 1½ teaspoons cinnamon
> 1 teaspoon nutmeg
> 7 cups pecan halves (do not cut up)
> ¾ pound chopped canned cherries
> ¾ pound chopped pineapple
> 1 pound golden raisins
> 1 cup butter
> 2¼ cups sugar
> 6 unbeaten eggs
> 3 teaspoons brandy flavoring

Sift together into a mixing bowl the flour, baking powder, salt, cinnamon, and nutmeg. Add pecans, cherries, pineapple, and raisins. Mix until all fruit and nuts are coated with dry ingredients. Set aside.

Cream together the butter and sugar until light and fluffy. Add unbeaten eggs one at a time, then the brandy flavoring. Mix this into the fruit mixture.

Spray a 10-inch tube pan with nonstick spray or put wax paper on the bottom. Pour mixture into pan. Bake in oven 275 degrees for 3 hours.

Cool cake completely before removing from pan. Wrap tightly in foil and store.

Goldie's Cook's Notes
This was my grandmother's recipe. Written on notepad paper in her handwriting, it has been passed down from my mother to me and, one day, to my daughter.

Pineapple Upside-Down Cake

¼ cup butter
1 cup firmly packed brown sugar
¾ cup chopped pecans
20-ounce can of pineapple slices, drained, reserving
     5 tablespoons juice
1 cup all-purpose flour
1 teaspoon baking powder
½ teaspoon salt
3 eggs, separated
maraschino cherries

Preheat oven to 350. On low heat, melt butter in 9-inch cast-iron skillet. While the skillet is still warm, add the brown sugar and pecans; stir well to thoroughly combine. (Turn off heat. You don't want to "cook" the mixture.) Next, arrange 8 pineapple slices in a single layer over the brown sugar mixture in your skillet.

Set aside flour, baking powder, and salt in a separate bowl.

In mixing bowl, beat the egg yolks at medium speed until they are thick and bright yellow. Continue to beat while gradually adding the flour mixture (that you set aside) and reserved pineapple juice to the sugar-yolk mixture.

In separate mixing bowl, beat the egg whites until stiff peaks form. Fold the whites into the cake batter. Spoon the batter over the pineapple slices as evenly as possible. Bake skillet at 350 for 40–45 minutes. Let cool for 30 minutes then flip skillet onto a serving plate. Top each pineapple ring with a maraschino cherry.

Vonnie's Cook's Notes
Move over pumpkin dessert, David has a new favorite. And I have to admit, it's one of mine too. I guess great taste runs in my family.

Larry's Fudge Bars

½ cup butter
1 egg yolk
2 tablespoons water
1¼ cups sifted flour
1 teaspoon sugar
1 teaspoon baking powder
2 cups chocolate pieces
2 eggs
¾ cup sugar
6 tablespoons melted butter
2 teaspoons vanilla
2 cups finely cut nuts

Beat ½ cup butter with 1 egg yolk and 2 tablespoons water. Sift flour, sugar, and baking powder. Stir into butter mixture. Press into greased 9-by-13-by-2 pan. Bake for 10 minutes at 350 degrees. Sprinkle with chocolate pieces immediately; return to oven for 1 minute. Remove from oven, spread chocolate over top.

Next, beat 2 eggs until thick; beat in ¾ cup sugar. Stir in 6 tablespoons melted butter and vanilla. Add nuts; spread mixture over top of chocolate.

Bake at 350 degrees for an additional 30–35 minutes. Cut in 1½-inch squares.

Yield: 4 dozen squares.

Donna's Cook's Notes
Okay, I admit it, despite the fact Larry is not my favorite person, I took one of his fudge bars to try later that night. And yes, it was good, and yes, I did finally ask him for the recipe—though I made sure he understood my interest was nothing personal.

Tiramisu

1 pound (16 ounces) mascarpone cheese
3 tablespoons sugar
4 tablespoons coffee liqueur*
1 cup heavy cream, whipped
24 ladyfingers, split
1½ cups cold espresso or strong coffee
1 can Solo or 1 jar Baker almond filling
3 ounces semisweet chocolate, grated

Combine cheese, sugar, and coffee liqueur, mixing well. Fold in whipped cream. Set aside. Line bottom of a deep 3-quart, straight-sided glass serving dish with a layer of ladyfingers, cutting some to fit as necessary. Drizzle with ⅓ of the cold espresso. Spread with ⅓ of the almond filling, then ⅓ of the cheese mixture and ⅓ of the grated chocolate. Repeat layering two more times. Refrigerate thoroughly and serve *semifreddo* (cold but not frozen).
Serves 16.

*For those who don't like the idea of a coffee liqueur, try the following substitutes: espresso, non-alcoholic coffee extract, or coffee syrup.

Lizzie's Cook's Notes
Tiramisu is considered a classic Italian dessert. Since its "invention" it has become my all-time favorite dessert. Every time I eat out, I look to see if tiramisu is listed on the dessert menu, trying it at various dining places.

Hot Cocoa for Adults

> 2 tablespoons cocoa
> 2 tablespoons sugar
> pinch of salt
> ½ cup boiling water
> 2 cups scalded milk
> ¼ teaspoon vanilla

Mix cocoa, sugar, and salt together in top of a double boiler, then blend to a smooth paste with the ½ cup boiling water. Place over direct heat, bring to a boil, and cook rapidly for one minute, stirring constantly to form a syrup. Add milk and heat to scalding over boiling water. Remove from heat and add vanilla. Whip for a minute with an egg beater and serve steaming hot.

Yield: 3 servings.

Goldie's Cook's Notes
Wonderful, wonderful drink to sip on a cold winter's night. This has long been one of our favorites. I don't know why it's called "Hot Cocoa for Adults," but that's the way it reads in the cookbook my mother gave me when I married Jack.

Easy Biscuits

> 2 cups sifted flour
> 4 teaspoons baking powder
> 1 teaspoon salt
> 1 teaspoon sugar
> ¼ cup shortening
> 1 cup milk

Sift dry ingredients together then make a well (or hole) in the center. Place shortening and milk into the well. Mix with wooden spoon until smooth. Pat dough on generously floured board. Turn over. Pat dough again, then cut with round biscuit cutter. Place cutouts on baking sheet. Bake at 450 degrees for 12 minutes.

Yield: 6–8 servings.

Donna's Cook's Notes
I know, making biscuits actually involves cooking. But this easy recipe is a good compromise on my "avoid turning on the oven" creed. Plus, as I only eat two biscuits at a time, I can save the rest for the freezer, to microwave for yet another day.

Stuffed Cabbage Rolls

1 small head of cabbage
1 pound ground beef
2 teaspoons chopped onion
1 egg, beaten
½ cup milk
1 teaspoon salt

Trim off soiled leaves of cabbage and remove core. Cover with boiling water and let stand five minutes or until cabbage leaves are limp. Separate leaves carefully, reserving five of the largest leaves for the rolls. Combine meat thoroughly with onion, egg, milk, and salt. Place ⅕ of the meat mixture on each leaf and fold up envelope fashion. Fasten with toothpick. Lay, flap down, in Dutch oven or saucepan. Add ½ cup water and cover rolls with rest of cabbage leaves. Simmer, covered, for 1 hour. Serve with tomato sauce recipe.
 Yield: 5 servings.

TOMATO SAUCE
 1 14½ ounce can tomatoes
 1 teaspoon grated onion
 ½ teaspoon salt
 ½ teaspoon sugar
 2 tablespoons butter
 2 teaspoons flour
 ¼ teaspoon Worcestershire sauce

Combine first four ingredients and simmer for 15 minutes. Melt butter, blend in flour, and add tomato mixture and Worcestershire sauce, stirring until sauce boils and thickens.

Evangeline's Cook's Notes
Could this get any easier? I think not! And when you serve it, your family will think you slaved all day. A huge thank you to my friend Lizzie!

367

Chicken and Chutney Finger Sandwiches

> 3 cups diced cooked chicken
> 1 cup canned pineapple chunks, drained (reserve juice)
> ¾ cup sliced celery
> ½ cup mayonnaise
> ¼ cup sour cream
> 3 tablespoons prepared chutney (I use store bought)
> 1 teaspoon curry powder
> ½ cup crushed Chinese noodles (or ½ cup almond slivers)
> 1–2 small loaves Pepperidge Farm sandwich bread

Trim crust from bread slices. In a large bowl, combine chicken, pineapple, and celery. In a separate bowl, use a wire whisk to blend 3 tablespoons of your reserved juice with the remaining ingredients (except almonds or Chinese noodles). Stir into chicken mixture.

Cover and refrigerate at least 1 hour. Stir in crushed Chinese noodles or almonds, then spread on bread. Top with bread slice to create sandwich. Slice each sandwich into 3 or 4 finger slices. Serve immediately or freeze on baking tray. Place in baggies. Defrost and use as needed. If you plan to freeze, omit Chinese noodles, else they will get soggy.

Yield: This makes over 5 cups of sandwich filling and can serve 6 as a salad (on bed of lettuce) or will make several dozen finger sandwiches, depending on how thickly you spread the filling.

Lisa Leann's Cook's Notes
I've scaled down this recipe for you. But note that with so many nut allergies out there, I never use nuts in my catered cooking. I've found crushed Chinese noodles can work as a great replacement.

Cabbage and Apple Salad

2 cups shredded cabbage (¼ head)
2 cups apples, chopped
2 cans mandarin oranges
1 cup seedless green grapes

DRESSING
½ cup whipping cream
1 tablespoon sugar
1 tablespoon lemon juice
½ cup Miracle Whip
¼ teaspoon salt

Beat whipping cream until stiff. Add the rest of the ingredients.

Evangeline's Cook's Notes
It doesn't sound appealing when you think of cabbage and apples together, necessarily, but you'll be more than pleasantly surprised by the deliciousness of this recipe!

Baked Ham

> 1 12-pound ham
> 1 cup (packed) brown sugar
> 1 tablespoon dry mustard
> ½ cup spiced fruit juice
> whole cloves

Preheat oven to 350 degrees, then put ham in oven. Insert meat thermometer into ham's center. When the meat thermometer registers 130 degrees, remove the ham from the oven. Next remove the rind and score the fat. Spread a mixture of brown sugar, dry mustard, and fruit juice over the ham. Insert cloves into scored ham fat. Return ham to oven for 15 to 20 minutes or until ham is glazed.

Lisa Leann's Cook's Notes

Hams are perfect for big galas. I like to use my electric knife to slice it thin, though for smaller groups, thick slices are nice. One 12-pound ham can serve 30 to 50, depending on portions. So, if I'm serving ham to 200, I'll cook 4 or 5 of them, depending on how many other options are available on the menu.

Easy Oatmeal Crispies

½ cup butter
½ cup margarine
½ cup sugar
1 cup flour
1½ cups quick oats

With electric mixer, cream butter and margarine. Next, add sugar, flour, and oatmeal, one at a time, into mixing bowl and blend. Chill dough for 1 to 3 hours. Shape dough into teaspoon-sized balls.

Place cookie balls three inches apart on a greased baking sheet. Flatten balls with bottom of glass dipped in sugar. Bake at 350 degrees for 12–15 minutes. Let cool.

Yield: 4 dozen.

Donna's Cook's Notes
I always need a little sweet to tide me over. But I don't want to overdo the sugar. This is a good compromise, as it's low in sugar and high in oatmeal. I like to bake a couple of batches to freeze in large freezer bags. Then, I just pop the cold cookies, straight from the freezer, into my lunch. They're perfect for my afternoon break.

The Recipe for Friendship

2 heaping cups of patience
2 handfuls of generosity
1 heart of love
a dash of laughter
2 well-rounded scoops of respect
2 heaping measures of trust
1 head of understanding
sprinkle generously with kindness
add plenty of faith and mix well

Spread over a lifetime and serve everyone you meet.

How to Have a Christmas Tea

Evangeline Benson

If you have suddenly found yourself as the grande dame of a Christmas tea (as I did), and whether or not you are forced to share these duties with someone else (as I was), I'd like to share a bit of wisdom I've acquired.

First, set a date. Many churches find that having the tea the first of December works best for the ladies of the community. After all, people have lives, and the holidays seem to bring out the best in folks and the worst in their calendars.

You will also want to plan where. Most church-sponsored Christmas teas are held either in the church sanctuary or fellowship hall, though there may be a lady or two in your church or community with the perfect home setting for your tea. If you decide to have the tea in your church building, account for both setup time and breakdown time. (Oh, and you'll want to coordinate with the men in your community or church so you'll have some brawn to help with table setup and breakdown; perhaps the husbands, sons, or fiancés of the girls.)

Next, decide if you want to have an evening or an afternoon tea. Or, you could do both, and in this way—should you have your tea on a weekday—the ladies who work outside of the home and those who work inside of the home can all find a way to attend.

Then, get the ladies of your church or organization to sign up as table hostesses and helpers as early as possible. I cannot stress this enough, and I suggest giving them at least a month to six weeks lead time. Instruct your hostesses that they will be responsible for the setting and theme of their table, which should hold no more than six to eight, typically. This is also a lot of fun, seeing the themes for the first time the day of the tea. For the most part, women simply love to get out all the pretty stuff and play.

Have one of your ladies be responsible for decorating a greeting table in the front entrance, reception area, etc. I suggest that this be done a couple of weeks before the tea so as to add to the promotion of the tea.

Promoting the Christmas tea is never difficult. Bible studies, potluck clubs (like ours!), church bulletins, flyers about the community, an announcement in the local paper, something on your church website—the list goes on and on. If you are having a special speaker or music (and don't get me started on the mess Lisa Leann created this year), make sure you give adequate information. You might want to add photos from past teas on your flyers or invitational letters as well.

When it comes to organizational meetings, I suggest you hold two meetings specifically for the table hostesses, the first about four weeks out, the second a week from the event. Always call the ladies before the meetings, because with so much going on during the season with a Reason they could easily forget. Have a list of details ready to share with the ladies and be sure to remind them that the focus of the tea is Christ and glorifying God (some people we know need reminding of this more than others).

Checklists for the hostesses should be passed out at the meeting.

Now here's a little ministry tool you might want to consider: ask that the centerpieces for the tables not be secular in nature. No reindeer, Santas, or snowmen. This gives those who are unchurched something to focus on that might, in turn, become a seed planted. Of course, Lisa Leann vehemently disagrees with me on this, and I'm not saying I'm for it 100 percent. I've seen some secular centerpieces that'll thrill you to pieces. I'm just saying consider it. You know your group better than I do.

374

While we're on the secular versus religious issue, I have two other comments.

1. This is a *Christmas* tea. Not a *holiday* tea. If God had wanted us to call it a holiday tea, he would have called his son "the Holly" rather than "the Christ." That's my opinion, anyway.
2. But on the other hand, I see no problem with having a little Bing Crosby "White Christmas" on the stereo system followed by Perry Como's "O Holy Night." For pity's sake, if Barbra Streisand can sing "Silent Night" and "O Little Town of Bethlehem" on her Christmas album, then why not?

Make sure the hostesses have the correct date and time, and especially when the venue for the event will be open to them so they can come in and decorate their tables, etc. If you plan the tea correctly, you can actually have a tea decorating party the evening before the event.

Some churches choose to sell tickets for the tea (either to support their ministry or another ministry or to supply funds for the speaker or musical entertainment, etc.). If you do—and you certainly shouldn't feel bad about doing this—keep your hostesses apprised as to how many tickets are selling. You may have to invite additional hostesses to join, and wouldn't that just be grand! (I suggest having two or three additional tables set up for unexpected guests.) One last thought on this is to be sure to have a ticket receiving table where additional tickets can be purchased the day of and where name tags can be picked up.

Though the event is called a tea, be sure to offer other drinks as well, such as coffee and wassail. Prepare all of these as early as possible (about three hours ahead of time) and try to get one-hundred-cup pots for brewing and then thermal serving pots for serving. (Of course, for the tea, you will simply need to get thermal pots of hot water ready with a nice assortment of teas.) Offer an assortment of cold drinks as well. Consider having the young ladies of your youth ministry help with the preparation and distribution of the drinks, allowing them to apprentice in the art of hosting a tea.

For food setup and distribution you have a couple of choices: either setting up long tables (we, at Grace Church, like the round tables for tea and long tables for serving) and having the ladies serve themselves one table at a time or having servers wait on the ladies. Some churches have the fellows in their congregation take on the role of servers, dressing them up in penguin suits and draping a white towel over their arm.

Food can either be catered in or brought in by the good cooks of your church or community.

A Christmas tea should reflect the personality or personalities of those who are giving it. Create or organize fun games and activities (nothing too flamboyant; after all, this is a tea not a three-year-old's birthday party). Have door prizes. Perhaps a dramatic sketch or reading. Above all, give the gift of love, a fitting thing during the holiday season.

Linda Evans Shepherd has turned the "pits" of her life into stepping stones following a violent car crash that left her then-infant daughter in a yearlong coma and permanently disabled (see LindaAndLaura .com).

Linda is the president of Right to the Heart Ministries and is also an international speaker (see ShepPro.com), radio host of the nationally syndicated Right to the Heart radio, guest television host of Daystar's Denver Celebration, the founder and leader of Advanced Writers and Speakers Association (see AWSAWomen. com), and the publisher of Right to the Heart of Women ezine (see RightToTheHeartOfWomen.com), which goes to more than ten thousand women leaders of the church.

She's been married twenty-seven years to Paul and has two children, Laura and Jimmy.

Linda has written more than eighteen books, including *Intimate Moments with God* (co-authored with Eva Marie Everson), *Tangled Heart: A Mystery Devotional*, and *Grief Relief*.

Award-winning author and speaker **Eva Marie Everson** is a Southern girl who's not that crazy about being in the kitchen unless she's being called to eat some of her mama's or daddy's cooking. She is married to a wonderful man, Dennis, and is a mother and grandmother to the most precious children in the world.

Eva's writing career and ministry began in 1999 when a friend asked her what she'd want to do for the Lord, if she could do anything. "Write and speak," she said. And so it began.

Since that time, she has written, co-written, contributed to, and edited and compiled a number of works, including *Sex, Lies, and the*

Media and *Sex, Lies, and High School* (co-written with her daughter, Jessica). She is a Right to the Heart board member and a member of a number of other organizations, and is a mentor with Christian Writers Guild.

A graduate of Andersonville Theological Seminary, she speaks nationally, drawing others to the heart of God. In 2002, she was one of six journalists chosen to visit Israel. She was forever changed.

For more fun with the Potluck Club, go to: www.PotLuckClub .com